To Jodie, Connor, and Aster.
My best world is with you.

The Lotus and the Barley

Anthony St. Clair

rucksack
universe

Rucksack Press
Eugene, Oregon

CONTENTS

"It is said that the mythical bird the phoenix burns and then is reborn from its own ashes. The same can be said of London, once the heart of a global empire and the jewel of what was then known as the United Kingdom. London burned to the ground during The Blast, and the empire broke apart. Today, construction continues in the capital of England, drawing everything from large multinational corporations such as Deep Inc. to tourists seeking a pint of Deep's Special Lager or Galway Pradesh Stout at the Mirror & Phoenix, or commemorating The Blast at the Square of Ashes."

"A reminder about First Call Brewing and the Irish language: 'grúdaire' (pronounced 'gruh-duh-ruh') means 'brewer' but only a grúdaire can brew Galway Pradesh Stout. 'Na Grúdairí' (pronounced 'nah gruh-duh-ree') is the name of the collective order of the brewers of First Call." While nice to know, London visitors would find this more useful if the brewery offered tours, which at this time it does not."

— Guru Deep, *London Through the Third Eye*

AFTER THE ALARM

NO ONE KNEW ABOUT the problem until the alarm rang, but Feckniss imagined the man in the orange suit at the top of the world was the only one who smiled about it.

From Feckniss's cubicle much lower down the world on the third floor of the Lotus, the phone line clicked, then droned. Guru Deep had ended the conference call. A few minutes later, Feckniss's gray-suited manager Blanders stepped into the cubicle. He stood next to the "ILLUSION IS REALITY" poster, which some said was the true mission statement of Deep Inc.

"What's going on, sir?" Feckniss knew they could speak freely. At this late hour, no one else was in the Lotus except for Blanders, the assistant Nia Fox, and

Guru Deep himself, the man in the orange suit at the top of the Lotus, London's highest skyscraper and currently the world's tallest building. Despite the third floor being empty, for a moment Feckniss thought he heard a snicker, brief yet packed with cruelty and condescension. Then he thought of Guru Deep, and Feckniss shuddered with awe and relief.

Guru Deep hadn't said a word during the briefing call. He never did, but anytime Feckniss and Blanders were in a meeting, the line was open to Guru Deep's office. Only Blanders and Feckniss did the talking, but Guru Deep's silences resounded more than any words, a presence like a stalking tiger or a thunderhead filling the horizon. But Feckniss could imagine him standing there: Guru Deep. The Great Leader, He Whose Third Eye Saw All The World That Was And Could Be, was the President and CEO of Deep Inc. Dealing in finance, self-help seminars, travel guidebooks, breweries, and other initiatives—that Blanders hinted at but never explained—over the last few decades Deep Inc. had become of the world's largest and most powerful companies.

On this call too Feckniss could feel the brilliant gravity of the leader's presence as they discussed the enemy's latest disruptions—and their effects on quarterly profits—of less-than-public Deep Inc. operations in Marrakech, Mexico City, and Moscow. "Guru Deep sees all and hears all," Blanders said, "even if you don't see or hear him. Guru knows. These developments trouble him. The enemy hasn't been such a problem for Guru Deep since Kyoto, and that was decades ago."

"What happened there?"

"At the rate you're progressing," said Blanders, "perhaps you'll get to visit his office someday and ask him about the two curved swords behind his desk. It is quite a story."

Feckniss could picture it as clearly as if he were beside the Great Leader himself. Guru Deep would be staring out over the dark London night from the north window, forty-two stories above the city that had rebuilt itself after being burned to the ground by The Blast a hundred and thirty years ago. The Lotus had recently opened as the bright, brand-new, orange glass-and-steel world headquarters of Deep Inc. In the black of the evening, Guru Deep's trademark orange suit, a deep saffron like the flag of India, would shine like the sun against his brown skin and eyes. And there, somewhere near his massive desk, where he led his empire, two curved swords would shimmer with the power of the story they had to tell.

Feckniss shuddered at the mere idea of being there, in that office, with the man whose empire spanned businesses and industries around the globe. And one of those industries, what was about to happen, had been the subject of their call—

"Of course I can't say for certain," Blanders said, his voice flat as a coffin bottom and returning Feckniss's mind to the third floor. The pale taut skin over his skull always reminded Feckniss of a balloon about to pop. Smoothing the impeccable gray wool of his lapel, Blanders smiled, which meant the corners of his mouth briefly twitched upward, then fell back down as if embarrassed to be caught trying. "But I believe we can safely surmise that the enemy has taken it."

"Just as Guru Deep expected," Feckniss replied. "Though wasn't the Lotus designed to keep out that individual?"

Again the near smile. Blanders tapped the side of his nose. "Guru knows. Though I'm sure he'll have Ms. Fox order a full security audit to find and remedy whatever lapse or flaw led to this breach. Damn new building and new protocols—of course the enemy managed to find some weakness, no matter how small, that he could exploit."

Feckniss nodded. "Of course. We are so close now. Guru Deep knew the enemy would come, didn't he?" Again the brief grin. "I see. Guru Deep *wanted* him to come. Will it affect the plans? Will it disrupt our progress toward Operation—"

"Only in ensuring our success," Blanders replied. "All endeavors are easier when your enemies complete your work for you."

"Does he know the secret?"

"It doesn't matter," Blanders said. "What we have long ago set in motion, his actions cannot stop. All that matters, Feckniss, is that through our teamwork and Guru Deep's guidance, the time has come. Tomorrow proceeds as planned."

"It will be no more?"

This time the smile remained. Bloodless lips curved into an upside-down scythe. "Its end," he said, "is only the beginning."

I

THE MAN IN BLACK ran across the plaza, and the guards followed. After all, that's what guards do. Especially if they want to continue doing things like receiving paychecks and having a pulse.

Outside the massive building, the clanging of the alarms faded in the distance, dominated by the sounds of a vibrant city at night, and stopped cold by glass that, it was rumored, could stand up to a grenade blast. Now the sounds of pounding feet and fast breathing were all that could be heard. That, and the usual cries of things like, "Stop, Faddah Rucksack, stop!" and "We will shoot!" and "Who the hell would've thought he could run so fast?"

The first cry made Rucksack chuckle. Did anyone ever follow such ridiculous commands?

The second cry was something he had known going in, but it still concerned him. Ever since the incident in Hong Kong years back—the memory still made Rucksack shudder—the world had decided it was tired of guns. It was rare you saw firearms, other than with specialized military units or certain hunters. But he couldn't allow himself the luxury of surprise. Of course Guru Deep's guards would be armed. Rucksack thought of the small briefcase he held by the handle in his gloved left hand. Given what he'd taken, he was surprised they weren't shooting already.

At least he could find comfort and humor in the third remark. Despite the humid summer evening making sweat bead on his bald brown head and dampen his black silk clothes, Rucksack couldn't help but smile. Not that he liked running, but you didn't survive as long as he had without being able to leg it faster than the people trying to kill you. Rucksack believed the world was best experienced at a rambling walking pace, though briskness was acceptable if you found yourself late for happy hour. But at his age it was nice to know he could still outpace the young guards, despite how they kept fit both by Guru Deep's PEFFER program, the Personal Everyday Fulfilling Fitness & Empowerment Regimen, and a soul-deep fear of what would happen if their physical conditioning was found not to be up to snuff.

He couldn't let such thoughts distract him though. The smile faded to a line as firm as the horizon. The timing now was everything, and if it was off even by a few seconds...

Rucksack ran faster.

The Maya Plaza fanned out from the Lotus in all directions. In the daytime the park was serene and lovely, a bright public square with a dark private heart. Now the shrubs and trees were black. He'd planned the escape route to keep well away from the lighted paths, but now the trees were working against him. Dark branches snagged at Rucksack's clothes, plucking at the knotwork buttons that ran down the center of his long untucked black shirt, scraping his neck above the mandarin collar, and pressing like tripwires over his shins where long ties wrapped the bottoms of his pants for extra silence.

The shouting voices were closer.

He ducked around a tree, pausing a moment to evaluate where the guards were. By now they were converging from all sides, with some surely heading to the edge of the park to trap him inside. But if he made one slight change to his course...

Rucksack started running again, leaping a row of shrubbery and dodging more trees.

A high root grabbed the toe of his boot.

Instead of resisting the change, Rucksack followed the new direction. He launched forward, tucking his body and holding the briefcase more tightly.

He winced. The damn left hand had been all but useless ever since The Blast. He would have preferred to hold the briefcase in his other hand, but he had to keep the right free, no matter what.

Soft grass cushioned his back as he somersaulted. With the momentum came a memory, an old power, an old trick that had always worked well. Momentum to energy, energy to force. The focus was everything, and he focused now, pulling the energy from the grass, the ground, and his body, compressing it, targeting it. When his feet hit the ground, as he stood from the roll, he unleashed the force inside. A tremor like an earthquake passed through the park. Men yelled. Some stumbled and fell.

Rucksack grinned. It was almost like the old days. More importantly, it bought him time—but he knew he'd pay for it later. Assuming there was a later.

He passed through the last row of trees. Beyond the green of the Maya Plaza, the steel, glass, and concrete of London surrounded the park. Night muted the colors, but come dawn the reds and oranges, the blues and greens of the city's bright buildings would make the park seem dim and monochrome, as if it should try harder to enjoy itself.

The voices of the guards were so near now.

Rucksack listened more closely.

So was another sound—a low, deep rumble—the difference between escape and capture, or worse.

There was still time.

The first shot rang out. Behind him, bark exploded.

The guards closed in on him. Fifteen men, all taller and broader than he was. All with guns out. It had been decades since Rucksack had seen one, let alone fifteen.

Rucksack's boots hit the sidewalk that ringed the Maya Plaza. A few meters of concrete were now all that separated him from escape. At the far edge of the sidewalk, a low metal railing marked the edge of one of London's busiest roads.

The guards still yelled. Another shot ruptured the air. This one passed by his shoulder blades, ending in a loud *ping-bop* when it hit the lamppost nearby.

But Rucksack ignored the guards and the guns. He focused only on the sound, focused only on making the timing, the angle, the momentum just right. The approach, the moment, had to be perfect. He was nearly there, and from the sound, so was it.

Then, from behind a mailbox, a sixteenth man stood and blocked Rucksack's path. He stood taller and broader than the others. Rucksack couldn't see his face, only a smile, only a motion that could be anything—

The tremor had been taxing. Using so much energy now was risky, potentially too risky. But it was the only thing he could do if he wanted to escape.

He swung. His left hand roared with agony as the metal briefcase hit the man's outstretched hand. Something clattered on the pavement, out of sight, but Rucksack kept hold of the briefcase. It was still latched. Everything depended on what was inside. But he was out of time. He didn't stop, couldn't stop—it was everything or nothing. Rucksack hadn't survived what he had survived only to die now, hadn't regained what he had lost just to lose it all now, on a dark sidewalk south of the River Thames, to some patsy guard who had no idea what he was really doing or what it really meant for him, or for London, or, for that matter, all the world—perhaps all of existence itself.

Rucksack's swinging hand led his body into a spiral. As he turned he planted his left foot. He spun his body and his right leg rose, bent—and then one kick showed the sixteen men with guns what real firepower was.

The guard flew backward, but the power behind the kick had only begun to strike. As Rucksack lowered his foot to the ground, a flat smacking sound rolled past his ears as the man bounced off the low metal railing. But the sound was more than sound.

Behind him, guns clattered on pavement as the shockwave made the other fifteen guards double over or stumble back. The guard at the railing fell to his knees and his forehead thudded on the pavement. Rucksack ran forward. The other guards recovered quickly, some running toward him while others scrabbled in the shadows for their weapons. Men lunged. A hand slid off his shoulder. Fingernails grazed his wrist.

But that could not matter. He listened to the rumble again. It was here.

One guard's fingertips glanced off a boot and smacked the concrete. One foot braced on the back of the hunched-over guard, Rucksack's brown-black eyes winced at the blinding gaze that stared into his very soul. The railing clanged under the next step.

With a roar, Rucksack leaped toward a red wall.

Like a charging tiger, the terrible sound paused all hearts and breath. Then Rucksack was in midair, hanging over the pavement, flying toward a street teeming with speeding traffic.

The driver of the bright-red double-decker bus shifted gears and sped up, aiming to beat the stoplight before it changed. The engine's rumbling was the sweetest sound Rucksack had ever heard. He reached out his right hand, grabbed the handrail just inside the open doorway at the back of the bus, and stepped on as lightly as a sunbeam, swinging the briefcase to his side.

The guards stood open-mouthed and watched the bus rumble away.

Grinning, Rucksack waved to them until the Maya Plaza and the Lotus were out of sight at last.

Then, unable to stand anymore, he collapsed on a seat and began to shake.

WHILE HER SISTER ZARA handed another small cup of beer across the small table to the old man in gray, Branwen watched a trembling man in black enter the Mirror & Phoenix and take a seat at the bar. A small briefcase, black with chromed steel edges and corners, clattered when he set it on the polished mahogany. He wiped sweat from his bald head. His skin was brown as Tibetan dirt, but nonetheless he looked pale, clammy, like a thin shell left after the insides had been hollowed out.

"I'd drink this every day," said a woman Zara had given beer to earlier. "Na Grúdairí must be so proud." She carefully pronounced the Irish word for "beer brewers" as "*gruh*-duh-ree."

From their little table at the far end of the pub, Branwen could feel the tightness in the air around her sister, like the moment after a lightning strike before the forest catches fire. Zara's short purple-and-yellow hair didn't stand on end and her black combat-booted legs didn't lash out in one of her vicious kicks or knee strikes, but her dark brown eyes, the same as Branwen's, widened. The two women had been enjoying pints at this pub for as long as they could legally drink, but drinking those pints wasn't what

Zara ultimately wanted. The bartender, Jade London, had reminded Zara of that as they set up their homebrew sample table that evening. The people were just trying beer, Jade had said, not making pronouncements on Zara's personal destiny.

Zara stared at the woman and said nothing, only gave a thin smile as the woman disappeared into the crowd that filled the pub. "I'm going to pour more samples," she said, her face a little pale as she leaned over to move the white tablecloth and pull tasting cups from a box under the table. She set a cup under the brass spout of a squat black cylinder on the table. Brass piping gleamed in the pub lights. A thin glass vial running up the side told Branwen the pressurized miniature keg was getting low, but they could still pour a few more samples. Zara turned a four-point black handle above the brass spout, and dark beer flowed into the tasting cup, foaming as it landed.

Branwen tucked a wayward lock of black hair behind her ear. She tried not to stare at Jade the bartender, but it was always hard to look away. Jade was medium height, slender yet solid—Branwen had seen what one punch could do to a man twice as tall and three times as broad. Jade's rich dark brown skin gleamed beneath the overhead lights. Her hair was cropped close, except for a long section near her forehead that flowed down her cheek to her jawline.

Wearing her usual white button-down shirt, black pants, and a blue bow tie, Jade the bartender didn't take the man in black's order, but moments later she set a pint of Galway Pradesh Stout in front of him, as if she had been expecting him. The black beer was the night sky poured into a pint glass; the thick white foam on top always made Branwen think of new snow. Relief passed over the man's face. The tension in his body eased. Beer slopped on the bar as his shaking right hand lifted the pint. Even from where she sat, at her and Zara's white covered table at the end of the pub, she could see that his left hand, clad in a black leather glove, was smaller than his right.

The man took a long, deep swallow of the stout. For eons Galway Pradesh Stout had been the world's most popular beer. Today GPS was brewed on every continent except Antarctica—though many said it was drunk enough there to compensate.

For a moment he paused. Branwen knew he was savoring the stout's smoothness, the interplay of roasted barley with a sharp bitterness of hops, underlaid by a tang that was a counterpoint to both flavors yet also a connecting thread. Branwen recognized the moment well, given all the times she and her sister had spent tasting GPS, examining every nuance of flavor, texture, aroma, and finish.

Sometimes I wonder if we should get some sort of best customer status, Branwen thought. *But it's all for one purpose, one goal—*

A horizontal fountain of beer blasted out of the man's mouth and showered the bar below.

Jade the bartender went over. Branwen couldn't hear their words, but she had an idea of what was going on.

I thought Zara and I were the only ones who'd noticed.

After a heated exchange, Jade did something Branwen did not expect. She took away the pint. Then Jade the bartender pointed at the sisters.

* * * * *

TAKING HIS BRIEFCASE, the man got up and Jade the bartender followed. When she came out from behind the bar, the two walked side by side, and she carried an empty pint glass. They seemed to know and respect each other, yet a wariness lay between them. As they approached, Branwen thought she heard the bartender say "ghost," and the man shook his head and tapped the top of his skull. The bartender only shrugged in reply, as if acknowledging good effort to avoid saying it wasn't quite enough.

"Good evening," said Jade. "Zara Porter and Branwen Porter, meet my friend Faddah Rucksack. He is finding our current GPS stock... disappointing."

"You think my opinion o' it is merely disappointed?" Rucksack's accent clipped the "th" sound into a mere "t."

What's his story? Branwen thought. *Irish voice with a Tibetan face. Even here you don't come across that every day.*

"I've drunk horse piss that tasted better than that sour swill. I'd bet my two old swords there isn't a worse keg in all the world."

"What a safe bet," Jade replied, "since you don't have those swords anymore."

"And how I wish I could find them and get them back." Rucksack waved his hand. "Details, details. But off the point. How in the world could you put that keg on, Jade-bloody-London?"

Jade's elbow moved so quickly Branwen almost missed the dig into Rucksack's ribs.

Zara stared hard at the man. Then she smiled. "I hated to tell you, Jade," she said, "since you were so nice to let us have our homebrew tasting here. But there is something off about the GPS. It's not just the

Mirror & Phoenix, though, and we know you're the best in the city about storage and cleaning. At least the past year, every pint of GPS we've had hasn't been right. But lately, and especially today, it's just been terrible. The balance is off. The sourness isn't just a note; it's a whole damn out-of-tune band. And what's up with the bitterness? There's hardly any lately. It's like they're not getting enough hops for the brew."

"I'll talk to my supplier," Jade said, coolness in her dark eyes. "In the meantime, I thought if my beer was unacceptable, Rucksack might be interested in your homebrew."

Rucksack grimaced. "Now, come on, Jade, you know I only drink GPS."

"Not at the moment you don't," Jade replied. "Though if you're going to be so damn stroppy, I suppose I could always give you a Deep's Special Lager on the house. Not like you pay for anything anyway."

"The source o' my credit always compensates you," Rucksack replied. "Just because I have drunk horse piss doesn't mean I want to repeat the experience."

Zara laughed. "That would be preferable. At least horse piss would taste like something. Deep's Special Lager is like eating snow. About all you can say for it is it's cold."

Rucksack stared hard at the sisters, then he smiled too. "All right, all right, Jade," he said. "You're trying to do me a kindness. Please forgive my rudeness. I'm not exactly at my best right now."

For a moment Branwen thought Jade was going to smile. "Given the circumstances," Jade replied, "I'll give you a pass. But remember, you even being here is still... tentative, as far as The Management goes."

Branwen could hear the capital letters, as well as a lot unsaid in the silence that followed. "No one has forgotten Hong Kong," Jade added. "And what just happened in India will be remembered for many years to come."

"As, I hope, will be the fact that there continue to be years to come," replied Rucksack. "But I promise I'll be a nice lad."

Jade chuckled. The lights of the pub danced on the dark skin of her high cheekbones. "Sure. And I'll just go fall off the beer truck."

"And what do you have to do with this beer?" Rucksack asked.

Jade smiled. "It's all the sisters," she replied. "It's out of my influence."

Rucksack said nothing, but his eyes widened. He and Jade stepped back as some men came to the table. "Ah," Zara said, "your timing is perfect. We were just closing up."

Branwen looked at her sister. "I thought we—"

Zara poked her in the ribs, then handed over homebrew samples.

Branwen glanced back at Jade and Rucksack, who were talking about something, but too low for Branwen to hear anything except Rucksack saying he would leave the briefcase with her later. Then Jade and Rucksack stared hard at each other, as if reading something.

Zara and I have been coming to the Mirror & Phoenix for years. I've never seen Jade act like this before. Who is this guy?

Then Jade went back to the bar, and Rucksack walked up to the table. Closer to the man in black now, Branwen could see the pain and weariness in his face, an agony in the brown-black eyes like a dying fire begging for more fuel. "Are you okay?" Branwen asked.

"You're kind to ask," Rucksack replied, pulling up a chair, sitting down, and setting the briefcase on the table. "Suffice to say that I've had a rather busy day and it took more out o' me than I expected." He smiled. "Sometimes I forget I'm not as young as I was. That... sometimes things are different."

Zara removed the empty sample cups and pulled off the tablecloth, revealing an ordinary pub table. "Well, it's not GPS," Zara said, "but we think it's pretty darn close." She picked up the empty glass Jade had left. Reaching under the table, Zara pulled out a large plain brown glass bottle and another empty pint glass. "The little keg is empty. Fresh one for you, sir." She popped the cap and a hiss made Rucksack smile. Then Zara began to pour stout into both glasses.

"You pour it like GPS," Rucksack said.

Branwen nodded. "My sister and I clone it at home."

"That's quite a challenge. I've encountered, shall we say, attempts at it, both commercial cons and homebrew hopefuls. No one has ever been able to clone GPS."

Zara paused to let the initial pour settle. "And how would you know that?"

"GPS is a... passion of mine." Rucksack nodded his approval at her pour.

"There's a line between passion and obsession," said Zara. "When it comes to GPS, which side are you on?"

"Never was much for lines," Rucksack replied. "I've had my share o' other beers, for what they're worth, which combined doesn't add up to one perfect pint o' GPS. If you name a pub anywhere in the world, I can tell you how the GPS tastes there. Who pours it best, who rushes, who needs to clean their lines. I can tell you which brewery the keg came from. I've drunk GPS in just about every place in this world there is to drink it, for longer years that you'd care to count. It's been quite a while since I was in London, and I've had a... difficult day. Let's just say you have no idea how ready I am for that pint."

"It's almost ready," Zara replied, topping up the pints. "You should know the pour can't be rushed."

Rucksack smiled, but he still trembled. "GPS has a secret," he said, "something special that makes it unlike any other beer. Trouble is, no one knows."

Zara let the full glasses settle again as the rich foamy head collected on top. "Don't get all mythical and mystical on me. There is no secret to GPS. We just make damn good homebrew, and First Call makes GPS. They're the biggest brewery in the world, and they know what they're doing. Brewing GPS is all just impeccable ingredients, perfectly designed and fabricated equipment, and flawless brewing technique. That's all you need to make a perfect GPS."

"The First Brewer invented GPS thousands of years ago," said Branwen, glaring at her sister. "There's lots no one knows, but we've learned as much of the lore as we could. It's hard to separate fact from myth."

"That line is far blurrier than most people realize," said Rucksack.

"So you think you know GPS?" Zara asked.

Rucksack nodded.

Zara handed over one pint of homebrew and raised her own. "Okay," she said, "then tell me about this beer."

"ZARA KNOWS EVERYTHING ABOUT tasting beer," said Branwen. "She can taste a hop substitution while stuffed up with a head cold."

Rucksack and Zara locked eyes and grinned. Then they each took a long draw of their pints.

"You bottled this ten days ago," Rucksack said. "And since you did the boil on your stove, there's some caramelization." He took a smaller sip, moving it around his palate before swallowing. "But you anticipated that and compensated by adding more hops to increase the bitterness."

"Is that all you notice?" Zara asked.

"The New Galway Gold hops have been less bitter this year," Rucksack replied. "All that damn rain in Ireland. Ah, o' course. So you also bumped up the roasted barley and used a hotter roast," he added. "That was risky. Easily could have come out too astringent, out of balance."

It's like he was there with us, Branwen thought. *It's like he's reading my notes.*

"But it didn't," Rucksack continued, and Zara's eyes brightened as he said, "Because you lowered the temperature while steeping the malted barley, to enhance the sweetness of the sugars being drawn out!"

They all clinked glasses and drank more stout. "It's been ages since I could talk that level o' detail," Rucksack said. "Thank you."

"Same to you," Zara replied. "I'm... impressed. You really know your beer."

"I didn't know we had a brother," Branwen said, nudging her sister.

"Oh, saying I was long lost would be putting it mildly," Rucksack said.

"You're not going to hit on us, are you?" Zara asked. "Because to put it mildly, you're wasting your time."

"Thank goodness," Rucksack replied. "For a moment I thought you were going to hit on me." He drank more of his pint, which was now almost empty. Then he stared at a spot over Zara's head, then Branwen's, almost as if he were reading something?

"You two really know your stuff," Rucksack said. "This homebrew is amazing... but it's not a clone o' GPS."

The smile fell off Zara's face. Branwen's breath paused.

"It's the closest I've ever encountered," Rucksack continued. "It's a damn sight better than the swill passing off for it here tonight. It's certainly making me feel more myself. But it doesn't have the secret."

"So we've kind of made GPS," said Branwen, "only not GPS as it's supposed to be, but as it is right now."

"I suppose you could put it that way," said Rucksack.

"How are we supposed to figure out what *na Grúdairí* themselves don't know anymore?" Branwen asked. "That magic, that secret—it's gone."

Zara snorted.

Branwen stared at her sister. Before she knew it she said, "You don't believe in the secret, but something can be real without anyone else believing it. Existence is truth, and it doesn't give a damn about being believed in. You don't believe in the secret, that's your deal, but don't mock me for what I think."

Eyes wide, Zara sat back and said nothing.

Rucksack stared from one sister to the other. Again he stared above their heads. Then he was silent, as if he had traveled deep inside his self, into some private world that even from the outside felt as big as the universe. "You said you had studied the lore o' GPS," he said slowly. "What have you learned about what it was, and what it is now?"

"For eons there has been the beer," said Branwen, "and some have said that without the beer the eons wouldn't have happened. Wherever there has been joy or grief, a hard day or a good day, a lonely drink or a lively party, there has been Galway Pradesh Stout. All around the world, from taps and bottles, the beer has poured. No beer has been as popular or long lived as GPS."

"Exactly. Today should be like any other day," replied Rucksack. "People went to the pub after work. Couples opened bottles at dinner. Friends clinked glasses as they watched the match. Some savored their last pint, some their first. Solitary drinkers ordered another GPS, thick and black, with a pillowy-white head like a snowdrift. The stout brings it all into focus, the boldness o' life, the black and white, the grays and bright colors. It's said that a pint o' GPS can make the world make sense, if only for a while. So dry and bitter on the tongue, GPS snaps people back to life, but what really brings them back, time after time and pint after pint, is what's hidden inside."

Branwen nodded. "Something was different that day. The beer wasn't right, but that wasn't all of it. People realized the beer hadn't been right for a while."

"That's exactly the thing," said Rucksack, "and it's been happening all over the world."

"Where have you been to notice?" Branwen asked.

"Last place I stayed a while was India. I had to deal with some nasty business, but that's another story for another time. I just got to England a couple o' days ago. Crossing Asia and Europe I kept encountering dodgy pints, and I realized there was more afoot than dirty lines or a keg left in the sun."

"And now you're really noticing that something is wrong with GPS," Branwen said. "Because this is where First Call Brewing is headquartered?"

"That's it in one," Rucksack said. "All this time, people have turned to GPS because it brings them a sense o' the universe filling them up. It gives a moment when the world makes sense. That moment hasn't been happening for a while, but people are malleable, forgiving, forgetful. They ignored it, figured it must be them. But it's happened too many times, and what's more, the beer is getting worse. Something's wrong with GPS, and people know it now. But more than that. Something's rotten in the brewery o' London. I've tried and tried over the years to appeal to the brewmaster. His second-in-command, Gabsir, and I go way back, though not necessarily as best mates. They don't want my help."

Zara sat forward. "Because of Guru Deep, I bet." Bitterness cut through her voice. "Branwen and I can't stand him."

Rucksack smiled a thin, sharp smile. "That makes three o' us. I'm going to sort this out. From the brew kettles o' First Call, all the way up to Guru Deep's office at the top o' the feckin Lotus if I have to."

"But Deep Inc. took over First Call decades ago," Branwen said. "What with Galway being destroyed in The Blast, First Call was weakened, had lots of problems, and eventually Deep Inc. took advantage of that. Brewmaster Samara was still in charge when it happened, before she passed leadership to the current brewmaster, Arthur Celbridge. Now Deep Inc. owns two breweries. First Call makes Galway Pradesh Stout, and Deep Brewing brews Deep's Special Lager. Are you thinking Guru Deep is trying to do something to First Call and GPS?"

"Yes," said Rucksack, "because it will do what he seeks: hurt me and hurt the world." A darkness had fallen over Rucksack's eyes. Long-simmering hostility radiated from him like heat from a boiling brew pot.

"Sounds like you two go way back," said Zara.

"I'm a thorn he can never quite get out o' his side, though I try harder." Rucksack grinned. "I've been opposing Deep Inc. since the company's early days, back when it was run by his grandfather. I've always considered the Deeps a pack o' shysters at best."

"Deep Inc. began about fifty years after The Blast," said Branwen, glaring at him. "You look pretty young for a hundred and thirty."

"It's not nice to ask a fella his age," replied Rucksack. "Deep Inc. was mostly fake medical cures then, and tent-revival sermons about the illusion of the world, but always accompanied by the reality o' the collection plate." Finishing his pint, Rucksack leaned forward. The clamminess had left his skin and the sweat had dried. His eyes were clear. Behind the darkness, a fire burned. "A few decades ago, Guru Deep came up in the company, doing inspirational talks and self-help books, got famous for his 'Find Your Third Eye In Half The Time!' feel-good enlightentainment shite. Today he's got that, the breweries, his travel guidebooks, and various complicated financial dealings. Over the past few decades he's built a global empire. Now we're at a culmination. I'd bet a year's pints that Guru Deep took over First Call precisely so he could eventually destroy the brewery and the beer."

"He's just a big business blowhard," said Zara.

"Some say Guru Deep is ridiculous, a sparkling nothing with a big smile and a bright suit," said Rucksack, lowering his voice. He looked over his shoulder and scanned the pub, then turned back to the sisters. "He's a showman for sure. But make no mistake. He does far more than all the things we just said. For months I've been disrupting Guru Deep's operations. At three in particular—in Marrakech, Mexico City, and Moscow—I saw things that made me wish I was having a nightmare: experiment pits. I shut them down, but the people there... those who had survived... I did what I could, but I can only hope they'll find a way to live again without screaming. Guru Deep had huge labs where shady and discredited scientists were using people as lab rats. It's not fake cures anymore. He's experimenting with reality. Poking at it. Trying to tear it. And seeing what happens to people when you do."

The sisters leaned back. The air in the pub and the blood in Branwen's veins felt cold. "Why... Why would he do that?"

"Some people want to rule the world," said Rucksack. "Guru Deep considers that a lack o' ambition. He has his sights set far higher. There are those who say the world is an illusion, the dream o' a sleeping god."

"That would figure," said Zara. "Let me guess: Guru Deep doesn't want to wake the god. He wants to take its place."

Rucksack nodded. "He hides it well, but everything he does conceals his true self and his true purpose. Guru Deep is one o' the most dangerous people in the world. Whatever his ultimate plans are, he's setting them in motion."

"What can you do about it?" Branwen asked.

"Luckily," said Rucksack with a smile, "I'm one o' the most dangerous people in the world too."

"Who are you, anyway?" Zara asked.

"I'm Faddah Rucksack," he replied. "The world's only Himalayan-Irish sage. The hero o' old and the hero o' now. He who flew and he who fell. He who lost and he who is trying to regain and restore. I am ten thousand years old. I am the fire o' life, the tiger's roar. Time and again in history, I have been the one who kept this world not only turning but thriving, saving lives and ensuring tomorrows. And I am the one who, yet again, will stand against Guru Deep."

Branwen grinned. *I've been searching for the secret,* she thought. *I think I might have found it... And now I have also found someone who can tell me I'm on the right path.* She looked at her sister—and even Zara had a brightness in her eyes beyond her usual smoldering hardness and skepticism.

Rucksack's smile fell away. "I've a horrible feeling that I can't stop him though."

"What?" said both sisters.

"You are amazing brewers," said Rucksack, "and I believe we're meeting for a reason. I trust you—it's in the beer, who you are, how you make it. You know something I don't. Something Guru Deep doesn't. Something even na Grúdairí and the brewmaster don't know anymore. I can't stop Guru Deep." He looked from Branwen to Zara and back to Branwen. "But I reckon *we* can."

"How?" Zara asked.

Rucksack nodded at the briefcase. "How about I show you?"

THE OLD MAN HADN'T noticed the man in black before, but if he had, he didn't know what he could've done differently. Picking at loose threads on his ragged gray coveralls, he drank the rest of his sample and stared at the man in black while making sure he couldn't be seen.

The man in black drank the women's homebrew as if it were GPS itself.

Staring down at his empty cup, Gabsir Abrigs hated to admit it, but it damn near was.

It was missing one thing though—only he didn't know what. Not even the brewmaster knew anymore.

Before he could look away, the smaller of the two women, the quiet one, caught his eye. Before the man in black could turn around and see him too, the old man left the pub.

He had to get back to First Call. It was infuriating enough that Faddah Rucksack was back in London and sure to meddle. The brewmaster would be angry too—angrier even than about having to hear about the Malt and Hops sisters again. But he really needed to change his mind and try some of their homebrew.

AS THEY GATHERED AT the small table at the end of the kitchen, Branwen was impressed that Zara had offered their flat.

Sitting between the sisters, Rucksack set the briefcase on the table. "What would you think," he said, "if I told you that the First Brewer and his wife spent centuries discovering the secret and creating the beer that would become Galway Pradesh Stout? And what if I told you that the first good batch, made with the secret, was brewed over a tricky peat fire on the west coast o' Ireland, in a beaten copper kettle that had to be patched up before they could brew with it? Or that the fermentation was done in a cave, in a hollowed-out boulder with a hot spring nearby that kept the temperature right, but that also allowed a bit o' souring to happen?"

"That's ridiculous," Zara replied.

"You'd be surprised how often truth sounds absurd."

"It fits," Branwen said. "Given what we know of GPS. If they're centuries old, are they... like you?"

Zara stared at Rucksack. "You're their son, aren't you?"

"The First Brewer's name was Jagathi," said Rucksack. "Together with his wife, Kailash, they created GPS. Kailash had other... plans, but the perfection o' GPS was Jagathi's reason for living."

"They were so devoted to brewing beer," said Branwen. "But it wasn't really just about the beer."

"People easily lose their way in life," replied Rucksack. "It's hard to understand the difference between what matters and what doesn't, what is real and what is dream. The First Brewer understood that there was a secret to life that could be brewed into the very beer itself. GPS became a way to express life's purpose."

"I get the reality part," said Branwen. "When I brew GPS, I feel... whole. Alive. I know that every move I make is with purpose, intent, truth. I know I'm doing what I'm meant to do." *Why am I saying so much to him?* she thought. *I don't even tell Zara this sort of stuff.* "But even with knowing that what I do is right, I can't say I understand some deep universal truth about the beer or life or existence or whatever. So what is the secret?"

Rucksack sighed. "That's the bear o' it," he said. "I don't know either."

Branwen's eyes widened. "You don't know?"

"I was never a brewer," said Rucksack. "Lacked the aptitude. So my dad never told me. I've drunk oceans o' GPS during my life. I like to think I live the secret o' GPS, even though I don't know the actual literal truth o' the secret behind it."

"Is that enough for you?"

Rucksack shrugged. "Perhaps the secret o' life is living the truth one knows as best one can. There's more to life than getting the words right. You're okay as long as you're getting the living right."

He unlatched the briefcase and laid his right hand on the lid. "And that brings us to this," he said, "Tonight, before I came to the pub, I broke into the Lotus and stole something o' Guru Deep's. Something essential to his plans. If GPS expresses the purpose o' life, then what's inside this case erases it."

He pulled up the lid. The sisters stared, their eyes wider with each moment.

"Whoa..." Zara said, her voice trailing off.

"Wow..." Branwen added.

They both reached out for what was inside the briefcase.

Rucksack closed the lid.

"The last thing any o' us wants to do is touch that," he said. "We'd mean well, but things certainly wouldn't end well."

"How can we help you?" Branwen asked.

"I can weaken Guru Deep," said Rucksack. "You can strengthen GPS."

"You're saying we can bring back the beer," said Zara.

"I'm saying that in all the years I've wandered this world, I've never encountered anyone like the two o' you," Rucksack replied. "What happens next to the world depends upon the chance meeting o' a fallen hero and two women trying to make their dream into their reality." He looked from one sister to another. "Helping me can help you. Will we work together?"

Zara nodded. "Meet us in the Maya Plaza tomorrow."

"What will we do?" Rucksack asked.

Branwen smiled. "We'll get to work."

* * * * *

THE ANNOUNCEMENT WOULD HAPPEN at ten a.m., said the flat radio voice in the morning. *As if we don't know already,* thought Branwen as she carried her purple bowl and Zara's yellow bowl to the kitchen. Well, almost. The short stretch of counter gave a passable impression of being a kitchen, but only if you were good at juggling and didn't mind moving the plug-in kettle, the dish drainer, and the messy meters of clear plastic tubing when you wanted to make a cup of tea. Or set down the breakfast dishes.

Branwen yawned and tried to remember what time it was when they had finished talking and Rucksack had left. After the late night, more tea sounded good. "Zara?" she called, balancing two bowls on one hand while she made room. "Weren't you going to clear up the brewing gear and the dishes?" *Again.* Branwen glanced at the narrow door on the wall past the counter. She smiled. *At least it's almost ready.*

A horn blared. Outside the window over the sink, four floors below, Branwen stared down at London. Red buses, thick crowds, and the city's iconic orange taxis bustled. They teemed around the diversions, detours, and delays of construction sites. "ALWAYS TIMELESS. ALWAYS LONDON!" beamed the bright, colorful signs all over the city. The colorful traffic swarmed around the black, as if momentum could help them ignore it. The blackened rocks, the blackened patches of ground, the black moods that still could take the city when they stared too long at what was black. What was black had once been burning.

There was a long time when black had been all that was left of London.

But not anymore. The morning man on the radio had reminded Branwen of that. A cloud dimmed the early sun, and Branwen stared out the window at the city below. People in brilliant colors walked on the wide sidewalks. Taxis swerved around lumbering red buses and the riots of purples, oranges, pinks, and greens of small delivery trucks and large lorries. Buildings grew like trees. And in London, no one wore black and nothing was colored black. Down below, the city was all whites and brights. Up above, Branwen looked at her purple shirt, white leggings, and purple cowboy boots. *Including me.*

But something about the city had shifted. Maybe it was the clouds settling over the sky. Maybe it was the lack of smiles on the people walking by. *Or maybe it's just that I got about two hours of sleep,* Branwen thought.

Over the sound of water coming out of the bathroom tap, Zara said, "Szzyahfgt."

Branwen shook her head. "I don't speak toothbrush."

A wet splat, then the water was off. "Sorry," Zara said as she came out of the bathroom, flicking her purple-and-yellow bangs out of her eyes. "I forgot about the washing-up."

"Well I'm not cleaning it up," Branwen said quietly. *Yeah you will,* she thought.

Zara glanced at the clock hanging above the shoebox kitchen sink. "It's eight already. We're going to be late for work if we don't hurry, and we still have to check it before we go."

Branwen shrugged and looked at the floor.

"Oh come on!" Zara grinned and flicked out a hand, lightly slapping her sister's shoulder. "You should be excited. It's our best yet! When it's ready, we'll get past the gate for sure."

"That's what you always say." Branwen shook her head. "But we never do."

"It isn't that we never do," Zara replied. "It's just that we haven't yet."

"Ugh. You sound like Guru Deep. Next thing I know you'll be wearing orange suits."

"We've dumped batches better than that draingush. We should be fine," Zara said, changing something in her voice, "As Long As I Never Sound Like I Talk Slowly, Each Word Perfectly Distinct With Profound Importance, As If Each Word Is Capitalized."

The laugh snuck out before Branwen could stop it. "That was so close it's scary."

Zara shrugged. "I get a lot of practice."

"He's making some sort of announcement at ten. Sounds like a pretty big deal."

"That's what they were talking about on the wireless?"

"The word is 'radio.'" Branwen looked up and rolled her eyes. "You sound like Mum. Or Gran. It's not like this stuff was invented yesterday."

"All right," said Zara, glancing over her shoulder at the door next to the kitchen. "I'll tidy up. You check the beer and grab a sixer to take to the gates."

Branwen sighed.

"We do good work," Zara said. "That's why I know it's going to pay off. Think of how much people liked our beer last night. These last couple of batches have been our best yet, little sister. This is it. I can feel it."

The excitement in Zara's voice had climbed with every word. She could see it, feel it, as if it were already happening. Branwen closed her eyes a moment and let herself go, following her sister along the wild ride that would follow. The dream come true at last. The gate opening, the welcoming handshake, the joyful camaraderie that came with the clap on the back from the other men and women as they walked inside together. *I couldn't care less that we'd be the first hired in years,* Branwen thought. *This is what we were born to do. Who cares that there's a hiring freeze? All we need to do is impress them, and it will all change. We'll be where we're supposed to be.*

Branwen smiled at her sister. As she opened the door to the boxroom, her smile faded when she remembered she knew what was inside, but she was the only one who did.

WHEN THEIR DREAM CAME true and it came time to leave the little flat, Branwen wondered if they'd get back their deposit. The landlord never complained, since they always dropped off some homebrew at his door. But as Branwen stepped inside the dark boxroom, earthy yeast and floral bitterness filled her nose. Branwen suspected the room would never really air out, though they did try to keep anything from soaking into the hardwood floor.

Once it got into you, it never left. Branwen breathed in deeply. *I hope this smell always makes me smile like this.* Then she thought of where that smell was going to take them, and she knew it always would.

She flipped on the light and went to one of the floor-to-ceiling shelves on all the walls. The shelves covered with plastic tubing, metal fittings, a large pot, worn brushes, and on the shelf where Branwen now stood, a massive pile of blankets with a rise in the middle, like a high mountain peak surrounded by smaller hills. Branwen had made sure that organizing and maintaining the equipment shelves was her job. It kept Zara from finding things she shouldn't.

Branwen pulled off the blankets and stared at what was underneath. Guilt plunged through her again.

I hate keeping secrets from you, big sister, she thought, *but there are some things you just shouldn't know.*

Where the blankets had been, a dirty, empty carboy sat on the shelf. Branwen thought of all the late, sleepless nights brewing the wort, monitoring fermentation, and checking the beer, all while her sister slept. A week ago, in the middle of the night, Branwen had siphoned the stout from this carboy and bottled the stout that she and she alone had brewed. Last night, after Rucksack's visit and while Zara dreamed of their dreams coming true, Branwen had drunk one of her beers and thought about what she had seen in the small briefcase, and what she should be able to see in a perfect pint of GPS.

The secret was there. So bright and simple, as obvious as exhaling after inhaling. Branwen couldn't believe she hadn't noticed before.

As she drank the stout and stared into the bottle, the understanding moved through her like breath, like blood.

And then, as she gazed into the dark heart of the bottle, a little light, like a distant star, began to shine.

Hands shaking, she took another long quaff from the bottle.

And Branwen saw. The world, life, decisions, destinies—all there. Faint, like a radio playing down the street. Dim, like the low sun through thin misty clouds. Just for a moment, a fleeting glimpse. Then gone. But it had been there.

I've done it, Branwen thought, though as she admitted it to herself a crack tore through her heart. *This isn't just a clone of GPS. It is GPS—the way it should be. I did it. But I wish we had done it.*

The guilt stung, but it faded as a conviction shone through her like the full sun breaking up a storm.

This beer is better than anything we've brewed together.

And there in the morning, her head still foggy, both exhilaration and sadness came back to her. Branwen took down one of her six-packs and stared. Inside the bottles shone little sparks. *If anything can get us through the gate*, she thought, *this will.*

Branwen replaced the blankets, crinkling them just so and making note of the telltale folds. She left the boxroom and Zara put the six-pack in her bag. "This is it, little sister," she said. "We've got the secret. Now let's get to work. Got a big day, what with the announcement and all."

If you only knew, Branwen thought as they left the flat. "And we have our new trainee," she said.

For a few blocks, the sisters walked in silence. Around them rose the grid of London, just north of the Thames. They passed shopfronts and cafes, taking in English rock and roll, Indian spices, and English subsidiaries of Hong Kong banks.

"At least we can walk there now," Zara said.

"So the glass is half full?" replied Branwen bitterly.

"I prefer to think of it as halfway to another glass."

Around another corner, down another street, past another block, they saw it.

The brown-and-black brick building rose only three stories from the ground, but the squat, dark hulk spread over four square blocks of precious London real estate. Steam rose from the roof, creating a thin fog in the cool air that made the place unearthly, unreal, as if they stared at a dream through mist.

No matter how many times they came to it, Branwen's heart beat faster.

Around the windowless brick building, with spiked bars ten feet high, ran a rusted iron fence, dotted with black spots of the original paint. Every ten feet a crumbling brick pillar interspersed the fence. The sisters walked along, staring through the bars.

They came to the gate and stopped.

Zara and Branwen gazed at the building beyond. The black doors through which only the best of the best could go—na Grúdairí.

Branwen looked at the engraved, dirty, tarnished brass plaque on the gate in front of her nose:

FIRST CALL BREWING COMPANY

A SUBSIDIARY OF DEEP INC.

GLOBAL OFFICES & LONDON BREWERY

Zara tugged on the gate, but it didn't budge.

"It's always locked," Branwen said.

"You never know," Zara replied. "Maybe one day it won't be. How will we know if we don't try?"

Branwen looked at her watch. "I know we'd better not be late today."

"We'll come back after work, stand here as long as it takes. We're not leaving until they at least take the homebrew." Zara smiled. "We will each be the best of the best of all brewers in all the world. We will each be a *grúdaire* of First Call." She said it again, slowly, "*Gruhd*-uh-ruh," savoring each syllable like a long swallow of stout. We're going to make it, Branwen. I know it."

"We're already really good brewers, Zara."

Zara nodded. "We are. But that's not enough. There are brewers... and then there are na Grúdairí."

With a last, longing look at the gate, Zara and Branwen continued walking to work, dreaming of the day when at last they would walk together through the gate, then the black doors. The first new members of na Grúdairí in decades. But not today.

AT THE MAIN THOROUGHFARE the sisters caught the bus that would take them across London Bridge. Zara always insisted they sit on the top deck, at the front, so they could see what was ahead of them. Just south of the far bank of the Thames, the glass monstrosity of Deep Inc. rose above the bright sandy-yellow tenements and the new but much smaller office buildings, so bright in their reds and blues. They stared; everyone always stared, or at least glanced up. All found it hard to look away.

The lower blue-green glass cylinder rose like a stem for thirty-five stories, which already would have made it the tallest building in London, and it was currently the tallest in the world. Hong Kong and New York were said to be racing along with taller buildings, but for now the corporate world headquarters of Deep Inc. was enjoying a big spotlight. Even though it would never remain the tallest building, Branwen knew it would always be one of the most unique. The bottom thirty-five stories were nothing special, though the wide, flat, public park and plaza that surrounded the building was a beautiful part of the city.

The top, however, was what ensured that the building would always be among the most distinct in the world. Those final seven stories defied architecture, physics, and reality as anyone thought they understood it.

From the top of the box, an orange flower rose. Panels of gold-sheen glass rose in narrow curves and angles, building on each other up and around the building like the petals of a flower. Or like the circle and spires of a crown, the cynics and critics said. But a flower was what it was, as Guru Deep had explained in hundreds of interviews all over the world, his wide smile the only thing brighter than his trademark orange suit, white shirt, brown-and-black shoes, and orange tie.

"At Deep Inc. we strive to think higher and clearer, to See Beyond What Is To What Should Be," he had said the day not long ago when the building had opened for business but had not yet been dedicated. "Today, we take our first steps into the Lotus. This is not only the new world headquarters of Deep Inc. The Lotus is far more than a flower of glass and steel. It is the heart, soul, and center of the company that I and my dedicated employees all over the world have built and continue to build into The World's Best Place To Work. It is a beacon that we all may look upon, when we need to see what lies beyond the reality that binds, blinds, and mires us. As all who enter our grand lobby will see, in the words etched upon the wall at the center, 'The Lotus Opens To One Who Knows There Is No Lotus.'"

Branwen knew that no other building would ever surpass its notoriety. *And none will be as clean,* she thought as the sisters got off the bus at the edge of the Maya Plaza.

Faddah Rucksack was waiting for them, looking uncomfortable and frumpy in a red tracksuit.

"You look terrible," Zara said.

"Don't I know it," Rucksack replied, "but at least it's different from my usual. I'd stick out like coal on a snowfield." He plucked the bright red fabric. "I never thought I'd be so happy to change clothes, and that's including being seasick during the storm I barely survived while sailing from the Mediterranean to Ireland."

"Then you'd better come on, FNG," Zara said.

Rucksack raised an eyebrow. "FNG?"

"Feckin new guy," Branwen explained. "Though how is this going to work? If Guru Deep knows what you look like, won't he find you and trap you? Not to mention sack us, if we're lucky?"

Rucksack smiled. With a bob of his head the sisters followed him into the empty plaza and behind a stretch of trees.

"I could explain the history behind what I'm about to do, but we don't want to be late for my first day. Besides, the tale would take all week," said Rucksack. "I don't usually show this. But by asking you to trust me I've asked a lot. I want you to know I know that. So I'm going to show you how much I trust you. My family has—had—a secret. A skill we acquired to help us survive. It can be a bit... disconcerting to see, but I'll trust you'll keep this to yourselves."

Before the sisters could say anything, Rucksack closed his eyes and lowered his head. A soft white glow surrounded him, obscuring his features.

When the glow faded, another man stood before them.

Zara stepped back. "What the hell?"

"When we met last night," the man said, "I told you we were meeting for a reason, and that I had stolen something from Guru Deep, because o' something I believe he is planning for GPS and First Call."

"That's true," Branwen said, touching her sister's arm.

"I'm still me," he said. "For the sake of simplicity and duplicity, call me Jeremy. Jeremy Ruckley."

"Your accent is gone, and your face is all narrow instead of round," Zara said. "Your skin is lighter, more like you're English."

A breeze rustled the tracksuit.

"You're a lot to take in," Zara said.

Rucksack chuckled. "The part you see is just window dressing, little more than clothes, really." He took the glove off his left hand and held it next to his right. Both hands looked the same. "Though it'd be a helluva lot easier to live up to all that guff if my hand were better."

"What did happen to your hand?" Branwen asked.

"Accidentally smashed it with Guru Deep's *London Through the Third Eye* guidebook," said Rucksack, staring at the left hand. "Making the hands the same will be tiring as all hell. If I need a breather, could you explain I have a medical condition or something?"

"Sure," said Zara, "but I don't think you really need to worry."

Rucksack raised an eyebrow. "What do you mean?"

"You have to understand," Zara replied, "what it's like working inside the Lotus. Everyone walks around as if they were sleepwalking. They Talk Like Every Word Is Capitalized, because most of what they say are platitudes from Guru Deep."

"That won't matter as much as you think," Rucksack said. "It will still be dangerous."

"How dangerous?" Zara said.

"Extremely," Rucksack replied. "If Guru Deep finds us out, the worst thing I can think o' is probably the nicest thing he'll start with."

"But if we don't help," Branwen continued, "then the stakes are high. First Call. GPS."

"Higher," Rucksack replied. "Bigger. London. The world. All life and the universe itself."

"Okay," Zara said. "Then we'd better get to work. Literally, before you're late for your first day."

The three crossed the Maya Plaza and walked to a nondescript narrow door at the back of the building.

Once buzzed inside, they handed over Jeremy Ruckley's papers and were waved through. They walked down a dim corridor lined with pipes, conduit, and posters that said things like "WITHIN LABOR, LIBERATION WAITS." They pointed Rucksack to the men's locker room, then ducked into the women's.

When they all emerged wearing their gray coveralls, the sisters took Rucksack to the storage closet.

They'd hardly closed the door behind them when the new executive manager, Blanders, stopped them.

His gray suit and tie made the dim lights drabber, and he carried a large bundle, wrapped in brown paper, under one arm. "Spic and span, ladies," he said. "Today is the big day. Guru Deep has instructed me to personally oversee operations, right down to even your duties." He sneered.

"The dedication," Zara said. "We'd never forget."

"You were nearly late," Blanders replied.

"We had to get our trainee settled," Branwen said.

Blanders turned his gray gaze to the man behind them. "And you are?"

"Jeremy Ruckley, sir," Rucksack replied.

"Keen to clean, are you?"

Rucksack shrugged. "A job's a job sir, as long as the work is honest. And the people too."

Blanders stared, searching his face. "Guru Deep knows where your dedication lies," he said at last. "And remember, whatever you do, say, or think here, Guru knows. Guru Deep knows all. Now, if you are done running late—"

"Nearly late," Zara cut him off, "is not late."

"For Guru Deep, On Time Is Late. Early Is Everything."

"Then with respect, sir," said Zara behind gritted teeth, "since this dedication is such a big deal for Guru Deep's announcement, may we get to work?"

"Of course," Blanders said, stepping aside to let them pass. "Just remember something for me."

"What?"

"The dedication is nothing compared to what he's really going to announce." Blanders smiled. He started to walk away, then stopped. "All that glistening repartee," he said, "I nearly forgot."

He lifted the bundle under his arm and handed it to Rucksack. "These were just printed this morning. We had an incident last night. I want these posted every three meters on every wall in the lower thirty-five, and from thirty-six to forty. And one in each cubicle, office, restroom, restroom stall, break area, and non-public conference room."

"What about forty-one?" Branwen asked, trying to keep the breathiness out of her voice that everyone else used whenever they talked about the floor of executive managers directly beneath Guru Deep's.

"Forty-one is unnecessary. Ms. Fox and I have already briefed the upper management. I want all of these hung by the morning tea break."

Zara's mouth hung open. "What? In addition to everything else we need to do? We'll be here till midnight!"

"'Tis Not The Time But The Task That Matters," Blanders said. "And as you sagely mentioned before, I really must let you get to work." A smile fluttered then died. "Oh. One more thing."

"Sir?"

"I'll have a special task for you later as well. After the announcement. Happy hanging." Blanders stepped close to Zara. "Guru Deep thanks you for your silent efficiency and determined commitment." Then he left.

"So that's the boss?" said Rucksack. "He's a one-man air conditioner."

Branwen nodded and rubbed her arms. "Now that he's gone, I think the temperature just went up five degrees."

"I can hardly believe Blanders came down from up high to micromanage us," Branwen said. "He's not our boss though. Our manager is old and sweet, but not exactly on top of things."

"He also has an easy signature," Zara added.

"And doesn't exactly count his personnel forms," said Rucksack, nodding. "Nicely done."

Zara pointed at the bundle in Rucksack's arms. "So, Jeremy, what are we wasting our day on?"

Rucksack tore off the paper. They all looked—then gasped. "Well I'll be," he said at last. "Not a bad likeness. If you want to take one home, I'll autograph it for you."

He set the stack on top of the cart, but Zara stepped away from it. "Thing's heavy enough without those," she said. "FNG, you can be the cart mule today."

Rucksack sighed and started pushing. Armed with their brooms, mops, and the stack, the janitors of the Lotus got ready for a long day's work.

THE SIGHT OF IT still startled Feckniss. The original Tower of London had once loomed over the city, but its thick walls and long history had been no match for the fires of The Blast. Some said the very blocks had melted and flowed into the Thames. Others said the Tower had exploded into dust and ash. Every day when Feckniss rode by on his bus, he tried to imagine what the original Tower must have looked like. But it was hard to imagine when its original grounds were now the site of Tower Park, all rolling lawns and soaring trees. The Tower itself now was but a replica, built at a scale that was a fraction of its size, yet still large enough for people to walk through. Feckniss had loved strolling through the hallways as a schoolboy, a giant among the tiny rooms, imagining the kings and queens of old cowering before him.

The bus lumbered onto London Bridge, crossing the Thames to the south bank. Downriver the black, twin-tower hulk of Blast Bridge—or Blasted Bridge, as it was known when traffic backed up—almost shone in the morning sunlight. During London's long rebuilding, the black bridge with its towers and double drawbridge had been the first built to span the Thames, reconnecting north and south London by road for the first time in decades.

Rumbling through the traffic that packed the wide streets, the bus rounded a corner. Feckniss held his breath.

At last.

Every morning he never felt awake until he saw it. Tower Park, the bridges, they were all just a warm-up compared to what he saw now. Every day he longed to be there, and every night he hated to leave. The bus pulled up to his stop at the edge of the Maya Plaza. Feckniss beamed as he stepped down, knowing that each foot in front of the other brought him closer to his true home.

Something out of the corner of his eye made him pause. Feckniss turned. The hole in the lamppost hadn't been there yesterday morning. But at least it had been patched, if somewhat hastily and shoddily. He made a note to tell Blanders, who would ensure the appropriate maintenance personnel could be dispatched.

So tall and vast, so high above the rest of London, the top of the Lotus could be heaven's basement. Feckniss walked with his head high and eyes wide, staring across the Maya Plaza to the tall flower where he worked. Only on the third floor, but it was a start.

"I will work myself up," he said, smoothing his tan overcoat and the dark blue suit beneath. He'd chosen his favorite orange tie today. All his ties were orange, as a show of respect to Guru Deep, but this tie was special. Blanders had given it to him a year ago, the day he had added Feckniss to the project.

Feckniss noted the stage that had been built for today's announcement, then slowly gazed up the building, along the tall blue-green stalk, then up to the flower. Behind the gold-orange glass of the Lotus's petals, the main managers guided the day-to-day operations of one of the world's biggest companies. They answered to the people on forty-one, the home of executive managers such as Blanders. The executive managers answered only to Guru Deep himself. At the south side of forty-one, Guru Deep's personal assistant, Nia Fox, guarded a lone elevator. That elevator was the only way up to Guru Deep's private domain on the forty-second floor.

Next to the elevator door, a poster said, "TO RISE IS TO FALL. TO FALL IS TO RISE."

How high up can I go? Feckniss thought. *How long will it take to go from the third floor to forty-one?* It had been long, hard work just to earn and keep his place on the third floor, but Feckniss knew he was Aiming Higher To Fly Higher, just like Guru Deep had said in yesterday's company motivation speech.

After the speech, and after a long day and a long evening, Feckniss's manager had clapped him on the shoulder. "We're ready," his manager had said, grinning. "You've earned the tie."

And he had. Feckniss thought back over the late nights, all-nights, and early mornings of the past year. Document after document. Presentation after presentation. Phone calls in the middle of the night—never from Guru Deep, of course. Feckniss wasn't that important. But his manager had said that Guru Deep was aware of and satisfied with Feckniss's work. All the while, he labored under the poster that covered the entire ceiling above the block of cubicles where he worked. A red line graph showed a sharp line falling, falling, falling. Above it, the orange words glared:

WHAT IS THE SOUND OF NO PROFIT RISING?

Like the others around him, Feckniss worked silently, knowing what hung over him.

Throughout that hard year, Feckniss had struggled, had doubted, but persevered. He had worked so hard not only at the work, but at calming the doubts and questions he would not answer, would not consider. "Hard Choices Require Hard Feelings," Guru Deep said. The strain had been hard. So hard. So hard that yesterday—after the alarms and the news of the theft, of the enemy's infiltration—Feckniss felt something inside crack.

But it had just been nerves. "Yesterday's Struggles Birth Today's Triumphs," Guru Deep had said. Now the time had come. In a little over an hour, Guru Deep's voice would be heard all around the world. He would officially dedicate the Lotus.

Then shake the world.

Straightening his tie, Feckniss took a deep breath and walked from the bus stop, across the wide sidewalk, to the ring of the low-growing sacred fig trees that marked the perimeter of the park surrounding the Lotus. In order to build the Lotus here, city government had required Deep Inc. to make the surrounding area a public park, where all could go free and unchecked. Feckniss knew that still rankled his manager, and even Guru Deep, but they'd had no choice. Still, one day it wouldn't matter. Not once it happened, not once Operation—

But Feckniss put it out of his mind and tried to enjoy his stroll through the calm park. Feckniss's stride was slow and smooth, as cool as the morning, and Feckniss couldn't help but let his shoulders slide deeply from step to step. *I'm on my way*, he thought.

From the eastern edge of the plaza, Feckniss followed the path that went straight from the street, through the trees, past the grass park spaces and the ponds, to the Lotus itself. Seven other paths, one for each of the eight main points on the compass, came in and out of the Lotus, representing the principal winds that marked the main ways of the world. Throughout the day, Deep Inc. gardeners groomed the paths, smoothed the stones, and removed trash. The paths always looked as if you were the first person to set foot on them.

Feckniss thought of the perfect compass line that he was walking on. The sun rose from the end of the eastern path and set at the western edge. He knew the paths stopped at the street, but something about them seemed to keep going. Across England and Scotland, crossing the official yet informal border between the two countries. Across Ireland, though even the path must shudder to pass by the lifeless ruins of Galway, still blackened and desolate a hundred and thirty years after The Blast. The paths ran south through France and Western Africa, and east across Asia, and through the oceans and glaciers, mountains and plains...

All around the world. The massive, massive world.

Faintness jellied Feckniss's knees. The coolness fell out of his stride. He slipped, barely caught himself on a tree trunk. The rough bark scraped his smooth face.

The world beyond London was a place he never wanted to go. Just thinking of it made him weak and tired. Feckniss closed his eyes. His breath caught, but he tried to breathe, tried to remember his little solitary flat and the bus route he took every day. He thought of the chippie where he got dinner on Friday nights, and of his favorite orange tea mug.

You never have to leave London, he thought. *Your Work Is Your Anchor, just like Guru Deep says. You never have to leave London. Never. Never ever ever.*

Gradually his racing heartbeat calmed, and his breath came more easily. Feckniss opened his eyes. He was still in London. The Lotus still rose in front of him, waiting for him to come through its wide glass doors.

Everything was okay. The world was still and quiet. He brushed off his coat and suit. No damage done, though his face felt raw and sharp in a few places. No one had seen him fall.

Then why do I hear someone laughing? he thought.

Feckniss turned around and around, looking for the person who must have seen. But there was no one but him in the empty park.

As he came to the doors of the Lotus, he could still hear the laughter.

The doors closed behind him. Feckniss's heart pounded. He thought for sure he could hear its thump resounding through the vast open space of the Lotus's lobby, bouncing off the white marble floor, the floor-to-ceiling windows, the security and reception desk, and the central elevator bank. But all was quiet, except for the sounds of shoes as more Deep Inc. employees arrived.

Then the laughter began again. And it resounded everywhere, off the floor and windows, off the ceiling so high up, Feckniss was sure he could see clouds there sometimes.

But no one else seemed to hear it. Or if they did, they ignored it, fleeing instead to the elevators, to their cubicles or to the rare offices for the department managers. Feckniss shook his head, and at last the laughter ceased. He quickly crossed to the elevator and fled to his cubicle—where someone waited for him.

The face stopped him at the open entrance of his cubicle. There he was.

The enemy.

Instead of the orange that colored the letters of all the other motivational and inspirational posters around the Lotus, these words were black.

WANTED.

THIEF. PROVOCATEUR. INSURRECTIONIST.

Faddah Rucksack

PROMOTION & REWARD

REPORT TO FORTY-ONE

Beneath the name was a face, but Feckniss wasn't sure if it was a photograph or a painting. The face was at once both completely real yet unreal, a man and a dream. Feckniss took in the bald head, the brown skin, and above all the piercing brown-black eyes that, even in the poster, seemed so filled with joy and sorrow that the man could have been there at both the beginning and the end of the world.

Feckniss realized he'd been staring at the poster for a long time. He heard the laughter again. No words, but the insult in the sound was clear. He looked around, but no one was paying any attention to him. They never did. His colleagues tended to their morning tasks, or walked silently, their faces blank as they went from one part of the third floor to another. Feckniss wondered if other offices were as quiet. But it did make it easier to get on with work—and that would make it easier to move up to the fourth floor. He looked up. *And keep on going.*

Switching on the radio in his cubicle, Feckniss listened to the detachment and anticipation in the voices of the announcers. No one knew what Guru Deep was going to do or say, but everyone had their theories. Some suspected he would run for public office. Some anticipated the announcement of a major merger. Others wondered if the time was finally coming for Guru Deep to name his successor—it was no secret that young as he may look, the decades-long head of Deep Inc. wasn't getting any younger.

At nine o'clock, Blanders and his smile came in and slapped a newspaper on the desk. "It's everywhere," Blanders said. "Isn't it wonderful?"

"Just as we planned," Feckniss replied.

"Guru Deep is pleased." Blanders sat on the edge of Feckniss's desk. "I spoke with him before coming down to you. He told me, 'That Feckniss,' Guru Deep said, 'that Feckniss, he sees the answers as if he knows the questions.'"

Feckniss puzzled over this apparent compliment, but at last he gave up. "What does that mean?"

Blanders tapped his finger to his nose and chuckled. "Guru knows."

In the bland fluorescent lights of the third-floor offices, Blanders's suit seemed to suck in the light and turn it into a gray sludge. Even his white shirt somehow seemed gray. Everyone else liked to make fun of him, how well suited he was to his name. But Feckniss knew the truth. Behind the dim, gray clothes was the sharp, bright mind of a man Feckniss respected with all his being. You couldn't be one of Guru Deep's top people without being the best of the best. As far as Guru Deep was concerned, excellence and perfection were only a good start.

"Now, Feckniss," said Blanders, "what is your assessment of this morning's chatter?"

Feckniss began outlining his analysis. Together they conferred on the likely fallout from the announcement, and various ways the company could respond.

At ten minutes to ten, Blanders nodded. "We're ready," he said. "Do you remember what I told you last night?"

Feckniss nodded. "This is the end. But it's only the beginning."

"Of what?"

"I don't know, sir."

Blanders nodded. "Of everything. Of nothing." He smiled. "Guru knows."

"Is that the secret, sir?"

Blanders shook his head.

"What is the secret?"

With a smile, Blanders leaned forward until his mouth was next to Feckniss's ear. "It's simple, my dear boy." Feckniss felt the smile grow wider. "The secret is that there is no secret."

Feckniss tried to understand or think of a reply. Blanders rose and left the cubicle. "I'll come back after the announcement, and then we'll debrief." Alone, Feckniss tried to think of what his manager meant. He thought and thought, and almost had it, but then the clock struck ten. On the radio, in the office, all over the world, the voice of Guru Deep began to speak.

WITH A NOD OF thanks to Jade London, Gabsir picked up the brimming pint of GPS and ignored the annoying pop music on the radio. His pale skin and patchy long hair matched the beer's white head, but his tattered, faded gray coveralls were more reminiscent of dishwater than the beer he had devoted his long life and remaining years to. Even the name tag on the left side of his chest, with "Gabsir" embroidered in white thread over a black rectangular patch, was pale and threadbare. Glancing out the window of the Mirror & Phoenix, the sun at last had burned off the morning's misty fog. Across the

Thames, despite the daylight glinting like sparks on its petals, clouds gathered behind the Lotus.

"What troubles you?" She turned the radio down.

He shook his head. "Stop staring at the top of my head. If I wanted my future read I'd go to a carnival."

No one else was in the pub. Jade came out from behind the bar and sat on a stool next to him. "It's destiny and decision," she said. "They're like a helix, rising from each person like rivers, diverging, intertwining. I'm not trying to read your fortune. I'm just trying to understand where you are and where you're going, so I can help you. All these years you've been coming in. Gabsir Abrigs. The white shadow behind the brewmaster of First Call. I've seen you angry. I've seen you sad. I've never had higher praise than when I've poured you a perfect pint." She smiled. "And I've never felt a sharper tongue than when you thought the beer was off."

"It was off," Gabsir replied, smiling despite himself. "Damn keg must have expired weeks before you remembered to dig it out of the sewer."

"You had a cold," said Jade. "You were more off than a light switch at the end of the night."

Gabsir looked around. "Are those kooky damn bosses of yours around?"

"The Management?" Jade shrugged. "Probably not. From what I understand they're still busy cleaning up all the mess in Agamuskara."

"From what I've heard that India business was pretty nasty. Didn't something happen to your... counterpart there?"

Jade shrugged. "Company policy prohibits me from discussing such matters."

"So they're not that gone."

"Gone enough not to care about the ramblings of an old man drinking stout at ten to ten in the morning."

"Even if he's a lifelong brewer of the beer none of you can meddle with?"

"You know they stay out of your affairs." Jade's amber eyes narrowed. "As long as you stay out of ours."

Gabsir took a long swig of his pint.

"You look exhausted," Jade said. "Rough night at the brewery?"

He sighed as he set down the glass. "One of the worst we've had in years. It's bad enough, Guru Deep owning First Call. He has his global empire already, thousands of dopey-eyed worker bees droning away, what with the guidebooks, those self-enlightenment seminars, and deities know what else. But him owning First Call? It wasn't enough to take advantage and pull us into his domain. All he ever wanted to do was suck us dry. I don't know where the profits go, tailoring more orange suits or whatever he does. But these last few years? People say that all you need to make beer is malt, hops, yeast, and water. You know what ingredient they forget? Perhaps the most important?"

"What?"

"Money." Gabsir took a long swig of his pint. "That sonofabitch Guru Deep is strangling us. Every quarter, more budget cuts. Every year, more staff reductions. There's parts and equipment that should've been replaced ten, twenty years ago—can't forget when he stopped us investing in new technologies. The stuff we've got now, the whole damn brewery, is held together with fencing wire, duct tape, licks, promises, beer sludge, and one person on a job where we need three." After more beer Gabsir continued, but his voice quavered. "Last night some of the lads and I spent hours piecing together a pipe run that blew. From the brew kettle, too. It's a miracle we weren't running boiled wort down the damn thing when it happened. We would've been stewed in our own beer."

"No one was hurt?"

Gabsir shook his head. "We even saved the batch. We haven't missed production yet, but it's only a matter of time. And what is going out the door..."

"What about the brewmaster?"

Gabsir shrugged. "Arthur does what he can. Always has. But I'd told him earlier to get some rest. He wasn't on the floor when it happened, so I took care of it. This morning, I must've looked like I'd seen The Blast. Arthur told me to get some air and not come back till after lunch."

"What have you been doing all this time? You were first through the door the minute I pulled the bolt."

"Walking around London," Gabsir said. "Looking in the windows of other pubs. Seeing GPS in the coolers of shops. Wishing like hell I could still believe that tomorrow, or six months, or ten years from now, that's how it will be. But now... Now I just don't know anymore. That sonofabitch is up to something. I know it. This announcement? It's nothing good. Not if you're na Grúdairí, that's for damn sure."

"Sure you don't want something stronger?" Jade said. "I've got a wonderful whiskey in from western Ireland. I'm told it was bottled the day of The Blast, then lost, and uncovered only a year ago."

He shook his head. "Today might be a terrible day, but it won't be the last day of this life," Gabsir replied. "You know good and well that's the only day I'll drink something other than water, coffee, or GPS."

Jade patted his hand. "I hope you'll make an exception for me."

"What are you talking about?"

"We've known each other a long time," said Jade. "When the time comes for me to leave, I hope you'll have a drink with me. Of that whiskey."

"Leave? Enlighten an old man."

"Jades move around," she said. "Like queens in chess. We go all over, do what needs to be done. The Management eventually want to move me onward, and get a Jake in here to be London. He'll then be here as long as he's one of the Jakes and Jades."

"A king?"

"In chess. The comparisons end there. And still not even. In chess a king moves one space at a time. But a Jake moves only once. Twice if you count... departure."

"Where will you go?"

"Where I'm needed. That's the life. The duty. I think you understand."

Gabsir nodded. "I wanted to be a grúdaire from the moment my dad let me have a sip of GPS when I was a nipper. The moment they finally unlatched the gate, I ran in before they changed their mind. I've always loved it. And I reckon I'll always be there, till the day they cart me off."

"How long have you been there now?"

"Long enough to point out that's like asking a lady her age instead of remembering her birthday." He smirked. "Long enough to know more lore than probably anybody but Arthur."

"Such as?"

Gabsir smiled. "Did you know it's believed that the First Brewer created The Management? Created the Jakes and Jades, and all the crazy elixirs you have that influence people's decisions and destinies?"

"I've heard rumors, but The Management aren't exactly forthcoming about the truth."

"My favorite story, though, is how GPS all began."

Jade nodded. "How did that happen?"

"Lightning."

"What?"

"That's the story. The First Brewer was a man named Jagathi. He and his wife, Kailash, lived in what we now know as northern India. As best as we can ascertain, Jagathi had been part of a band of nomads. Kailash was from the Heart of the World, in the Himalayas."

Jade whistled. "One of those folks, walking the very Earth," she said. "I can hardly believe it."

"They loved each other from the moment they met," said Gabsir. "Traveled together, the leaders of their group. They found a place to call home, settled there, and began to farm. A heavy rain spoiled some grain, giving them the first inklings of beer." Gabsir stared at his pint. "Ah, beer," he said, "the drink that makes the world vibrant and bright, that brings a music from the body and soul, as if the essence of reality itself has gone traveling through your veins." He looked at Jade again. "After that, well, as you can imagine, they began to grow more barley. The crop was strong and the field was full. Then one night, just before harvest, there was a terrible storm."

Gabsir drank more of the black beer. "Lightning set a field afire. When the clouds rolled away and the flames died, the field had been reduced to char. Jagathi despaired. They needed the crop for food—his wife was pregnant."

Jade leaned forward. "What did they do?"

"They despaired, but then Jagathi got this sense, this feeling, that there was something there," said Gabsir. "Not just something that had survived the fire. Something new. For hours he walked through the still-smoking field. Kailash thought he'd gone mad. But at last, Jagathi came back. She thought it must be out of sadness and surrender, but when he returned he was smiling. He held out his hand and showed her three grains. They were black, not the pale brown of barley ready to harvest. She thought they were just bitter and burnt, but Jagathi said there was something different about them. They had been kissed by fire, he said, and now were different. That barley would not make flour or bread or dumplings. But the sky's fire did not destroy what the earth grew. Fire gave it a secret, a sweetness locked behind the bitter. With water and time, he believed it was a secret that would be told, a secret he and Kailash could learn. And from that secret, they would create a different beer. A new beer. Something that took the elements—fire, wind, water, earth—and combined the very stuff of reality into something we can bring into ourselves."

"And they did," said Jade, staring at the nearly empty pint glass. "It must have taken years."

"Centuries," Gabsir replied. "Oh, don't look shocked. It's not like your years actually match that fresh face of yours. Jagathi and Kailash... Something happened to them, something that took away their mortal lifespan. They spent centuries trying to unlock the secret of the fire-kissed barley, devoted their all to it. But they didn't age anymore—and that made people afraid. Fear—and a mob waving torches—drove them out of India. Gradually they made their way across Asia, through Europe, coming at last to Ireland. There, where it was cooler, where there was hops, they finally unlocked the secret." Gabsir picked up the pint and looked at the dark liquid. "They created Galway Pradesh Stout." He drank the rest.

They said nothing. Even the radio went quiet.

Then the announcer came on. The moment he said two words, Gabsir tried to relax the tension in his body, but he knew it was no use.

Jade picked up his glass and stood.

The voice, honey-smooth yet as resonant and powerful as a rolling thunderstorm, froze them both. The lightning of the words struck.

Jade dropped the glass, and it shattered.

"You bastard," said Gabsir, running for the door.

ALL ACROSS LONDON, all across the world, the words rolled on.

In a flat on the other side of the city, a man and a woman shook their heads in disbelief, then ran to the nearest shop.

In a hostel on the western edge of Ireland, a redheaded woman ran from her hostel to the pub. Though separated by miles, mountains, oceans, and years, she felt the same rage go through her sisters.

In France, the men and women of the stripes shrugged and returned to their sacred duties. What did they care? They had wine. But still—something was not right, and they too were troubled.

Anger and confusion bubbled and flooded up from every person listening to the voice. From Cambodia to Chile, Australia to Austria, Kenya to Kazakhstan, the words struck. The world yelled outrage and shuddered in futility, but the voice was in control, and the voice said there was an end. What could they do?

Jade London eyed the empty pub, then ducked under the counter to the secret cabinet that no one could see. Well, no one but Rucksack, and she really wished The Management would explain that one sometime. She opened the cabinet, reached beside the racks of bottles, each with a colored liquid that could steer a person's decision and destiny, and pulled out something far more influential and important. Opening the briefcase, she squinted in anticipation of the bright light. She closed the case and said, "What are you up to?"

In a janitor's supply closet in the Lotus, Zara, Branwen, and Rucksack huddled around the radio on the cart and stared at each other. Branwen hadn't seen tears in her sister's eyes since their mum had died. Loss and anger surged through Branwen. So did something else, though she couldn't figure out what it was.

Rucksack slowed his breathing, sought the fire and calm that made him who he was, that made him able to face anything. Even this. He hoped.

But when Guru Deep's voice boomed over the pub's radio, the shock shattered Rucksack's brittle calm. His breath caught. A fire leaped in his eyes, but there was no smile beneath. An ancient rage burned instead—

and as Guru Deep spoke, that rage blazed higher than ever.

Higher up in the Lotus, Blanders and Feckniss smiled. Everything was going according to plan.

The voice faded. As the world tried to make sense of what it had just heard, Rucksack's own voice blazed up. Gaze bright and hard, he stared up, thinking only of Guru Deep, and he thumped his left hand on the wall.

"Like feck you will."

THE WORDS LAUGHED AT the black iron gates and punched through the thick doors and walls of First Call Brewing. Gabsir stopped running, and wheezed for breath as he pulled out his large keyring. As usual the gate's lock froze and clunked. He swore as he jiggled the key and smacked the rusting iron.

"Gabsir?"

He looked up. The courier stood there in his orange jumpsuit, head down. He held out a large, thick brown envelope.

"What is it this time?" His clanking, clattering keys scratched more paint off the gate.

The courier shrugged. "All I know is it's from the Lotus. And it came from the top."

"So not full of large-denomination bills," said Gabsir. At last the gate squealed open. Gabsir took the envelope and signed for it.

"I heard it on the way over," said the courier. "I'm sorry."

Gabsir nodded and raised an arm toward the brewery. "Step inside. Take some beer with you before you go."

At the door he stared at the faded, splotchy paint and sighed. "First job they ever gave me was to paint this door," said Gabsir. "I spent all day on it. Got chewed out—it was one thing to be thorough, but it was quite another to be slow about it."

The courier on his way with a case of GPS, Gabsir locked the gate and then closed the door. He took a deep breath in the dim room. The roof above the lobby had developed a leak five years ago. While they had tried and tried to patch it, dampness had set in, and the wet, stale scent of mold saddened him. At one time the lobby had been bright, and was full of displays and memorabilia from the long past of the world's favorite beer—old advertising posters and billboards, coasters through the ages, the evolution of the distinctive curved pint glass that defined GPS almost as much as the beer itself.

It was all gone now. Guru Deep had sold it to a museum.

The empty lobby now was cracked tiles, faded woodwork, and empty light fixtures. Gabsir was certain he saw more holes in the wood paneling from some sort of damn insect.

He caught his breath and held the envelope tighter. It had happened at last. His insides writhed like a batch of wort bubbling up to a boil, but that couldn't matter. Right now it was time to be Gabsir Abrigs again. The white shadow behind the brewmaster. The man who made sure the kettles boiled and the beer flowed and the fermenters kept the right temperature and the kegging and bottling lines were clean enough for birth.

He just wished his hands weren't shaking.

"It's one thing to be old," said Gabsir to the mold in the ceiling and the bugs in the walls. "It's another thing to feel old."

He steadied his hands as best he could while he carried the large brown envelope through the lobby and down one of the rounded passageways that cut through the brewery like a rabbit warren. The way was dim; most of the bulbs had burned out and hadn't been replaced. Nonetheless, he could see the occasional gleam of the rectangular white tiles that covered the tunnel and floor. The brewery might have been dilapidated, but na Grúdairí could make even dilapidation gleam.

Goodness knows we've had enough practice by now.

Skipping the openings that led to other parts of the brewery—grain storage, milling, hops cooler, lab, yeast propagation, fermentation tanks, conditioning tanks, keg line, sensory evaluation room, bottling line, beer storage, offices—he followed the passageway to the end. Steam met him.

Gabsir paused, and smiled.

All those years, and still the sight dazzled him. From the enclosed, tight quarters of the tunnel, he emerged in a wide-open room, larger and as high as the lobby of the Lotus, gleaming white from the tile that covered the walls and the floor. The floor was two meters lower than where he stood now, the resulting wall studded with ladders every few feet, so one could escape in the case of a flood of wort. They'd nearly needed those ladders last night. At least only a few rungs had rusted away over the years.

All around, steam rolled up through the air, toward ventilation shafts all around the room. The way the brew room's air currents eddied and flowed, Gabsir couldn't help but give himself over to a moment of whimsy. Did the water of London love becoming GPS so much that, as steam, it played through the air like a happy excited child?

The massive copper kettles could boil an army, though right now they were filled only with a stewed concoction of malted barley, roasted fire-kissed barley, and loads of pale green cones of New Galway Golds hops. The bittersweet scent filled Gabsir's nose and his soul. Men and women saw him and waved, then went back to their tasks. Gabsir waved back, but seeing his fellow brewers, their silent work, their endless dedication despite what had happened—the anger ripped through him.

None of it was right. Na Grúdairí deserved better. They should have the best facilities, best equipment, best ingredients—the best of everything to match the best brewers in the world. No matter what little they did have, no matter what challenges constantly confronted them, they still rallied. Even if they were no longer making the best beer the world had ever known, Gabsir took some small comfort and much larger pride that they were still making the best GPS they could with what they had.

If only it had been enough.

Gabsir never expected to feel such rage and hatred, to have to fight so hard to hold back the urge to rip the envelope into small pieces, burn the fragments, and then grind the ashes into dust.

He got in motion. If he stayed still, he knew he'd give in. But he couldn't. He was just another courier, and the envelope's fate wasn't his to decide.

Walking around the raised floor that ran around the brew room, Gabsir turned down a passageway. Relieved to reach the door with the envelope intact, Gabsir raised his hand to knock and took some comfort, though tinged with desolation, at the words there:

ARTHUR ARDCLOUGH CELBRIDGE

BREWMASTER

"Come," said the tired voice, just as Gabsir knocked. He opened the door, came up to the brewmaster's desk, and handed over the envelope. The golden light of the brass desk lamp only made the brewmaster look more tired. Gabsir stared into Arthur's eyes, the dark brown of polished wood, as dark as his skin, and surrounded by more wrinkles every day. The short curly hair was now more gray than black, but Gabsir was certain that hadn't been the case even a year ago. Arthur's raised hand shook as he touched the envelope, as if shocked or suddenly in pain. On a nearby table, a radio told the world what Guru Deep had to say.

"Malt and Hops walked by again," said Gabsir, hoping to get him to talk about it.

"They can keep walking," Arthur replied.

"What about Faddah Rucksack? If he's in London it's to do with Guru Deep. I don't like Rucksack any more than you do, but maybe he could help."

"If Rucksack wanted to help, he could've been a grúdaire like his father before him."

"He's assisted First Call in the past."

"You mean meddled. He's the last thing we need.

Besides, do you really want another Dublin with him?"

The memory stung—the harsh words, the dumped kegs spilling GPS down the city's drains.

"No," said Gabsir at last. "You're right, we'll get by without the likes of him around."

Arthur opened the envelope, saying nothing as he read. Gabsir read the brewmaster's face; the words struck like blows, but not as a surprise.

Arthur set down the paper and rubbed his eyes. He had read only the top sheet of a small stack. "Formalities, of course," said Arthur, bitterness dark in his voice. "He's nothing if not officious and official. I always wondered. That bastard."

Gabsir sought for something other than defeat and venom in his leader's eyes. Some little spark of hope. But Arthur's eyes were dark, as if looking only inward and not liking what they saw there. The two men stared at each other in silence, Gabsir trying to accept what had happened, but Arthur having already known.

GABSIR FOLLOWED HIS LEADER. Around them the work of the brewery continued, as if the broadcast hadn't happened. Before Arthur had read the letter and shown Gabsir what it said. Now the letter was in Arthur's pocket as the two men made their way through the heart of First Call. Gabsir thought of what lay in his own pocket.

"We are na Grúdairí," said Gabsir, surprised at the ceaseless bustle around them. "Love and duty drive us. I understand that. But how can they be working as if nothing has happened?"

"They don't know what we know," replied Arthur, his voice heavy. He and Gabsir shifted aside as two men passed, carrying sample trays of recent batches. "As far as they're concerned, batches still need to be tested to make sure they meet our visual, aroma, texture, and flavor profiles. Mash tuns need to be cleaned, so we can steep more barley in hot water to make wort. The grain silos need to be filled so they can be emptied again. Trucks need to be packed so their axles groan as that fresh, London-brewed GPS can flow across England, Scotland, and Wales."

"But everything has changed," replied Gabsir. "Are they dedicated to the point of denial?"

Arthur shrugged. "They're dedicated to the point of ignoring all they consider irrelevant. They weren't listening to the broadcast. You know them as well as I do, if not better. How they cope with Guru Deep is by acting like he doesn't exist. Anytime something orange gets delivered from corporate, does it ever make it to the walls?

Gabsir chuckled. He'd burned a fair bit of those deliveries himself.

"The moment they heard about Guru Deep's announcement," said Arthur, "they turned off their radios and got back to work. As far as they're concerned, they have beer to brew and that's all that matters."

"It's only going to make this harder," said Gabsir. *And everyone will be wondering what you are doing,* he thought. *Respect you though they do, lately sometimes days go by without you leaving the office.*

Arthur stared into Gabsir's eyes, showing both deep sadness and something else Gabsir couldn't yet recognize. With a sigh and a shake of his head, Arthur replied, "Nothing could make this easier."

As the brewmaster and his second walked through the brewery, the dry, thick, bitter sweetness took over the air. From Arthur's office, you could still notice it, but the scent was weaker there, back near the accounting offices, the marketing and publicity folks, the regional sales departments. But through the hallways connecting the administration offices to the heart of the brewery, the scent grew stronger, becoming not so much an aroma but another state of matter: solid, liquid, gas, plasma—and wort.

At its heart, Gabsir reflected, brewing is a practical alchemy that transforms sunshine into joy. The sun helped the barley grow, and the hearty grass could grow all over the world, in places where wheat withered, from the flat sun-parched fields of the USA to the high valleys of Tibet. Once harvested and the grains separated out, the barley began a process called malting. First the barley was moistened, and water tricked the seeds into germinating. Then the grains were dried, stopping the sprouting process and redirecting them from one destiny—more stalks of barley—to another: beer.

Some GPS barley met a different fate. Instead of being malted, the raw barley was roasted. The bitter notes and dark color made it the heart of GPS. But in the beer, what could have been astringent and harsh became something else: refreshing, strengthening, emboldening, revealing.

Roasted barley. It was part of the heart of GPS, Gabsir knew, but it wasn't the secret.

The narrow hallway ended at a choice: left, right, or across. Opening on to another open space, the floor ended and down below, the brewery bustled at the point where it all began. To either side, catwalks went around the space, gleaming white from the tile walls. But Gabsir followed his leader's choice: the catwalk that crossed the dozens of meters between where Arthur and Gabsir now stood, and the opposite side of the space.

As they crossed, Arthur stared at the people and the equipment below. Large gleaming tanks shone silver-gray and rose from the floor like mountains. The two-meter-wide stainless steel cylinders rose to a height of ten meters, then at the bottom of each tank an inverted cone tapered to a point. Flowing across, between, and all around, pipes connected the tanks and kettles like arteries and veins. Steam hissed from a pipe as a grúdaire adjusted a temperature setting on the mash tun, an open pot large enough to be a small swimming pool. Inside, malted barley and roasted barley soaked in hot water like the world's largest cup of tea, converting the barley's starches into sugars that yeast could eventually eat and create alcohol.

Halfway across the catwalk, Arthur stopped. So did Gabsir.

Down below, all the activity stopped too. Men and women stared up at the brewmaster of First Call. The title had been passed down from man to woman, woman to man, for centuries beyond what Gabsir could wrap his mind around. Just like anyone who worked anywhere else, they didn't always like their boss. They didn't like how things had been for the decades since Deep Inc. had taken over First Call, but they also knew it hadn't been all Arthur's fault. What had happened was before his time. He had just been the one who had to deal with it.

Na Grúdairí didn't always like their leader's decisions, not more than anyone always liked their leader's or boss's every decision, but even when they disliked the man, they respected his role. Gabsir thought back to the two women, their short rakish hair rustling in the morning breeze, the longing and excitement, the fear and determination in their eyes as they stared at the brewery.

Some of Arthur's decisions leave a lot to be desired.

"Here?" said Gabsir. "I thought we were gathering everyone in the main room."

Arthur ignored him and pointed to a man next to a kettle. "What's the step?"

Every grúdaire knew the question. Copies of the recipe for GPS were posted at every station of the brewery. At a moment's notice any na Grúdairí could recite exactly where he was in the brewing process, and explain any technical issues or on-the-ground changes that had happened or were being dealt with.

The man stepped forward. His reddened face told Gabsir he'd been standing over the mash tun, where the hot grain and water created the sugary wort, where the crushed barley first began to tell its secrets.

"We just ran off the wort to the kettle and are firing. Not up to boil yet, but we're on the way."

Arthur nodded. "What do you smell?"

"Chocolate and coffee. Mum's porridge and a January morning. The day I met my wife."

"Good signs." The brewmaster nodded. "But it's missing something."

The grúdaire shrugged. "I'm following the recipe."

"Of course you are. But you're forgetting, we got the third round of hops, not the first. Our lot is lower in alpha acids, so the bittering is lower—not for what the recipe calls for, but what the end result must be. You can tell in the aroma: it's too sweet. Yes, it should evoke the day you met your wife. But you should also be remembering the day your gran died." The brewmaster paused and took a deep breath, tapping the bar of the catwalk while he thought. "Add twenty percent more New Galway Golds to the kettle now, again in thirty minutes, and then another fifteen percent just before flameout. We'll get the bittering right and retain just a touch extra aromatics so the nose isn't bored when it's hovering over a fresh pint."

The grúdaire nodded. "I'll get more hops."

"Wait," Arthur said. "Everyone. This is an all-brewery announcement." His voice cracked. Arthur paused a moment and stared at his shoes. "Meet in the main room in five minutes. Tell the others."

"But sir," said the grúdaire, "we're brewing."

"Turn off the kettle," Arthur replied gently.

The brewery stopped. The men and women of na Grúdairí turned and stared at Arthur. Except for cleaning and what they laughably called maintenance, the brewing kettle was always on, always ready for the next batch of wort that would become GPS.

The words hit Gabsir like a punch in the gut. *But not today,* he thought. *Everything became different today.*

"For now," added Arthur.

The brewers left the brewing area, spreading the word and making their way. Arthur and Gabsir reached the other side of the catwalk and began walking down another white hallway.

"The brewmaster has to be the brains of the brewery," said Arthur. "Sometimes the heart. But always the brain. Lately, it seems the last thing I can afford to have is heart. Thank goodness I have my second. You've been my eyes and ears for so long, Gabsir."

"And still a while to come."

"I should hope. You've often been my heart too." Arthur sighed. "Of all the times to be a brewmaster, this time had to be mine. It's no secret how hard it's been. I want to thank you, Gabsir. You are the best second that a brewmaster could have hoped for."

"Thank you. That's most kind."

"Simple truth," said Arthur. "There was a time I would've thought you'd be my successor. You served Samara as a most capable second. To this day I'm still surprised she chose me."

Gabsir shrugged. "As I've said every time you mentioned it, I'm far too old. Besides, I'm the one who told Samara to choose you."

"No wonder I keep you around. I'm in your debt. How old are you, anyway?"

"Old enough but still young enough."

"Someday I'll get a straight answer out of you. We don't even have it in your personnel file."

"Maybe I'm so old the paper crumbled away. Besides, I don't even remember."

Arthur laughed. "Are you getting feeble on me?"

"I can still recite every step, word, and punctuation mark of the GPS recipe," Gabsir said. "Shall I demonstrate? Step one..."

With a wave of his hand, Arthur politely declined. "I would never doubt you, old friend. But I do have to tell you there is something you don't know."

"Of the recipe?"

Arthur nodded.

Gabsir whistled. "I didn't know that."

"You didn't know you didn't know it." They stopped walking and Arthur looked around. By now all everyone would be in the main room, waiting for the head and heart of First Call. "After we do this," said Arthur, "come back to the office with me. I thought I'd show you this someday, in a happier time, but today will have to do. Now let's get this over with."

The men walked on and came to the main room. In front of them, dozens stood silently, staring, wondering.

"What's going on, brewmaster?"

Arthur took the letter from his pocket and began to speak.

"AFTER LONDON BURNED TO the ground in The Blast," said Arthur, "this brewery was one of the first buildings rebuilt. Across the sea, na Grúdairí survivors in Ireland rebuilt not in the desolation of Galway, for nothing would grow or live there again, but away from the epicenter, in a grief-stricken village that grew and grew and became known as New Galway."

Arthur's voice was even and strong. *Soft too,* Gabsir thought, *but only like velvet over a hammer.*

"In both places, within months GPS flowed again. Our beer slaked the thirsts of thousands who worked to help those who lost so much in The Blast, and those who rebuilt in the aftermath of the burning. The Blast has defined our world and our time, yet it is still but a moment in the history of GPS and na Grúdairí. For eons we have brewed. Struggled and fought. Retreated and rebuilt. Whether by fire or in peace, we have brewed. From Ireland and England, First Call Brewing has brought Galway Pradesh Stout to all the world. We are na Grúdairí. For us, to brew is to live."

Arthur sighed. "But it is no secret that this has not been easy. While we recovered from The Blast and continued brewing, the brewery is also a business. And businesses have vulnerabilities. My predecessor, Brewmaster Samara, fought a brave fight. But as you know, in the end we lost that fight. First Call was weak—and Guru Deep's company took over First Call."

"He owns the company," said a grúdaire, "but he'll never own the beer!"

Cheers and shouts went up from the gathered women and men. Arthur raised his arms, and silence again covered the room. "How I wish it were so easy." He shook his head. "Or that it were true." Arthur unfolded the letter. "Just now, while you continued the excellence of your life work's, Guru Deep made an announcement to the entire world. He sent the same words to me. To us. He was gracious enough, however, to send me a copy of his speech."

Gabsir could just imagine Guru Deep, standing on a stage in front of the Lotus and addressing the world. His orange suit, white shirt, and orange tie would have been shining. His ludicrously large smile would have been reflecting the morning sun.

The evenness broke in Arthur's voice, and he paused. Gabsir could see the fight in his eyes, the sadness and the strength, the anger and the fear. *Is it because she couldn't thwart that bastard's plans?* Gabsir thought. *In the end, do you blame Samara? Is that why—?*

The strength surged in Arthur's eyes again. As he gazed out over the people who trusted him, relied on him, followed him, Arthur began to read the letter.

"People of the world, on this day we celebrate beginnings and endings. Today, after years of dreams and plans, hard work and striving, we dedicate the Lotus, world headquarters of Deep Inc., and open its spaces to the world so we all may know only what is real and see beyond the dreams that blind us.

"For every beginning, something else must end. So with a heavy heart, I also must make a graver announcement. For years, centuries, even eons, the beer known as Galway Pradesh Stout has been brewed by the brewers, or na Grúdairí, of First Call Brewing, a subsidiary of Deep Inc. Your mothers and fathers, grandparents and ancestors beyond memory or measure, have likely enjoyed what has usually been regarded as the world's most popular beer.

"But you, like me, know that of late something has not been right. The Galway Pradesh Stout of today has not been the stuff of legend, the beer of old, the reality in a glass that so many over the years and all over the world have claimed it to be. Is it good? Of course. But it has slipped. It has fallen. And what was, is now no more. The mythology of this beer for too long has stood in the way of new ideas. Galway Pradesh Stout is outmoded, less popular than it once was, and no longer as good.

"After much time and heartache, after much hard work and difficult decision-making, my team has given me their recommendation, which I unfortunately have no choice but to agree with.

"Galway Pradesh Stout will be discontinued. In six months' time, it will be no more. Instead, we will increase production of our popular beer Deep's Special

Lager, lovingly known the world over as DSL.

"However, the skills and staff are different and do not cross over. Galway Pradesh Stout is the only beer First Call produces. At the end of the six-month transition, First Call will be liquidated, all equipment and property sold. Staff will be provided for so they may relocate to new employment. The recipe itself will be no more. It is the end of an era. But one end is always another beginning."

Arthur reached the end of the letter and stopped, staring from the paper to the men and women before him. Gabsir could feel the confusion and anger brewing in the room. Fires seemed to grow in the eyes of the men and women who were proud of their work and dedication, na Grúdairí who could brew the world's best beer—

But it isn't, Gabsir thought. *It hasn't been for ages. Arthur and I knew it. Damn Guru Deep figured it out. The world noticed too. And now it's come to haunt us, just as I told Arthur it would.*

"He can't be serious," said Rookdale.

"This can't be happening," added Heffen.

Shouts, confusion poured out. Arthur said nothing.

Until, at last, one voice rose above the others. "What now, brewmaster?" said Gabsir. The room quieted. "What do we do?"

"You answered that this morning, when no one listened to Guru Deep's announcement," Arthur replied. "We do what we have been doing. We be who we are. We brew GPS. If there is a way out of this, I will find it. But in the meantime, we must be na Grúdairí. We must remind people of what they love, and be the best we can be at what we do."

"But we'll be out of jobs," said a grúdaire. "What about our families?"

"Throughout the day," said Arthur, "Gabsir will bring each of you to my office. I have details on how the company will take care of each of you."

"We don't want anything from that bastard," said another grúdaire.

"Your family also can't eat pride," Arthur replied. "I will make sure that you receive enough to help you find something else. New work. Maybe even create new breweries. Who knows? And from every penny I can wrench from our joke of a budget, I will do him one better. You have my word not only as your brewmaster, but as a fellow grúdaire. You aren't taking anything from that bastard," Arthur said. "You are getting what you should from the work you have done."

"So we should get back to work?" said a grúdaire.

"If any of you wish to leave and speak with your families, go; the time will be paid. If you wish to work, please stay. Make the choice that your heart says is best."

Are you, Arthur? Gabsir thought.

"As for me," said the brewmaster, "I indeed will be getting back to work. Fire up the kettle when you are ready." He turned and said to Gabsir, "With me, old friend."

AN EERIE SILENCE HUNG in the brewery like a fog as Arthur and Gabsir made their way back through the brewery to the brewmaster's office. Arthur had put the letter back into his pocket. Gabsir wondered if that paper felt as heavy as the hope and burden he carried in his own. "How could it be true, Arthur?" Gabsir asked once they were inside. "How could we have fallen so much in the world?"

Arthur closed his eyes a moment. Gabsir had the sense his leader, his friend, was again battling something inside. "Guru Deep's not lying," Arthur said at last. "GPS is still popular but isn't drunk as much as it once was. So much that we should be shut down? No. For years he's tried to control us and failed, tried to influence the beer and failed. Reduced our budget to a pittance and failed. While the sales agreement doesn't allow him to set foot in a First Call brewery, that only does but so much. If he can't control us, all the better for him to destroy us."

"All this is just an excuse to destroy First Call?"

"Guru Deep fears only what he can't control," Arthur said. "He's been able to own the business and the rights to the beer, but not us. Better we be gone and helpless, scattered and without what we love— we're less of a threat."

"To what?"

"We just brew the beer, Gabsir. I don't know what he thinks or why he thinks it." The brewmaster walked to the dark shelves that covered one of the walls. Gabsir glanced at Arthur's desk, covered in stacks of papers. Like an island, an envelope, the paper yellowed with age, sat on a clear patch of desk. The black ink said only "Arthur," but Gabsir recognized Brewmaster Samara's handwriting. On another cleared patch lay a thick document, also yellowed.

"Arthur, is that what I think it is?"

The brewmaster followed Gabsir's gaze. "People think that conflicts have to be resolved in grand battles. Sometimes they do. But the smart ones know that often their best weapons lie hidden behind paper shields." He nodded. "That's the original sales document of First Call Brewing to Deep Inc. I've been going over it to look for loopholes. Escape routes." He shrugged. "Hell, I don't know, secret ultimate weapons."

"You knew this was coming. I could see it in your eyes earlier."

After a long silence, Arthur nodded. "Guru Deep never told me. Neither did any of his lackeys, such as that damned Blanders. But I knew it was coming, could read it in everything that wasn't said in meetings or memos."

"What do you think you'll find in the document?" said Gabsir.

Arthur shrugged. "Maybe a miracle. Maybe nothing but what it seems—a bunch of dry legal speak. If it shows us a way out, a way forward, I'll go through anything and everything." He touched the old leather spines of the massive volumes on the shelves. "Do you know what these are?"

"The journals of your predecessors," said Gabsir. "All the way back to the beginning, to the First Brewer. They have notes from every day, they have recipes and modifications to the recipe depending on changes in the malt, or the hops, or the yeast, or the water." Gabsir pointed to the desk, where Arthur's own journal lay open. "When the time comes, that book will join its brothers and sisters."

Arthur grimaced. "It's a miracle they survived. Some say the First Brewer knew The Blast was going to happen, so he sent his second to the village before catastrophe struck. The reason, he claimed, was to create a test brewery, a lab where na Grúdairí could experiment in a different environment, get fresh ideas in the fresh air, that sort of thing. But the First Brewer insisted the second take all the journals with him." Arthur shook his head. "They should still be in New Galway. We only moved them here when Deep Inc. took control of First Call and had to make London the primary brewery and administrative headquarters."

"You wish we were back in Ireland?"

For a moment the strength fell away from Arthur's face. A hunger burned there, a yearning. But he only said, "I wish for a lot of things."

Arthur removed four books from the shelves, then pressed a part of the wall that looked the same as the rest of the deep polished wood. A hatch sprang open silently. Arthur reached inside and with both hands pulled out a large sandalwood box, as long as Arthur's body was wide and as tall as a pint glass.

"What is that?" Gabsir asked.

"It's what I had always hoped to show you in happier times," replied Arthur. "But this will have to suffice. It was the First Brewer's."

"That makes it... ancient," said Gabsir. "If the lore is true."

Arthur raised the lid. Despite its age, Gabsir could still smell the sandalwood, undercut with the scents of malt and hops, of fire and old paper. "We don't have much of the First Brewer's," Arthur said. "Some things were lost in the storm that drowned all but him, his wife, and son as they sailed to Ireland after fleeing India. We know he planted the first barley in Ireland, dug the earth with his bare hands and knew that at last they had found their truest home, the place where the beer could come to full fruition. Three things were never brought here from Galway—it was thought they shouldn't be close to Guru Deep. But what we have here are some of the First Brewer's letters, some papers, some personal effects." He rifled through the stacks and items in the box, then took out a sheet of parchment, yellowed with age, but unflawed except for a ragged, burnt edge at the bottom. "And this."

Gabsir's eyes widened. "It's the original recipe!"

"Written in the First Brewer's own hand," said Arthur, nodding.

Gabsir read through the ingredients, the instructions. Little was different from what was posted all over First Call today.

"You will note, of course, the bottom," said Arthur.

"The most important part of brewing true GPS," Gabsir read.

"Is this secret," Arthur finished for him.

Below that, the page ended in jagged black.

Gabsir handed the incomplete parchment back to the brewmaster. "What happened to it?"

"We don't really know," Arthur replied. "It's thought that the First Brewer kept this with him in Galway, and that it survived The Blast but was damaged."

"Bloody miracle that anything survived," said Gabsir, "much less a piece of paper. Parts of Ireland and England are still black."

"The Blast changed the world, and most would say for the better," said Arthur. "Even in all that death and destruction, one never knows what may survive. All the more important, though, is what this recipe doesn't say yet still tells us."

Gabsir stared at the paper. *Maybe I am getting feeble,* he thought. "I don't understand."

"The true nature of Galway Pradesh Stout is what Guru Deep has always gotten wrong. He's thought it was the company, or the brewery, or the ingredients, or the process."

"But in order to brew a beer on the scale that GPS is brewed," Gabsir replied, "you have to have all those things."

"You do," Arthur conceded. "But you are making the same mistake as Guru Deep. GPS, true GPS, is anything but just another beer. That's the trouble. The secret of GPS. We don't know anymore." He put the parchment back in the box. "It's not the damaged recipe," said the brewmaster. "It's not the sales graph trumping up Guru Deep's decision. A vital ingredient is missing. Over time, after The Blast, more and more of us lost the secret, down to the very brewmasters."

"But does that really matter?" said Gabsir. "Guru Deep has made it clear. He's going to destroy us. Not just our jobs or the most widely drunk beer in the world." Gabsir pointed at the shelves. "All these books. Right down to that parchment."

"Oh, this?" Arthur shrugged. "This is history. Even Guru Deep can't destroy that. He can mess with the records, but he can't erase what happened, what our predecessors and ancestors did. That's writ on the soul and fabric of the world. Not even Guru-bloody-feckin-Deep is that powerful."

"He is going to destroy us. First Call. Na Grúdairí. GPS." Gabsir swept an arm around the room. "And everything here. I'm not disagreeing with you, brewmaster, but your words sound more like hope and sentiment. We need to preserve this. GPS is what it was, no matter what Guru Deep does. It has to be."

"I almost wish that were true." Arthur put the journals back on the shelves, covering the closed hatch. "But Guru Deep can't destroy what we've already lost. That's the problem. He isn't destroying us. We are destroying ourselves. Right now, the secret is that there is no secret. That loss is the undoing of all we love."

The men sat silently for a while, the uncomfortable silence between them spoiling like wort left too long in the air. Then Gabsir got up. "I hope you're wrong, sir," he said. "That there's a way."

Arthur shrugged. "It's going to be a long day. Start bringing people in when you're ready."

Gabsir left the office. Though everyone had gone to work, silence and sadness, anger and confusion filled the heart of the brewery. Gabsir tried to encourage them to focus on their work, to focus on the moment, to do what they loved, but with every back he clapped and every gaze his dark eyes failed to hold, he choked on the hollowness of his weak words.

He turned to his own office, far from Arthur's and closer to the heart of the brewery. Just as he reached his own door, Gabsir stopped. *Dammit, Arthur,* he thought. *I always feared you would bring us to this.*

There was only one thing to do. The brewers could wait. The piles of paperwork in his office could wait. Gabsir walked away from his door. The hallway beyond was dim, and unused now that Gabsir had moved the janitor closet to a different part of the building. *I wonder if Arthur even remembers this space is here?* he thought.

Down the hall, past a closet, Gabsir tucked himself into a small alcove cut into the wall. Unless you were staring right at it, the door was all but invisible. Gabsir reached into his pocket, down to the bottom, through the flap into the small secret pocket beyond. Taking out the key, he unlocked the door and pushed it open. A sound like a heartbeat made him grin. Gabsir disappeared inside. The door closed, and all was silent once more.

"EVERY LINE IS BUSY," said Feckniss. He pointed at the papers spread out on the conference table. "The announcement had hardly finished when people began calling. Shouldn't we bring on more operators?"

"The first step of aftermath: control the response," Blanders replied, his voice monotone yet Feckniss could've sworn he detected a threat of mirth. "You know this as well as I do. We control the response by limiting who can reach us. For every call we answer, another twenty will fail to get through, and they will give up. Frustration will dissolve into helplessness. Helplessness will turn to weakness, futility, and the resignation of will—a begrudging, shoulder-slumping acceptance of circumstance. 'It is what it is,' I believe, is the usual phrase. That is as it should be. That is the plan. You know this. I know this."

Blanders glanced at the black phone in the middle of the table, where a small red light shone. "And Guru Deep knows this too."

"Then we are doing the right thing," Feckniss replied. He looked around the room. Next to a wanted poster of Faddah Rucksack, a poster on the wall showed a gray fog, but over it were bright orange letters: "ALL IS UNREAL EXCEPT THE PLANS OF THE GREAT."

I will be great too, Feckniss thought. *Blanders knows. And Guru Deep knows too.*

Then the sound again.

"What is it?" Blanders asked.

"Sorry, sir," said Feckniss. "Thought I heard someone laughing." Feckniss tried to put a smile back on his face. Instead he caught a glimpse of himself in the window's reflection, and turned away.

"Probably some mirth from your colleagues," said Blanders flatly, rising from the table and walking over to Feckniss. "It will have an impact on productivity, of course, but sometimes we have to know when to let a little laughter slide." He squeezed Feckniss's shoulder. "That sort of discretion and seeming kindness is what it takes to rise to forty-one."

The extra significance of the floor below Guru Deep's made Feckniss's eyes widen. "Forty-one?" he said, wonder and excitement flooding him. "People always say the corporate ladder is all ruthlessness."

"Those on the bottom say that," Blanders replied. "Or those who lack the quality Guru Deep demands. Those who are worthy will find challenge, but also family. They will find a place, a belonging. You Have What It Takes, Feckniss, just as Guru Deep himself would say if he were here. As Guru Deep implores us to do, you 'Breathe The Dream Yet Reach For The Real.' This project was just the beginning."

"Of what?"

Blanders smiled and glanced out the window. Feckniss waited, but when his manager said nothing else, he went over to the window and looked down too. The third-floor conference room looked out over the eastern plaza, where staff already were dismantling the stage Guru Deep had left an hour ago. As Guru Deep finished speaking, the buzz around the office had exploded. So much secrecy had now erupted into surprise, gossip, and speculation. People looked at Feckniss with curious glances; for the past year, at Blanders's orders, he had lied about what he was working on. Now his cubemates all stared, wondering how deeply he had been involved.

They didn't know, he thought. *Didn't need to know. Unlike me.* Then Blanders had returned and led Feckniss to the conference room, away from the hubbub. *I wonder what they're saying now.*

The third-floor people seemed in a state of both celebration and disbelief. It had really happened, he knew it had, but any understanding of that new reality still hung over him like a haze. *The plan is underway,* Feckniss thought. *This should be the best day of my life.* He felt the smile fall off his face again. *Why do I feel so sad? So confused? Why do I feel like I shouldn't be here?*

Feckniss stared out the window, at a London shining in the summer sun. Beyond London lay the cities and fields of England, and beyond that lay a bigger, different world, full of people who weren't wearing suits, full of people who weren't waking every morning to rush to work along with everybody else.

I'm where I should be, thought Feckniss. *Why do I suddenly wish I were somewhere else?*

"So much will be happening now," said Blanders, still gazing out over London.

Feckniss turned away from the window and sat back down. Out of the corner of his eye, he thought he saw his reflection laughing at him. "Sir?"

"We've worked so hard, you most of all. You helped me build the case. Once we had the evidence, Guru Deep knew what the right course of action would be. But you had the vision. And what, Feckniss, is vision?"

Feckniss smiled. "Vision Is Seeing What Cannot Be Seen."

Blanders returned to the table. "The people below? The people outside? They may have many things, but they have no vision, Feckniss. They cannot see. You can. The public can rail and protest all they want, but they cannot dispute the facts. That is thanks to you. Guru Deep must make and enforce the decision. But you made that possible. Guru Deep is grateful."

Through the silent phone line, Feckniss basked in the radiant satisfaction.

"What we've done today is only the first step," said Blanders. "This next phase is treacherous. Even we cannot know who may try to stop our plans. I need you to be more steadfast than ever, Feckniss. I know you have worked hard—but that will seem as nothing compared to what's next. It's going to be difficult, and I will not ease your mind with kind words. As Guru Deep would say, 'You Must Be More Than You Ever Thought You Were.' There must be changes. So, now we turn to some different, thankless business."

Blanders stood and went to the door. His blank face was hard. "This meeting is over. Go back to your cubicle and wait."

The red light turned off.

Feckniss left, walking awkwardly with the surprise of the abrupt ending. *Did I do something wrong?* he thought. *Didn't I do what he said needed to be done?*

Doubt poured through him as he sat down at his desk in the little cubicle. Again he thought he heard someone laughing at him.

Sometimes people like me are cut loose, he thought. *We're too close but not important enough. What if I'm now some sort of liability, some weakness that they can't afford to have?* Doubt set into fear.

"Everyone. Your attention, please."

Feckniss sat up, startled. *I thought he was going back to forty-one.* Standing up, Feckniss looked out over the top of his cubicle.

The third-floor people gathered at the front of the room, all staring silently at Blanders, who stood in front of the window. The morning sun outlined Feckniss's manager in gold.

"It has been an exciting morning and you all do so much," said Blanders, his monotone relaying anything but excitement. "Yet I must ask you for something else. Today brings not only new beginnings, but difficult news. Please listen, all of you."

Feckniss tried to listen, but he kept looking around the room, afraid to leave his cubicle, surrounded by the laughter. It was everywhere, bouncing off the walls and ceiling. Blanders was speaking evenly but loudly. It should have been easy to hear him. But the laughter kept drowning out everything. Feckniss heard only gasps and cries. Then, Blanders and all the third-floor people turned and stared at Feckniss.

THE SHARP, HARSH STINK of disinfectant and sweat was everywhere. The Lotus might be new, but as far as Branwen was concerned the janitors' work had already seeped into the building's secret hallways, the locker room, and even the small break room down the hall. Sitting at their favorite of the three small tables, by the wall, beneath the intercom, Branwen tried to breathe in the aromatic steam from her fresh cup of strong tea, as did Zara, but even the rough tannins weren't enough to keep the reek of work and cleaning at bay.

"If it already smells like this," said Branwen with a thin attempt at a smile, "what'll it be like in a year? Stench might make the place spontaneously combust."

Zara forced a slow nod but said nothing. *She's been silent since the announcement*, Branwen thought. An unease washed through her, far beyond her dislike of the stink. Zara was always the strong one, the one in charge. Zara led and Branwen helped. It had always been that way.

"At least Rucksack's handling it well," Branwen said. He'd been fatigued from keeping his hand transformed, so during his lunch break he had left the Lotus to rest and try again.

As schoolkids growing up near the River Lea in east London, the sisters had always dressed differently, talked differently, acted differently, and cared nothing for what anyone else thought about it. Others cared though, and being different had made the sisters targets. While Branwen cowered, Zara would stand up to anybody. With sharp words and bloody knuckles, Zara eventually won out—maybe not with friends and affection, but at least with respect and fear enough to keep people at a safe distance.

When their bodies changed, so did the smirks and putdowns. "You never kiss any boys," people would chide. "What's wrong with you?"

Branwen could never think of anything to say, but Zara came to the rescue. "You stupid tart," she'd retort, "as if who we fancy is all we are?"

When they had snuck out to the pub as teenagers, Branwen was certain they'd be chucked out right away. After a ridiculous Career Day at school, where Zara had been told she'd be a teacher and Branwen told she'd be a baker, the day had already been packed with disappointments. But Zara had pushed on, and Branwen had followed. The bartender, Jade something-or-other, had looked at them skeptically. Branwen was sure they'd soon have the door to their backs. Then the bartender had stared and stared—not really at them, but more at something above their heads. *Not really stared,* Branwen thought. *It's like she was reading.* In the end, Jade something-or-other had waved them to the bar. Zara hadn't said a word, but the look on her face screamed, "I told you so!" The girls had gone straight to the liquor, a gin for Zara and a scotch for Branwen. Even now, ten years later, when Branwen thought back to that night, she thought something in the scotch, if only for a moment, made all her world seem clear, her destiny a set path that was so easy to choose.

Then they had ordered two pints of GPS. They'd long before had first kisses, but the rough-smooth black liquid had touched their lips with more excitement, tenderness, and passion than any kiss. "Wow," Zara had said, waving over the bartender. "Who makes this stuff?" Then Jade something-or-other had told them about First Call Brewing, and its breweries all over the world, and the stout that was the oldest, most popular beer on the planet.

"Bugger what those losers at school told us," Zara had said. "Our real Career Day is right here. I'll tell you what we're going to do for a living, little sister. We're going to brew this stuff."

We're still trying to, Branwen thought, staring at her sister through the steam rising from their tea. Raising her mug, Branwen said, "I really wish this was a beer."

Zara shrugged.

"What do we do now?" Branwen asked. "How can we become na Grúdairí if there won't be a First Call?"

Still nothing.

"Maybe we were wrong," said Branwen. *If hope won't work, might as well try despair.* "All these years, but First Call won't even check our qualifications or try our homebrew. Half the brewmasters have been women, and there are as many women na Grúdairí as men. First Call won't give us a second glance." Branwen shrugged. "Being janitors isn't so bad, you know. It's steady work, and we at least have plenty of time to do things we care about. We can save some money instead of spending everything on brewing equipment and ingredients. We can still have a good life, Zara. Or who knows, maybe there's another brewery out there somewhere that we could try. Guru Deep can't control everything, and there's no way all the world's beer is going to wind up being Deep's Special Lager."

Zara snorted. "Humpf. He'd like that. Probably what he's trying to do."

Branwen nodded, and in her sister's downcast eyes saw the first spark of Zara's usual fire.

Fan the flame.

"We could leave the six-pack in the Brewing VP's office," said Branwen. "We need to clean his office later today, and he's the one in charge of DSL production."

Zara sat up. "If we took our worst, most failed, most disgusting batch of beer ever," she said, "dumped it down the drain, ran it through a sewer line, and then bottled it, that bastard still wouldn't be worthy of one drop of our beer."

Now we're getting somewhere. "If we got our foot in the door," Branwen replied, "we'd at least be working in a brewery. With First Call gone, what's left?"

"That's not even beer!" Zara thumped the table. "DSL is all rice and food coloring. I bet they don't even use yeast, probably just mix in grain alcohol. Probably not fermented at all."

"But you know what Guru Deep says," Branwen added. "Your Dreams Are The Only Reality."

"Living in dreams is how you avoid reality," replied Zara, her face hard. "We will make our dreams true, make them our reality."

She's going to call the shots, Branwen thought. *She'll lead the way. I did it, I pulled her back. Again.* Branwen could get back in line behind her sister, hide safely in the brash shadow. Her fear faded.

"No, we won't be sucking up to that feeble draingush fake of a brewery," Zara said. She leaned forward, held her sister's gaze, and took Branwen's hand. "I'll tell you what we're gonna feckin do, little sister. I don't care if First Call's going to be gone in six months. I don't care if it's going to be gone next week. Na Grúdairí are still waking up and going to work every day. GPS is still being brewed."

"What does it matter though?" Branwen asked. "It's not like they're going to be dying to hire new people."

"Oh, they'll take us. That current brewmaster might just hide in his office all the time, he might want nothing whatsoever to do with us, but he is going to have to consider us. He is going to know who we are and what we can do. And then, if he really deserves to be a brewmaster, then he will bloody feckin hire us."

Zara stood and dumped her tea down the sink. "After work, we're stopping by the gates. We'll wait an hour. If no one comes out to talk to us, we're leaving the homebrew."

"And then?"

A smile blazed up Zara's face. "Then we'll see if na Grúdairí are good enough for us, not the other way around. Not anymore."

Branwen felt her own smile rise in reply. *Maybe we can do it after all,* she thought. *If Zara believes it can happen, it can happen. We—*

"Break time's over," came the crackling voice through the intercom. "Report to the third floor for office transition." The intercom went silent again.

"Great," said Zara. "I guess we're getting our workout for the day."

"I wonder what happened," said Branwen as the sisters stood and left the break room.

"You know as well as I do," Zara replied. "'Office transition' is usually company nice-talk for 'clear out this stuff. We just sacked someone.'"

RUCKSACK LONGED TO CATCH the bus that crossed the Thames, then hide inside the Mirror & Phoenix. There he could rest. There he could be himself. There he could stop shaking from the strain and fatigue. Besides, no one in London could pour a pint like Jade, and he wanted to see the briefcase, make sure the object was still safe in her keeping. But there wasn't enough time. The pub down the road would have to suffice.

His body shook, so he forced more precious energy into the change. It had to hold. For just a little longer.

People passing by gave him strange, questioning looks, then hurried past.

Rucksack's feet dragged as he limped along. He looked behind him, eyes squinting at the cloudy yet bright sky. At last. The Lotus was out of sight.

He ducked into an alley to change back into the red tracksuit and revert his appearance. He stashed the coveralls behind some discarded pallets and stared at the horror of his left hand.

The memories came back.

He remembered how the orange robes billowed as he flew, the air splitting with a roar like a tiger's. For a while he'd also worn red, as an homage to part of his Himalayan heritage, but he'd always preferred the orange, the holy orange that in later years would grace so many, from the monks of Thailand to the wide-eyed sadhus of India, ash in their hair as they slept in the junkyards of skeletons and the ends of lives.

But back then. Back then, he recalled, in those glorious days. His flight blocked out the sun like an eclipse, and his long black shadow trailed on the ground like a hunting dog or a horse. All who saw him in the sky, all who saw that shadow along the ground, they knew Rucksack was there. Rucksack would save them. Rucksack would do the right thing.

The people would smile as he passed.

All who did wrong would frown and cower, or

otherwise try to find a way to defeat him. But none could defeat Faddah Rucksack, the hero of old, the hero of now, the hero of always. The fire of life itself. He thought of the world transformed by his actions, the course of decision and destiny altered by his existence and his involvement.

But it hadn't been enough.

He could save the world from people's deeds, but he could not save people from themselves.

He'd barely kept ahead of the torches that night, beating the mob to the cave where his parents were checking their latest attempt at the dark beer. That beer had been a failure too—a relief, really. Father would have wanted to take it with them otherwise, and there was no way Rucksack was carrying a barrel on his back. They had fled with so little, heading west, following the setting sun, stopping here and there, but all the while seeking somewhere that could be home.

Halfway around the world, across a sea, in western Ireland, in a place that one day would become Galway, the city of foreigners, they'd found it at last. With time, they had also found the ability to alter their appearances—subtly, but just enough to keep fitting in as years became centuries and generations gave way to generations. Of course, the beer helped too. People will overlook just about anything if you give them beer.

Father had at last found a peace he had always sought, the home where the land was as himself. How he had loved tending the barley fields, and the herbs they used in the beer, and the green fragrant conical flowers that were heady and bitter. Mum had loved Ireland too, though she also longed for the mountains of her birth and her heritage. Especially she longed for the world mountain, the true biggest mountain that compared to Everest made Qomolangma seem a small hill. Sometimes, she said, she saw the mountain in her dreams. As the years went on, she began to see the mountain everywhere, and then, she said, seeing the mountain began to feel more and more like looking into a still pond and seeing your own reflection.

Those years, those centuries, had been peaceful times. Wonderful times.

A shame how they ended.

Faddah Rucksack shook his head. The brick of the alley wall was cold under his hands, the right so strong, the left so crooked and small. All but useless.

He put on the glove.

Remembering the good times wouldn't change anything and wouldn't do any good.

He made his way to the pub and ordered two pints of GPS. It wasn't what it should be, broth when he wanted a huge meal. Then again, maybe broth was all he could take right now anyway.

The now was what mattered. The now was all he could live in. All he could change.

So Faddah Rucksack sat and drank the dark beer. He thought of the briefcase, of what was inside. Guru Deep was still trying, and Rucksack knew this was only the beginning. But he had the briefcase now, and the gleaming object inside. That was the key. Without it, Guru Deep couldn't realize his plan, his true, long-sought, terrible plan, that damnable Operation—

But he put that out of his mind, and Rucksack's body became calmed, restored. And by the time two empty pint glasses were all that remained, Rucksack returned to the Lotus with a plan of his own.

WHEN THE POLITE APPLAUSE began, Feckniss knew he was about to puke. As his stomach convulsed and he fought to keep his breakfast down, he bent over, straightened, bent over, straightened again—*don't throw up, don't throw up*—and the clapping got louder. *What do they think I'm doing?* he thought, *Taking a bow?*

Stronger and stronger, the heavings racked his body. Yet again, he heard the harsh laughter that had surrounded him all morning. His stomach threatened a return of this morning's tea and toast, all he could stand to eat from the nerves. *This is it*, he thought. *I hope no one gets splattered.*

The applause stopped. Everyone's blank eyes looked away from him and back to Blanders, who began speaking again.

Feckniss ran to the men's room, barely avoiding a collision with two janitors who'd just gotten off the elevator.

"He should be back by now," he heard one say.

When he came out of the cubicle, the gray walls rang with the sound of flushing. A sour, acidic stench wafted through the otherwise sterile air. Leaning in front of the mirror that stretched the full width of the counter with its three white sinks, Feckniss bowed his head and closed his eyes. "I can't believe that just happened," he said. "But what just happened? I didn't think I'd get so scared in front of people anymore."

His terror of attention stung him, circled him, trapped him. As a child he'd avoided speaking in class or in front of a group; for any school event or play that required being on stage, Feckniss always came down ill and didn't have to go on. For years he had avoided attention, fading into the background, a quiet listener who spoke only when spoken to. He had heard that some of his classmates had gone on from the school stage to the major stages of London, and beyond, to greater cities such as Hong Kong, the current World's Greatest City. Feckniss found refuge in the theater's darkness and silence. Since everyone was looking at the stage he never had to worry about anyone looking at him. Sometimes he wondered what it must feel like to be in front of thousands of people, to recite memorized lines with conviction and passion, to deal gracefully with things that went wrong.

Feckniss shook his head. He preferred the calm waters of indecision; in decision there was pain and the chance of failure. But where someone else made the choices, he could simply float on the currents of what others did. He knew nothing of the great joys or achievements, sure, but he also spared himself the crushes and despairs of defeats, failures, and mistakes.

Opening his eyes, Feckniss stared at the sink. He knew the mirror was there, but couldn't lift his head to see how bloodshot his watery blue eyes must be. Instead he smoothed his short, straight blond hair, splashed water over his pale face, and made sure his suit was free of vomit.

"Holy crap," said a voice, harsh and brash, sharp and ragged, like a fist made of broken glass. "Just when I thought you couldn't look worse."

Eyes wide, Feckniss stood up straight and looked around. "Who's there?"

A snort and a chuckle bounced off the hard floors and the mirror. Feckniss opened the doors of all five toilet cubicles, but no one was inside.

"No wonder you needed to puke," said the voice. "After seeing that, it'll be weeks before I can keep anything down."

He stood on a toilet and stared into the ventilation shaft beyond. Something glinted in the darkness. He went back toward the counter.

"You're always looking in the wrong place."

"Who are you?" Feckniss said, turning in a circle, his eyes wide. "Where are you?"

Silence.

Feckniss leaned on the counter again and closed his eyes. "I'm going to lose everything," he said. "First my breakfast, then my job, then my mind."

"Of course you're not going to have anything," said the voice. "You always were a nothing. A nothing can only have nothing. And nothing about you has changed. Well, you're taller. And uglier."

Feckniss spun around, his back to the mirror, body heaving. "Stop saying things like that!"

"Always a loser," the voice replied. "Now you can lose everything. Poor feckin feckless Feckniss. Didn't all your school chums used to call you 'Feckwit?'"

"Only at first. They mostly called me Fu—"

"Feckwit Feckwit Feckwit." The reflection laughed. "I'd forgotten what a good ring that has."

"Why are you doing this to me?"

"Ask yourself."

"I've never done anything—"

"Right in one!" said the voice. "You've never done anything, and that's what you've done. Tell me,

Feckwit, when was the last time you even had a date."

"I'm too busy for that sort of thing," replied Feckniss. "But if I go out sometimes, you know, like for a drink at the pub, women, you know, look at me. As if they are interested."

"And what do you do about that?"

"I finish my drink and leave. I'm tired and want to relax. I work long days. My job wants enough as it is. A woman just wants more."

"You're too scared to talk to a woman." The voice chuckled as if spitting at him. "Too scared to do anything but hide and retreat. That's you, Feckwit. You could talk to any woman, but you don't. You could've been the lead in those school plays, but you didn't give dare. After school you could've traveled, gone anywhere. Your mum and dad even wanted to help fund the trip. But you were too scared to leave London. As if the world would eat you. Please." The reflection snorted. "World wouldn't eat you. You'd make it sick. You've spent your whole life making yourself invisible and insignificant. Now you aren't worth the attention, but you made yourself that way."

"Why do you hate me so much?"

"I don't hate you. I just see you as you are and react in the only natural way possible. Feckin feckless Feckwit. That's you. It's okay though. I bet you're getting sacked. Those two janitors—you know, the ones you nearly plowed into on your way to liberate your tormented toast from your lame little insides— they're here to clean out your cube, buddy-roo."

"No." Feckniss punched the wall, but hardly noticed that he felt no pain. "I did everything Guru Deep needed and wanted. Blanders wouldn't sack me."

"Do you think you'll end up on the dole? Or will they be so unable to notice such a stupid little nothing like you that they won't be able to sign you up?"

Feckniss stared, silent, as the words sank in like blades. Then he ran out of the restroom. Harsh laughter trailed him out the door and all the way back to his cubicle.

Blank eyes barely registered his passing, and noticed nothing else.

Feckniss stopped at the opening to his cubicle. "What are you doing?" he asked.

The two women nodded at him but said nothing. They continued putting his papers, trays, and binders onto a cart. Not that they would have much to do, Feckniss knew. Unlike his colleagues, he had no knickknacks or framed photos. Only his work.

"I have things to do," Feckniss said. "High-priority items." He pulled some papers off a cart and set them on his desk. "Whatever you were told, it must have been a mistake. Or you have the wrong cubicle."

The janitors said nothing. They just put more things on the cart, and Feckniss took them off again. "I helped bring down GPS, dammit!" he said. Blank faces looked up from their cubicles.

The eyes of the two women widened, then narrowed. "That was you?" said one of them, purple and yellow streaks in her rakish hair, not as short as the other.

"Yes," replied Feckniss, "so whatever you were told, you must have gotten it wrong. There's no reason for you to be here." He grabbed more papers off the cart.

"Standard office transition," said the other quietly. Her eyes were dark brown, quiet but bright.

A booming voice said, "Feckniss!" Blanders stepped to the cubicle entrance. "Pardon me for not joining the party," he said, "but it is a little cramped in here." He slapped Feckniss on the back. "Good thing we're changing that, huh?"

"I've done nothing wrong," Feckniss replied. "I only did what you said to do."

"What are you talking about?"

"Why am I being sacked?"

Blanders stared at the janitors, at Feckniss, at the papers clenched in his white hands. "Didn't you hear what I was announcing?"

"I'm sorry, sir," Feckniss said. "All the tension must've gotten to me... I, I felt a bit ill."

"Understandable. I've been working you hard. Accepting your physical frailty is a sign of interior strength and a higher mind. Good man." Blanders slapped him on the back again. Feckniss wondered if the bruises would be another sign of interior strength.

Blanders nodded at the janitors. "You," he said. "What's your name?"

"Zara, sir. With a zed."

"I suppose not everyone's mum and dad can afford the letter S." He pointed to a note taped to the cart. "Sara, tell my associate what your instructions are."

Zara pulled off the card and held it up. "'Feckniss, office transition, from floor three, cubicle three-seven, to forty-one, office east.' Signed and instructed by Blanders. That would be you, sir."

"Very good. Glad you can read. Surprisingly clear diction."

Feckniss stared at the card, then at his manager. "Sir?"

"What?" Blanders glanced at the papers still clenched in Feckniss's hands. He gently pulled them away and set them on the cart. "These are busy people, son. Let them finish their work. We are busy too. You have a lot to get used to."

"Sir, she said forty-one."

"Of course."

"I don't understand. I've never even been to forty-one."

"Apparently I needed to speak more loudly," said Blanders, his tone flat but his eyes gleaming. "My dear boy, we could not have pulled off this new strategy without you. Guru Deep himself knows that you provided what he needed to bring about the end of that unfortunate, misguided, unprofitable endeavor."

The two women paused. Their breathing hitched, like a hiss, or as if they'd been punched. But Blanders continued, as if he hadn't noticed. "The last thing in the world I would do is sack you, Feckniss. But I can't have you down here anymore. You're needed by my side at all times—and that means you need to move." Blanders smiled. "Correction. You need to rise. You're going to forty-one to be my personal assistant, in the office next to mine. My right-hand man, my sergeant. The one I can always rely on to get things done."

"Me?"

"Do you see anyone else in the room who looks like you?"

A loud broken laugh bounced off the walls and ceiling. "For their sake," said the harsh voice, "I hope not!"

"Stop saying that!" Feckniss shouted.

"Saying what?" replied Blanders.

The janitors just stared.

"You didn't hear the laughing, and the cruel things it said?"

Blanders stepped back from the cubicle. "Follow me, son," he said. "Let Sara and... this other janitor finish their work. I don't want them to fall any further behind than they already have. Let's start getting you acquainted with your new home. Then, well, I have been working you hard, and I can understand if you fear negative interactions with your former third-floor workmates." Blanders smiled, then leaned in, as if sharing a secret. "I never liked the smell down here anyway." He glared at the janitors. "See what you can do about that, Sara."

A quiet voice said, "Zara and I will be along presently."

Blanders stared at the small woman as if the desk had spoken to him. "I would expect no less. Not from anyone who wishes to continue in the grace of Guru Deep's employment, that is."

As the men walked away, Feckniss was certain he could feel the quiet woman's eyes drilling into them. He wanted to run but forced himself to walk a hair behind his manager. Inside the elevator, Feckniss shrank back to the gleaming brass and dark paneling. Anything to avoid the glass walls whose gaze both stared out over London and bored into his soul.

"You're stepping into a new world, Feckniss," said Blanders as the doors closed. Feckniss locked his gaze on his manager. "From now on, you will answer only to me. And I, as you know, answer only to Guru Deep. Anything you do, anything I instruct, is as if it came directly from the Great Leader himself."

"I understand, sir. And I appreciate this honor."

Blanders smiled. "I need you to understand something, son. The end of GPS is the beginning of something bigger. Your actions today, your actions over the past year, have proven that You Chose To Be On The Winning Team. I can't say the future is without rockiness and difficulty, but for those of us who follow Guru Deep, there is a paradise to come."

Feckniss nodded. No reply was expected, only understanding.

The elevator rose up the side of the Lotus. His body shook. *Maybe I'm afraid of heights too.* Feckniss's gaze tried to wander toward the glass, to look out over London as he rose higher than he'd ever been before.

He caught himself in time. "Sir?"

"Yes?"

"What is the forty-second floor like?"

With a nod and a flat chuckle, Blanders replied, "Answers."

"What are the questions?"

A corner of his manager's mouth twitched. "Guru knows, Feckniss. Guru Deep always knows."

"That's the answer?"

"And the question."

Blanders looked to the glass. Paleness washed over his face. "What's that?" He stared harder. "It can't be."

Oh no, Feckniss thought, closing his eyes. *What does Blanders see?*

"I can't believe it," said Blanders.

Feckniss heard the laughter again. So loud. It boomed and bounced, so harsh and rasping, Feckniss was sure the glass was cracking. *This is it.*

"How could he be here again?"

Feckniss shook his head. "What?" He blinked. The laughter was gone. He opened his eyes.

Blanders stared down from the smooth, polished glass, to the Maya Plaza below. From the green of the plants to the streets beyond the plaza, London bustled. People teemed, busy with their days, their clothes as bright as the sun hidden behind the clouds. In the midst of all the motion, Feckniss saw what Blanders was staring at: a small, still darkness.

Dressed all in black, a man stared up at the Lotus. No, Feckniss realized. *He's staring at the elevator. At us.*

Then Blanders said, "But of course he'd come back." A calm, radiant smile made his face serene. "All the better, really." He locked his gaze with that of the man below. Between them, Feckniss felt determination and will collide—and a long-smoldering rage blaze anew.

THE JANITORS SAID NOTHING until the doors of the freight elevator had shut and they were alone.

"So that was him," said Zara. "This knob moving up the Lotus to be Blanders's pet is the one destroying our future."

"I don't know which one's the bigger jerk," Branwen replied.

Zara punched the button for forty-one. "Me neither."

Instead of going up, the freight elevator went down.

"What the hell?"

Three. Two. One—

The doors opened.

Rucksack stepped inside, dressed in his pale face and his gray janitor coveralls.

"It's about time you got back," said Zara. "I take it you're better, Jeremy Ruckley?"

"For now."

"We've got a lot to tell you," Branwen added.

Rucksack's mouth was a hard line. "You don't know the half of it."

Branwen pushed the button for forty-one.

"Why are we going up there?" asked Rucksack.

The sisters filled him in. Then Rucksack did the last thing they expected. He smiled. "This works perfectly with what I had in mind."

"And what's that?" asked Branwen.

Rucksack stared at the furniture and Feckniss's work effects, then nodded at the janitor cart on the other side. "We carry tools, right?"

Zara nodded, then reached into a bucket and took out a screwdriver. "I think I know what he's got in mind, little sister. Shall we?"

"Oh," said Rucksack, "we're just getting started."

Branwen smiled. "I'd hate to fall behind on such an important project." As the elevator rose, so did Branwen's spirits.

ELATED AFTER THE DAY'S work, the sisters paused to gasp and tremble in front of one of the wanted posters. Rucksack shook his head and said nothing, except that if they needed him he would find them later. But they were glad to see him grin as he left.

Standing in the Maya Plaza and wearing their bright street clothes, Zara and Branwen took a deep breath absent of disinfectant and mischief. They smiled at each other.

"Let's do this," said Zara, and Branwen followed.

Weak early evening light filtered through the clouds and dulled the gates of First Call. Branwen took the six-pack out of Zara's bag and set it on the ground between their feet. A fresh pang of guilt shot through her, but it was too late to go back now. While London streamed and teemed behind them, the sisters stood still, said nothing, only stared at the dark building just beyond the gates. They waited.

After the first half hour, the elation had worn off.

During the first hour, Branwen's feet went numb.

During the second hour, Zara had locked her knees and nearly passed out.

During the third hour, they shivered in the evening's chill and tried not to think of how hungry they were getting.

At the end of the fourth hour, they wondered whether or not to give up. But they stood. Just a little longer. Just a little longer. Just a little...

"SIR," said Gabsir as he poked his head into the brewmaster's office, "I know you don't want to hear this. I know it's been a long day and you don't want to be disturbed. Especially with this."

Arthur sighed. He'd finally seen the last of the London na Grúdairí and had finished preparing memos for head brewers around the world. "But you're going to tell me anyway." He waved Gabsir inside. "What is it?"

"I'm telling you because I believe it's important."

"As my second you know I trust your judgment. I take it nothing is about to blow up?"

"No sir," said Gabsir. "We haven't had any pressure problems. At least not today."

"As long as everyone's being mindful of the damn timers and gauges and bleeding off the valves at the right times, we shouldn't have anymore problems with the pressure redlining." Arthur paused, then added, "And don't call me sir. Makes me sound old. I would prefer you remain our expert on that. So what is it?"

Gabsir sighed. Stared. Hesitated.

"No, you're right," Arthur said, "I am in a damn terrible mood. You've been keeping the brewery going. I've spent my day talking about how it's all going to end, and how na Grúdairí here and the world over will have to deal with it. So if you're going to interrupt this jolly feckin good time, then out with it."

Standing straight with his arms at his sides, Gabsir said, "Malt and Hops are here again."

For a moment it hung between them.

"We've discussed this. Time and again." Arthur pinched the bridge of his nose. "No new staff."

"But we need new people."

"We don't have the budget."

"We have the need."

"We don't have time to train up FNGs."

Gabsir took a deep breath. "I believe one of them has learned the secret."

Arthur was silent. His dark eyes pierced Gabsir. "We don't have a point." Arthur shook his head. "Soon there won't be a secret. Won't be a First Call. Won't be a GPS. No stout, no secret. No secret, no need for na Grúdairí wannabes. Leave them be."

"They come every day. And their homebrew is excellent. They did a tasting at the Mirror & Phoenix last night. To put it mildly, I was impressed. There's something there, Arthur. Brewmaster. Sir."

Arthur stood up and his voice rumbled. "I don't care if they're the First Brewer back from the dead. Leave them be."

"They've been outside for hours. They brought homebrew to give to us. At least try it, Arthur, then you'll see. Through them we might find a way."

"This discussion is over."

"But there's one more thing you should know."

"Is there now?"

Gabsir nodded. "Rucksack has met them. Has had their beer. He was impressed too."

"That lout had better not be outside the gate too. He's sure as hell not coming in either."

"He's not here. But no matter what you think of Rucksack, sir, no one knows GPS better. We have to at least talk with them, brewmaster."

"Gabsir. I'm ordering you..." But the door had already closed. "Dammit," said Arthur.

Then he came to his decision.

BEYOND THE BLACK GATE, the doors opened.

Brewmasters always handpicked new members of na Grúdairí, and Branwen had expected Brewmaster Arthur Celbridge himself to come out. But the thin, wiry old man who came down the steps was the very antithesis of the brewmaster. Branwen thought he looked vaguely familiar, but she couldn't quite place it.

"Who are you?" Zara asked.

"Not who you would prefer," the old man replied. "But I am who you get. My name is Gabsir Abrigs. The rest doesn't matter."

He nodded at the six-pack. "Every day you come. Some days you stop only a moment. Some days you stay an hour. Some days you leave homebrew. You think no one sees, yet still you come. I notice. Every time. Every day. And I was in the pub last night. I tried your homebrew. It was really good. The best I've had. On par with what we expect from na Grúdairí."

"You!" Branwen shouted. "You were staring at us."

Zara stood up straighter. "We were born to be—"

Gabsir stopped her with a wave of his hand. "I know why you're here. I'm old, not feeble." He stared into Branwen's eyes, then into Zara's. In his gaze, sadness and kindness collided. "You are young and have much you could do," he said, shaking his head. "Go do it. You will never be na Grúdairí."

The women looked at each other. The words rocked Branwen like a punch, but in Zara they burned like her own personal Blast.

"I'm sorry," said Gabsir, and Branwen thought she saw pain in his eyes. "There is nothing here for you. There are thousands of us all over the world, and soon there will be nothing for any of us. Live your lives. Do something else. Leave." He started to walk away.

"You're wrong," said Branwen. "What do you know anyway? You're not the brewmaster. He's the one who picks na Grúdairí. If anyone is going to send us away, it can be him. Not some weak old man. I've seen dehydrated yeast less dried-up looking than you."

Zara's eyes widened and she jumped as if she'd been poked. "Branwen!"

They expected loud yelling, but when the old man came back to the gates, Branwen was certain he was suppressing a smile.

"It is true that I am not the brewmaster," said Gabsir. "But every leader needs his second. If the brewery is for the wort, the brewmaster is for the recipe and the process."

"Then what are you?" Branwen said.

"We are na Grúdairí. We make beer."

Branwen returned Gabsir's stare. "Brewers don't make beer. Yeast does."

The corners of Gabsir's mouth twitched, breaking the hard, flat line of his mouth. "Well observed. If the brewmaster is the wort, then the second is the yeast." He pointed at the six-pack. "Let me guess," he said, "another GPS clone."

"Our best yet," Zara said.

"And let me guess," Gabsir replied. "You think you know the secret."

Branwen snorted.

Gabsir started to say something, but another voice stopped his words.

"For as long as there has been GPS," said Arthur, coming down the stairs to stand next to Gabsir, "there has been speculation about the secret."

He was tall and grand, almost regal. He drooped some now, Branwen saw, from the burdens of age and duties, but still, she could see the strength and pride there, in the set of his broad shoulders and the power in his thick torso. But she saw fear there too, in the dark eyes. And something else—

"Yeah," said Zara. "The secret. But it's all just brewing. You know it. We know it. Try our homebrew. You'll understand. The announcement doesn't matter. Bring us on. Train us up. We'll help you brew GPS so amazing, Guru Deep will have to change his mind. The public will force him too. They'll be too in love with GPS again to let First Call die."

Branwen chuckled.

Arthur stared at her. "What's so funny, wannabe?"

"The secret," Branwen said. "Do others always go on and on about a secret?"

"Why?" Arthur asked, his face close to hers. "Do you think you know what it is? Everyone else does."

Branwen stepped closer. "The secret is that there is no secret. There is only finding the light inside the dark."

That's going to do it, Branwen thought. *Impress enough that it won't matter. Make him open the gates and give us a chance. At last.*

But instead, Arthur stepped back. Anger clouded his face. "Oh, you think you're so damn smart, don't you?" He reached through the bars and pulled the six-pack through. "There is no place for you here. Never was. Never will be."

Arthur went up the steps and stopped at the doors. "Go away," he said. "Don't waste your time here anymore."

Gabsir scrambled to get back to the brewmaster's side. Arthur raised his arm. Branwen could see the dark beer slosh inside the bottles. But she also saw a little hint of light, a gleam in the dark—

Arthur swung his arm down. The six-pack shattered on the ground.

Gabsir said nothing, only stared at the brewmaster. Without another word, Arthur went inside the brewery, Gabsir following, and slammed the door behind him. The beer bubbled and foamed as it soaked into the concrete.

* * * * *

BRANWEN STOOD AS SILENT as her sister, mouth open, their hands gripping the iron bars. All the work. All the testing. All the certainty. Branwen's empty stomach wanted to leap out of her mouth. Zara's face was as pale as her clenched hands. After all this time, all the hours and days, all the brewing, all the beer left at the gate, all the learning and experience and trying and failing and trying again and at last, the understanding—someone had come.

And this is what had happened.

There was nothing to say on the way home. Nothing to say once they were inside the flat. They didn't cry or rage or console.

Zara punched the wall, then left without a word.

Alone in the flat, Branwen pulled one of her six-packs from the boxroom and sat at the table. The hiss as she opened the bottle was the only kind sound she'd heard in hours. She stared at the plain, brown, unlabeled bottle. The glass muted the light, making the black beer inside seem indistinct and unreal. Usually Branwen loved to savor the aromas and flavors of the homebrew, but tonight all she cared about was the buzz of the alcohol knocking down all the pain and hurt inside.

Yet she kept being drawn to stare at the bottle. It was brown-black inside, dark as the middle of the night. She stared and stared. Nothing. She blinked— and saw it. Looking directly at the beer, there was only glass and liquid. She looked away. From the corner of her eye, she saw it again. Not a light. Not a brightness.

But the barest hint of a gleam.

Branwen opened the beer and tried to force the tears to stay in her eyes. The slam of the door still rang in her ears, from when Zara had stormed out. It hurt as much as the crack of the glass on the concrete.

"He threw it away," Branwen said to the beer bottle. Tears stung her eyes. "No. My beer. Maybe we got what we deserve. I lied to Zara. If we'd brought the beer she said to take, maybe this would have been different. Maybe that's why Zara wouldn't stay. Why I'm alone now."

She emptied the bottle and opened another. The beer wasn't doing much for the hurt inside—and it wasn't blunting the truth inside either.

What are we going to do now? Branwen thought. *Are we really just going to be janitors forever? How will Zara cope with that?*

How will I?

Branwen stared at the little flat and thought of their two little rooms, hers purple and Zara's yellow. *I can't be happy with just being a janitor. I've come too far. I know what I should be.*

In her room, Branwen pulled out her notes on every beer they had brewed. Zara wasn't much of a note-taker, but Branwen recorded everything. If they added an extra amount of chocolate malt for richness and flavor, Branwen wrote down the details—how much, how they crushed the grain, the temperatures at which they steeped it—and later analyzed how that batch compared to prior batches. Now she turned to her notes from the latest batch, the one she knew was her best ever, the one that now enlightened the concrete in front of the steps of First Call.

It had something to it, Branwen thought, *something different, something I've never tasted in any of my beers before, or in any other beer before. It's almost like it was alive.*

Ew, she thought. *No. Not alive... but aware.*

And to think that jackass threw it away. What is he so afraid of?

The knock made her look up.

"You forget your keys, sis?" she called as she went to the door. "Or do you want to talk?"

"I am not your sister," said the voice behind the door, "and neither are you."

Branwen looked through the peephole.

Gabsir stared back.

"WHY THE HELL ARE you here?" Branwen called through the door. "Once First Call closes, it's not like we're taking flatmates."

"For years I have refused you entry into my home," Gabsir replied, his voice soft, kind—even apologetic. "I have no right to expect you to treat me any differently. But I do hope you will forgive me and grant me the chance we have yet to let you have."

"Then answer my question," said Branwen.

"Please open the door," said Gabsir, "and I'll show you."

"You clearly have never been a woman living in a big city," Branwen replied. "We usually don't just swing open the door for random men. Turn around slowly and show me your hands."

Gabsir did. Then he held up the empty brown glass bottle in his right hand.

"Arthur hardly ever leaves the brewery nowadays," said Gabsir. "It was a total surprise when he followed me outside. I've rarely seen him so angry. When he took the beer and went up the steps, I feared the worst. I don't know why he did it. I don't know what he's doing sometimes, or why he can be so resigned to First Call being shut down. But he was so focused on destroying the hopes of you and your sister, that he wasn't paying attention to me, his second, his most trusted of all na Grúdairí."

"You slipped a bottle out of the pack," said Branwen.

Gabsir nodded.

"But it's not like you were all words of support either," she added.

"No," said Gabsir. "That was to protect you."

"Cruel to be kind?"

"I've lived a long, long time," said Gabsir. "Despite how little it's worth, I hope you'll one day understand the depth of that kindness and the greater sharpness I was trying to spare you from."

"Did you drink it?"

"That's why I'm here."

Branwen opened the door. "Would you like a beer?"

He nodded. Branwen opened the fridge and pulled out a bottle. They sat at the table and for a while said nothing, just drank their beers and sized each other up. Branwen looked closely at the old man for the first time. Now she noticed not only how deep the lines on his face went, but also how bright and lively his eyes were. "Where are you from?" she asked. "You don't exactly look like a Londoner."

Gabsir smiled. "I'm from here and there," he said. "I used to be more a wanderer than anything, but my love of brewing won out over my love of vagabonding. It's not easy to haul a fermenter around."

Branwen laughed. "Zara and I grew up in London. Never been anywhere else. Yet."

"You say that as if it pains you."

"I've always wanted to see the world," she said with a shrug. "Different places. Different people. London is great... but it isn't everything. The world's a big place."

Gabsir smiled. "It still amazes me how both big and small the world is." He took a long drink from the bottle of homebrew. "So tell me something..."

"Branwen. Branwen Porter."

"Okay, Branwen. Then tell me why just now you gave me a beer that you and your sister brewed, instead of one of the beers you brewed."

"It's the same as earlier." Her gaze pierced him.

Gabsir chuckled. "I have tried every beer you left at the gates," he said. "You and your sister are excellent brewers. The homebrew you served at the pub the other night was your best effort yet, but like the others it lacked the spark, the vibrancy, that we need in a First Call beer. Until today. That beer was different. It was as real as reality—and that is the stuff of true Galway Pradesh Stout. You have found a secret, but we all have secrets. I certainly do. So I also know you are keeping one of your own."

Something hot was burning through her, and Branwen looked away. "I don't have any secrets."

"But you do," replied Gabsir. "You and your sister brew together. I can perceive what is you and what is her. Your calm and her fury, your unsureness and her drive. The beer you gave me earlier doesn't have that. You may indeed have learned the secret of GPS. That beer you brought to First Call earlier? You brewed it yourself." He smiled. "But even that's not your secret."

"So what is my secret?" Branwen replied, her voice small, refusing to look him in the eye.

"You are a far better brewer than your sister will ever be." Gabsir leaned in. "And you know it."

A hot tear came down her cheek. "I didn't mean to be."

"You should always mean to be who you are," Gabsir replied. "Of course, it's cruel to strive to be a better brewer just so you can hurt and diminish your sister."

"That's not why I do it!"

Gabsir took a long pull off his beer. "Then you have nothing to feel guilty about. So why do you brew?"

"Because it's who I am." Branwen couldn't help but smile. "It started out as Zara's idea. She was the one who always said we were destined to be na Grúdairí. She brought me to it." Branwen stared at the old man. "We always brewed together, and when we weren't working we've always been learning."

"But it all started to change, didn't it?"

Branwen nodded and wiped her eyes. "About a year ago. Your rejections, how First Call ignored us. We used to just brush it off. Lately it's been getting to Zara. She's frustrated. Angry."

"Because we wouldn't give you a chance that you thought you deserved?"

"That's part of it but not all," replied Branwen. "I couldn't talk to Zara about it. She's technically capable. She knows as much about beer and brewing as anyone else in na Grúdairí. The more we've brewed lately, the more Zara is just... stuck. I learned everything from Zara—but I've also learned all from her that she has to offer. She will never progress beyond where she is. The hardest part is that I think she knows it too."

"Does she know that you've surpassed her?"

Branwen shrugged. "I don't know. Sometimes I think she doesn't. Sometimes I think she does and just can't bear to admit it."

"I know your sister loves you. It would be unfair of her to hold you back."

"I don't think it's that," said Branwen. "For years now, we've been all each other has. Our mum has passed on. We visit our dad, but he's just trying to enjoy being retired. Zara always said we'd make our way together, and that's all we've known. If I went on to be a grúdaire and she didn't, I don't know what we'd do without each other. I think the thought of it terrifies her."

"That's a reality you're going to have to face," said Gabsir. "Like it or not, Branwen, you have what it takes to be na Grúdairí." His voice was soft. "You sister doesn't. The question is: Which do you choose? Do you stick with the comfort of what you've known, for the sake of sparing your sister pain, or do you stay true to who you are and who you could be?"

Branwen shook her head. "I just can't leave her behind."

"When you let someone find their own new path, even when it's different from yours, you aren't leaving them behind. You're trusting them to find their own way. That is one of the greatest loves possible."

Another quaff from the bottle left it empty. Branwen set it down and said, "Why are you here? Really?"

Gabsir emptied his own bottle and set it next to Branwen's. "What I told you earlier is true," he said. "First Call will be no more, and Arthur has made it clear we aren't hiring."

Branwen's eyes narrowed. Before she could catch herself, she said, "Why does he hate us so much?"

She expected him to be defensive or evasive. But he just sighed and said, "I wish I knew. I've known him for years and was there when he started as na Grúdairí."

"When Samara was brewmaster," said Branwen. "Right before Guru Deep took over First Call."

"You know your history."

"Not like it does me much good."

Gabsir smiled. "Arthur has always had a problem with being brewmaster, with leading and guiding First Call. He's not just some boss. He's the living repository of all the lore, knowledge, and experience of na Grúdairí, all the way back to the First Brewer. But he's also the first brewmaster to serve a full tenure in a company that no longer controls its own decisions and destiny. Arthur always respected Samara, but he was always uneasy around her too, especially after the company lost its independence and she named him her successor. After Samara retired, none of us noticed at first that Arthur had stopped hiring. Stopped going out as much to events or tastings. Over time, we realized that all he does is work in his office, and occasionally go through the brewery and run through process with na Grúdairí. I've confronted him about it, but he says it's just part of being the brewmaster in these difficult times. And all the while, we've lost customers, lost favor, gone down in the world."

"Did you believe him?"

"I didn't drink my first pint yesterday," Gabsir replied. "But there's not much I could do. As you said, whoever becomes part of na Grúdairí is ultimately up to the brewmaster. I can influence Arthur on many things, but I've never been able to on this. He wasn't always like this. He used to love the outer world, though he preferred the world of the brewery. Over time, especially these last few years, he's stopped leaving entirely. Today is the first time he's set foot outside First Call in I don't know how long."

Branwen nodded. "Is it just that he has a hard time with his... superior?"

"Arthur never said much about it," replied Gabsir, "but I'm sure that for years Guru Deep has been trying to bring down the brewery. Arthur's been resisting it, fighting it, but he can only defend and never go on the offensive. Dollar by dollar, person by person, year by year, Guru Deep has been chipping away at us. He could never get into the brewery, could never compromise the integrity of na Grúdairí, but he didn't have to. Instead he strangled us from the outside. Now it's finally worked."

"Why are you telling me all this?"

"I can't make Arthur give you and Zara a chance." Gabsir stared hard at Branwen. "So if I'm going to trust you, then you deserve to know what I know, so I can earn your trust in return."

"To do what?" said Branwen. "Watch the last of the beer get drunk before Guru Deep sells off the company and burns it all to the ground?"

"No." Gabsir leaned forward. "To help me save it."

"What?"

"You have a gift," said Gabsir. "It's rough and unpolished. In some ways your brewing is totally ignorant."

"Great," Branwen spat back. "More insults—"

"But there is also ability, talent, drive. Maybe even genius. And today, you proved you have grit. Being a grúdaire isn't just about technique. It's about change and adaptation, steadfastness and trust, and above all, perseverance and love. I believe you have found the secret that even we have lost. It's not fully expressed in your skills yet, but it's there, like a flower just beginning to open." He sat back. "I'm offering you an opportunity to be not officially na Grúdairí, but to brew with me. The thing is, Branwen, I have a secret too. If you help me, I will share it with you. I can't save First Call by myself. But we just might be able to save it together."

"What about Zara?"

"Your sister's destiny is not yours, nor is it your responsibility. The time has come for you to decide your destiny," said Gabsir. "We have little time. If you want a chance to be a grúdaire, then you must come with me right now. We will need to meet regularly. You have much to learn, much to practice. And your sister cannot know."

"You're going to teach me to be a brewer of GPS, even if I'm not officially in the club."

Gabsir nodded.

"My sister or my future?" said Branwen. "That's one hell of a choice."

"You're strong enough to make it."

"It's not that simple."

"Things that don't seem that simple are usually still that simple," Gabsir replied. "No matter what, you must decide whether you choose love or choose fear. How much do you love and trust your sister? How much do you love and trust yourself? And how much are you afraid of each?"

Branwen sat back. "I love my sister."

"You still will."

"What happens if I say no?"

Gabsir shrugged. "I will thank you for the beer and leave. You'll never see me again. And no matter what happens, even if First Call can avert being closed and destroyed, you will never again have a chance to become one of na Grúdairí."

"But if I go with you, Zara might never speak to me again."

"Your sister might admire your courage—and she might be furious if you gave up your future for the sake of her feelings."

It's right in front of me, Branwen thought, *like two shining rivers. My sister. Or my future. Why not both? I love my sister. I never could have come this far without Zara.*

But I can't go any further with her.

Branwen picked up a pen and a piece of paper.

"What are you doing?" Gabsir asked.

"Telling Zara not to wait up," Branwen replied. "Telling her I needed to go out and clear my head. That I love her and we'll figure it out."

Branwen got her keys and set the note on the table, where she knew her sister would see it. Then, with a sigh, she locked the door behind her.

As she and Gabsir wandered through the cool London night, Branwen said, "So you really think I could be a brewer?"

"I haven't fully decided what I think you could be," Gabsir replied. "It will be a long time before I tell you anything I have decided."

"Wait," said Branwen. "Do you think I can do this or not?"

"What I believe you can do and what you will do may or may not be the same thing."

"So you think I still might let you down."

Gabsir smiled. "I didn't say that at all."

"Yes you did."

His chuckle rattled in the air. "You are assuming you will fail. Now, it will be difficult. But when it comes to what I believe you can do, I know full well that you may surpass any dream or expectation I could have had of you. Make no mistake, though. You think you know brewing? During these early days, I'll work you so hard you'll doubt you know the difference between malt and hops." He chuckled again. "Coincidentally, that's what we call you."

"Great," said Branwen bitterly, "but as nicknames go, Dream and Expectation sound pretty lame."

Gabsir laughed. "No. Malt and Hops. You're Malt, and your sister is Hops."

"Are you saying I'm sweet and she's bitter?"

Gabsir shrugged and bobbed his head. "I'd add that you know as well as I do that malt and hops are more complex than that."

"But my sister isn't good enough."

"Once she stops seeking a path where none exists, your sister will find her way."

They arrived at First Call. Gabsir took a ring of keys from his pocket, unlocked the gate, and held it open. Branwen walked up to the opening and stopped. She looked at him. "There's no turning back, is there?"

"If you think this is only a lark, or a job, or some silly fancy," Gabsir replied, "then you can turn back."

"I don't feel that way at all."

"Then you already know the answer," said Gabsir. "If this is really what you want, if this is really what you love—"

Branwen nodded. "Then forward is the only way worth going."

She walked through the gate.

Inside the brewery, Branwen followed Gabsir through the winding passages. They said nothing and saw no one. Eventually, they passed a door, came to a hallway hidden in shadow, and down that, Gabsir stopped at a door that all but blended in with the wall. When he opened it, Branwen heard the sound like a heartbeat and smiled.

Gabsir smiled back. "Are you ready, Branwen? Are you ready to become who you were meant to be?"

She stepped inside and he followed, letting the door click softly closed behind them.

THE FIRST THING THAT struck Feckniss about forty-one was that there were no posters. No cubicles, only offices. No gray walls and beige curtains, only sumptuous woodwork. No fluorescent lights, only wall sconces and chandeliers. Soft music floated out of impeccable speakers, inconspicuously hidden in the ceiling's light wood paneling and adding height, airiness, and majesty to the lofty, brightly yet gently lit story.

Yet despite having a new office on forty-one, Feckniss hadn't seen it all morning, afternoon, or evening. Instead he'd visited every other floor of the Lotus—and their motivational posters, from "There Are No Prophets But Profits" to "Your Dreams Are

The Only Reality." He'd met possibly every other person who worked in the building, beginning with an in-depth getting-to-know-you tour of forty-one, and all the managers and assistants who worked there, from his counterparts to Blanders's management colleagues, and a one-on-one discussion with Nia Fox that left Feckniss wondering why his cheeks felt hot. Now, at last, Blanders opened the door and showed him inside the spacious, comfortable, well-appointed office that was now his home away from his flat.

"I'll let you get settled in," said Blanders. "I have a special meeting with Guru Deep, to discuss our change to strategy due to the object's temporary departure. Goodness knows you've done enough today. Head home soon and rest up."

"Big day tomorrow," Feckniss said.

"On forty-one, all the days are big—but few will rival the ones to come," replied Blanders as he left.

Feckniss took in the rich wood paneling, which complemented the cream carpet. Open curtains, their stately gray like marble statues, framed the bright lights of London at night. Feckniss crossed the room to look out the window and saw his office reflected in the glass.

He ran and closed the curtains.

Breathing hard, he put his back against the window and closed his eyes. "There's nothing to be afraid of," he said. "I'm just afraid of heights. That's all."

A voice blared. "That's bollocks and you know it, Feckwit."

Before he could reply, a million farts blasted through the office—or at least the sound did, brapping and brapping and brapping. Feckniss could almost feel the spittle flying from the unseen tongue and lips.

Then the broken-glass laughter came, blasting through the window, through the vents in the ceiling, from under the door.

"What's wrong, Feckwit? Don't like being on top?"

"Why are you doing this?" Feckniss shouted back. "Show yourself!"

The laughter got louder and louder, bouncing off everything in the office, its terrible drumbeat pounding in Feckniss's head like hammers on concrete.

Then a knock on the door, and at once all was silent.

Nia Fox stepped inside the office.

"Everything okay?" she said.

Feckniss glanced around the room. She must not have heard it. Or else was being really polite to a new colleague.

"Umm... yeah," he said. "I just... Heights freak me out. I've never been up this high before."

She nodded. "It takes some getting used to. But just wait until the first project that requires you to ride in an airplane." Her looks reminded him of women from India, but her flat yet bright voice suggested the USA, perhaps the West Coast. "Few things are weirder than looking down and seeing the world look no bigger than your childhood toys. It still amazes me sometimes that we can fly."

"Flying?" Feckniss felt his hands get clammy.

"You never know where this job may take you," replied Nia. "Sometimes I've needed to accompany Guru Deep when he's visited other parts of the company empire. The company name might be Deep Inc., but Guru Deep's reach is broad, not just deep. We are everywhere, Feckniss. Every continent and country. 'Every Day We Touch Every Person's Life,' as Guru Deep would say. So yes, you'll travel all over. Different countries, different continents. Just getting there can take ages." She smiled. "But I do love looking out a plane window at night and watching the stars."

He gulped. But the fear wasn't as acute as he was expecting. "The ocean must look so far away."

"Don't worry," said Nia. "If you dislike heights, it's too dark at night to see how high up you are." She grinned. "When you're flying over the ocean at least. Flying over land, the city lights are a giveaway. You'll want to pull down your window shade for that one."

Feckniss couldn't help but chuckle, though at the same time he wondered if the sounds and laughter would come back. But with Nia standing there, all was silent, as if his tormentor had been scared away or else was too afraid of Nia—or at least of her proximity to Guru Deep—to continue his games with Feckniss while she was near.

Nia Fox. Feckniss realized that in the rush of people he'd met today, she was the only one he remembered. When Blanders had brought him to meet her earlier, she stood up from her desk, the guardian next to the elevator that led to Guru Deep's private domain above. She was the same height as Feckniss and looked about the same mid-twenties as himself. A vast, serene intelligence glowed in her dark eyes, a light that you could always find your way by. Long, wavy black hair flowed down the rich brown skin of her neck to her bright blue shawl and purple dress. When she held out her hand, he could see the muscles in her arm, the power in her torso, not stick-thin like so many women in London, but healthy and confident, poised, and fully and completely herself.

He'd never encountered any woman like her before.

"Your mum and dad must be proud," Nia said.

"I wish I knew," he replied, his voice low. "They died in a car crash when I was ten."

"I'm sorry," she replied. "My parents... are alive as far as I know."

"As far as you know?"

"Let's just say that their politics have always been a health concern. When I was a little girl we moved around a lot, but once I was on my own they went into hiding so deep I don't even know where they are."

They stood in silence for a moment, looking at each other. Then Nia smiled, politely yet genuinely. "Would you like some tea?" she asked as they stood in Feckniss's office. "Though if your first day on forty-one is anything like mine was," she continued, "between seeing the building and meeting everyone, and also getting briefed on the private details of Guru Deep's schedule, I was ready for something rather stronger." She winked. "I keep a bottle of bourbon in my bottom drawer for such cases requiring special resuscitation."

"That sounds perfect," replied Feckniss. "It has been an overwhelming day."

"You'll do fine," Nia said. "Blanders clearly thinks highly of you. And while technically he's supposed to be in the same position and authority as the other senior managers on forty-one, everyone knows he's really the one in charge here." She glanced up. "Well, in charge except for one. As far as assistants go, if you play your cards right, I'll be the only one above you."

Feckniss wondered why he was blushing. "I don't think I ever knew he was that powerful. Or that I could be."

"He's an amazing man," said Nia.

"Guru Deep or Blanders?"

"They both are." Nia leaned forward and cocked her head to one side. "May I give you a bit of unsolicited advice, one assistant to another?"

"Anything that might help me swim instead of drown," replied Feckniss.

"Deep Inc. can take you anywhere," said Nia. "Both sublime and terrifying. As long as you try to see things as they really are, you'll find your way." She smiled at him. "I'll go get the tea and bourbon."

"I can help you with the kettle."

Nia chuckled. "Another rule of being an unparalleled assistant—always anticipate three things: no, yes, and needs. I already knew you'd want the tea. In fact, it just finished steeping. As for the bourbon..." She winked and stepped out of the office for a moment.

All the air and light went with her. Feckniss thought he heard a chuckle, as if something was coming closer—

Nia came back in, holding the bottle and two glasses. "Feel free to start without me," she said. "I'll be right back with the tea."

Though she was gone, all remained silent.

"This just might work out after all," said Feckniss as he sat behind his mahogany desk for the first time.

Then he heard Nia shout.

He started to get up, but the air whooshed out of him as the wheels snapped off and his chair thudded to the floor. The shock made him slam the bottle and glasses on the desk. The sharp aroma of bourbon pricked his nose while the amber liquid spilled down the desk and onto his pants.

The desk legs collapsed and the desk thudded to the floor. His new brass lamp slid onto the carpet, and there was a tinkling smash as the bulb broke.

Feckniss tried to get his breath back, but the sounds didn't stop.

All over forty-one, furniture crashed. Nia ran inside his office. "The tea counter fell over!" She stared at the wreckage around him. "Is it an earthquake?" she shouted, retreating to Feckniss's doorway.

Behind him, the curtains fell off the wall. Feckniss stopped himself from turning around.

He and Nia just stared. Blanders ran into the office, and Nia stumbled forward as he knocked her off balance. "What is going on?" he said, tremors of panic in his voice.

"I don't know sir!" Feckniss said. "I don't know what to do!"

Nia said nothing either. Even Blanders just stood there with them. The tremors and crashes echoed from thuds and smashes happening all over forty-one —and from below too, from all over the Lotus.

I'm going to die, Feckniss thought, *and I never even got my bigger paycheck.*

Above Blanders, a wood panel broke. He leaped backward just in time, as the splintered wood bounced off carpet that still had the indentations of his soft gray shoes.

"Sir?" said Feckniss, watching.

But Blanders said nothing. He and Nia just watched too.

Despite all the crashing and chaos in the rest of the building, the white piece of paper floated as if it had no care in the world. As it fell, the crashes faded, the thuds lessened. Within moments the building was silent again, and all that Feckniss could hear was the pounding of his heart.

Blanders snatched the paper out of the air and unfolded it. His face got even paler. The line of his mouth became so flat it seemed hard and sharp, like a sword ready to do what swords are made for.

"The enemy," said Blanders, "is here." He held up the paper, refusing to speak the words printed there.

Feckniss's mouth fell open as he took in the bold black writing, which said simply,

BRING BACK THE BEER.

II

"EVERYONE THINKS THIS IS about GPS," said Rucksack, glancing one more time at the empty Mirror & Phoenix. Through the window, across the street in the dim early light he could see another occurrence of what had popped up all over London during the past month. Black letters painted on a white wall said, "BRING BACK THE BEER."

With a smile he opened the briefcase, but when he stared at the gleaming object behind the light, the smile fell away. He still wouldn't pick up the thing inside. "The end o' GPS was just the beginning, an opening move. Damn near a mere ploy. The reality is much worse."

"It never can be simple." Jade London stood next to him and stared into the briefcase. "What's the legend again? Whoever holds the key wields the power to cross the boundary between the real world and the world of the dream?"

Rucksack nodded. "Or worse," he said, "destroy the line." He closed the briefcase. "The border o' life and nothing, reality and dream, has stood for billions o' years. But no matter how long it's stood, any wall can be breached."

"Existence and dream collide. The story of the real and the dream plays out." Jade traced her finger over the briefcase's cool metal. "All around the world, in every culture, there are myths about how everything came to be," she said. "Space and the planets. Land, sea, and sky. Plants and animals. You and me. First there was nothing, then a god or goddess decided there should be something. The Management explain to us that there is a wall between our reality, which is the universe as we live it, and a sort of anti-universe of dreams and nothing on the other side." Jade shook her head. "Some say the wall is the god or goddess itself, and that what we believe to be real is in fact nothing but a divine dream. As long as the dream is dreamed, we exist." Jade smiled. "I've never held with the idea that we are just a dream."

"What do you say?"

"Real is real," said Jade. "If there is a dream, we aren't it. Anyone saying otherwise is trying to sell you something."

"I believe like you do," said Rucksack. "We are. All is. And I believe, above all, that life and the world are worth protecting and should continue." He shrugged. "And then there's Guru Deep. He isn't about increasing shareholder value for the company. He doesn't care about people, or his talks, or any o' the things his company does. All that makes him gobs o' money, but that's only a means to an end."

"Guru Deep believes we're the dream, that we're on the wrong side of the wall." Jade chuckled, but there was no laughter in her eyes. "And that daft bastard wants to tear it down."

"I've seen the line," said Rucksack. "You know, back then. I've peeked beyond. If Guru Deep tears down the wall, he believes existence would pass into perfect, eternal bliss. The divine would wake and the dream would end—meaning there would be no more world. No people, animals, or plants. No creation. No love. What he considers the ultimate everything is in fact the worst nothing. Beyond imagination or comprehension. If that wall came down, so would everything we know and love."

"Annihilation," said Jade. "And not just us or London. The world of the dream and the world of our reality are never supposed to collide. They'd destroy each other. All life wiped out would be only the beginning, but it wouldn't stop there. All existence, all our world, the entire universe, would be destroyed."

Rucksack's eyes narrowed. "That's the power inherent in this key," he said. "And I'd never heard o' it before."

"Neither had we," Jade replied. "The Management are learning everything they can, but we don't have much to go on yet."

"All the more disconcerting," said Rucksack. "This key is more powerful, more terrifying, than anything I've ever faced. More threatening than anything I've ever preferred not to have to square off against." He shook his head. "And to think it was unknown, just sleeping in the ground like a child tucked into bed."

"It was unearthed in the ruins of The Blast a few years back, right?" said Jade. "After that business with your father's three relics and the Awen of Ireland?"

"That's the one. Thank goodness this hadn't been found yet. That all could've turned quite nasty. We might be having a very different conversation right now."

"Or no conversation at all." Jade stared hard at him. For a moment they said nothing. Jade put away the briefcase. "What connects the key and GPS?"

Rucksack sighed. "Me."

"As much as I appreciate your reputation, not everything in the world actually revolves around you."

His left hand clenched and opened. "Thank goodness for that."

"Are you ever going to tell me what happened to your hand?"

"Just know that my struggle to invent the oven mitt was not without pain and sacrifice."

Jade sighed. "One of these days, Rucksack." She looked at him. "Does the key have something to do with your mother and father? A relic they had that you didn't know about?"

"That would make it easier, frankly. But no. This isn't because o' my mum and the First Brewer. Guru Deep is taking down GPS because it's a sort o'... guardian."

"The beer?"

"Not so much the beer, as its effect." Rucksack nodded toward the secret cabinet behind the bar. "When The Management are training you lot to become Jakes and Jades, do they tell you why all those fancy elixirs can influence destiny and decision, yet can't be used with GPS?"

"No. But they tell us they aren't going to tell us."

Rucksack chuckled. "Your influence on destiny and decision comes from them being relative, fluid, and changeable. GPS represents something different. It reminds people o' what's most real about themselves, about the world. Destiny and decision are relative. Reality is absolute. What's real, is. What's unreal, isn't. GPS reminds o' what's real, because it's about as real as reality gets."

"As you like to say, 'Nothing makes the world clear like darkest beer.'"

"Exactly. I'm not just being fanciful."

Jade raised an eyebrow.

"It's nice to be around one o' you who's not so damn serious, you know that? I said not *just* being fanciful. When you're my age you're entitled to a little poetic license." Rucksack smiled. "Guru Deep is getting rid o' GPS because drinking GPS makes people more aware o' what's real. That awareness, in turn, makes the line between dream and reality stronger."

"Remove GPS, weaken the line."

Rucksack nodded. "Weaken the line, it will be easier to use the key to destroy the line."

"What does that have to do with you?"

"Guru Deep knows I'm the one who can derail his plans."

"You're the only one who can oppose him, huh?"

"Others can resist him. But I see my own path again, Jade London. I can see who, in the end, must be the one to stand before Guru Deep and stop him once and for all. You could say he's part o' a very, very big quest for me. Stealing the key put a big hole in his plan. But now we have to find a way to reverse him destroying First Call."

"Did he know you would come?"

Rucksack nodded. "He's been trying for me ever since he became aware o' me, ever since I began opposing him years ago. He's tried deceptions and traps and all sorts o' larger-than-life stratagems to capture or destroy me. Most have been so outlandish as to just put me at risk o' breaking a rib from laughing my arse off. A few have nearly gotten me. He knew I'd come to London to stop him destroying GPS. But I don't know yet what he's going to do about it."

"At least you got the key."

Rucksack shrugged. "That's less comfort than you think. We still don't know what else he has in mind. Guru Deep's plan is unfolding, but the real work for us has only just begun."

"YOU'RE LATE," said Blanders. He closed the door to his office and sat down behind his large desk. Outside the large window, a cloudy sky transformed the sun from a star to a matter of conjecture. The brightest thing Branwen could see was Blanders's orange tie. It was hard not to squint. She wondered if it would bother her so much if her body wasn't throbbing and sore, and so tired she could barely stand.

"We're on time," Zara replied, Rucksack and Branwen standing behind her. Branwen had seen Zara so little lately that her own sister's voice sounded unfamiliar.

"As I said." A corner of Blanders's mouth twitched. "Not that it matters. Do you know why you're here?"

Branwen forced her mouth to stay completely still. *Yup.* Even her face felt sore.

"Our morning assignment said we were to report straight to your office," said Zara. "Sir."

"How perfunctory."

Branwen saw the muscles tense under her sister's gray coveralls. Zara said, "Did you mean to ask us why we're here from a metaphysical or existential perspective? Sir?" Knocking her feet together, straightening her spine, and looking past Blanders, Zara recited, "Your Dreams Are The Only Reality. Sir. As Guru Deep says. Sir."

"And what is your dream, Sara?"

Zara said nothing.

My dream is to be na Grúdairí, Branwen thought. *Though for now I'd settle for muscles that didn't feel made of boiled barley.* Gabsir had warned her it would be hard, the physical toil of lifting heavy bags and stirring the large batches of boiling liquid. And twisting and scrunching her body to squeeze inside and clean the tanks until she was satisfied—and then clean them some more, until Gabsir was satisfied. And sitting with him, hour after hour late at night, reading the old recipes, being quizzed on all the lore of GPS and First Call and na Grúdairí, and, her favorite, sneaking into Arthur's office and reading the journals of past brewmasters.

"Ah, a bit private for the workplace, I suppose," said Blanders. "I'll hazard a guess though." He leaned back in his chair. "Do you dream of disrupting productivity? Of harming this quarter's revenues, at a particularly precarious and strategically essential time in the history of Deep Inc.? Were you under the impression that small janitor mice such as yourselves could halt the massive works of a giant such as Guru Deep?"

"We just keep the office clean," said Zara, still staring at a spot above Blanders's head. "Sir."

"Then you must have been so professionally affronted by the incident a few weeks ago, where every chair, desk, table, and cubicle wall fell over. We lost weeks of productivity. Had to close the building for three days. We're still making repairs."

"I'm aggrieved." Zara's mouth twitched. "Sir."

"Then you naturally have wondered what we would do when we discovered the culprit behind the failures." Blanders shook his head. "Pardon me. I misspoke. I meant sabotage."

"It could seem that way, sir," replied Zara. "However, most of the equipment in the building was purchased secondhand, so it is entirely possible that old parts past their useful lifespan had simply given way—"

Blanders thumped the desk. "Enough."

"Sir?"

Blanders stood. "The three of you sabotaged this office. This building. This sacred space and its sacred productivity. We can only be grateful that your antics did not cause anyone harm. And, thankfully, you had no access to Guru Deep's office. He alone was unaffected. Which must be such a disappointment, given your grand plans otherwise."

Zara stared.

"You have nothing to say for yourself now, Sara?" Blanders leaned forward more, resting his elbows on the desk and tapping his fingertips together. His head drew upward like a cobra. "If we didn't have bigger beer to drain, I'm sure I could be troubled to be more severe with such wastes of skin. For now, dismissal will suffice. Effective immediately, you are—"

"They didn't do it!"

Blanders sat back, surprised.

Rucksack stepped in front of Zara. "It was me, sir," he said. "All me. They were tasked with training me, but that was all they did."

Shock resounded through Zara and Blanders, but he shook his head and said, "No mere trainee could have had the access and knowledge it took to do all this."

It's not enough, Branwen thought. *Not anymore, no matter what Rucksack may have thought.* She took a deep breath. *No turning back now.*

"He's right." Branwen stepped forward too, standing beside Rucksack and in front of Zara. "I helped him. The company's decision to get rid of GPS made me angry. I suppose I was overcome. Incensed. Out of my mind. I wanted Deep Inc. to suffer for what it had done. So I took advantage of Ruckley's newness. Plus he was angry too. Together we sabotaged all the office equipment. But Zara had nothing to do with it. No knowledge. No participation. Had she known, she would have stopped us. And reported us."

"Branwen!" Zara grabbed her arm. "Stop this!"

"Be quiet, Zara!" Branwen locked her gaze onto her sister's for a moment. *Please please shut up. You have no idea why I'm doing what I'm doing. Nor can you.* She forced herself not to think of all the missed evenings, skipped brewing sessions, all the times now when

Zara was alone. "You are not going to pay the price for what I've done."

"You two are sisters?" Blanders leaned forward.

Branwen nodded.

Blanders looked back and forth between Branwen and Rucksack. For a moment his gaze paused on Rucksack. *Don't figure it out,* Branwen thought. *Please don't figure it out.*

"Ruckley. Branwen." Blanders stood. "You are terminated. Effective immediately." He looked at Zara and grinned. The air in the room cooled. Goosebumps broke out on Branwen's skin.

"Sara," said Blanders, "you will continue with your work here. I trust your attitude will improve alongside your dedication. You are, however, barred from speaking of any work matters with your sister."

Zara stepped forward, and Branwen saw the fire in her sister's eyes. Before Zara could say anything, Branwen grabbed her sister's arm. "Thank you, sir," Branwen said. "My sister and I are humbled and honored by your mercy."

"Leave." Blanders sat down. "I don't want to see you and Ruckley again. Sara, stay a moment. The less I see of you, the better for you it will be. However, before you go, we need to have a little chat, manager to employee."

Zara stared at her sister, and Branwen could read the questions there. *What the hell are you doing? Why are you leaving me behind?*

But Branwen said nothing. She looked away, making sure the door clicked shut behind her.

As soon as the elevator doors closed and they were alone, Rucksack said, "What the hell was all that about? The plan was solid. And why did you take the fall with me? You know damn well that if we were getting found out, I was to take the blame. Not you. Not you and me. Just me. That was the plan. What were you thinking?"

Branwen shrugged. "It had to be done, Rucksack. I can't tell you why. Not now."

"Plans within plans, eh? Is that how it's going to be? For feck's sake. You ruined our chances o' finding out what Guru Deep has in store next. We were that close to figuring out how to get to his office."

"Zara is still there. She'll help us."

"Zara believes you just sacrificed yourself to save her." Rucksack thumped the elevator wall. "Though given that she'll be in the Lotus without you, she may think it's the other way round. And you know just as damn well as I do that Blanders wants her here because she's your sister. He knows that if need be he will use her against you, to keep you in check. Or if he figures out my involvement, he'll use her to get to me. Do you have any idea how much danger she's in?"

Branwen's eyes narrowed. "My sister and I have looked out for each other all our lives. Long before we ever met you. If you think for one second that I'm not aware of the danger, or looking out for her still, then by the time I'm through with you, you'll wish it was only your hand that hurt."

Silence crackled between their locked gazes, and Rucksack looked away. "I shouldn't have said that."

Branwen nodded. "Zara will be okay. She's always been the strong one. There's nothing Blanders can throw at her that she can't handle. Even without her mouse of a sister around. I... I have another part to play now."

Rucksack took a step back. "You can't tell me?"

"Not yet. I'm sorry." Branwen stared into Rucksack's eyes. "You once asked us to trust you, and we did. Now I'm asking you to trust me."

Rucksack stared back. "What's done is done," he said. "I know better than most how things can't be undone, you can only do better going forward. I'm going to trust you. But I wish I'd known."

Me too.

"But you know what really gets me?" Rucksack chuckled. "How did they find us out?"

Branwen took a deep breath. "Remember what I just said."

"About Zara?"

"About trusting me."

"What are you saying, Branwen?"

No turning back now. "I tipped them off," she said. "Anonymously. But I made sure Blanders got what he needed to know."

Rucksack stepped back. "You... Why?"

"Please. Trust me."

"This is... This is outrageous. Impossible. How can I possibly trust you?"

"Do you want to bring back the beer?"

Rucksack paused and stared at her. "Yes."

"Then you want to trust me."

The elevator reached the maintenance level. Rucksack and Branwen went to their separate locker rooms to get their things. But Branwen made sure to leave before he did, so Rucksack couldn't follow her.

* * * * *

THE TWO MEN SHOULD have been as brothers. That was the point of na Grúdairí, Arthur reflected as he and Gabsir ran down the corridor toward the heart of the brewery. Na Grúdairí were like family, but tighter knit, bonded not by fate but by choice, love, dedication, and a shared goal: brewing the best beer in the world. Na Grúdairí were meant to bond, to stick together during the good times and the bad.

Then again, there had never been a time as bad as this. *Even when we lost control of the brewery to Guru Deep,* Arthur thought, *that was a dim, difficult time—but at least there was still an us.* In the month since Guru Deep had announced the end of Galway Pradesh Stout and First Call Brewing, each day had had its bad times, its angers and futilities. They were manageable. Far harder were the days when a grúdaire didn't show up anymore, their absence a notice of resignation.

No, Arthur thought, *of surrender. And of my failure, because of all I have to hide from those I care about the most.*

Beyond the usual hisses and burbles of the never-ending brewing, there was always the sounds of the brewers. The calls and banter combined into the life and breath of First Call. It was like the little sounds that told you a newborn baby was still breathing. Brewers compared different batches of malt. Sniffed hops and checked lab results. Discussed yeast cells and how many parts per billion were in a batch. They would gather in small groups, adjusting the process of recipes to fit the reality of ingredients so that every time, no matter what, each batch of beer brewed met the ideal of Galway Pradesh Stout. After checking fermentation levels, then conditioning levels of more mature beer, brewers at last would prepare to fill bottles, cans, and kegs that went to beer drinkers throughout the world.

Sometimes there were raised voices. Even shouting. There wasn't usually screaming.

At first Arthur had ignored it, burying himself instead in the piles on his desk. *I never knew that getting rid of something would create so much damn paperwork,* he thought. He picked up a document, skimmed it, got to the bottom, and realized he had no idea what it said, then tried to read it again. Still nothing. He started to read it one more time, then looked up.

The shouting was louder.

Arthur glanced down at the paperwork, then looked up. Instead of the closed door, Gabsir stared at him. "It's pretty bad, sir."

"Injury?"

Gabsir shook his head. "Worse."

Bracing himself, Arthur followed Gabsir as they ran from the office toward the heart of the brewery. Harm could come from brewing. Arthur knew it as well as any. Heavy materials, hot liquids, steam, pressure. The long years of na Grúdairí had their share of injuries and deaths, all mourned not like distant co-workers, but as siblings and children. Problems happened between them too. They might be as family, but every family had disagreements and conflicts. Still, the only thing worse than injury—

"Who's dead?" Arthur asked.

Gabsir shook his head. "Worse."

"What the hell could be worse than death?"

Then the two men emerged into the large open room where the kettles bubbled with boiling wort, hot enough to take the flesh off a person. Arthur saw.

Arthur heard. Arthur nodded.

A wet heat covered the room. Usually the best of friends, two brewers stood nose to nose, faces red as they shouted. One held a heavy steel brewing paddle. Around them, other brewers stood, watching, talking slowly and calmly, trying to get the men to listen.

Disagreements happen, Arthur thought. *But there isn't usually fighting.*

"Na Grúdairí!" Arthur called.

The two men didn't seem to know he was there.

"Bleed off the pressure!" shouted the man holding the paddle, sweat rolling down his face. "You could make the place blow sky high!"

"What does it feckin matter if I do?" the other replied. His voice dropped and cracked. "It's not like we've much longer to be here anyway."

No punches had been thrown, but Arthur felt like he'd been smacked in the gut with the paddle. "Lads," he said. They ignored him. "Ron. Michael."

At last, they looked at him. "Oh," said Michael. "Did you remember we existed?"

Arthur ignored the jibe. "Why haven't you bled the pressure off number six? Ron's right."

The scrunched anger on the man's red face reminded Arthur of a furious child. "I was having me tea."

Then again, Arthur thought, *he has reason to be angry.* Arthur saw what was worse than injury. Worse than death.

Mutiny.

Betrayal and futility burned in Michael's blue eyes. Behind the emotions, Arthur saw the words in the ash they left behind.

I don't care.

Arthur knew why. He could see it in everyone's eyes when they looked away from him, could hear it loudly in all the things they didn't say when he was around.

This is all your fault.

Arthur knew they blamed him. Guru Deep's takeover—what everyone now called Samara's Folly—may have happened on Brewmaster Samara's watch, but even that paled before Brewmaster Arthur's calamity. *It's on my watch that First Call's death sentence was announced,* he thought. *That will always make it my fault, my weakness, my failure.*

Gabsir went over to a long vertical pipe. "Sir," he said, "we're redlining." He put his hand on the wheel of a relief valve. "I'm going to bleed off the pressure."

"No," said Arthur, his voice even and low. The simple, solo word bounced off the hard white tile of the brewery and struck each person gathered.

"Sir." Gabsir stared at him wide-eyed. "Ron's right. Feel how hot it is in here. This has been left so long, if we don't bleed it now this whole area will blow."

"Step away, Gabsir. It's not your job."

For a moment, Gabsir stared and said nothing. Then he nodded and stepped back.

A piercing beep began to sound. Pipes began to knock and rumble as the steam inside sought escape.

Sweat rolled down Arthur's own face as he turned to Michael. "I remember the first time you came to me with the improvements to the pressure systems, to deal with the part shortages we were having due to the latest round of Guru Deep's budget cuts." He let himself smile a little. Not too much to seem false, not too little to seem harsh. "You'd found a design flaw—even walked me back through old reports of ten people who'd been injured and three who'd been killed over the years because of it. You remember that?"

Michael glared. Then he nodded.

"Some of the finest engineering work I've ever seen," Arthur said. "Made me all the more glad you became na Grúdairí. You were hard at work on the new design, doing the fabrication and change-out, as I recall, when your mother died."

The color went out of Michael's face. "You told me to take all the time I needed," he said.

"Remember that night I found you under the floor, changing out fittings?" Arthur let out a chuckle. "You'd hardly changed out of your funeral clothes."

"You said you'd be back," Michael said. "A few minutes later, you were wearing coveralls and carrying two beers. We toasted my mum, sat a minute in silence, out of respect, then you got under the floor with me and asked how you could help."

"I hadn't been under the floor in ages," Arthur said. "Thank goodness you were so patient with me. Do you remember what you said when I asked why you were here, instead of home with your grief?"

Michael nodded. "I said, 'Mum told me that when I lost something and it hurt, go to what I loved. There I would find comfort and a way forward.'"

Arthur stepped closer to the grúdaire. "We've all lost something. But we still have what we love, if only we will go to it."

Behind them, a cloudy jet of steam hissed out of a pipe. Gabsir grimaced. Arthur felt it too. The room was stuffy and hot. Too hot.

Michael went to the valve and turned the wheel. Then he went around the room, turning more valves.

Gabsir let out a long-held breath. "Pressure is dropping."

They waited, barely breathing, the heat in the room still blazing, then Michael spoke. "It's back in normal range now."

Arthur looked long at Michael and said, "Thank you. And I'm sorry."

Michael shook his head. "I shouldn't have let it get to me, sir."

With a smile Arthur said, "Something I tell myself every day lately."

You've got their attention, he thought. *Use it well.*

He stared at the faces around him, could feel them about to break from this moment and get back to one of the last times they would do their tasks, their incremental everythings that combined into Galway Pradesh Stout. "Na Grúdairí," Arthur said, "can I tell you something I've never told anyone?"

Everyone stood still and looked at Arthur.

"When Brewmaster Samara was dying, I sat with her and asked her how I could possibly keep things running right when First Call was no longer independent. When we were trapped inside Deep Inc. You know what she told me?"

He paused, waiting, letting the words sink in.

"She told me to never stop. That no matter what Guru Deep did, no matter what happened to First Call, to remember what I was here to do." He sighed. "Look, I understand. More than you might think. Na Grúdairí were chasing me from the gates when I was a teenager. The day they let me inside, I knew I'd never leave. First Call isn't my job. It's my home. It's my love. It's my life. The reality that it's being taken away from me, from all of us, sickens me and angers me every day. But as long as we are here, we can do what we do best. Guru Deep can take away the brewery, but he cannot take our love, and he cannot take our pride. I come here every day to do what I was meant to do, as best I can. I hope you do too."

Around him, people nodded and exclaimed. Here and there, he thought he saw wet eyes. "There's one other thing." Arthur stood up straight. Old strength poured through him, the conviction and love that drove him day after day. The fear was there too, along with the disgust and helplessness. They were old but strong, and they gnawed with sharp teeth. He pushed them back, out of his way, and forced himself, yet again, to continue. "As long as we are here, doing what we do and what we love, we have a chance to make things different. To find a way out. I'm here because I won't stop until I've tried everything. Will you be there with me?"

The yeses and the shouts rang up around the room, not of exultation but of relief, of purpose, of commitment and readiness. Of rekindling.

Na Grúdairí went back to work. As he and Gabsir left, Arthur saw Ron and Michael shake hands.

Down a corridor, Arthur looked at Gabsir and said, "Thank you."

"For what, sir?"

"For trusting me. I know you could have bled off the pressure."

"But it wasn't the point. We all have our roles and we all have our duties."

Arthur nodded. "Michael needed to remember he's part of something. I understand if people feel angry or futile. I just don't want them to surrender to it."

"An impressive speech," said Gabsir. "That was tricky handling."

"They are scared, hurting," Arthur replied. "All I can do right now is remind them to find the love beyond that pain and fear."

"Who would've thought brewing beer took so much heart?" said Gabsir.

"Anyone who understands what it takes to make the best of anything," Arthur replied.

As they turned into an empty corridor, far away from the calls of the brewers, Gabsir stopped. "Can I ask you something?"

"Anything. Of course."

"Did you believe what you said?"

Slowly Arthur nodded, making sure his face and eyes didn't betray the truth. "I know people think I'm weak. That I'm helpless and terrified. Maybe they're right. Maybe someday I'll realize all the things I could have and should have done differently to prevent this from happening. But today, Gabsir, I'm just another grúdaire trying to do my best. The love is still there. If it wasn't, I would've given up and left long ago."

"I think you won them back today," said Gabsir.

"Sorry I almost blew up the brewery to do it."

"Next time you give a speech, I hope you don't mind if I listen from across town."

They both laughed.

"Perhaps that could be today's only crisis," Arthur said.

Gabsir shook his head. "Afraid not."

* * * * *

ARTHUR SHOOK HIS HEAD. "What now?"

"Well, less crisis and more... opportunity." Gabsir looked at the floor, then met the brewmaster's eyes again and saw a gleam there. *If you're going to do this,* he thought, *you have to go all the way.* "What if I told you that someone had regained the secret?"

Excitement, mingled with a fragile hope, flooded Arthur's face. "Which grúdaire is it? Let's go talk to them right now. It could be the chance we need. If we can make GPS the way it should be again, the people would love the beer the way they used to. The public pressure alone would force Guru Deep to leave First Call open."

"I'll show you who it is."

Gabsir and Arthur came out of the brewery corridors and walked through the front lobby. "All I'm going to say, sir, is that no matter what form this chance takes, we go for it." Before Arthur could reply, Gabsir opened the front door and the men stopped in the entrance.

Outside, the thin daylight was timid, dim, and sparse. Clouds over London threatened wind and rain. Painted in bold black letters on the red brick across the street, BRING BACK THE BEER glared at them. At the gates, standing small but straight beneath the large dark clouds, Branwen stared at the two men. Excitement lit up her face and wide eyes when she saw not only Gabsir, but Brewmaster Arthur himself.

"That's Malt," Gabsir said, his voice low. "Hops isn't na Grúdairí material. Malt's the one. Her real name's Branwen. She needs training, direction, the help that only we can provide. But if we do... Arthur, if we do, she can bring us back. She's figured out the secret. I don't know how, but she has. Branwen can bring back the beer. I know it. Hell, someday..."

Gabsir stopped talking, afraid he'd said too much. He was grateful that Branwen was silent too. Over the past month he'd broken her down and helped her find her way back up, stronger and more aware. They'd studied every ounce of lore and fact of GPS, First Call, and na Grúdairí. It wasn't the way he'd prefer to train up such a promising grúdaire, but under the circumstances he knew he had no other choice.

Now it was time to try. Gabsir looked from his protégé to his leader.

What he saw chilled his heart.

Instead of excitement and possibility, Gabsir saw a battle. Hope was in Arthur's face, but fear smothered the brewmaster's eyes. And bewildered Gabsir. What was Arthur so afraid of? What could be worse than losing First Call, losing GPS? For a moment, Gabsir thought he could see Arthur about to step outside. To tell Gabsir to unlock the gate and bring Branwen inside not only the brewery, but into the fold, into the family of na Grúdairí. To save the beer.

Arthur slammed the door. Gabsir thought he heard Branwen gasp, then shout.

"Sir?" Anger flared in Gabsir. "What are you doing? We need to give her a chance!"

Arthur's eyes narrowed. Anger sharpened his brittle, jagged voice. "So much we have to do. The next time she or the other one come, then you know what to do. Ignore them. Send them away. Why are you wasting my time with this?"

"She's persistent," Gabsir replied. "A quality I believe you mentioned using to your own advantage."

"That was different. I'm different."

"How? Branwen wants to be na Grúdairí and she has what it takes. That's all that matters. At least, that's all that used to matter."

"Circumstances change."

"And look where that's gotten us." Gabsir fought back his anger. "Why won't you give her a chance?" He leaned forward. "You haven't even tried her beer."

"I'm not interested in homebrewer wannabes."

Gabsir shook his head. "She's not. I've had more of her recent homebrew. A GPS clone. She has much to learn, but sir, she has the secret. What else matters? The beer she brewed wasn't GPS. At least, not as we brew it. But it's what GPS *is*. Surely that means something to you. Sir."

For a moment, Arthur said nothing. Was that a gleam of interest in the brewmaster's eyes? Then fear pounced, and Arthur's voice was hard. "What do you want me to do about it?" he replied. "Tell Guru Deep that First Call has to stay open because a newbie should have a chance to make her dreams come true?"

"This all began with a dream," Gabsir said. "It did for all of us. You've said as much in other speeches over the years. If you don't have the dream, you don't have the love. And if you don't have the love, then all the technique and knowledge in the world won't make you part of na Grúdairí. 'What we do, we do from the heart,' you say. You tell us we have to understand that purpose. That's the light we have to find in the dark." Gabsir felt his voice rising and tried to bring it down again. "I just want you to remind yourself of that."

"We're closing in less than five months," Arthur said. "I already have so much paperwork to do, you can fill my grave with it instead of dirt. The last thing I need is a trainee getting tangled under my feet." His voice dropped to a harsh whisper. "And you know we don't bring on new hires anymore." He looked away.

Gabsir took a deep breath. *You're standing at the damn line,* he thought. *Now cross it.*

"Why?"

Arthur glared at his second in command. "You've never questioned me on this before."

"It's never been so important before." Gabsir leaned forward, meeting Arthur's stare. "I don't care about closures and budgets or anything else. This woman is na Grúdairí in all but name. We're about to lose everything. I show you we have a chance, but you won't take it, and all because you don't want to bring her on? Yes, I'm questioning you. Why are you doing this? Help me understand, Arthur. We've lost. But with her, we have a way back. Our only way back."

Arthur closed his eyes and shook his head. When he looked at Gabsir again, his gaze was distant. "Despite all the years we've known each other, there is no way you could understand."

"It doesn't make sense." Gabsir waved toward the door. "She could help us. She could save us. Why not try? I thought we would try everything. I thought you were doing all you could to find a way out."

"I am. But not that. Not her."

"Sir—"

But Arthur was gone.

Gabsir opened the door and looked outside. He breathed in the mingled scents of exhaust, spring flowers, and the brewery steam that made the air smell sweet. He'd feared this day would come. Whatever fear consumed Arthur, Gabsir didn't know what to do about it. And now he had come to the choice he always knew he might have to make.

He walked to the gates. "Branwen?"

She stepped out from behind a brick pillar.

"I'm sorry," said Gabsir. "I thought he would understand. Thought he would finally be willing."

Branwen shrugged. "At least I'm having better luck than you are today."

"You're no longer at Deep Inc.?"

She shook her head. "Just as we planned. I'm here full-time now." She tried to smile. "Assuming you'll have me, anyway."

"Let's get inside before there's another damn crisis," said Gabsir. "We've got a lot of work to do, especially now that Arthur's decided we have to do this the hard way."

Gabsir unlocked the gate.

SLAMMING THE DOOR TO his office, Arthur locked himself inside and dumped his body in the chair. Ignoring the paperwork that covered his desk, he opened a drawer and took out a thick sheaf of papers, yellowed with age.

He read it again and again. Then he picked up the envelope tucked inside, but set it down again.

Samara, you said to open this only when the worst had happened. Things are dire, but we're not done yet.

Samara's Folly. Always Samara's damn folly. If the company had stayed independent, he could have just been a normal brewmaster with a good career.

Instead I'm trapped on a path I didn't set, on a journey I don't want to take, that ends with a destination I must reach but would give anything to avoid.

So much he had hoped and tried. Arthur forced himself not to look at the failures and rejections surrounding him. All the no's and not-at-this-times and the insufficient-credits. He looked at the safe underneath the desk, considered what was inside but decided against it. It wouldn't have been enough, and Arthur had resolved to keep it for na Grúdairí. Not for himself or for the plan Samara began and left him to continue. To complete. If he could.

The one thing I hate is the only thing I'm left with.

The fear and disgust came back with their terrible teeth. He couldn't resist anymore. Arthur put his head in his hands and cried.

BRANWEN HAD JUST CLIMBED out of the large steel kettle and collapsed on the floor when Gabsir shook his head.

"More cleaner," he said. "Scrub it again."

"I've scrubbed it twice." Branwen's eyes narrowed. Exhaustion had turned her muscles to wet malt. Everything felt heavy. Except the concrete floor in the secret brewery. That was surprisingly comfortable. "I scrubbed the way you showed me, with cleaners mixed precisely to your exact ratios."

"It's not clean enough."

She shook her head. "I'm starting to think you're trying to sanitize me."

"Again."

"You've got to be kidding me!" Branwen thumped the floor. "You tell me I'm going to be part of na

Grúdairí. You tell me I've got what it takes. But mostly you just have me scrub and carry. I thought I was leaving being a janitor to become na Grúdairí. I'm still just a damn janitor."

Gabsir kneeled in front of Branwen and looked her in the eye. "At least it smells better here."

"There is that, I suppose."

"I'm hard on you."

"Yes."

"No harder than I am on myself," Gabsir replied, kindness in his voice. "No harder than my teacher was on me. Brewing GPS isn't glamorous, Branwen. A lot of it is heavy, dusty, wet, mushy, and exhausting as hell. If the equipment isn't cleaned and cleaned and cleaned again, there is always a chance some damn microbe could offset the yeast and ruin the beer."

"I've done exactly what you said."

"And what I've said is we clean it twice to believe it's clean enough. The third time is so we know beyond any doubt."

Branwen sighed. "I thought being na Grúdairí would be... nicer than this."

"Oh, there's that too." Gabsir smiled. "It's just that it's an all-or-nothing package. If you can't accept the hard parts, you can't appreciate the good parts. I'm hard on you because my expectations are high, not because I'm singling you out. It was the same for all of us, from the First Brewer, to me, to Samara and Arthur, to you. Before na Grúdairí, scrub tanks and carry malt bags. After na Grúdairí, scrub tanks and carry malt bags."

"That stuff is a lot lighter when you're only making five gallons at home."

"But now you're making GPS for the whole of England and beyond," replied Gabsir, a brightness sparking in his eyes. "And who knows where you might end up. The journey of na Grúdairí can be a world's wander and wonder. India. Australia. Canada. The USA. Brazil. Japan. South Korea is especially hot for us right now. I think they're angrier than the Irish about the demise of GPS."

Branwen sat up. "It's hard to imagine going to all those places. Especially now. You talk as if there's still a chance of GPS being saved, but you know as well as I do that there's nothing Arthur can do."

A shadow quenched the light in Gabsir's eyes. "I know. But I hope you'll forgive an old man if he acts to the contrary." He looked away, then looked back. "Being na Grúdairí, brewing GPS, is my life. I can't imagine another anymore." He tried to smile. "If I could have my pick," he said, low and soft, "you know where I'd go?"

"Where?"

"New Galway."

Branwen nodded. "You miss Ireland."

"More than you know. New Galway and Ireland are part of me. I've been na Grúdairí so long, if you cut me I'd bleed black. My bones are peat and limestone. If I cried, my tears would smell like a spring rain."

"You certainly have that sense of poesy the Irish are known for."

"A relic of better days," said Gabsir. He held out his hand and Branwen took it. Together they stood up.

They walked over to the brite tank, where their latest batch of finished beer had carbonated and was ready to pour. Gabsir picked up two glasses and opened a small valve. "Time was we had the finest equipment, the best ingredients, and enough na Grúdairí to make everything run as if everything was always brand new, as if we always had the process down to both the tightest science and the highest art." He shrugged as the beer settled. "Now everything is held together by wire and duct tape."

"Listening to you in here," Branwen replied, "I would have guessed prayers and curses."

Gabsir laughed. "Fine senses but a coarse tongue make the best na Grúdairí." He patted the brite tank and handed Branwen her glass. "Now if I can just teach you to swear better, that's all you'll need to have made this latest batch even better."

"You mean that?"

"I only say what I mean," Gabsir replied. "Unless I'm lying, but I only do that in the direst of circumstances."

"How do I know these don't qualify?"

"I wouldn't spare your feelings." He shrugged. "I'd let the door bump you on the arse to get you out of here faster."

Branwen nodded. "At first I think I would've cursed you for how hard you are on me."

"And now?"

"Now you're still an arse at times. But at least you're an arse with a purpose." She looked at the beer. "I do curse you some. But mostly... mostly I'm grateful. You gave me the chance. You're doing all this. Thank you."

Gabsir shook his head. "It's I who will be thanking you." He clinked his glass to hers. "Your good health," he said. "Sláinte, Branwen."

They drank, then Branwen said, "It's hard to imagine how different things are for you now, compared to then."

Gabsir nodded. "It's such a shame for you to see First Call like this. Not just the demise hanging over us. But the dilapidation. Guru Deep has been starving us out financially for decades. At first little pinches, little cuts. Now he does the budget with an axe."

"You've all still managed."

Gabsir nodded. "Aye. Part of what's good about knowing the lore is you understand the fancy equipment has more to do with consistency and scale than with actually being able to brew beer. The First Brewer used fire and open pots, barrels and rainwater. He had to go around the world, from India to Ireland, to get the right ambient temperature, since he couldn't control temperature to the same degree we can."

He tapped the gauge on a pipe. Knowing the cue, Branwen came over and helped him turn the pressure relief valve. "Damn wheel," said Gabsir. "Always sticks."

When they were done, he continued. "Of course, our biggest problems here can be pressure. Bleeding off steam and heat when we need to. The system is terrible, frankly. Used to be better. But then again, that was when we actually had a budget. This cobbled-together stuff... even in here, where I could scrimp and pull in whatever I could and set up the system to my own specifications, blast it all if half the time I'm not terrified that one day this room is going to just blow sky high."

"Do you ever wonder what it was like for the very first na Grúdairí?" Branwen asked.

"We actually have a good idea of that."

"How?"

"Kailash, the First Brewer's wife." Gabsir's eyes shone. "She wrote an account of when the first five brewers came to her and the First Brewer to become na Grúdairí. Luckily for us, that telling was one of the things that had gone to New Galway just before The Blast."

Branwen's eyes were wide. "What does it say?"

"Five came on a full-moon night, three women and two men," Gabsir said, "to the edge of one of the barley fields near Galway."

Branwen could see the moonlight on the dark stalks, could hear how they rustled with gentle whispers in the soft breeze.

"What people don't often understand about na Grúdairí," Gabsir continued, "is that we don't do oaths or swear loyalty or give up who we are for the sake of becoming na Grúdairí. That all began that night."

"Some say na Grúdairí are like monks or nuns in the church, though," Branwen replied.

"Like I said. People don't understand. They believe that being part of something means giving up who you are. We've always disagreed. For us, being na Grúdairí means enhancing the whole of who you are. You work toward something bigger than yourself, yes. But you are still you, and who you are, the decisions you make within the destiny you've chosen, they determine the fate of that bigger something. We all understand that, and we have from the first."

After another drink of their stouts, Gabsir continued. "The five kneeled in a line. The woman in the middle said that they were ready, that they would dedicate their lives to Kailash and the First Brewer, would take any oath they required. And that's where na Grúdairí were proven, then and for all time."

"What do you mean?"

"Kailash told the five, 'Then for life's sake, get up.'"

Branwen laughed.

"As you can imagine," said Gabsir, "the five were surprised. They feared they weren't worthy. Then the First Brewer told them that their worth was exactly why they weren't going to kneel like servants or worshippers. The five said that they would serve, but Kailash told them that they were not seekers and servants, but doers—and brewers. 'You've known kings and queens,' the First Brewer told them. 'Those who stand and command. Those who kneel and know only to follow. Now it's time to learn something new.'"

Branwen raised an eyebrow. "What oath do you give for that?"

"From what Kailash related, she and her husband had deliberated for weeks," said Gabsir. "After all, humans both strive for liberation and hunger for submission. But Kailash and Jagathi had seen what could happen when people followed oaths and followed blindly, forsaking their own judgment for someone else's. They knew that for what they wanted to do, that would never work."

"But surely they also knew that something was needed," said Branwen. "Something that helped connect them, something that helped them hold together when they doubted or when times were hard. People need something to follow, too."

"That they do," said Gabsir. "So the First Brewer told them, 'You know why you are here. You know what you seek. If you must have an oath, I won't ask you to take one for me. I would instead have you make a promise to yourself.'"

"They were to be true not to the First Brewer," she said, "but to themselves and what they sought to do."

"Kailash then stepped forward," said Gabsir. "As she walked to each man and woman she said something simple, but as real and true as real and true can be." Gabsir smiled. "Feel free to say it with me, Branwen."

Gabsir put his hand on her shoulder and recited, "In all things there is universe and nothing, life and death, decision and destiny, the reality and the dream. I choose to live, decide, make, do, and love. I pledge my life to na Grúdairí and to the beer. For as long as I choose and am able, I will make the best beer that I can make, the beer that is life and reality itself."

As Branwen repeated the words, she understood. *These aren't just words,* she thought. *I can feel their meaning in me, becoming part of me, the essence of who I am and why I live.*

Gabsir smiled. "We are now family and friends. We are the brewers. We are na Grúdairí. I will teach you all that I know, and together we will make the beer."

"That must have been an amazing night."

"Just as amazing as this moment right here, right now," said Gabsir. "With those words and the feeling behind them, those five people became na Grúdairí." He smiled. "Just as you now are, Branwen."

"What? Me?"

"You are just as worthy as they were. I've put you through hell these last few weeks. You've done all I asked, met all I expected—and more. You are part of na Grúdairí now."

Branwen took a step back. "I... It's..." She shook her head and looked Gabsir in the eye. "Thank you."

"You're welcome. Grúdaire."

"I've got to get used to that."

"You will," Gabsir replied. "I know I finally did."

"How long did it take?"

"Both no time at all and an eternity. Sometimes I still feel like I hardly know enough to be worthy of what I do."

"I hope I get there," said Branwen.

"You will." From his pocket, Gabsir handed her a black key, small yet heavy. "The brewmaster and the second traditionally are the only ones in a First Call brewery who have keys to the gates and the main doors," he said. "But I see no reason why an exemplary grúdaire such as yourself shouldn't have one to this room." He smiled as she looked at the key. "This little brewery is as much yours as it is mine now," he said, then raised his glass and toasted her.

They drank, then Gabsir said, "One other thing you should know about that day the First Brewer and Kailash created na Grúdairí. After they spoke the words, Kailash told them something difficult."

"What was that?"

"She told them there would come a time when she and the First Brewer would be gone. One among them had to be more than just a grúdaire. She explained that one must hold the knowledge we hold, keep it safe and keep it striving. One must ensure na Grúdairí continues, for as long as there is life, love, reality, and universe. That person would be the brewmaster, and she or he would serve until such time as they passed on that joy, burden, and duty to another."

"Who became that first brewmaster?"

"The woman in the middle," said Gabsir. "She was strong and capable, she knew the beer, and she understood brewers. Much of what we do and know today is because of her. Much was expected from her —but what she did was beyond all expectations."

"That's a lot to live up to," said Branwen.

Gabsir raised his glass. "Fear not, grúdaire. One day, Arthur will be gone too. And so will I. Someone must ensure na Grúdairí continues."

Branwen smiled. "That kettle still needs its third cleaning," she said. "I'd better get on that."

THE PHONE RANG, but as Feckniss leaned forward to reach for the receiver, the wheel fell off his chair again. The chair thunked to the floor, throwing off his hand as he reached for the phone, which thunked on the desk.

A faint voice came from the receiver. "Sir?" The receptionist paused. "Sir?"

Feckniss scrambled out of his chair and grabbed the receiver. "Yes?"

"You'll need to leave now in time to meet your lunch appointment."

"Of course. Thank you."

The hook on the back of the door gave way. His coat became a puddle of worsted wool on the floor.

"Are you okay, sir?"

"Send maintenance up while I'm gone," said Feckniss. "I need a new chair. And they need to fix the coat hook. Again."

He hung up and shook his head. While the rest of the offices and cubicles in the Lotus had been repaired, all month his office had teetered on the edge of falling apart. Desk drawers stuck. The ventilation shafts clogged, leaving his office either blazing or frigid, depending on the day. Pictures fell off the wall. He hadn't said anything to Blanders, wanting instead to Take Initiative And Find a Way, but this was becoming maddening. *It's a brand-new building,* Feckniss thought. *None of this is happening to anyone else anymore. Why me?* Lately he wondered if one day the floor would simply fall out from under him.

But none of that was the worst.

Feckniss turned around to the window that was the back wall of his office and was glad he had opened the heavy curtains when he came in. Bright morning light streamed in. For a moment it made everything quiet. Feckniss wanted to smile, but the day was too dim and cloudy for smiling. The buildings below, usually as bright and colorful as a child's crayon box, were now all but gray, drained of life and vibrancy.

Looking down on London, Feckniss tried to remember the triumphant feeling that day a month ago when Blanders had brought him to forty-one and showed him this office. *I've made it,* Feckniss thought, *so why do I keep feeling it would have been better if I'd been sacked after all?*

Feckniss got his bearings and stared north over the city. Only a few offices had that orientation, and Feckniss knew it must be a sign of Guru Deep's approval. North, Blanders had said, was the same direction his desk pointed. The same as Guru Deep's. Not east to birth, Blanders had said, or west to death. Not south; to Guru Deep that was like looking backward. Only north. Forward.

I see the city the same way Guru Deep does. Feckniss stared. *So what does Guru Deep think of that?*

Before he could stop himself, Feckniss raised his gaze to the rooftop across from the north side of the Lotus. And there it was. The thing that mocked him, challenged him, taunted him. For a moment Feckniss heard the terrible laughter, but even that was put out of his mind by his anger and terror at what stared at him from across the sky. The letters were white on black, and must have been taller than him and Blanders put together:

BRING BACK THE BEER.

The laughter came back. It stopped only when Feckniss closed the curtains.

A loud *ping* made Feckniss jump. The curtain rod snapped. Fabric whooshed past him. That was all it took. For just a moment, he saw what laughed.

No, Feckniss thought. *No.*

A loud knock tore Feckniss away from his reflection.

The receptionist opened the door. Feckniss tried to ignore both the confused look on her face and the sweat on his own. "I tried to call, sir," she said, "but the phone wasn't working. I'll have maintenance look at it while you're out." She handed him a folder. "Here are the directions to where you're meeting your appointment, and our notes on the consultant. The meeting itself is at the Mirror & Phoenix, across from the Square of Ashes. Your taxi is waiting."

"Sounds straightforward." Feckniss picked up his coat from the floor and brushed it off.

"Sir, there's one more thing."

"Yes?"

"Mr. Ruck asked if you would first meet him in the Square of Ashes, by the Moon of Hope."

"Did he say why?"

She shrugged. "Why do consultants do anything?"

Feckniss chuckled at the joke, one of Blanders's favorites. "Because they bill by the hour."

They left the office. As Feckniss closed his door, the doorknob fell off. His mouth dropped open, but no sound came out.

The receptionist hardly blinked. "I'll add it to the list, sir."

AS THE TAXI DROVE away, Feckniss walked toward the Square of Ashes. The Square commemorated the burning of London during The Blast, as well as all the death and destruction it had caused the world over. Tall black columns rose from each corner of the Square of Ashes. Rounded gray stone surrounded the base of each column, symbolizing the ash remaining after the last fires had finally burned out. At the top of each column, fire flew. Bright red and orange phoenixes unfurled wings of gold.

So many lost. So much destroyed. Yet the people of London endured. Rebuilt. Re-imagined. Kept going. And remembered.

Feckniss tried to imagine what the world must have been like right after The Blast. Every schoolchild around the world learned that on October 16, 1834, Night's Day, the first day of year o AB, After Blast, a mirror eclipse had shone with a dark sun and a white sun. To this day no one knew why it had happened—

but only a few months ago, the world had paused again, holding its breath when the sky shimmered under another mirror eclipse. No one yet understood what had happened in Agamuskara, India, on that far too recent day, and those rebuilding the city would not talk about it. Deep Inc. operatives had been there, trailing Rucksack, but before they could report back they had died in the disasters that had destroyed much of the city.

The Blast had begun in Galway, then blossomed outward like a terrible flower, changing the entire suffering world. Fires swept over Ireland. Galway had been decimated. Today its lands remained blackened and uninhabitable, yet England had fared far worse. As the power of The Blast swept west over the Atlantic Ocean and east over Ireland, it crossed the Irish Sea and set fire to the fields and cities of England. Today there was still The Char, a wide black band that stretched from Galway in western Ireland to the Black Cliffs of Dover at the edge of southeastern England, the burned lands of the path of The Blast. One hundred and thirty years later, people were only just beginning to return to many of those regions.

As England burned, its global empire had shuddered—and fallen. Beginning with three heroes who rose in Ireland, Scotland, and India, in the wake of The Blast, in the midst of the confusion and loss England had suffered, the colonies had rebelled and regained independence, most with little or no loss of life. The island of Britain shattered into three countries, and a whole and free Ireland quickly rebounded. Simmering tensions between countries and peoples cooled—having seen enough devastation, peaceful resolutions to difficulties resounded throughout the shuddering world.

In the British colonies military and business forces relented. Most cared only for what had happened at home, boarding ships for England to learn the fates of loved ones, to see the devastation with their own eyes. But above all, the soldiers and clerks, ambassadors and businessmen, had left the former colonies for one simple reason. In one moment, much of England had become a black and desolate land—but that didn't matter. It was still home, and home had been hurt, so they returned to do what they could for where they had come from.

Of all the damage, all the lives lost, London had fared the worst. Some now talked of the decimation of London as similar to the Great Fire of 1666, when much of the city burned, destroying the homes of over seventy thousand in a city of eighty thousand. But far more had died in The Blast than in the Great Fire. Despite all the rebuilding, despite those who had come from other lands, many accepting English citizenship in exchange for helping clean up and rebuild, London still felt like it wore clothes that it hadn't grown into yet.

As Feckniss walked through the Square of Ashes, he thought about the former city of Galway. Once a hub of trade and culture, the ruin of Galway was now a blackened place where none could enter but the specialized scientists who worked at the research center there. It was said that Galway now had ash instead of dirt, and the very air was gray, as if it still singed. All the land was black, as were the waters of Galway Bay. Despite years of study, no one knew how

The Blast had happened, what it was, what caused it—and whether or not it could happen again.

Feckniss passed over the stone plaza, famous for its delicate, subtle shading that progressively lightened from black at the edges of the plaza, to gray, until the center. In a circle at the very center of the square, calm waters shimmered in a clear, shallow pool of milky white stone called the Moon of Hope. Behind the pool, at the edge of the plaza, a tall column was topped by the golden Sun of Tomorrow.

A man gazing into the waters turned to Feckniss and said, "Do you ever wonder what London would be like if The Blast hadn't happened?"

Feckniss shrugged. "This place would probably just commemorate a battle or something."

The man nodded. "Interesting speculation."

"People are people," Feckniss replied. "The world has known a lot of peace since The Blast. But sooner or later, people may decide that getting along isn't good enough anymore."

"And what are people?" said the man.

Feckniss pondered that a moment. "Afraid," he said, standing back from the pool and looking at the man instead of the water.

Slowly, the man nodded.

Feckniss didn't know what had just happened, if he'd been confronted with some sort of test or what. Then a hand was in front of him, but the man kept his other hand out of sight. "Jeremy Ruck," said the man, his smile nearly as bright and big as Guru Deep's. "Just call me Jeremy."

"First name?" Feckniss replied, smiling back. "That's so un-English of you. I'm Feckniss."

Jeremy laughed. "My dealings with Americans. You get used to a first-name basis." His smile was bright, Feckniss saw, but his expertly tailored black suit was more somber and subdued on his large frame. It gave Feckniss the impression of a confident man who could handle himself, but whom you needed to fear only if you brought trouble on yourself. Behind the matching vest, an orange tie lay over a crisp white shirt. The face and bald head were nearly as pale as Feckniss's, with a hint of tan to suggest time in the sun, but not too much. Brown-black eyes gleamed, and in their gaze Feckniss felt himself relax. To be near this man was to be safe, to shelter in the presence of a deep joy and an inexhaustible power. It was like being near Guru Deep.

"Are you based in London?" Feckniss asked.

"My dealings take me all over the world," Jeremy replied.

"Must be an interesting place."

"I like to think so."

"I'll stick to London," Feckniss said. "That's home for me."

Jeremy shrugged. "Home can be anywhere. You just have to find yourself in wherever you are, and find wherever you are in yourself."

"A curious observation," Feckniss said, thinking Jeremy Ruck just might be off his rocker. "Then again, you chose a curious place to meet."

Jeremy nodded. "I come here whenever I visit London," he said. "It reminds me that every beginning has an end, and every end has a beginning. But it also reminds me that every end has an end, and every beginning has a beginning too."

This is a very weird consultant, Feckniss thought. *But Business Is Business, Blanders would say.* "What ended here?"

"Our futility."

"Futility?"

"Humans are so good at being futile. At not seeing beyond the moment, especially when that moment is difficult. Yet the day The Blast happened, the entire world suffered, as did every person. The world's path changed. I like to think it was for the better. Despite all the suffering. All the loss. I like to think that the good that came of it outweighs the terrible." Jeremy stared at the golden sun atop the column. "I like to think we learned that when faced with such tragedy and adversity, such disaster and decimation, if we could do such good to one another that day, then maybe we could every day."

Feckniss stared at Jeremy Ruck. *What exactly did he want to see me about, anyway?*

"But you're a busy man who didn't come here to listen to me ramble," said Jeremy. "Shall we get to business?"

"Here?"

Jeremy shook his head and pointed across the plaza. "There's a lovely pub there. Have you been?"

"I don't get out much," Feckniss replied. "Work, you know."

"Indeed. Amazes me how much work gets in the way of living. Best not waste another moment."

Why do I get the feeling that what he meant is different from what he said?

Feckniss followed Jeremy's fast pace across the plaza.

* * * * *

PASSING BY THE RED-and-black exterior of the Mirror & Phoenix, Feckniss and Jeremy Ruck stepped into the quiet pub. Feckniss took in the polished wood and the worn but gleaming brass. Jeremy raised two fingers. The bartender nodded, but she had a deliberate way of barely looking at Jeremy.

"You'd think the Mirror & Phoenix would be just another tourist place," Jeremy said, "but it's not. Place went up same time as the Square of Ashes, first for the workmen, then for those in London who needed something."

"Beer?"

Jeremy grinned. "Not just that. Perspective."

"Is that what we're here to discuss?" Feckniss asked, more than ready to steer the conversation to business. "To see what perspective you can bring to Deep Inc.?"

"More specifically, to you," Jeremy replied. They sat at a booth, far away from the other few people in the pub. As they looked over the lunch menus, the bartender came over and set two pints of Galway Pradesh Stout on the table, took their orders for fish and chips, and left.

Feckniss leaned back, away from the black beer. "Why not a Deep's Special Lager?"

"Gotta get GPS while we can," Jeremy replied. "You're looking at your pint as if it's grown a tail. Do you like GPS?"

Feckniss traced a finger down the condensation on the glass. "I've never had it before."

Sitting back in his seat, Jeremy Ruck opened his mouth, then closed it.

Wow, Feckniss thought, *that made him shut up.*

Jeremy shifted forward and raised his glass. "Well met, then," he said.

"What do you mean?"

"You had a lot to do with Deep Inc.'s decision to shut down First Call, did you not?"

"I'm Just Part Of The Team," Feckniss replied.

"But word gets around," Jeremy said, though for a moment his flat speech seemed to have a hint of Irish. "If you helped bring about the end o' GPS, then you may as well have one before it's all gone."

Reluctantly, Feckniss picked up his glass and lightly touched it to Jeremy's. He took a small sip.

"Not like that," he said.

"Not like what?" Feckniss replied. "It's beer. That was my mouth. The beer went into my mouth. Isn't that how it's done?"

Jeremy drained a quarter of his pint and set it down. "You have to taste it properly." The Irishness was gone from his voice, as if it had been nothing but an aural illusion. "Try again. This time, take a good long pull, a big mouthful. Breathe in the aroma. Feel the sparkle and the smoothness on your tongue. Taste how the bitter and the sweet come together, opposing but harmonizing."

"Is this a metaphor for life or something?"

Jeremy took another quaff of his pint. "Some would say GPS is life, or at least as real as reality gets."

Feckniss shrugged. "Some would say This Is All A Dream."

"You work for Guru Deep," Jeremy said. "That's to be expected. Just try giving that pint a proper swig, especially if it's to be the only one you have."

"Why does it matter to you?"

Jeremy smiled. "Did you know that some say there's a secret to GPS? Something na Grúdairí knew about the beer, about life, that they fused together in the stout?"

"I've heard that, sure," Feckniss said. "Figured it was all marketing."

"I don't know the secret," Jeremy replied, "but I believe it exists. If you try hard enough, sometimes I think you can taste it."

"Doesn't matter much now," Feckniss replied, taking a long drink of stout. *Let's just get through this,* he thought. *This guy was clearly important enough to get the meeting with me, but I have yet to understand what he wants to do with me, much less with Blanders and Deep Inc. I'm just going to tough this out, get back to the Lotus, and close myself in the office for a while. As long as the door doesn't fall—*

Then he felt it.

Everything Jeremy had said. It was true. It was beer, just beer, but throughout it and every sensation it caused, he sensed something else. Something more real than anything he'd ever known. As the stout washed over his palate, Feckniss then realized what else was there—or rather, what wasn't.

Jeremy Ruck sat back and smiled. "You notice too, eh?"

"A hole," Feckniss replied. "That's the best I can describe it. There's so much there, so much real, but then there's this... this void, like something should be there but isn't."

"That's just it," Jeremy said. "You're right. That absence is what you attacked. The weakness you exploited. That's why Guru Deep was able to bring down GPS."

"Is there something wrong with the beer?"

"Yes. It's still amazing. Tastes great, not particularly filling. But it's not what it's supposed to be."

I know that feeling. Feckniss drank more of his pint. "That's only part of it," he said, surprised both by the words and by the bold feeling buzzing through his veins, his breath, his soul. "He told me there was a line, a prison of a line, between what we think we know and what really is. And that I was helping Guru Deep erase that line."

Jeremy said nothing that Feckniss could hear, but Feckniss had the feeling that behind the man's blazing dark eyes, words were exploding like an internal Blast.

As if by magic, two more pints appeared at the table, along with their food. "Why are we here?" Feckniss asked.

"Is that a philosophical question?"

"A practical one. Why are we having this meeting? You're a consultant. What do you want to consult with Deep Inc. for?"

Jeremy Ruck finished his first pint. "Ah. I don't."

"Then I don't understand."

"I'm not here for Deep Inc." Jeremy smiled. "I want to consult with you."

"Me? I don't think I can afford your rate."

"My consulting is the sort you can't afford to do without," said Jeremy. "And there's no charge."

"What is this about?"

"Are you happy?"

Out of the corner of his eye, Feckniss thought he saw something out the window. He looked again, but it was nothing.

"This moment will pass and what you fear can pass along with it," said Jeremy, who looked from the window back to Feckniss. "It's just a reflection of who you are right now. At the moment. A snapshot. But that can change. You can change."

"I don't see how that's relevant," Feckniss replied. He thought about getting up, but something was holding him to the table. Maybe the beer. Maybe—

"Happiness is relevant to all things. We like to think it's not," Jeremy replied. "The Blast taught us that too, oddly enough. We can survive, but sooner or later we have to find ways to thrive."

"I'm fine," Feckniss said. "I have an amazing job with the best company in the world. I'm a step away from Guru Deep himself."

"That doesn't make you close. To him or to anyone. Have you ever left London?"

"No need. Hong Kong can boast all it wants, but as far as I'm concerned London is the greatest city in the world. I don't need anywhere else."

"But what do you want?"

Feckniss drank his second pint, quickly draining the glass. Before he realized it, he didn't know where the speaking was coming from or why the voice sounded like his own. "I want to see everything. I want to see the world. Always did. But was always too scared. I always thought I'd do what I was supposed to do. Get a good job with a good company. Have security. Work and work and work some more. Retire someday. Be happy then."

Jeremy Ruck leaned forward. "What if I told you that you could do something else? That all you had to do was tell yourself the truth, and walk away, and then begin doing what you really want to do?"

Feckniss stared at the strange consultant. The impossible words echoed around his mind. The truth. "You're saying I could do it," Feckniss heard himself say. His mind screamed. *Listen to him. You've always wanted something more than what you were told you were supposed to do. Say yes. Not to him. But to yourself. Say yes. Free yourself. Go.*

The words battled inside him, as if meeting on a cracked battlefield in his soul. No and yes. Yes and no. Was there a difference? There was, and Feckniss could feel the difference all around him, both as walls pressing in and as an endless sky.

One answer held fear, terror. The other held joy.

Jeremy leaned forward. "Do you truly want to work for Guru Deep?"

I could go anywhere. I've never wanted to go anywhere. I could be free. I don't need to be free. I'm safe, I'm alive.

But I'm not really living.

Feckniss looked at Jeremy Ruck, at the right hand covering the left hand. "Who you are, who you were," Jeremy said, "is not who you have to be."

Deep inside, Feckniss felt something break, snap, but if something had shattered or been freed he did not know. He said only, "Do I want to work for Guru Deep?" Then deep inside Feckniss felt a word win, felt his mouth open again—

"Of course he does."

Jeremy's eyes widened and he stood up. Feckniss turned.

"Feckniss knows exactly what his place is," said Blanders, standing at his full height by the table, his gray suit and gray voice sucking all the color and life from the room. His voice was as flat and level as ever, but in his eyes a rage smoldered. Feckniss had never seen him so angry.

"Sir!" Feckniss said. "I'm sorry, I was just meeting with Mr. Ruck as the schedule had said."

"It's okay," Blanders replied. "You were just doing what you were told. You didn't know that what you were being told was a lie." He leaned toward Jeremy. "Isn't that right, Faddah Rucksack?"

For a moment Jeremy Ruck said nothing. Then he smiled and stood. "Funny how hard it is to get to talk to a young man," he said, the Irish now clear in his voice, "who's done nothing wrong other than work for Guru Deep."

"It is when it's you trying. So you thought you'd try a ruse, a fake identity, a different look? How quaint, Rucksack. Really. All these years, and you still can't learn a new trick." Blanders turned to Feckniss. "Back to the office."

"But sir, the schedule—"

"The schedule has changed."

"He doesn't want to go with you," Rucksack replied.

"Oh no," Blanders said. "He wants to give notice, right? Wants to trade his crisp suit and his nice flat in the city he loves for ragged t-shirts with stupid-wishing-they-were-witty sayings on them, a backpack heavier than he is, and a trip around the world, right? Wants to vagabond, hungry and directionless, never knowing where he's going or understanding where he's been. That's all you ever have to offer. Filthy hobo ruffianship in the deluded guise of liberation. The world has seen enough of you and those like you,

Rucksack. My assistant and I are leaving. You will never go near him again."

Rucksack came out from around the table and stood inches from Blanders. "Feckniss can make his own choices."

"As long as they're yours?"

"I could ask you the same."

Blanders's arm blurred.

Rucksack's eyes went wide and his mouth opened into a large O. He froze, then doubled over, coughing as he wrapped his hands around his belly. As he bent over, for just a moment Feckniss could have sworn the left hand looked small and... wrong.

"Come, Feckniss," said Blanders, and the two men walked away from the wheezing man behind them. "I'm sorry it had to come to that. As you know, the enemy is a longtime... irritant of Guru Deep's. Now and again he likes to make trouble. Had I known it was him, I never would have let this happen. I'm sorry he wasted your time."

"I'm sorry too, sir," Feckniss said. "I didn't know. But I'll never trust him again or let him near us."

Blanders nodded. "I would have expected no less. But we must be getting back. We have a meeting."

"With who, sir?"

Blanders looked around and smiled at Rucksack. "Why, with Guru Deep."

Rucksack sprang forward, but the two men had left the pub and quickly gotten into a waiting car. Feckniss turned around and saw Rucksack standing in the road, fear and anger smoldering in his dark eyes.

Then Feckniss realized something. "Sir?"

"Yes?"

"The enemy still has what he stole. Why didn't you bring security and subdue him, bring him to the Lotus so we can get it back?"

"Guru Deep knows, my protégé." Blanders smiled. "The time is not right. Faddah Rucksack is not the only one who can take something of value. When the time is right, we won't have to pursue Rucksack. He will gladly, freely, return to us what he has stolen."

Feckniss turned away, trying to understand. Trying to listen only to Blanders. Trying to forget what he had almost said.

"ZARA!" called Branwen as she closed the door behind her. But the flat was silent. Even the wanted poster of Rucksack on the wall by the door, which usually always seemed ready to crack a joke, instead had a foreboding quiet to it.

"Sis?" She went into the kitchen, which was covered in its usual post-Zara detritus. Toast crusts petrified on a plate. An empty beer bottle sulked on the table. Tea sludge in a mug turned to tar.

Branwen wandered through the flat, checking each room. No sign of Zara. No sign that she had returned home from work. Everything was as it had been when they had left that morning.

She went into the boxroom. *Something's not right.*

Looking through every shelf, checking every tube and carboy, it was only when Branwen came to the secret covered area, the area that Zara always left alone, that Branwen realized what was wrong.

The old blankets had been moved and put back, but not exactly how Branwen had left them. The telltale folds weren't right. She lifted the blanket.

A six-pack was gone.

But that's not all, Branwen thought. *You looked right past it. Thought it was just more of the usual cleaning-up.*

She ran back to the kitchen and grabbed the empty bottle. *This isn't one of our usual bottles. If Zara saw it, she'd know that immediately. This is from the new batch, and I'd just brought it home yesterday. The batch Gabsir toasted me with today, when he named me part of na Grúdairí.*

Her joy turned to ash. The fears tore through her again. Rucksack's words. The flicker in Gabsir's eyes when he had told her to stay away from the brewery that evening, that he couldn't get away and she might be found out. The warning in her own heart.

What if Zara's figured out that I've been brewing behind her back? She'll know I've surpassed her, Branwen thought. *But it's worse than that. What if Blanders learned it too?* She recalled Blanders asking Zara to stay in his office after he dismissed Branwen and Rucksack. *What if they came here and realized what's been going on? What if they've taken her?* She shuddered. There were stories about the Lotus, whispers that deep in the ground were special sub-basements, prisons... dungeons.

Branwen left the flat, barely remembering to lock the door behind her.

"WHAT THE HELL DO you mean, it's all off?"

Arthur stood in the middle of the brewery, surrounded by confused na Grúdairí.

"We don't know what happened, sir," said Ron. "We were in the middle of the boil when suddenly the heat was gone. No gas in the lines. We've all checked and double-checked and triple-checked. There's no gas in the brewery. No gas, no fire. No fire, no boil."

"Same with us, sir," said Michael. "We were pouring the water to start the next batch, when the tap ran dry. Not so much as a drip now."

"No boil, no beer," said Arthur. "No water, no wort. And you've checked every line?"

Each nodded, and Arthur knew they meant it. Each one would have gone over every inch of pipe, every switch and valve.

This wasn't a mechanical problem.

"Sir?" Another grúdaire pushed through the group until he was in front of Arthur. "There's a call for you."

"At least the phone works," said Arthur. "Unless it's the gas or water utility, tell them we're dealing with an emergency."

"I, uh, I think he already knows."

"Who is it?" But suspicion grew in Arthur. *Not a mechanical problem,* he thought. *A political problem.*

The color went out of the grúdaire's face. "It's Guru Deep."

THE DOOR OF THE Mirror & Phoenix bounced off its stop and nearly smacked Branwen in the face as she came in.

Jade London looked up from the bar. Clearly she had seen what had happened, as had everybody else in the packed pub. Branwen fought back the sudden urge to smack the grin not only off the bartender's face, but off the booze-swilling mouths of each and every person in the room.

Jade must have noticed that too. Her grin fell away as she pointed to a table in the corner. "They're over there."

"They?"

Jade nodded. "Rucksack's been here all afternoon, after a rather difficult lunch, uh, disagreed with him. Poor bugger's still exhausted. This sort of thing takes a lot more out of him that he realized. Sometimes I think he should meditate on the phrase 'You're not as young as you used to be.'"

"That's nice. What about—"

"And your sister got here half an hour ago."

Branwen's heart pounded. "Zara's here?"

"Unless you have another sister."

Branwen ran to the back table, relief flooding her when she saw the spiky hair, the smoky eyes, the angry face. She wrapped her arms around her sister. "Oh thank goodness," she said. "I'm so relieved you're okay."

"Okay? What the hell are you talking about?"

Branwen stepped back. "Blanders. All his weirdness toward you after he sacked me and Rucksack. He hates you... and I was scared, big sister, I was really worried about you—"

"But not so worried that you stayed." Zara set down a beer bottle. "Not so worried that you didn't take the fall for Jeremy Ruckley here, letting him take the fall himself, the way we'd planned all along. Not so worried that you didn't at least let me join in the self-sacrifice brigade. No, clearly you were just beside yourself with worry. And then, as Rucksack tells me, you disappeared after the two of you split off for your respective locker rooms. He looked all over for you, but no go. It threw him off when he tried to pull off another plan to get deeper into Deep Inc., but that fell apart too."

"Zara—"

"We trusted you," said Rucksack, setting down his own bottle. "Both o' us. Zara and I thought we were all in this together. Equal. But we weren't. I told you the truth. Zara has been open with us. But you." When Rucksack picked up his bottle and pointed at Branwen with it, she realized what he and Zara had.

The six-pack missing from the flat.

"You've been brewing without me," said Zara, her mouth a hard, thin line.

"Not just brewing without you," Rucksack added. "Brewing somewhere else. This doesn't taste the same as the beers you make at home. The water's different. The malt is different."

Zara nodded. "And the only place you'll find these New Galway Golds is at First Call Brewing, right here in good ole London." Her voice dropped even lower. "How'd you do it, little sister?" The pleading tore at Branwen's heart. "You got in. But why did you leave me behind?"

"Let me explain," said Branwen.

"No," said Zara. "Let me. It all makes sense now." The sharp edge of Zara's voice cut through Branwen, each word deeper and deeper. "Even at work you've been using duties or claims of problems as an excuse to be wherever I wasn't," said Zara. "And outside of work the distance has grown too. Missed drinks at the pub. Not eating dinner together at home. Hell, you weren't even brewing with me anymore."

The tears pulled at Branwen, not for the first time, but this was the closest yet they'd come to falling. *We've been so close for so long,* Branwen thought, terrified at how her sister sat across the table from her yet was so far away.

How can what we love most be what's tearing us apart?

When Branwen didn't answer, Zara shook her head and took a long drink from her bottle of Branwen's stout. Around Rucksack and the sisters, the crowded pub bustled with the after-work relief and kvetching of a cross-section of London. They came here all the time, usually after work or for the occasional night out. Half the city seemed to be there this evening, unwinding, relaxing after a long day. Gestures and motions kept catching Branwen's eye, though she knew she was just letting herself get distracted. Anything to keep from looking at her sister.

"I figured you must have met someone, and for some reason didn't want me to know who she was yet," said Zara. "I wanted to give you space, figured you'd tell me when you were ready. It's not like either of us has cared much about dating, so I figured you just wanted to see where it went, see if she was going to be important enough for me to meet her, just like I would do before introducing someone to you." Zara chuckled. "I was looking forward to explaining what would happen if she hurt my sister."

Branwen tried to keep her voice steady. "I would have told you." Zara tried not to sound hurt or angry, but Branwen knew she was. They told each other everything. Always had. Until now.

And Zara would have told her, Branwen knew. Just as Branwen would have. At one time. Far worse than the anger, the quiet pleading in Zara's voice cut Branwen to her soul and nearly brought her to tears. It laid bare the wish, the dammed-up desire to again tell her sister everything that was her and listen to everything that was her sister.

But Branwen had lost her chance to tell the truth. The beer had told all instead.

"It was really hard to feel so cut off from part of your life." Zara shook her head and the anger seemed gone. "I wanted to understand. But today, after everything at the Lotus..."

"What happened with Blanders?"

"Nothing of note," Zara replied. "He told me he was disappointed at what had happened, but was relieved I wasn't involved. He said he was hard on me because he could tell how hard I worked, so he held me to a Higher Standard. And with that came an expectation that I would surpass that standard."

"Then what? What did he try to get out of you?"

"He asked how I took my coffee."

"What?"

Zara shrugged. "We had coffee. We talked about janitorial, what we needed, what was working. Then he thanked me for my dedication and sent me on my way."

"That's a relief."

"Please," said Zara. "He's a boring, condescending, patronizing prat, and I was tempted to sock him between the eyes with the hard end of my mop. But I figured that could wait for another, more gratifying occasion."

"I'm glad you're okay."

Zara shook her head. "I'm not okay, little sister. I'm far from the far side of being okay." She slammed the bottle on the table. "I came home, completely confused. I thought you'd be there, but you weren't. I really wanted a beer, to decompress after this hellish day. We didn't have any in the fridge, so I went into the boxroom. Looked all around. Found nothing. Could hardly believe we were out."

"My fault," Rucksack added. "That sort o' thing happens a lot when I'm around."

"Then I peeked under that little blanket of yours on the shelf. The one you always seem to want to keep me away from. And what do I find?" She picked up the beer bottle. "I find GPS. In bottles that say First Call. And beer that screams Branwen. It wasn't that you'd found someone special. It's that you were being someone special. Someone brewing in secret."

"That's not true," said Branwen. "Well, okay, no, it is kind of true. But not the way you think. I couldn't tell you, Zara. I wanted to. But I couldn't—"

Zara's eyes narrowed. "You decided you were better than me, and you left me behind."

"You weren't the only one," said Branwen, anger rising up from her sadness. "I've always gone along with what you wanted. Always let you be in charge. I wanted to be na Grúdairí because you wanted to. At least, that's how it began. I learned everything I could about brewing, tried my best at it, because I knew how much becoming a grúdaire meant to you. I didn't make him decide that I was the only one worthy!"

"What do you mean?" Zara asked.

The tears fell down Branwen's face now. "The old man at the brewery. Gabsir. The day the brewmaster broke our bottles. That night, while you were gone, he came to the flat and found me. He told me that I had the makings of na Grúdairí... but you didn't."

Branwen stopped. Zara's eyes dimmed as she slumped forward, as if something holding her up had given way. *I'm sorry*, thought Branwen. *I would have traded with you in a heartbeat, would have spared you all this pain. Except that... except that...* But she couldn't bring herself to think the rest, much less say it.

"All I ever wanted was to be na Grúdairí," said Zara, her voice barely above a whisper. "How could it be you instead?"

But inside Branwen, something hardened, strengthened. Before she could stop herself she said, "Because brewing is who I am. I love it. I understand the beer. What it needs. What it is. That's what Gabsir saw in me. This past month, he's been working with me nearly every night. I've been spending every spare moment at a secret brewery he has there. Not even the brewmaster knows about it. Gabsir's taught me the history of GPS, shown me old recipes. He's taught me everything he knows and everything na Grúdairí knows." Branwen looked down. "The beer you're drinking is the first GPS I've brewed that Gabsir thought was worthy of being bottled. Today he toasted me with it and said that I was now a grúdaire."

Zara shook her head. "You lied to me."

"I wanted to tell you. I've wanted to tell you all along. But I knew this is how it would be. Your dream wouldn't come true but mine would. You wouldn't be able to handle it."

"No," Zara said. "It was our dream, Branwen. It was supposed to be you and me. All this time all I wanted was for us to get inside, to get our chance—but you already had it. You were already in. And you couldn't even tell me. So instead you left me behind." She nodded, then stood. "Fine. I'll do some leaving too. Good luck. Grúdaire."

Branwen glared at her sister, ready to say more.

"Be quiet!" Jade London shouted. "There's something on the radio." Voices fell, but some murmuring conversations remained. "Shut up!" she yelled, and the pub fell silent. "Guru Deep is making another announcement."

Rucksack and the sisters went rigid. As Jade turned up the radio, Guru Deep's bright voice boomed across the silent pub.

"WHEN LAST WE SPOKE," said the voice of Guru Deep, as if having a pleasant yet unfortunate chat with loved ones, "I came to you with news triumphant and sad. As you know, after much difficult deliberation, it was declared that production of GPS would cease in six months. It pains me to say that even the most experienced businessman can be wrong."

In the silence that followed in the eternal pause, Branwen wondered how many people across the city, around the world, were listening.

Not to mention holding their breath.

"Due to circumstances that I cannot explain at this time, GPS production will not end in six months."

Did he change his mind? Branwen thought. *Did Arthur find a way after all? Maybe Gabsir and I were wrong.* The hope sank in. *If they found a way, if they really found a way, then I won't just be a grúdaire in name. Gabsir will reveal me. Arthur will have to accept me. If this can work out, then come what may, Zara and I can be okay, we can figure it out, we—*

"GPS production," said Guru Deep, "has now officially ended. Tonight, all breweries around the world ceased operation."

He paused again, as if knowing a loud, global uproar had followed his words.

Jade London quieted down the pub, and the voice continued. "I know what a shock this must be. Therefore, tonight only, after this announcement, all orders of Galway Pradesh Stout and Deep's Special Lager are on me. Tomorrow begins a new era for lovers of good beer. And for tonight, I bid you farewell. Cheers."

The voice was gone. In the pub, anger swelled—but so did something else.

Rucksack shook his head. "Free beer," he said. "Only Guru Deep would know that as angry as he would make people, he could get them right back on his good side."

People rushed to the bar and soon had it surrounded, five people deep.

"Bugger this." Zara stood up. "Free or not, Guru-feckin-Deep's not getting another moment of us. There's homebrew in the fridge, and it'll be more GPS than anything pissing out of the taps in here." She nodded at Rucksack. "Would you like to join us?"

She and Rucksack started walking away, but Branwen didn't move.

Zara stopped. "Branwen?" she said. "Little sister?"

"I'm sorry," said Branwen. "I can't."

"Can't come drink homebrew at home with your sister and a friend? Can't commiserate this crappy, crappy end to a crappy, crappy day?"

Branwen shook her head and fought back tears. "There's something I have to do." She started toward the door, but Zara stepped in front of her.

"There's always something you have to do lately," said Zara. "How about you be bothered telling me what the feck it is?"

Branwen started to reply, but before the words came out, once again Jade London's voice cut through the noisy pub. "Zara!" she shouted. "Branwen!"

The sisters stopped. The bartender stepped out from behind the bar. "It's time," she said.

AS FORMER BREWMASTER ARTHUR Celbridge came out of his office, he wondered how pale he looked. The door clicked and he turned around.

Na Grúdairí filled the corridor. At the front of the group, Gabsir locked eyes on his leader, and his face filled with concern.

Oh, Arthur thought. *That pale.*

The dread and horror that filled him surrounded him. Except that Arthur's was now tempered by something else: the terrible relief of finality. It was an unwanted gift, but also one he had no choice but to share. He took a deep breath and stared into the faces of each man and woman around him. They were all there. *At least I only have to say this once.*

"Guru Deep lied," said Arthur, and it was met by murmurs but less surprise than he might have expected. "He changed the timeline. Instead of five more months, he shut us down tonight. All of us around the world. That's why there's no gas or water. First Call Brewing... Galway Pradesh Stout... Na Grúdairí... We are no more."

Ever since the first announcement of their end, Arthur had wondered how the brewers would react when the final moment came. And when he hung up the phone not two minutes ago, he had feared. Would there be simple resignation, private sorrows released later and drowned in the company of family or friends or fellow na Grúdairí? Would anger boil over into something worse? Arthur wondered who would rage at him, the last brewmaster of First Call. He wondered how the disappointment at his failure would look, and if it would crush him or tear him apart.

He hadn't expected this.

No one spoke. Na Grúdairí bowed their heads. As one, they turned and began walking away. Resigned. Crushed. Surrendered.

Except for Gabsir.

"That bastard," said the former second, a familiar fire in his eyes. "You couldn't have known. We never could have accounted for this."

"I don't know if he planned it all along," Arthur replied, "or if something forced his hand."

"What do we do?"

Inside Arthur, the dreaded words waited. Yet when he spoke them, the relief he also felt surprised him. "We let go," he said. "We start moving on."

Gabsir shook his head. "It's not that simple."

"Nothing ever seems that way," Arthur replied. "That's why it's always that simple."

"Most of us hadn't gotten that far," said Gabsir. "Some of them have families. They don't have things finalized. They thought they had more time."

Arthur nodded and opened his door. "Bring out everything we have, Gabsir. Every keg, every bottle, every can."

"It's not much, sir," said Gabsir. "We were just at the end of a big distribution pickup. The cooler's pretty bare."

"Whatever we have. They can have it here, they can take it home, they can do whatever the hell they like."

"A going-away party?"

Arthur's mouth was a flat line. "More like a wake." He stepped into the office. "And Gabsir?"

"Yes?"

"Beer won't be the only thing we're cleaned out of tonight." Arthur tried to smile. He bent forward and leaned under the desk. Small whirring sounds filled the air. "Tell everyone to make sure they see me in the lobby before they leave."

Gabsir almost smiled. "Why?"

"Guru Deep ended First Call. He ended our livelihood and took away what we love most." Arthur sat back up. Some of the color came back into his face. "But he can't take away how we treat each other. I promised that each grúdaire would be taken care of. Tonight, I'll make good on that."

And with thump after thump, Arthur reached into the steel-and-brass floor safe and started throwing stacks of cash onto the desk.

JADE LONDON PULLED OUT a tin box lined with brass, the size of a case of wine. Branwen, Zara, and Rucksack stood still, watching her.

"C'mon, you lot," she said. "If you thought you had more time, you don't. If you thought you'd wait for the last minute, the clock just stopped." Jade pointed at the sisters. "If you're a regular, either you know Zara and Branwen Porter, or you at least know their homebrew. If you don't know them and their beer, we're going to correct that oversight. That bastard Guru Deep might have gotten rid of GPS, but he's got nothing on these two. They want to be brewers. Hell, they wanted to be na Grúdairí. It's been their lifelong dream—only Guru Deep just threw their dream in the dirt and stomped on it." She paused and looked out over the silent crowd in the pub, then continued. "Guru-feckin-Deep. He can stop these two from becoming na Grúdairí... but he can't stop them brewing. For now they at least need to keep going with their homebrew. Maybe you're looking at the next masters of a new brewery, pumping out beers that give Deep's Special Lager a run for its money."

"What the hell is she doing?" Zara whispered.

"Why Jade London, you softie," said Rucksack with a smile. He winked at the sisters. "Just wait."

"If you care about good beer," said Jade, raising the box high over her head, "then you care about Zara and Branwen." She reached into her pocket, pulled out a wad of bills, and put them in the box.

Then she handed the box to a person at the bar and said, "Now pony up."

The box went around the pub, to each and every person there, until at last it came back to the hands of the bartender, who smiled, gave a simple thanks, and then walked over to the sisters.

"Zara," said Jade. "Branwen." With a grin, she held out the box. Their hands shook as each sister grabbed a side. Branwen tried not to look at her sister, but she was certain she saw the same overwhelmed look in Zara's eyes, the same tears barely clinging.

"Guru Deep will regret the day he took GPS away," said Jade London. "Now give him hell. Wait. No. Give him damn good beer." Jade thumped the bar and chanted, "Bring back the beer! Bring back the beer!"

All around the pub, people began thumping and chanting, thumping and chanting.

With a wink, Jade London went back to the bar and started serving what was left of the GPS. And the sisters looked inside the box.

It was packed to the top with cash.

"Singles... fivers... tens..." Zara's eyes widened.

"Twenties," Branwen said. "Fifties. Hundreds!"

Zara looked at her sister. "How much do you think is in there?"

"Enough for us to brew whatever we want," Branwen replied, "until we've used all the malt in England."

Then the smile was gone from Zara's face. "Yeah," she said. "If you ever have the time again." She took the box in both arms. "I almost forgot. You have somewhere to be. Or has something changed your plans?"

Branwen hung there, thinking of Gabsir in First Call, and of her sister right in front of her. *This is it,* she thought. *As if I haven't chosen enough.*

She started to talk, but Zara cut her off. "It's okay," said her sister in a tone that indicated it was anything but. "I already know what you're going to say. I'll save you the trouble. You've cut me off. Cut me out. Fine. I'll do the same."

For a moment Branwen watched Zara and Rucksack as they went ahead of her. *Oh big sister,* she thought, each word painful, *if only I could tell you.*

Zara and Rucksack left the pub, turning toward the sisters's flat. Branwen left too. And headed toward First Call.

IN THE PRESENT THERE was no future, so Arthur looked instead to the past. Stacks covered his desk.

Arthur ignored them. Each piece of paper he signed was just another bleeding cut, another nail in the coffin lid, another reminder that his life's work was dead and gone.

Instead he had cleared a space at the edge. There he had brought over some of the journals, which he read as often as he could for comfort, and the letter, which he had never opened.

The journals held the thoughts, concerns, observations, goals, and lives of the long line of brewmasters. They discussed everything from day-to-day operations and the challenges of the times, to their admiration of their fellow na Grúdairí and their love of Galway Pradesh Stout. Their thoughts and feelings lived on there, their days and their lives, their hopes and their challenges. Their very souls were on the page.

And I am the end of the line, thought Arthur.

The reminder cut into him. The life's work of dozens upon dozens of men and women, come to a brutal halt. *I've let you all down, my kindred,* Arthur thought. *I'm sorry.*

Tears stung Arthur's eyes. He set aside the journals and picked up the letter. Calm replaced sadness.

Arthur had held the unopened envelope hundreds of times. His fingers had given the paper a sheen. So too, he was certain, there was now salt in the fibers from all the tears that had dried there.

On the front of the envelope, Brewmaster Samara had written "Brewmaster Arthur" in her elegant script. He turned over the envelope. On the back, in simple, stark block capital letters, she had added, "OPEN ONLY WHEN THE WORST HAPPENS."

"We tried to make things different," said Arthur to the empty room. "After she was gone, I kept trying, just as she told me to. But she always knew it would come to this." He sighed. "And so did I."

The worst had happened. He raised the slim silver blade of the letter opener toward the envelope.

A knock on the door made him stop.

Gabsir stepped inside the office and stood in front of the small table by the door. Arthur slid the letter beneath one of the stacks of papers covering his desk.

"I've sent them off, sir," said Gabsir, his voice steady but for a slight tremble. "They took every remaining pint with them, in bottles or kegs or their bellies... or all of the above."

Arthur chuckled. "That's as it should be," he said. "At least something is."

"A few of them said they would take some around to the pubs too, to augment the stores for one last proper quaff."

"Devoted, down to the last drop."

The silence hung like fog between them.

"You have been the best second a man could have asked for," Arthur said. "Thank you for being so diligent. And so trusting. For being not only my mentor and my colleague, but my friend."

"The honor has been mine," Gabsir replied. "I know that bringing you up had its controversies, but controversy comes with the naming of a brewmaster like bubbles come with a fresh-poured pint. Samara knew what she was doing. She knew she'd found the right person for the job that had to be done."

Arthur remembered. Others had been better brewers, or had known the equipment or the lore or the business better. Yet Samara had chosen him, though sometimes Arthur still wondered why. He couldn't stop the bitterness in his voice. "There was no right person for this job. There was just the one who would see it through."

"No glory. No pride. Just grit. Just never stopping until all is done. Sometimes that's all there is." Gabsir shrugged, then sat down. "I remember the day Samara declared you the new brewmaster, before us all," he said. "How she told us joy and grief were one that day. She would have known better than anyone."

Arthur nodded. "The illness was getting worse. She was so gaunt, but her strength hadn't faded yet. The sting of the sale was still sharp. That caused far more pain. People already called the sale Samara's Folly."

"She told us First Call was bought, but we were not beaten, and no matter what, we had to remember that difference. Given all that had happened, sitting up there must have been hard."

"She'd called me into her office, to this office, the day before," Arthur replied. "She had asked me if, given what had happened with the company, if I still wanted to be brewmaster. And she'd told me to consider that carefully. I could decline and go on with all my honor... but if I continued, it would be harder and more terrible than I could imagine."

"Samara never minced words," said Gabsir. "Always wanted people to know what they were getting into, understand what was and what wasn't."

"I considered it, too," Arthur said. "No longer in control of our own destiny. Not truly making all our own decisions. But she was right, Gabsir. We'd been bought, but we weren't beaten."

Everyone in the room had nodded, including Gabsir, who had stood next to Arthur on the small platform. All of London's na Grúdairí had stood assembled before Samara and Arthur, as did head brewers and other First Call representatives from around the world, listening through open phone lines. The men and women of na Grúdairí had stood shoulder to shoulder. Their faces represented every race, from the paleness of Samara's Irish skin to dark browns such as Arthur's own. He thought back to his family, who had left Kenya for England after The Blast, and wondered what they would think of this day, of what the next generations had created.

But he couldn't tell Gabsir what else she had told him, that day in her office before she named him the next brewmaster, officially marking an end to decades and decades of her leadership and guidance. He had knocked on the door expecting to go over the ceremonies. He'd been all the more surprised when he'd entered to find Samara, her long graying hair loose instead of pulled back, sitting behind the desk with a bottle of scotch and two glasses in front of her.

She'd asked him to sit down, and he did. He wondered when she would stop pouring, and the drink she handed him was heavy. "Let's make a toast," she had said. Her thin, wry smile could have been sardonic except for the warm light that, despite all that had happened to her and to First Call, still glowed. "To all that changes. To successes and mistakes." Her smile grew. "And to my folly."

They'd had their drink. Then Samara had set two things before Arthur. She opened the sales document that governed the takeover of First Call by Deep Inc.

They went through everything, line by line, until they came to a small paragraph. Samara poured them each another large scotch.

"I know what everyone says about me," she said. "And I know that everyone will say it about you too. I'm so sorry for what you are taking on. You and I have had each other to confide in. You will have no one. This path I began, the path you must continue, is lonely and terrible. Who you are must be separated from who you seem. What you do must give no indication of your true purpose."

"What about Gabsir?" Arthur asked. "Why can't we tell him?"

"What we are doing is devotion masked by betrayal," said Samara. "I won't lie to you, Arthur. There will be no rest for you. No mercy. No friends or companions. No light on a black path. Come the end, you will be alone. You will do things you cannot imagine. You will be reviled—but no one will hate you more than you will hate yourself." She shook her head. "Now imagine how terrible this is for one. Would you wish it on another?"

Arthur said nothing. Then Samara handed him the second thing: a sealed letter.

"I hope this will be a light in the dark," she had said. "I'm sorry I can't offer more comfort in the hard times to come."

"Samara," said Arthur at last, "your..."

"My fool's hope. My one little gleam in the utter darkness. It's okay."

"Is it really going to work?"

"If the circumstances are right." She gave a half-smile. "Maybe this gets renamed Samara's Brilliance."

"And if they're not?"

She shrugged. "Then a fool and her folly will never be parted.'"

Returning to the present, Arthur tried to smile at Gabsir. "Every day I still think upon what she told me, the same words her mentor and predecessor told her."

Gabsir nodded. "'Lead with love and wisdom, and the beer will be what it was meant to be. Be who you want na Grúdairí to be, and the brewers will follow.'"

The simple statement fired like an arrow into Arthur's soul. When it hit, the feelings came loose.

Deep inside, he saw the truth. For a moment, he hoped.

Then the fear roared.

"Hard words to live up to, in times like these," said Gabsir.

"Words, my old friend, that I'm afraid we no longer can live up to." Arthur sighed. "We always wondered what would happen, as time went on and Guru Deep sank his hooks deeper." Arthur shook his head. "I never thought it would come to this."

And I couldn't do it, Samara. I'm sorry. Your last little light has gone out.

Sitting back in the chair, Gabsir's usual vibrancy fell away and he just seemed old. Tired. Gabsir had been old even when Arthur was a new grúdaire. Back then Arthur had tried to joke about it with some of the others, but they made it clear that no one ever talked about Gabsir's age. Gabsir himself just claimed it was the result of taking in so much fresh beer over the years. But as Arthur stared into his friend's brown-black eyes, he wondered. *How old are you? Where did you come from?*

"Maybe it's time we went out for one more last one, then," said Gabsir. The vitality, the youthful, mischievous gleam, had returned to his dark eyes. It reminded Arthur of what the past brewmasters said in their journals: When you had a truly perfect pint of GPS, if you looked just right, you could see it: a light in the midst of the darkness, like finding a faint solitary star in a sky of endless black.

That was the secret. Or so it was said.

But those days were gone, and the star with them.

"You go," Arthur said.

"Arthur..." Gabsir looked away and stroked his chin, taking a deep breath, then looked back at Arthur. After a deep breath, he continued. "Tomorrow you're going to have to face the world outside anyway. Might as well get used to it now. Samara wouldn't have wanted you to be this way. Shut up inside. Never coming out. I won't press you. But please. It's the end. Come out with me. Just once. For the last chance we'll have to go to the pub and drink our own beer together."

Arthur shrugged and pointed to the stacks on his desk. "I'm the brewmaster, the captain of the brewery," he said. "I'll go down with the ship, even if that means drowning in the last of the paperwork."

"For me, then." In Gabsir's eyes, Arthur saw the pain, the longing, the concern. Not Gabsir's own, not for his own sake. But for Arthur's.

"I'm sorry, my old friend," Arthur said. "I have my reasons. Even if we're no more, I still have a job to do. Until the very end."

Gabsir stood and went to the door, but stopped before opening it. "You are diligent, Arthur," he said. "Always have been. But sometimes..."

"Sometimes what, my friend?"

"Sometimes you use that diligence to hide your fear."

Arthur sprang up from his chair, and anger sprang up too. But even as Arthur's eyes narrowed, he knew it was all just to shield the wound inside.

"What I do, I do because I must," said Arthur slowly, deliberately, biting down harsher words—and behind them, the harshest thing of all: the terrible truth Samara had told him that day. "Think of it, think of me, what you will. Have a pint for me, Gabsir. Whatever fear you think I live in, don't let it keep you."

Gabsir started to say something else, paused, then looked away. The door rattled when he slammed it.

Fatigue flooded Arthur as he collapsed back into his chair. Of all the people he couldn't tell, it hurt the worst to hold back from Gabsir.

But Arthur also leaned back and stared at the piles on his desk. The arrangements to finalize. The agreements to sign, no matter how little he actually agreed with their contents.

He read and signed, shifted stacks, placing documents into boxes for the outgoing mail and Guru Deep's inter-office courier. Piece by piece, stack by stack, Arthur cleared the avalanche on his desk. Then he saw it again. The envelope, with its elegant script and its stark block letters. The kindness and the warning.

His hands shook as he held the envelope. The light of the desk lamp gave the paper a golden sheen. "It's time," said Arthur. "Samara, the worst has happened. I'm ready to know what you needed to tell me."

* * * * *

ARTHUR SET THE TIP of the letter opener inside the flap. The envelope sighed as it parted, as if relieved to finally be opened. His hands shook. The folded paper slid free and fluttered down to Arthur's desk.

"After all these years, all these failures, what do you have to tell me now?" he asked. "Do you have a secret to reveal about Guru Deep? Something that could get us out of this after all, some new information, or another document, concealed until the time was right? Is this our secret weapon? Our miracle?"

Hope steadied his hands as he picked up the single sheet. He unfolded first one third and then the other. The passing of the long years had yellowed the paper, but Samara's elegant script was still easily read:

```
Dear Arthur,

If you are reading this, then all
seems hopeless and futile. You are
scared, angry, doubting, and alone.
I'm sure you're cursing me for this
heavy, impossible burden. But if you
are here, then it may be not that all
is lost, but that the chance is close.
I can give you only one small gleam in
the dark:

WHAT YOU WOULD SAVE, DESTROY.

Samara
```

Arthur stared at the letter, trying to find something he'd missed. "That's it?" he said. "That's all you have to tell me?"

He crumpled the letter and threw it across the room.

Stepping away from his desk, away from the letter, Arthur desperately wanted a beer. Gabsir would have a stash of GPS in his office. Arthur made his way to the door—then stopped.

On the small table next to the door, a bottle stood. Arthur thought back to that brief pause before his former second had slammed the door behind him.

There was no label, but GPS was behind the brown glass.

Arthur smiled. "Thanks for saving me the walk, old friend." He carried the bottle back to his desk and sat down again. Arthur started to lift his opener to the bottle when he saw something that made him pause.

He set down the opener and held the bottle closer to his face.

It couldn't be, he thought.

Arthur turned off the lights. In the pitch-blackness of the windowless room, he stared at the bottle again.

It was still there. In the center of the beer, as if he were staring not a couple of centimeters away, but across the long, unfathomable bend of the universe.

In the midst of the darkness, a spark. Tinged with silver and gold, a little white light shone.

Hands trembling, Arthur turned the lights back on, opened the bottle, and poured the stout into his glass.

It can't be, he thought. *I've never seen it in my lifetime...*

He thought back to the journals. That spark had been the pride of First Call. The gleam in the dark. The heart of the stout.

"We lost that." Arthur raised the glass to his lips. Before he drank, he paused. "Who brought it back?"

The perfect beer flowed not only over Arthur's tongue, but through his soul. The spark grew, shining like the sun throughout his being. Arthur saw Samara's words again, and he saw the future before him. He saw First Call, GPS, and the one simple, single chance. From where he had failed, it flowed.

Maybe that failure was just what I needed.

Then Arthur, last brewmaster of First Call, saw exactly what he needed to do.

Arthur drank the rest of the stout. Then he ran from his office.

EVERY TIME JADE LONDON thought there wasn't room for another person in the Mirror & Phoenix, somebody new squeezed to the front of the bar and ordered GPS. Pint in hand, they vanished into the mass of people filling every square inch of floor.

So it was all the more surprising when, after handing a round of pints to three women, she turned to see a clear space around a man. He stood in shadow at the far end of the bar. People not only were giving him lots of room, they seemed to be convincing themselves that he wasn't even there.

As she came over, she understood why. Desperation and futility poured off the man, who looked now shrunken, then broken. Then familiar.

Jade stopped in surprise. "Gabsir?

He shrugged. "Maybe I should have a different name now." His voice was small and empty.

"I'm sorry," she said. "That bastard Guru Deep. Shutting you down. It's wrong."

"It's done," he said. "Nothing to do but try to get on with something else. You know how it is. One door locks shut, you gotta kick open another. Something like that. Though I think I left some things unlocked on the way here." He shrugged. "Not that it matters anymore."

Gabsir nodded at the bar behind Jade, then stared back at her. "Jade London," he said, his gaze dark and his voice cold, "how about we have that whiskey now?"

ARTHUR LOOKED ALL OVER the brewery, from the bottling line and the primary brewhouse, to the break room and the toilets. It was only while staring into the empty dark cave of Gabsir's office that the brewmaster remembered his former second had left.

"So much for seeing clearly," Arthur said to himself, chuckling.

The lights shone with a halo, as if through mist. The mysterious beer buzzed through him, adding a vibrancy to the world that Arthur had long forgotten.

Closing the door to Gabsir's office, Arthur stepped back—and heard something he shouldn't have heard. Couldn't have noticed before, in a bustling brewery that day in and day out was full of the sounds of brewers and beer, equipment and liquids and endless, endless work.

But now, in the silent tomb of First Call, Arthur could hear it. The unmistakable sound. The sound he never thought he'd hear in these walls again.

As he walked down the hallway, the sound got louder. Arthur passed a door and kept walking. The sound got softer.

Pausing and listening, Arthur backtracked. As he did the sound got louder again. Again he walked past. Again the sound grew fainter.

Arthur stopped at a door. An impossible heartbeat reverberated in his ears and soul. He reached out and found the doorknob.

A small turn revealed the door was unlocked. "Oh Gabsir," he said. The spark, so bright a moment ago, died. "How long has this been going on?"

FROM WHERE FECKNISS SAT at nearly the top of the world, no stars lit the night sky. No clouds rolled over it either, only there was something strange about the darkness, something beyond the normal eeriness of nighttime. Feckniss tried to look more intently at the sky.

The dark just looks... darker, he thought. *What the hell is darker than night?*

He shook his head. *I'm exhausted. Must be fatigue. Seeing things.*

Or just dying for something, some sight, some sound, something to break the empty silence that had ruled the last few hours. No noises crossed forty-one now. Except for three people, everyone else had gone home. Feckniss sat alone in the break area at the south windows. After they had returned from the Mirror & Phoenix, Feckniss had followed Blanders to his office. He dreaded the dressing-down that was surely in store for him.

When they got there, Blanders had closed the door, sat at his desk, stared at Feckniss—and done nothing. Had said nothing. Had only glared at Feckniss with gray eyes that roared with disappointment. And Feckniss had been unable to look away, unable to speak or plead or anything. He could only see Blanders, and could hardly even remember what was behind his manager, whether it was the closed curtains or the larger floor-to-ceiling wardrobe in one corner behind the desk.

Getting my arse chewed would have been a relief compared to that, Feckniss thought.

Since leaving the pub, the only thing Blanders had said had been as Feckniss left the office. The flat voice had fallen, as if grieving a wayward child come to harm. "I have to be alone, Feckniss," Blanders had said. "Much must be decided right now." Then he said something else. Far more than the rest of the day, those words froze Feckniss to his soul.

Before Feckniss could offer another apology, or a way to make things right, or anything at all, Blanders had closed the door. Not a slam of rage or contempt. But slowly and gently, with utmost deliberation.

Feckniss would have preferred the slam. Head hung low, he had walked by Nia Fox, working at her guard post next to Guru Deep's private elevator to the forty-second floor.

Now he sat on a low, brown-black leather couch that faced the windows. Employees like him could come here for a break, or a quick face-to-face meeting with a colleague. With the long hours, Feckniss had come to love staring out the window as the sun set, the last light of day gleaming over London and making its colors dance.

There's a reason I never wanted to go anywhere else, Feckniss thought. *London was always enough for me.*

But he knew it would all soon be over.

I wonder what will happen when Blanders fires me.

He knew there was no other reason Blanders was being so deliberate. *All this time and I've hardly left his side,* Feckniss thought, *but the one time I was truly on my own, I botched it. I botched it so badly I didn't even know how big a mistake I was making, or even that I was making a mistake at all.*

The London evening got too dark. In the glass Feckniss could see more and more of the office around him. He looked away, but not quickly enough. From every corner and ventilation shaft, from every office and from under every chair, the terrible laughter rasped out at Feckniss. The insults followed, the verbal sewage sticking to him with an almost physical stench.

"You're still here," said another voice, gentle and strong. When she spoke, the insults and the laughter vanished.

Feckniss turned. Nia Fox held out a cup of tea and smiled.

Thanking her as he took the steaming mug, Feckniss said, "What do you mean?"

Nia sat in a blue-green chair at a right angle to the couch, next to Feckniss. "I mean that whatever you think went so terribly wrong today, you are still here. Blanders hasn't sacked you."

"Yet."

She sipped her tea. "If Deep Inc. has an employee problem, it's not all Right Fit Or Quit. That person is gone quickly. There's no debate. No question. HR isn't consulted, only notified. This company gets rid of problem employees faster than the body's immune system goes after disease."

"Maybe they're figuring out the best way to get rid of me," said Feckniss. "Maybe it's not even as simple as a mere sacking." He glanced downward.

Feckniss thought of the rumors he'd heard on forty-one, that the Lotus was more like a tree than a flower; the building ran as deep underground as it towered high into the sky. Below the basement parking garage, down and down and down, there were secret rooms, homes, apartments—and prisons. No one knew for sure, but even in the short time they'd been in the Lotus, now and again a situation came up, or an employee somewhere around the world was a problem. Soon came terrified whispers, about special arrangements, secret transport, and special class.

Above all, Feckniss had heard, there was a special room, the bottommost floor, deep in the earth. A dungeon. Designed not for any mere transgressor, not for any extraordinary discipline problem that went beyond the usual policies and procedures manual.

It was an unbreakable, impenetrable place, designed and built to contain one man.

The enemy.

And I, Feckniss thought, *had lunch with him this afternoon.*

"No," Nia replied. "You're not that kind of problem."

"Are they real?" said Feckniss.

"Guru Deep knows," Nia replied guardedly. "If they are, they aren't for you."

"I messed up though." Feckniss looked away for a moment. "The most dangerous man alive. The face on posters all over this building. The man we've been warned about time and time again. Faddah Rucksack, Nia. He posed as a consultant and took me to lunch. He... He's so persuasive. He can make you so at-ease. I told him things, Nia. Things I never should have said."

"Were you sharing company secrets?"

"No, but—"

"Did you hand over access codes? Travel schedules? Strategies? Sensitive financial information? Details about Operation—"

"No! Of course not. But it's far worse than all that."

Nia shook her head. "You see it like that now.""

"I told him doubts," Feckniss blurted. "Doubts about myself, my job. About working here and living in London. About not having traveled, about not..."

"About not what?"

Feckniss turned away from Nia and looked out over the empty office. Even as he looked away from Nia Fox, her face, her brilliant eyes, stayed in his mind. He felt her quiet power, her sense that if she looked at you she was reading you like the endless piles of paper she always processed so efficiently. And he felt something else: a sense, solid and unshakeable, that he could trust her.

As Feckniss turned back toward Nia, his gaze caught the darker than dark London sky. And in the city where the streetlights below outshone the stars above, Feckniss saw something.

A small point of light, a solitary star in the midst of the vast darkness.

Feckniss turned back to Nia. "When I was a kid, before I lost them, my parents used to take me to this hill, just outside London. We'd go only on clear nights. Mum would pack some snacks and sweets, and Dad would lay out a blanket on the hillside." He pointed to the window. "You know how it is in London. It's like the sky is empty."

Nia smiled.

"But there, on that hillside," Feckniss continued, "we were far enough away that we could see the stars. Sometimes I'd be there, feeling the cool night air on my face, and I'd wonder what it would be like to see the stars from other parts of the world. The mountains and deserts. The islands and vast plains. How many more stars I could see. How different the skies would look in the Northern Hemisphere versus the Southern Hemisphere."

"You've never gone?" said Nia.

Feckniss shook his head. "I like to tell myself I just love London. But the reality, the truth, is that I'm just too damn scared of the world to do anything else. My parents always told me that the most important thing I could do was work, make a life, settle down, and do what I was told. Once they were gone, that was all I had left, so I grabbed onto that advice and didn't let go. I'm good at doing that. But being good at doing something doesn't mean it's the right thing to do."

Nia sipped her tea and set down her mug. "I've seen a lot of the world. Sometimes for work. Sometimes for fun. I had to travel a lot as a kid, but for different reasons. Another story for another time, really. I love to travel though. Usually take my holiday time and go somewhere else. Sometimes anywhere else, maybe turn up at the airport and see where the next plane is heading, as long as it's somewhere different. Everywhere I go, the world is both totally different and completely the same. It's both exciting and comforting. There is so much variety to all things —but we have so much in common too."

"You must have seen some amazing things," Feckniss said. "I wish I had that kind of courage."

"What happened to you today? Yes, you met with Rucksack, and yes, he stirred up some doubts. But that's certainly not all."

"Blanders pulled me out," Feckniss said. "He must have figured out who had met me and knew I didn't realize what sort of danger I was in. And I didn't. Rucksack in person looked nothing like the posters we have up here. How could I have known?"

"You couldn't have."

"That didn't make it any better. When we got back here... Well, you know. Blanders pulled me into his office and closed the door. He never said a word, though the entire time there was a line open to Guru Deep's office. The look in his eyes told me everything. How disappointed he was. How treacherous and precarious the situation was. How I had no idea how much damage I may have done to important plans of Guru Deep's. I would have preferred screaming and yelling. This somehow feels worse."

But that wasn't all, Feckniss thought. The chill went through him again. *I can't tell you that, but Blanders told me how close we were to Guru Deep's ultimate plan. About how I was on the inside of the biggest thing to happen to the world since its creation...*

Unless my meeting with Rucksack had ruined everything.

Feckniss stood and walked to the window. He stared and stared, but the little star was gone. Instead, clouds gathered on the horizon. No. Not clouds. A darkness. He blinked—and the darkness was bigger.

Nia stared at him, a look on her face that Feckniss couldn't identify. "The streetlights will eventually go out, but the stars are always shining," she said. "The world is still out there too, Feckniss. No matter what happened earlier, Blanders isn't going to sack you. I'm sure of it." She smiled. "Even if he did fire you, all it means is you're out of a job. That's all. Nothing more. Nothing less. Maybe it wouldn't even be so bad. There's a big world out there after all. Maybe it'd be your chance to see those different skies at last."

Feckniss's reflection was serene like nothing he had seen before. Yet inside, Feckniss could feel two decisions marching toward each other, the same way the clouds on the horizon now marched toward London. The job or the world. Existence or living.

He turned and stared at Nia. A feeling, warm and powerful, hopeful and blazing, surged up through him. *Something I have to say,* Feckniss thought. *Something she has to know—*

A loud buzz filled the room.

"Ms. Fox," they heard Blanders say through the intercom. "Tell Feckniss to meet me at the elevator. Guru Deep requires a meeting."

OVER.

That's what it all is, Branwen realized as she stared through the gate to the hulking dark building beyond. *Over. I thought I had done something special. I thought I was going to be something special. But all I've done is lose my sister over something that doesn't exist anymore.*

She looked at the gate. *It's always locked,* she thought.

But Zara always checked.

Branwen pushed.

The gate swung open. The front door did too.

For the first time, Branwen stepped inside First Call Brewing on her own. Without the sounds of brewing and bustling, the brewery's silence had a presence of its own, heavy, ominous—and wrong.

Gabsir told me the work here never stopped. This place was always going and going.

Until now.

Branwen made her way down the corridors, trying to remember Gabsir's descriptions of brewery's rabbit-warren layout, with its combination of tunnels and cavernous rooms. She knew where she was going, if only the brewery would cooperate. Three times she made wrong turns, arriving at the bottling room, the yeast lab, and the break room.

This was a lot easier with Gabsir leading the way, she thought. *And where the hell am I going anyway?*

But even as she wondered, she knew.

Gabsir's not here. I know it. And that's okay. There's someone else it's time I see.

She turned around and tried again. This time she took the right combination of tunnels, and emerged outside of the door she sought.

I can't believe I'm doing this, she thought, her heart pounding. Her hand trembled when she raised it to the door and rapped her knuckles on the word BREWMASTER.

No answer.

She knocked again.

And checked the doorknob.

The brewmaster's empty office was eeriest of all. Branwen wondered where he was and what he was doing, on this horrible night when someone else's actions had ended his life's work.

When Gabsir had brought her here, he'd told her to be careful about not upsetting or moving any of the paperwork. But now Branwen didn't care about that. *Let Arthur wonder,* she thought. *Hell, I almost wish I wore perfume, so he could come back and wonder where the scent came from.*

Every piece of paper she picked up was some sort of contract, memo, or agreement, all dealing with the demise of First Call. She flipped through the large packet on the desk: the contract that sold First Call to Deep Inc. *How many times has Arthur read through this lately?* Gabsir had gone through it with her before, so she could understand that a death by a thousand cuts was nothing. Death by a thousand pages of legalese was far worse.

That first time she had eagerly trudged through the document, trying to unravel the text that was both clear and incomprehensible, trying to understand the past, and the fate of First Call, and what future there might be. Tonight she turned only to one section, marked with Arthur's frantic handwriting. *Why?* Branwen wondered. *Why did you do this to us?*

"Us," Branwen said to the silent room. "At least I feel like I belong in na Grúdairí." She shook her head. "Shame we don't exist anymore."

Then she saw something wrong. Arthur's office was packed yet meticulous—except for a piece of balled-up paper on the floor.

Branwen picked it up and, on the desk behind a stack, noticed something else: an empty beer bottle. Branwen looked at it more closely.

It's one I brewed, she thought. *The batch Gabsir and I just bottled. Arthur probably doesn't even know it, but at long last he had one of my beers.*

She looked up. *I wonder what it did to him.*

Smoothing out the paper, Branwen read the elegant script and the horrible words. She read it again. And one more time.

Then she ran out of the office.

Back into the tunnels she went, no longer caring if she made noise. She checked Gabsir's office, but only to confirm her instincts.

The shadows in the hallway were blacker than stout, and Branwen's heart raced again.

She reached into her pocket for the key Gabsir had given her to the secret door. Then she put it back.

The door was already open.

Branwen took a deep breath, trying to calm her mind, trying to figure out what in the world she would say, what she would do. There were no plans now. There was only another blind step forward, onto the next unknown part of the path.

She stepped inside the secret brewery. The man stood with his back to her. He stared at the fermentation tank and listened to the heartbeat of the next true batch of Galway Pradesh Stout, the sound of yeast fermenting wort into beer and releasing carbon dioxide into the air.

Branwen broke into a sweat and thought about running.

Then the man turned around.

GABSIR AND JADE LONDON had just set down their empty glasses when the haggard man staggered up to the bar. Gabsir's eyes widened. "What the hell are you doing here? Still letting your father down?"

"What do you know about my father, Gabsir? Certainly not his manners. It's always a feckin pleasure to see you too," said Rucksack, his breathing ragged as he set the box of money on the bar. "But this really isn't the time."

"Worst damn night of my life," said Gabsir, "then you have to turn up?" He shook his head. "You're gonna have to leave the bottle, Jade. Having a hangover the size of The Blast will be worth it just to endure this eejit."

Rucksack thumped the bar. "Not now, Gabsir! You know nothing, dammit!"

"I know enough."

"Both of you, shut up," Jade said, taking away the scotch bottle and pulling two pints of GPS.

The two men's mouths hung open. They turned from each other and looked at her.

"Whatever your problems with each other," said Jade, "either figure them out or put them aside. Tonight's bigger than your egos." She looked at Rucksack. "What happened?"

Fear and frustration filled his wide eyes. "Guru Deep's men," he said. "They got the jump on me and Zara. Too many for me to fend off. Not in this damn state, anyway."

Jade stared hard at Rucksack. "Where is she?"

Rucksack shrugged. "Probably the Lotus."

Now Gabsir thumped the bar. "And you let them—"

"Shut it"—Rucksack leaned toward him—"you cranky feckin codger."

"If you two start again," Jade cut them off, her voice hardening, "I'll boot you out of here so hard you'll have my footprint on your arses for a week."

The men were silent while Jade checked the pints. "She's right," Rucksack said at last. "Gabsir, we have to stop. Yes, our history is a problem. But that's old news and another night won't kill us."

"Maybe I should've come to you anyway, and hang that Arthur said not to." Gabsir shook his head. "I tried to tell him you might be able to help. But it's too late now."

"Not if we focus on the future instead o' the past," Rucksack replied.

"If you two are going to talk sense," Jade said, "then you can stay. For now." She finished the pints and handed them over, then added, "You know what the problem with you two is?"

Gabsir chuckled. "Rucksack can't tell a GPS from his own piss?"

Rucksack grinned. "The past few years there's been little difference."

"No," Jade said. "You're so damn similar it's no wonder you can't get along. Stubborn and living for nothing but your own sense of purpose."

Gabsir started to reply, but instead he nodded. His shoulders sagged. "You're right. As are you, Rucksack. About the stout. You would know. Your father certainly would have. We lost our way, and it's finally ruined us all."

Nonetheless, the men took healthy swigs of their pints. "Rucksack?" Jade said.

"Yes?"

"I'm sorry you've had such a hard time of it. I'm sorry that your plans keep going awry." She put her hands on the bar and leaned forward. "But you know what?"

"What?"

"I don't care."

Rucksack sat back.

"All these years after The Blast, you've been wandering the world," said Jade. "Freaking out The Management, searching out that lost damn destiny of yours, and in general being a pain in the arse."

"The Blast nearly killed me, Jade," said Rucksack. "I was away for a century."

"You took a long damn nap," Jade replied. "I know. Yes. Fine. You were recovering. But that time is done. Machinations don't work. Grand plans make for fun movies and books, but that's about the extent of their usefulness. You have your destiny in sight again, but you don't have your full strength back. You're getting used to being, well, *you*, again. Fine. But I don't care how tired it makes you. You will push yourself past any limit you ever thought you had. If you collapse from exhaustion, either you will dig down deeper and find new strength, or else I'll pull you up by your bollocks and kick you across the Thames. Your purpose right now is damn simple: Get Zara back. Stop Guru Deep. And bring back the beer."

She stared at Gabsir. "And you, you cranky self-pitying bastard—"

"Guru Deep just destroyed us!" he said. "I've lost everything I have and am."

Jade smirked. "Like that's never happened before. You're harder than oak and twistier than a corkscrewed snake," she said. "And you officially reached the end of your wallowing about ten seconds ago." She looked back and forth between the two men. "What's happening is beyond you. So it's quite simple: You two are going to work together to make things right. It's the only way." She shrugged. "Unless you prefer a world without GPS, and one where Branwen's sister is lost to Guru Deep."

"Branwen lied to me," said Rucksack.

"Because I told her she had to," replied Gabsir. "We had no other option."

Rucksack shook his head. "It makes sense. Damn you but it does. If you felt you could trust me, you wouldn't have had to do that." Rucksack took another long draw from his GPS. "But at least you understand now. I've been drinking GPS since the day my father first made it. You know Galway Pradesh Stout better than anyone save me and the First Brewer himself. It's about time you realized that she can make it just as well as he could."

"She can bring back the beer, Faddah. I believe it now. I know it."

"Don't call me Faddah."

"Sorry," said Gabsir. "We probably could have skipped a lot of nonsense, huh?"

"Yeah," replied Rucksack, "we probably could have."

The men shook hands.

"Jade," said Rucksack, "any update on the key?"

She shook her head. "We've never had such a hard time figuring out one of these damn relics. The only thing we know is what it can do, but otherwise we've found nothing."

"That can't matter anymore," said Rucksack. "If we're going to bring back GPS, I have to force Guru Deep's hand. That key may be the only way. Don't be surprised if I'm back later for it."

Jade shook her head. "You know what it will do."

"That's not what I mean," said Rucksack. "I know more than enough about mystical objects to know when to leave them the hell alone." He grinned. "But Guru Deep doesn't know that."

Jade nodded. "I'll wait up."

"There's one other issue," said Gabsir. "Branwen. Where is she?"

Rucksack sat back. "She's not at First Call? I figured she had gone there."

Gabsir's face went pale. "There? She... She must have been going there when I was on my way here." He stood up. "We have to leave. Now."

"But what about the Lotus and Zara?"

"Guru Deep isn't going to do anything to Zara," said Gabsir. "Not yet anyway. But Arthur is the only person inside First Call right now. If he finds Branwen..."

The men ran out of the pub. Jade shook her head and put the box of money next to the small black briefcase.

THE COMBATING EMOTIONS DISTORTED Arthur's face, shifting between rage, despair, and fear, revealed and naked. Combined with the hot, stuffy air in the small brewery, Branwen's own fear grew, and sweat poured off her.

Too late to run now.

"How long, Malt?" Arthur said, his voice breaking. How long has Gabsir been sneaking you in here?"

Branwen's eyes narrowed. "Malt is but one component of the beer we brew," she said. "My name is Branwen."

"I don't care."

"Yes you do," Branwen replied. "Gabsir told me you always make sure you know each grúdaire. Not just here in London, but every grúdaire in every First Call brewery all over the world."

"You are not na Grúdairí," said Arthur, pointing at her. "You're just a wannabe who's now trespassing. It was bad enough that it's all destroyed. Now you're ruining everything!"

For the first time, Branwen saw the glass in Arthur's hand. Glancing behind him, she saw the brite tank, where he must have poured off a sample of finished beer to try. Foam covered the interior in patches, and the glass was still about a quarter-full of stout. There may have been little left, but it was enough: a faint light shone. *Our beer,* Branwen thought. *The newest batch, brewed with my best-yet understanding of the secret.* Sweat ran down her face. *I don't know what's worse,* she thought, *how scared I am or how hot it feels in here.*

"You're wrong," said Branwen. "I am part of na Grúdairí. I recited the oath with Gabsir today. In this very room."

"He did no such thing!"

"But I did, Arthur," came the voice, strained yet calm. "I did."

Gabsir's face sank as he and Rucksack stepped into the room. "So much has happened tonight," he said. "I forgot to lock the damn door."

Branwen smiled. "And the gate."

Gabsir grinned back. "That was deliberate." But his smile fell away when he looked again at his friend, his leader, the brewmaster of First Call, and saw the anger simmering there. "How did you find it, Arthur?"

"I forgot that you'd left," Arthur said. "I went to your office... then I heard something. I followed the sound here. To this hidden little brewery, your little secret that you hid from everyone. Even from me."

"We all have our secrets, Arthur," said Gabsir.

"How did you discover the secret of GPS, Gabsir?" the brewmaster asked. With his every word, the pressure in the room intensified.

"I didn't," Gabsir replied. "I built this place a few years after you had taken over as brewmaster. We still weren't getting the beer back to where it should be. If anything, we weren't improving, we were failing. We'd focused too much on technique. On ingredients. On chemistry. All important, but in this case the wrong place to look. On top of all that, Guru Deep was slashing the budget left and right, to make sure we couldn't get back where we needed to be. I understood that, and here I've been trying to look in the right place. But I still didn't find the secret."

"Then who did?" Arthur yelled. He glared at Rucksack. "I know it wasn't you. Your father always said you were about as interested in brewing as barley was in stamp collecting."

Rucksack said nothing.

"And I know it wasn't you," Arthur spat at Branwen.

Maybe he's right, thought Branwen. More sweat trickled over her, and with each passing moment the room grew hotter and stuffier.

"Who are you, Branwen?" Rucksack asked. His dark eyes were gentle, but in his gaze Branwen also saw a strength, a conviction, harder than steel and more enduring than the world. "Do you know who you are? More importantly, if you know who you are, are you going to live that truth?"

Gabsir looked at Branwen. Her hands trembled and

she wanted to clench them into fists. *No, she thought. I am na Grúdairí. I am doing what is right. He's the one who is wrong. He's the one who doesn't understand.* Forcing her fingers to stay open, Branwen took a deep breath. She stepped forward. "It was me, sir."

"Don't call me sir. And don't tell me you're responsible for this."

Branwen leveled her gaze at Brewmaster Arthur. "What do you think of the beer?"

"You know as well as we do that she's done it," said Rucksack gently.

Arthur opened his mouth but said nothing.

"I was born to do this," said Branwen. "Gabsir had my homebrew and decided I deserved a chance, even though it meant defying you. He refined my knowledge and technique. Showed me all the ins and outs of GPS."

Gabsir chuckled. "That's all true. But I only showed you the path, Branwen. Once you chose to take it, the brewing was all you."

"I am a grúdaire," said Branwen. "I am part of na Grúdairí."

"You cannot. Not ever!" Arthur yelled.

"It's too late for that," said Gabsir. "Sir. Brewmaster Arthur, Branwen is a grúdaire of Galway Pradesh Stout, part of First Call, part of na Grúdairí. Same as you, me, Samara, and the First Brewer. She is one of us, in craft and in oath, in work and in spirit."

"I am na Grúdairí," said Branwen again, her voice soft but steady. "That's my true self—so that's how I must live and who I must be."

Rucksack looked at the brewmaster. "What do you think of the beer, Arthur?"

He said nothing.

Rucksack nodded. "Then I'll tell you, brewmaster," he said, his voice low but not quiet, steady yet resounding off the metal and tile of the small brewing room. "When you smelled the pint, the aroma was fresh like the woods after a summer rain. It made you think o' your parents, o' that hard journey from Kenya to England when you were a boy, and how refreshing it was when you tasted the rain here for the first time. You remembered that same taste the first time you tasted GPS, and again the first time you went to Ireland, to take up duties in New Galway. And you knew it again tonight, for the first time in decades. From the moment you saw, smelled, and tasted that beer in your hand, you knew it was more than just stout. Infinitely more."

He paused and stared at Arthur. The brewmaster's wide eyes were locked on the son of the First Brewer, and he clenched the glass tightly.

What is he so afraid of? Branwen thought. Then she remembered the piece of paper.

Rucksack continued. "Your first thought was that the roasted notes were spot-on, as was the bitterness from the hops. The beer had bite without being sharp, and was silky and soft without being weak. It was, to your surprise, a technically perfect example o' the brand o' beer known as Galway Pradesh Stout."

"Formerly known," said Arthur, bitterness cracking his voice.

"Always known," said Rucksack, shaking his head. "And we're not done. What really got you had nothing to do with the technical aspects. They were there, but there was more. It was as if you'd poured some o' the very fabric o' the universe into a glass. Your favorite day as a child, combined with your most cherished memories as a man. The harshest nights you've survived, intertwined with the exciting comfort that comes in the dark. When you drank that beer, when you relaxed your body and your mind and your soul, when you let the beer move not just across your palate but through your very being, you knew you were drinking sunlight and moonlight, the spring, summer, winter, and fall, life and death, and every truth that makes you want to live far more than you can endure just surviving. You drank the reality beyond the dream and you realized that the dream was still the reality. You drank a Galway Pradesh Stout that was exactly what GPS was meant to be. And you know it."

Branwen smiled, but Arthur looked at her as if her gaze were an arrow. Arthur trembled. He clenched the glass so tightly Branwen feared he would shatter it. He said nothing and looked away.

Gabsir stood close to both Arthur and Branwen. "I never could have brewed this beer," he said. "Branwen figured it out. She was capable before, but now she truly understands. More than that, now she is confident in what she knows. What you're finding in that beer—and I daresay, what terrifies you so—is the conviction behind the brewing that transforms this from mere beer to reality in a glass."

"No," said a broken, angry voice. "This can't be."

Branwen swayed. For a moment the room had seemed cooler. Now it was even hotter and stuffier.

"It will ruin everything!" Arthur yelled. He pointed at Branwen. "And she is not na Grúdairí." Arthur slammed down his glass. Shards sprinkled to the floor.

"Arthur," said Gabsir. "You know this is right. You know she's done it. What is your problem? She can bring back the beer, dammit!"

"No one can bring back the beer!" Arthur shouted.

"What you would save," Branwen recited, "destroy."

Arthur spun to look at her. "How did you—?"

"Before I came here, I went into your office to find you," said Branwen. "I saw the letter from Brewmaster Samara."

"You don't understand," said Arthur, taking a step toward her.

"Yes I do," replied Branwen, taking a step back. "GPS has had so much working against it. Including you and Samara."

Gabsir and Rucksack gasped. Gabsir looked hard at Arthur. "Is this true?"

Arthur stood in front of his second and looked down on him. "You need to remember your loyalties. You took an oath."

"That I did," replied Gabsir, returning the brewmaster's stare. "Just like Branwen did a few hours ago. In the very spot where you're standing, in fact. Funny ole world." He smiled and recited, "In all things there is universe and nothing, life and death, decision and destiny, the reality and the dream. I choose to live, decide, make, do, and love. I pledge my life to na Grúdairí and to the beer. For as long as I choose and am able I will make the best beer that I can make, the beer that is life and reality itself."

"Then you know your loyalties," Arthur said.

"Were you and Samara working with Guru Deep to destroy First Call?"

"No!" Arthur shouted. "You don't understand."

"Did you help Guru Deep ambush me and Zara?" Rucksack asked.

Branwen turned and stared at him. "What?"

"After we... went our separate ways at the pub," said Rucksack. "Zara and I were going back to the flat. Next thing I knew, Guru Deep's men attacked us. When I came to, your sister was gone. Guru Deep has her trapped in the Lotus. Gabsir and I came to get you, Branwen, so we could figure out a way to help her."

"I had nothing to do with that," said Arthur. "With any of it."

"Are you remembering your oath?" said Gabsir. "I've never forgotten it, brewmaster." Gabsir smiled. Now he and Arthur stood almost nose to nose. "In fact, Arthur, I'd say I know it better than you do."

"Your loyalty is to me!"

"And where does it say that, exactly?"

Arthur took a step back. "What are you talking about?"

"I pledge my life to na Grúdairí and to the beer," Gabsir said. "There's no mention of the brewmaster. There's no mention of you."

"It's... implied. It's there."

"No." The men looked at Rucksack, who continued. "My mother and father never wanted submission or obedience, and you know that as well as I do. They wanted women and men who used their hearts, souls, instincts, and minds. They wanted people who decided. Who *did*, out o' hope, trust, knowledge, and conviction. Not because they were bound by some damn paragraph."

Gabsir nodded. "That oath wasn't a chain binding us to the brewmaster. It was a commitment we made to brew the best beer that we could possibly make. You and I made that oath—but you know as well as I do that it's been many a long year since we lived up to those expectations. All I have done, I have done for the beer, for what it must do in the world again."

Rucksack nodded at Branwen. "She's not only taken the oath. She's done something far more important."

"What's that?" Arthur spat.

"She's lived it." Rucksack stood in front of Arthur. "If you aren't helping Guru Deep, then you want to beat him. If you want GPS to pour all over the world again, then whatever this fear, this poison, is inside you, it's got to be dealt with and let go, Arthur. We'll help you. You are a good man. Always were, always have been. But your fear blinds you. Your fear is destroying what you love. If you want to bring back GPS, then you have to accept Branwen. She's the one, Arthur. She's the one."

Arthur stepped back. He looked around the faces before him. "The beer is no more," he said. "And it must remain no more."

"Arthur," Gabsir said, "talk sense. What in the world do you mean?"

Arthur's eyes were as dark as GPS. "And I am *not* a good man."

Behind him, steam began shooting out of pipes. A shrill rushing sound filled the air.

A piercing beep began to sound.

GABSIR RAN TO THE pipes and looked at a gauge. "Oh Arthur," he said, "What have you done?"

"That's why it was so hot and stuffy in here!" Branwen shouted over the alarm. Then she ran to the brite tank. "The new batch! We have to do something! It's our only chance!"

"I told you," Arthur said. "The beer must be no more." Before anyone could speak or move, the last brewmaster of First Call ran from the room.

"He overrode the safety valves," said Gabsir. "Locked everything down and let the pressure skyrocket. This room is about to be nothing but flying shredded steel. Get out of here, now!"

Branwen's eyes widened. "But the beer!" she said.

"There's nothing we can do, Branwen. Just go." But Gabsir ran to the tank and grabbed a wheel. "With luck, we can pour some beer down into the packaging hold, away from this room, so we don't lose everything." He pulled, but the wheel didn't budge. "Damn valves are always stuck!"

Branwen and Rucksack ran to help Gabsir. He shook his head. "Dammit, get Branwen out of here!"

"I'm taking an interest in the family business," said Rucksack. "What do we need to do?"

"We can always make more beer," replied Gabsir. "We can't make another her."

"I'm not leaving," said Branwen, putting all her strength against the wheel.

"I'm old, Branwen," said Gabsir. "I've lived longer than you can imagine. I've brewed more beer than I could ever drink." He smiled. "No matter what else has happened, Branwen, grúdaire of na Grúdairí, I knew you. Come what may, I'll always have peace from that. I'll fix this or die trying. But let me be the only one."

"Touching speech," Branwen replied. "If I wasn't sweating all over, I'd probably be crying. Now put your damn backs into it, both of you."

Rucksack and Gabsir stared at each other, eyes wide, then they grabbed onto the wheel as well. Around them the room grew hotter and hotter. Sweat poured. Steam gushed from pipes. The screams of splitting metal tore at their ears.

The three of them pushed at the wheel. Above the tanks, a pipe split open and steam poured around them. They ignored the pain and the searing heat, straining to turn the stuck wheel.

"It's going to blow!" Gabsir yelled. "We're out of time!"

"A little more!" Rucksack clenched the wheel tighter, grimacing at the pain from his withered left hand.

"Almost got it!" Branwen shouted.

The rush of the loud steam drowned out the piercing alarm. The wheel didn't budge.

They pushed, and pushed some more—and then Gabsir let go. "We did it," he said. "The beer is flowing down below. Now come on."

Branwen and Rucksack ran into the hallway. The hissing and screaming sounds stopped, and with a final groan gave way to the pressure.

Gabsir stopped at the doorway, still inside the brewery. "Too late."

"What are you doing?" said Branwen.

"I lied," Gabsir replied. "I'm proud of you both. Now bring back the beer."

He slammed the heavy metal door shut and clicked the lock home.

"Gabsir!" Branwen shouted as Rucksack pulled her down the hall. "You can't, you have to—"

The explosion took away the rest.

* * * * *

FECKNISS WISHED SHE WOULD shut up so he could think. Nothing had made sense since... since... He looked away from the woman. Looked away from the window, and stared at the dark red walls and rich woodwork of Guru Deep's office, the entirety of the forty-second floor of the Lotus. He'd tried hard not to look, but at last he had seen. And he still couldn't believe what he had seen. He closed his eyes...

"Is this the part where I'm supposed to be scared?" said Zara.

He opened his eyes again. The bound, spiky-haired sister had regained consciousness not long after security had brought her to the forty-second floor and set her on one of the black couches near Guru Deep's private elevator. Feckniss wished they could have knocked her out again before they left. Or at least gagged her. *Even the voice is better than this,* he thought. *At least it stops talking sometimes.*

Zara nodded. "Do you usually intimidate people with your just-resting-my-eyes routine? Or are you trying out something new tonight?" She smiled. "Do I need to tip you? Because I could get to my pocket if you would just untie me."

Feckniss said nothing. He couldn't find the words for anything now.

Blanders had made him wait by Nia Fox's desk while he went up first. Feckniss stood, the minutes ticking by. Nia said nothing, though sometimes Feckniss thought she wanted to touch his hand. He certainly wanted her to.

She was about to speak when her intercom buzzed.

"Ms. Fox," said the voice of Guru Deep, "send up Feckniss." He paused. "And then go home. It's been a long day, and we gentlemen have a long night ahead of us." The intercom went dead.

The dismissal startled Nia, but still she said nothing, betraying herself only by the widening of her eyes.

But Feckniss had gone up, to the room where they waited, where he had seen—

"Oh," said Zara, staring at something behind him. "Who else is coming up? Are we having a party now?"

"What?" Feckniss whipped around and stood. "There shouldn't be anybody else."

The elevator doors slid open with a sound like an oiled snake slithering. Gray and white and smelling like hot grain, dust like a small cloud poured out.

"Who's there?" said Feckniss, coughing into a trembling hand as he stepped toward the open doors.

But there was only the dust. Feckniss stayed back enough so it wouldn't get on his clothes.

A heavy step pushed through the cloud, and a dusty black boot stepped onto the top floor of the Lotus.

The rest of the man emerged, and he looked like he'd been a castaway. Or trapped underground. Or pulled from the rubble of a burning building. Perhaps all three. His torn clothes were so choked with gray dust, Feckniss couldn't tell what color they'd been originally. Blood crusted over long scratches on his face. He looked like he could barely stand, but in his right hand he kept a death grip on a small briefcase.

"I'm going to tell you something," said the man. A fire in his dark face and his brown-black eyes made the room stuffy and hot. "Then you'll get Blanders and Guru Deep. I have some one-sided negotiating to do."

"I'm guessing you don't have an appointment," Feckniss replied, trying not to feel intimidated.

The man smiled. "Guru Deep will always make time for Faddah Rucksack."

Rucksack stared deep into the office, toward Guru Deep's desk. "Why that sly thieving bugger," said Rucksack. "So that's where he's had my old swords all this time."

Zara cleared her throat. "I'm fine," she said. "Thanks for asking."

"Already knew," said Rucksack, "but I'm sorry my courtesy is lacking." Rucksack's voice was steady, but Feckniss noticed a slight sway in his posture.

She nodded. "You look like crap. Is that what those guys did to you?"

Rucksack shook his head, but pain rippled through his face.

Feckniss took a step back. "You've had quite the bad night."

"Explosively so." Rucksack stepped forward. "What do you have to tell me?"

Rucksack's gaze softened, became kinder. "You're better than this. You are stronger than your fear."

"It doesn't matter."

Rucksack shook his head. "Who you are is far more than you've let yourself be so far. Leave here. Pick a direction and go. You'll be all right. Hell, you'll be better than ever. But get out o' here, out o' this job, this life. Get away from Guru Deep. You think you're on top, but you're barely surviving. Get out o' here, and you'll live. You'll thrive."

"You don't know what I've seen."

"I know you're the only one who can confront it." Rucksack smiled. "You have far more to look forward to than an office that breaks every day. Besides, I can't keep sabotaging your furniture forever. I have other things to do. Though depending on how you look at it, I'm either hopeless with a screwdriver or very skilled indeed."

"Why me?"

"You don't become who you need to be without getting shaken out o' who you are." Rucksack shrugged. "I just wish I'd done a better job. All this could've been avoided. Story o' my life today."

"I've learned the truth," said Feckniss. "Like them. Like Blanders and Guru Deep."

"They've forgotten more than you'll ever learn," said Rucksack. "They know how much you despair. They want to see how you tear yourself apart so they know how best to control you."

"Then what are you doing?"

"I'm getting Zara out o' here. And you too. I'm offering you a way out. Believe you me, Feckniss, I see what you fear. I understand. But you can beat it, Feckniss. It doesn't have to rule you."

He sees it too. The words reverberated inside Feckniss, bouncing off the parts of him that laughed and the parts that screamed. But Rucksack didn't run, though Feckniss had when he'd seen it earlier. *A way out... a different life... I could be happy,* Feckniss thought. *I could be brave. I could go so many places...*

"You won't be leaving with the girl," said Feckniss.

Rucksack sneered. "It's not the first time I've been blown up. If that hasn't stopped me, what teardropon-a-hot-griddle chance do you think you have?"

Behind Feckniss, a door closed.

Rucksack looked up and snarled. "You."

"Me," said Blanders. "Your conversation has been most fascinating. I hate to interrupt, but there is much to tend to."

"Starting with you telling your damn boss it's over," Rucksack replied. "Guru Deep is reversing his decision to close First Call. GPS will come back."

"Even for you, Rucksack, you look terrible," said Blanders. "A bit over the top though. Not your usual dusty appearance by any means. Don't you usually knock off some of the dirt first?"

"There was an accident at First Call. An explosion," said Rucksack. "The brewmaster is dead. So is his second. So..." He locked his gaze with Zara. "So is your sister."

"No!" Zara yelled. "But we... I didn't... No!"

Blanders rolled his eyes. "This is touching. Why should Guru Deep care?"

"This is why." Rucksack opened the briefcase. Bright light flooded the forty-second floor. Rucksack sighed, hesitated, then decided. He pulled out the key. "Guru Deep didn't think I'd do it, I know," said Rucksack. "Threaten the line. Do his dirty work for him. But there's more to this key than even Guru Deep knows. He thinks it's only a way to destroy? He forgets me. With this, I'll stop him."

Blanders smiled. "An impressive weapon," he said simply. "What do you think of this one?" With a swift, practiced move, Blanders reached into his suit jacket, drew a pistol, and shot Zara in the thigh. Her screams bounced off the wall. Feckniss covered his ears.

"I'm told there's nothing worse than being shot in the gut," said Blanders, pointing the pistol at Zara's stomach. "Shall we ask Sara her opinion on the matter?"

The light in Rucksack's hand shook, yet did nothing else but glow. "Dammit," said Rucksack. "Do something!" He stared at the key.

"What's the matter?" Blanders asked. "What's said about you? You have the very fire of life itself in you? Yet you can't find a way to use it with the most powerful relic in the world?"

Rucksack stared at Blanders, a helpless fury on his face. Then Rucksack lowered the key. "Spare her, Blanders. Don't kill her."

"Or what? I think you already know, but it's better if you say it yourself. I so hate miscommunication."

"Or..." The fire went dark in Rucksack's eyes. "Or you can have me. And the key. As long as she's treated for her wound and allowed to leave, safe and free."

Rucksack stood straight, his shoulders squared as he stared deep into Blanders's eyes. "So go get him," said Rucksack. "It's like his feckin birthday today. He gives up one janitor, he gets me, and he gets his damn toy back."

"On behalf of Guru Deep," said Blanders, "I accept your generous offer. And as a gesture of goodwill..." He put the pistol back in its holster. Then held out his hand.

"Rucksack!" Zara yelled. "Don't!"

"I failed, Zara," said Rucksack. "This is all that's left. I'm sorry."

He handed Blanders the key. Zara clutched her thigh and screamed again.

"Goodness, Sara, you do go on and on," said Blanders. "Have a sedative." He stepped forward and swung his hand. Zara collapsed, unconscious.

Rucksack took a step forward. "You—"

"Save it," said Blanders, waving his hand toward Rucksack. "She'll be better treated. But we can't have her screaming her head off when we still have business on the agenda."

"You've got me," said Rucksack. "Now go get him."

Blanders didn't move.

"Why are you standing there?" said Rucksack. "Let's get this over with."

Blanders smiled. Feckniss had never seen such a smile from his boss, as bright and brilliant as the sun.

"Oh Rucksack," said Blanders. "No one needs to summon Guru Deep."

The grays of Blanders's suit rippled, as did his face and hands. From the center of his chest, a white light grew, wrapping itself around the man. For a moment, Feckniss couldn't see his manager. Then the light faded.

Standing before them in his trademark orange suit with white shirt and orange tie, Guru Deep smiled. The office lights reflected off his bald brown head like a halo. "You see," he said, "I've been here all along."

"YOU..." said Rucksack. "How did you—?"

"I must thank you," said Guru Deep. "I'd shake your hand, but as everyone knows, Guru Deep doesn't shake hands. The famous Faddah Rucksack—the hero of old, the hero fallen, the hero restored—not even you could tell. You might not believe it, but that means a lot to me."

He shrugged. "But you're not important right now, Rucksack. You look so tired. I'd offer you a seat, but I already have to get Sara's blood cleaned off the furniture now, and it still has that new-leather smell."

Guru Deep raised the key. "And now," he said, "the time has come. I, Guru Deep, will show you the true power of this incredible relic."

He held it high in his left hand. Everyone in the room winced at the bright white light.

Then, with his right hand, Guru Deep reached up. There was a small click.

The light turned off.

Rucksack took a step back. "What?"

Guru Deep's laugh boomed across the office. "Isn't it great?" he said. "Next revolution in flashlights. At least, if we can figure out how to make the damn light blue. We're calling it the Luminescence Infinity Transmitter. LIT for short." He shook his head. "Name stinks. Marketing has to keep working on it. Feckniss, make a note."

"But the relic," said Rucksack, "the power..."

Guru Deep laughed again. "That's always the problem with you. You get so caught up in legend and grandiosity. I mean, okay, okay, fair enough. You are legend and grandiosity personified, but boy does it blind you sometimes. If this were your performance review, I'd note that as your Primary Improvement Area." His eyes narrowed. "That and not messing up my operations anymore. You're bad for business."

"You planted this light," said Rucksack. "Got word to me that it was something more."

"Right in one. My Communications guys and gals come up with, shall we say, a compelling story. The techs came up with this nifty battery." Guru Deep admired the lenses that comprised the entire surface of the light. "I just had to convince you I wanted it to destroy the world, all existence, 'tat sort o' ting,' as you would say in that ridiculous accent of yours. I knew destroying First Call would finally bring you here to London and draw you away from my sensitive operations."

"You mean your murder and mutilation pits."

"It's all a dream, Faddah. It doesn't matter." Guru Deep smiled. "If I could make you think I wanted to destroy the dream and bring about reality, well, it would certainly keep you busy. A man your age shouldn't be idle."

Rucksack's face was grim. "I'm touched for your concern."

Guru Deep sneered and threw the light to Rucksack, who struggled to catch it in his left hand. "Keep it," said Guru Deep. "Let it be a light when things get dark for you. Which, hey, coincidentally, they're about to. Now, I need a few words with my protégé, then we can finish up here." He turned to Feckniss.

"Protégé?" Feckniss replied.

"You must feel so confused right now, son."

Feckniss could only stammer. "Son? You're not? You're..."

"Feckniss, I am your father," replied Guru Deep with a wave of his hand. "No. Kidding. But I handpicked you to work with me, and at every step I have felt more like your father, like a guide and a teacher, than just your manager. I couldn't bring down GPS all by myself, you see. Powerful though I am"—

he winked at Rucksack—"*boss* though I am, every time I tried to order GPS discontinued and First Call shuttered, I faced too much opposition. I finally realized that if I couldn't do it by myself, then I would do it as someone else. So Guru Deep, with his bright orange suits and his sunshine smile, became the mild-mannered, even-voiced, gray-suited, flat-line-inducing Blanders."

"Why did you need me?" Feckniss asked.

"Rucksack is right," said Guru Deep, putting his arm around Feckniss's shoulders. "You are more than you realize, and luckily I do realize it. We brought down GPS and First Call *together*, Feckniss. You and me. Against all odds and all opposition. You found what I needed to make the case. We did together what I could not do alone. I know your potential. Ignore Rucksack. If he had his way, everyone would be flitting about on little global gallivantings, reeking of stale beer while losing their lunch in bouncing buses that move slower than the chickens they carry, and acting like the world is all just one big love-and-kindness, if only everyone would try." Guru Deep shook his head. "Oh, Rucksack," he said, "you at least were always good for a laugh. I will miss that."

Guru Deep put an arm around Feckniss's shoulders. "My dear boy," he continued, "you are far more than all that nonsense. You are bright. You have potential. I knew that if I guided you, you could help me do exactly what I needed to do." He beamed at Feckniss. "And you did! Now look! I have brought you up here, with me, on top of the world. I have mentored you personally. Feckniss, I trust you so inherently, so deeply, that *you now even know my deepest secret.*"

The words sank in.

"I have given," said Guru Deep. "I have trusted. I, one of the world's strongest, most powerful men, have made myself vulnerable to you, to prove how much I trust you. To show how far I think you can go. All the way, Feckniss. All The Way. So tell me, other than blather, what has Rucksack given you?"

For a moment Feckniss saw his reflection in the window. The room filled with insults and terrible laughter.

"Don't listen to him, Feckniss," shouted Rucksack. "It's lies. All lies. You're more than this. You're better than him. What I've offered you is the only thing he can't, but it's the only thing worth a damn, worth far more than the useless nonsense he's going on about. I offer you yourself. Your own path. Master o' your own self and soul. Freedom. It's all I have to offer, but it's the only thing that matters."

"You give it?" Feckniss asked.

"No," Rucksack replied. "No one can give freedom. It's already yours. You just have to accept it and live it."

"You see?" said Guru Deep. "He says so much to conceal that what he offers is nothing. You already know the right thing to do, Feckniss. First Call and GPS are only the beginning. Stay with me, and you will know all. You can be part of what happens next. But only if you stay with me."

Guru Deep turned. "Feckniss," he said, "please help Rucksack to his new room."

Feckniss stared at the two men: one resplendent, one staggering. Then he saw his reflection again, and recoiled.

"It's okay, Feckniss," said Guru Deep. "It's just more of Rucksack's tricks. Like breaking your office. Once he's gone, you won't see it again."

"That's a lie," said Rucksack. "You don't have to do this, Feckniss. There's still a chance. You can still be you and you can still be free. Just—"

The yell reverberated off every surface of the forty-second floor. Feckniss leaped forward, his right arm swinging out. He barely felt the impact of his fist on Rucksack's face.

Faddah Rucksack, barely standing already, fell to the floor.

"Thank you my dear boy," said Guru Deep. "He does go on and on and on, doesn't he?" He kneeled down next to Rucksack. "You're going to pass out," he said, leaning in close. "Before you do, I want you to know a few things. You will never wander the world again. I'm going to keep you here, a rare wild animal in my own private zoo, until I decide to put you down like the out-of-control animal you are. Oh, and this: that precious destiny of yours, that you've been trying to find for so long? You've got it now, but I'm afraid you forgot to be careful about what you wish for. You were always going to face me. And you were always going to lose."

Rucksack shook his head. He tried to stand, but fell down again.

"Oh no," said Guru Deep. "It's true. I never had anything to fear from you. Or from anyone. My determination is a sword, a spear that presses onward no matter how bloody things get. Someone wiser than you told me long ago, you see. Maybe it was someone you knew." Guru Deep smiled. "I'll even tell you what she told me: 'Never cease your course, then only a man born of man and a woman born of man shall harm Guru Deep.' Not bad, huh? Rather poetic really."

Guru Deep stood. "Not that any of it applies to you." A kick to the head, and Rucksack smacked the floor, unconscious.

"I'll take him to the bottommost subfloor," said Feckniss, surprised at the steadiness and confidence in his voice. "Her too," he added. "They can live in their futility as long as it pleases you."

"Initiative," said Guru Deep. "The Most Valuable Resource That's Always In The Shortest Supply. I've been preparing for this moment for a long time. After you're done with them, come back here. We have much to do, Feckniss. There'll be no rest, no time to reflect or pause—there will be not a moment to spare."

"What are we going to do, sir?"

Together, they stepped to the window and stared out over the lights of London. "We're going to destroy the enemy," said Guru Deep. "Once Faddah Rucksack is gone, we will change the world. Reality is sleeping, my dear boy. It's time to wake it from its dreams."

Feckniss tried to listen to the words, tried to look at the world beyond the window. In the distance, a darkness had grown. There would be rain in the morning. But Feckniss paid it no mind; all he could see in the dark glass was his reflection. He started to turn away—but stopped.

It's time to accept who I am, he thought. Feckniss stared into the reflection.

Red scars and bleeding pustules covered the twisted face. Patches of hair had come out of his skull, as if torn out by his own hands. The yellow eyes were like slits as they stared back at him.

But the worst was the mouth. Misshapen and lopsided, it opened into a sneer, revealing a black tongue and teeth the color of urine. Though Feckniss stood still, the reflection shook its head. "Oh Feckwit," it said. "What times we're going to have now!"

Then it threw back its lumpy head, and horrible laughter filled Feckniss's world.

III

IN THE DARKNESS, light came. Not gradually like the trickle of dawn that becomes a flood of sunlight, but with flickers, as if the light were uncertain of its strength, or anxious that it was in the wrong place where it had no right to shine. Eventually overheads around the ceiling, plus accent lighting in wall sconces, placed at tastefully selected intervals, all decided that they would stay on. At least for today, even if tomorrow was uncertain.

The rectangular room was long and narrow, with low white ceilings, untextured white walls, and a floor gray as the fog over a London morning. The custom furnishings in the middle of the room—the black coffee table between the single white couch and two white overstuffed chairs, the black radio, the black dining table with two black chairs—had been designed and selected with great care, in order to make the room appear comfortable. Long, gauzy white drapes hung at intervals on the left long wall.

Black floor-to-ceiling bookshelves lined the long wall to the right, broken only by a closed door in the middle, a door uncluttered by unnecessary features such as a doorknob.

From one short wall, lights flickered on through a narrow doorway. Along the other short wall, beginning inside three small side-by-side alcoves, three long narrow rectangles bumped out into the room, disrupting the carefully designed symmetry and harmony of the space.

Covered in thin blankets, two people lay on two of the concrete surfaces, which approximated beds in size and shape, but their hardness made it clear that comfort was not a consideration and rest was not a requirement. The people's breathing was ragged but even, the breathing of reflex that even the greatest exhaustion and fatigue could not yet stop.

Then, a gasp.

One figure started to slowly sit up—then slid off the slick surface and landed with a thud on the floor.

The room spun, and the person wheezed in and out, regaining breath and staring at the ceiling until the world stopped spinning. Everything hurt. Everything was wrong. But lying down wasn't going to do any good.

Faddah Rucksack stood and checked his body. His legs wobbled but held. "I have all my limbs and functions," he said. "That's a good start." He glanced around the room. "But where the hell am I?"

He hobbled to the door. Locked. Thick. Beyond the doorway on the opposite short wall, Rucksack discovered a bare yet functional bathroom.

Next he trudged to the windows and grabbed the drapes.

"Ah!" He pulled back his hand. The fingers and palm bled from several spots. Rucksack looked more closely at the drapes.

The rough fabric had been woven around small pieces of broken glass.

With his gloved left hand, he gently moved back the drapes.

The curtains covered a blank wall.

Rucksack stepped back and moved in a slow circle, staring, evaluating, calculating.

"We're trapped in a box," said a voice, followed by another thud—and a barely muffled scream.

Rucksack turned.

Zara had slid off another bunk. Already she was rising off the floor, but he could see the pain in her eyes. She hobbled toward him with the help of a pair of white crutches that had been left by her bed.

"How are you?" asked Rucksack.

"Guru Deep did at least have someone tend to my leg," said Zara, her voice bitter as she stopped near him. "It's patched and cleaned. For now he must want us alive. And I'm clearly on some sort of painkiller." Zara touched her right cheek, which was covered in a purple-black bruise. "It's better than the first one he gave me."

"He'll get it back in kind," said Rucksack, his voice low and angry.

Zara nodded.

He softened his voice. "How... else are you doing?"

Zara shrugged, but her body tensed. "We need to figure out where we are and how to get out of here." She looked at Rucksack's torn clothes and scratches. "How are you?"

"Every muscle and joint aches. I haven't hurt this much in a long time."

"You said there was an explosion." Zara's voice quavered. "You said my sister—"

"I said what I had to at the time," said Rucksack, "though I'm sorry to have hurt you."

"Are you saying Branwen's alive?"

Rucksack breathed in sharply. "I'm not sure. I had to throw Guru Deep off caring about her. I looked and looked for her. But Zara, I don't know if she made it and kept running. I don't know if she was trapped in the explosion and I couldn't find her. But I will promise you that when we get out o' here, we'll find out the truth."

Zara tried to smile. A tear streaked down her puffy cheek. "All the more reason to find a way out."

"Guru Deep might check, might send some people to verify. He'll find nothing but wreckage."

"What happened?"

Her face went from sad to grim as he told her.

"The entire brewery was destroyed?"

"Just about. The building had become so dilapidated and neglected, the explosion set off a series o' collapses. Ceilings, walls, floors, the whole damn thing came down."

"The brewmaster destroyed his own brewery?" Zara shook her head. "Because he was scared of my sister doing what he and na Grúdairí were supposed to do?"

"That's not the whole story," said another voice.

Zara and Rucksack turned. Arthur Celbridge, brewmaster of First Call, sat up on the third bunk. He started to say something else, but the words were lost. With a roar like a tiger, Rucksack pulled him off the bunk and threw him on the floor.

"WHAT THE HELL ARE you doing here?" Rucksack yelled as Arthur's head smacked on the tile floor.

So much to tell you, Arthur thought. *So much you don't know... So much I should've told you... told Gabsir.* A new pain ripped through him. *Gabsir—*

Rucksack kneeled over Arthur and punched him. Arthur's mind went white, then black, then flashed back to where he was.

"What were you thinking?" Rucksack yelled, punching Arthur again. "How could you? How could you?"

Red pain lit up Arthur's vision. "How could you?" he shouted back, knocking a fist aside and landing his own solid blow into Rucksack's stomach.

They rolled away from each other, panting and crouching on the floor. "You could've killed us all," said Rucksack.

"We're already dead," Arthur replied. "We just haven't stopped breathing yet."

The men circled each other. Then each winced and stepped back, rubbing sore kneecaps. Zara swung her crutch around again, and this time smacked each man on the ear. "Stop doing Guru Deep's dirty work for him," she said.

"Zara," said Rucksack, "he—"

"You think I don't know?"

Rucksack stopped talking. Zara stared Arthur in the eye. "Did you mean to blow up First Call? Kill Gabsir? Kill my sister?"

"No," said Arthur. "I wanted to disable Gabsir's secret brewery. I... miscalculated."

"I suppose I'll have to take your word for that, at least until we're out of here and I learn the truth." Zara locked Arthur's gaze. "But if Branwen is dead because of you, I will kill you with my bare hands."

Arthur took a step back.

Rucksack stared at the brewmaster. "Gabsir sacrificed himself to try to save us."

Possibly, Arthur thought, trying to wall off the pain that surged every time he heard his friend's name. *That old man's so tough he could have been standing next to where The Blast happened and tell stories about it in the pub later.* But he said, "I won't let that be in vain." He met Zara's gaze. "I wouldn't accept her. Gabsir tried to tell me, over and over. I made a mistake about your sister. But I don't think I'm the only one."

"Don't compare your actions to mine," said Zara.

"Oh?" said Arthur. "You wholeheartedly accepted that Gabsir took her into First Call, trained her up, made her a grúdaire—without you? You bought a round and praised her moving up in the world? You supported her dream and the truth of who she was? Who she could be?" Now Arthur locked eyes with Zara and stepped up to her. "You didn't, oh I don't know, rail at her and feel betrayed, and cast her away for having the audacity to be better than you?"

Zara said nothing.

"I can see it in your eyes," said Arthur. "The regret. The remorse. When you see them in the mirror every day, it's easy to recognize them in someone else."

"What else do you regret, Arthur?" asked Rucksack. "Being in Guru Deep's pocket too confining?" He stretched out his arms and gestured around the room. "How's this for a grand reward?"

"You don't know a damn thing, Rucksack," replied Arthur. "Never did and never let it stop you. Your father said that was always the problem with you."

"Just because you read a bunch o' old journals doesn't give you the right to talk about my father as if you were beer buddies."

"I know how worried about you he was, before The Blast," said Arthur. "Before The Blast, I know how he feared the mirror eclipse and how you might react."

Rucksack said nothing.

"Who knows what might be different," said Arthur with a shrug.

"Never found a trace o' Mum, but I found his body," said Rucksack at last, clenching and unclenching his left hand. "I was near dead myself, but I carried him. Carried him until I found a place to lay him down for good."

"Hate me if you want," said Arthur. "Though in case you haven't noticed, we're stuck with each other, and it's not as if we have much in the way of personal space. So if you want to detest me or cast me off or anything like that, do you at least first want to know what you don't know?"

"YOU MAY HAVE SOMETHING there," said Rucksack, his gaze fierce yet backing down.

"I'm listening," replied Zara, her voice hard but cracking. "A truce, then."

They all nodded. Rucksack glanced around the room. "We're under the Lotus, aren't we?"

Arthur shrugged. "How would I know?"

"It's what he said he was going to do, before he gave me this." Rucksack pointed at a large bruise covering the left side of his face.

"He could easily be lying," Arthur said. "For all we know, we're in the northernmost frozen hell of Siberia, or on some island off in the Antarctic Ocean.

Rucksack shook his head. "Not enough time. If you hurt half as much as I do, it's the next damn morning after the worst non-booze bender o' our lives. No, Arthur, we're under London. Under the Lotus, as down deep as Guru Deep ever had this damn place built."

"How can you be so sure?" Zara asked.

"GPS and First Call were only a small part o' his ultimate plan," said Rucksack. "Whatever that end game is, it's beginning now. Guru Deep believes he's unstoppable, and that's going to make him all the more unbearable. We're in the Lotus, alive, because he wants us close."

Arthur nodded. "So he can gloat."

"So he can torment us," said Zara, "while keeping us alive in case he needs something from us."

Rucksack swept his arm left to right. "We're not rotting in some rat hole with nothing but brackish water to drink and an overrun culvert to crap in. But we're in no paradise either. Nothing here is what it seems." He held up his hand, and the others gasped. "Don't try to open the curtains," said Rucksack.

Together they explored. At the bar at the end of the room, water poured from one tap, Deep's Special

Lager from the other. Guru Deep's own bestselling books, from his self-help tomes to his *Through the Third Eye* guidebooks, lined the bookshelves.

"I bet the radio turns on whenever there's something he wants us to hear," said Arthur. "And everything else will just happen. No choices."

"No freedom," said Rucksack.

"No joy," said Zara. "And everything that should seem simple and ordinary, will be a threat."

Rucksack nodded. "Just like him."

"He wants us not only to know he's going to succeed," said Arthur. "Guru Deep wants us to know we failed."

"Yes," said Zara. "And were helpless to do anything about it."

A whirring sound made them look at the dining table. In the middle of the smooth black square top, segments retracted. A moment later, the opening was filled with a tray holding a platter of gray squares and a platter of beige squares, a pitcher of water, and a pitcher of a yellow liquid.

"Do we trust this?" Arthur asked. He pointed to the yellow liquid. "Deep's Special Lager. I can smell the battery acid and mustiness from here."

"O' course we don't trust it," said Rucksack. "It could be drugged. It could be poisoned. Or it could even be poisoned in a way that will kill us unless we are here for the next meal, consuming poison and antidote in alternating amounts. I'm going to go by a rule o' the road, though."

"What's that?"

"Always eat, drink, and use the toilet when you have the chance. You don't know when you'll get another. The food might kill us. But starvation and dehydration definitely will."

Arthur and Zara sighed. They all went to chairs and sat down.

And immediately jumped back up, stepping away from the table, rubbing their backs and legs.

"What the hell?" said Zara. "I'm bleeding."

Rucksack leaned down. "Spikes," he said, standing back. "The chairs are covered in small spikes, just like the curtains are woven with broken glass."

Arthur walked around the room and came back. "The couch is covered in spikes too," he said. "The faucet is covered in razors. Even the toilet seat is covered in broken glass. Why not just torture us?"

"He is," said Zara. "Everything here is a trap. Everything here is made in some way to hurt us. To break us down—torment us through every moment."

"He expects to torture us slowly?" said Rucksack.

"No," said Zara. "He expects us to die. Only by degrees. Guru Deep wants to watch us break, inch by inch and breath by breath, until the final moment when he decides he's bored or has no use for us."

"Exactly," said Arthur. "He wants to be here when the lights go out in our eyes. Destroying the world is not enough. He has to break those who oppose him."

"You know him well," said Rucksack.

Arthur shrugged. "Like you, I've been trying to thwart Guru Deep for years."

"And failing."

"Also like you," replied Arthur.

Rucksack had no reply.

Zara stared at the food. "If the beds are made so we fall off, and the chairs are made so we can't sit..."

Rucksack sighed. "Then the food is made so we can't eat, and the water is made so we can't drink."

"Has he tampered with the beer?" said Zara.

"That swill is already unfit to drink," replied Rucksack. "Though tampering might be an improvement."

Arthur stepped away from the table, his face grim. "So we're going to risk starvation and dehydration after all."

THEY STARED AT THE food, then at each other. "What do we do now?" said Arthur.

"We start thinking," said Zara. "We work together."

Rucksack turned to the brewmaster. "First we need to deal with an unanswered question that I know has been vexing hell out o' me. What did you think you were going to do after blowing up the brewery?"

"I didn't know, honestly," Arthur replied. "I hadn't thought it through. I saw what Gabsir was doing, and I panicked. He was going to ruin everything."

"My sister has made the first true GPS in a generation," said Zara. "Doesn't that mean something to you?"

"My allegiance is far more than either of you know," replied Arthur. "Doubt me, dislike me, but do not for one minute think that I have turned my back on what I love. You have no idea how much I've sacrificed, how hard I've worked, how hard I've tried."

Zara sneered. Rucksack glared and said, "I think we understand 'sacrificed' rather better than you."

"You know nothing, Faddah Rucksack."

"Usually don't. But you'll be surprised what I figure out along the way." They stared at each other, then

Rucksack said, "What did you do next? After you presumably legged it out o' the brewery? And how in blazes did you wind up here?"

"I managed to get out of First Call," said Arthur, his eyes dark and his face grim. "A little scratched up, but nothing bad. For a while I didn't know what to do. I looked for all of you, hoped that you were okay. But I found no one. So I went to my office."

"Don't you mean what's left of your office?" Zara asked.

"I'm sure that Guru Deep is already poking around the wreckage," said Arthur, grinning. "He'll be furious when he discovers that in every First Call brewery, the main office is encased in two feet of solid steel. The one way in is a code that only the local head brewer and I know." He dropped his gaze. "Gabsir would have known it too."

"That'll keep Guru Deep busy for a while," said Rucksack, "but eventually he'll get in. He'll find all the originals of everything related to First Call and GPS: my father's journals, the original recipes, everything. He'll destroy it all."

"Not anytime soon," said Arthur, "and if we can find a way out of here we can get there before he does. After I made sure the office was sealed up, I went to the Mirror & Phoenix. Gabsir would sometimes go there for a drink, and he'd told me that's where he'd seen you. I figured if I had any chance of anything, I'd have to start there. The bartender told me you had come in, looking like hell, and then had gone to the Lotus. So that's where I went. I was going to help you. Show you my loyalties. And demand that Guru Deep reverse his decision, or he would regret it."

Zara chuckled. "How'd that go?"

"It didn't. He sent his lackeys, that Blanders and Feckniss, to meet me instead. I didn't even get to say anything. Last thing I remember is Feckniss walking behind me."

"He had quite the slaphappy evening," Rucksack said. "One thing you should know."

"Oh?"

"Blanders is Guru Deep."

"What?"

"I don't know how he does it. Didn't think anyone other than me, Mum, and Dad could. We could alter our appearances to fit in places, but it's only a... modification. We are inconspicuous, but not undetectable. But Guru Deep... he has the ability to completely transform how he looks."

"You never knew this?"

"Not till last night," said Rucksack. "Arthur..."

"What?"

Rucksack sighed. "Why would you never let me help?"

"I always figured our best course of action was to steer clear of you."

Rucksack shook his head. "I offered to help, you know. Offered many times over the years. I hate coming to London, but I would, just to try. For First Call, for GPS, I would have stayed as long as it took to help you and na Grúdairí find your way again."

"How far back do you two go?" Zara asked.

"A long time," Arthur replied. "Every brewmaster has known about Faddah Rucksack, the son of the First Brewer. Many of them have indeed worked with him."

Zara looked at Arthur. "Hasn't Rucksack always been regarded as a hero? What made you suspicious?"

"Before The Blast, his father was concerned about him. Concerned that he was unstable, and that something terrible might happen. Jagathi was supposed to go to New Galway before The Blast, but he stayed in Galway instead, to be near Rucksack. That decision killed him." Arthur shook his head. "To this day I wonder what would be different if he'd done duty to his life's work instead of to his son."

"Harsh words," said Rucksack, his voice quiet. "But deserved."

Arthur looked at the First Brewer's son. "How long have you known we'd lost the secret?"

"Since Samara," he replied. "She told me na Grúdairí were teetering, but I'd been tasting it in the beer long before that."

"Samara contacted you?"

"We were in regular correspondence, Arthur. She confided in me a great deal. But she never told me what the two o' you were doing and planning. You and I both have made mistakes over the years," Rucksack said. "But what we cannot do is change it. Dad is dead. But he'd always planned for that possibility. Want to talk about dislike? Want to talk about letting people down, Arthur? I was furious when Samara lost control o' First Call. I understood as best I could; I forgave her as best I could, but I was incredulous that it happened." Rucksack snorted. "And then there was you."

"Me?" Arthur shook his head. "And what did I do?"

"You were weak," Rucksack replied, his gaze burning. "The more restrictive you became, the more the brewery lost its way. Every brewery around the world looks to the brewmaster. Looks to you. And you closed the doors. Closed your mind. First Call didn't lose the secret o' GPS, Arthur. You cut them off from it."

Arthur stood taller. "I've done what I had to do."

Rucksack matched him. "I know that GPS is the stuff o' life, the stuff o' reality. And I know that when you disconnect the one from the other, both eventually die. You killed the beer, damn you. Now we just wait for Guru Deep to burn the world."

Arthur looked at the radio. "How do we know Guru Deep isn't listening to everything we say?"

"A distinct possibility," said Rucksack, "but I don't think we've said anything yet that he didn't know already. Thank goodness there's no way for him to watch us."

"I want to tell you everything," said Arthur. "Both of you." He shook his head. "But not here. It's not safe. I know you probably don't think I deserve it. But I'm going to ask you to trust me."

"Had you said that when I first realized we were here with you, I might have chosen the starvation," said Zara. "But I'm willing to give you a chance. For now."

"That'll do," said Arthur. "I'll try to deserve it." He turned to Rucksack. "There's something else. You know, of course, that your father left many of his personal effects to First Call."

Rucksack nodded.

"Some of these things have carried... instructions. Sometimes it's just a note on what something is for. But sometimes it's something rather different.

Sometimes we have notes, to take particular actions at particular times or under a certain set of circumstances. It's as if, somehow, Jagathi was looking into the future."

"That'd be Mum," Rucksack said. "She had a way o' looking ahead at things, not at what would happen, but at what was most likely and what was best for the world."

"Like now, then," Arthur said. "I'm going to give you a message from your father to you. He said it was for a brewmaster to tell you this only if First Call was lost, and the brewmaster would know when the time was right."

"Why didn't you say this before?"

"The time wasn't right then, but it is right now."

"It is indeed," said a booming, rolling voice.

Arthur stopped. The three turned and looked at the long wall. The door was open, and Guru Deep stood in the doorway, his orange suit the only color in their black-and-white world. "Arthur, you're looking grand," he said. "I'm so sorry our little chat turned so... physical."

"What chat?" Arthur said. "And do you prefer Guru Deep or Blanders?"

Guru Deep chuckled. "Ah, I assumed Rucksack would clue you in. We all have our secrets. You should be proud, Arthur. You put on a brilliant show. Worthy of you, Rucksack."

"Why are you here?" Rucksack said. "Surely not to get our feedback on the accommodations?"

"I wanted to offer my condolences."

"To?"

"To Arthur, of course, on the event of his death."

"What are you talking about?" Arthur asked.

Guru Deep raised his hand. The radio turned on.

"An industrial accident destroyed the London location of First Call Brewing last night," said the news announcer. "Two men are confirmed dead: Gabsir Abrigs, the second-in-command; and his superior, the brewmaster of First Call Brewing, Arthur Celbridge. We now ask for a moment of silence."

Guru Deep raised his hand again and clicked a button on something he held. "The captain went down with the ship. So sorry for your loss, Arthur. How is it, being dead?"

"You can let me know sometime," Arthur replied, his face drawn tight and his hands clenched.

"Oh, soon we'll all know," Guru Deep replied. "With the two of you out of the way, I can finally get some things done around this tattered old world."

"What happens to us?" Rucksack asked.

"You may listen and wait," Guru Deep said. "You may live." He smiled. "For the moment."

Then Guru Deep turned and walked away, the door whispering shut and locking behind him.

"What the hell are we going to do?" Arthur asked. "We're going to die down here."

"We do what people trapped in a locked room and an impossible situation always do," said Zara. "We find a way out."

LONDON TRUDGED. The dim morning muted the colors and quieted the sounds of the city. Fog pooled around rooftops and streetlamps. On the sidewalks below, people scrunched their coats tightly closed, trying and failing to keep out the chill. The engines of the buses and taxis worked harder, surprised to find it so hard to drive through clouds. For all the good it was doing, the sun might as well have been a gray egg.

Around the black gates of First Call, people gathered around the wreckage and rubble. Some of the people sang sad songs. Some attached flowers or other mementos to the gates. Some left cards and signs, all saying one thing: "Bring back the beer."

The rain began to fall, but the small group that was gathered at the gates ignored it. Some of them cried. Some were silent. Some were angry.

All were surprised when a pile of rubble rose off the ground.

The figure staggered toward them, dazed yet driven. It opened the unlocked gate, which squealed and clanged and stuttered—then fell to the ground.

The people stared, silent mouths agape.

The figure stared back at them, a fire in its eyes that the rain could not quench. Then it spoke.

"I don't suppose anyone could help a girl with some taxi fare?"

The group nodded. Moments later, Branwen was in a cab, and the people were on their way, still sad or angry or numb—but with a story to tell.

THE TAXI STOPPED AND Branwen got out. The rain was coming down harder now, drenching her filthy ragged clothes and making her cuts sting.

"They're not open yet," said the driver. "It's not even six in the morning."

Branwen shrugged. "They'll open for me."

The taxi left and she beat on the heavy wood door. "It's Branwen!" she called. "I need help."

No one came.

Branwen fought back tears of frustration and fatigue. "Dammit," she shouted. "I know you're in there. You're always there. I need your help. Open the door!"

Still silence. Exhausted, Branwen thumped her forehead against the door. The tears wouldn't stop now.

Everyone's gone, she thought. *I'm alone. I've never felt so alone.*

She turned away. Her vision clouded with tears and fatigue, Branwen couldn't see anymore. The last of her willpower drained away and her knees buckled. Clacks and clanks filled her ears—the sound of her world collapsing. Branwen began to fall, her body twisting around.

Into Jade London's arms.

Branwen's vision came back into focus. Instead of her usual dress shirt, black pants, and bow tie, the bartender wore a green sweatshirt over blue jeans. Behind her, Branwen saw the open door to the pub.

"Thank goodness you're okay," Jade said. "Now let's get you inside."

AFTER A SCOTCH, a shower, some tending of cuts and scrapes, another scotch, a change of clothes, and an excellent breakfast, Branwen and Jade London drank coffee while Branwen absorbed everything the bartender had just finished explaining.

"You say Gabsir's dead," said Branwen. Her tone rose in hope. "But if we survived..."

Jade shook her head. "I know what you're thinking, but Gabsir was in a very different situation from the rest of you. He shut the door on Rucksack to contain the explosion. When the equipment in that room blew, Gabsir was at the heart of the blast."

"I just can't accept that."

"I'm sorry, Branwen," said Jade. "He was my friend, just as he was your teacher. But he's dead. We both have to accept that."

"What do I do now?"

"I've had no contact from the others. So that says to me that Guru Deep has them."

"Where?"

Jade shrugged. "You were a janitor in the Lotus. You heard the rumors too."

Branwen nodded. "Underground. Down deep. In a secret prison."

Jade nodded. "So you know what you have to do."

"Yeah, but it's not like I have a company ID anymore. No one's going to let me into the Lotus so that I can sneak down to the bottom of the bottom disguised as a janitor."

Jade laughed. "You think they let Rucksack waltz in?"

"Of course not."

Jade laughed again—and winked. "Of course they did. Or rather, she did."

"Who did?"

"In that entire ashram rabbit-warren cubicle prison of an office, Guru Deep trusts no one," Jade said with a grin. "Except for one person. He might run the company, but there's one person there whose job is to run him. To make his arrangements. To mind the details." Jade leaned forward. "To tend to things he can't personally see to."

Branwen sat, puzzled, then her eyes went wide. "His assistant," she said. "Nia Fox."

Jade nodded. "She sets the schedule. She minds the appointments. She sees people on minor matters that do not require Guru Deep's personal attention or attendance. And she is the one we will turn to now, to get you inside the Lotus."

"She helped Rucksack?"

"Nia Fox and Faddah Rucksack know more about Guru Deep than anyone else alive. That's still saying only so much, but Nia knows that Guru Deep isn't... isn't quite right. That high-wattage smile and blindness-inducing suit serve a different purpose."

Branwen nodded. "The brightest lights don't illuminate," she said. "They blind."

"Exactly. Nia has been trying for years to figure out Guru Deep, what he intends, where he's weak," said Jade. "She lives in constant danger. Bringing you to her will be a risk, but she knows that freeing Zara, Arthur, and Rucksack is essential to stopping whatever Guru Deep has in store next. She'll help you."

"Okay then," said Branwen. "We have to get me to Nia Fox and get me into the Lotus. Shouldn't we have some sort of inspiring music going right now, to help us make our grand plan?"

"Every plan Rucksack made has fallen to ruin against Guru Deep," Jade said. "So have Arthur's plans, and even Gabsir's didn't really work out. This isn't some caper that we can meticulously strategize down to the snappy comeback and the soundless footstep. Guru Deep is the master planner, the strategist who can think through any eventuality." Jade smiled. "Except one."

"What's that?"

"The person who stops trying to plan like Guru Deep, and instead just acts in the moment, as themselves."

Branwen nodded. "I think I understand," she said. "But what do I do once I'm inside?"

Jade shrugged. "Get them out, Branwen Porter. Whatever it takes. Whatever you can figure out. Find them and get them out." She looked at the clock. "We'd better hurry. I called Nia while you were in the shower. She will be coming to the Lotus soon, and you're going in with her."

"Already?" Branwen said. "But I—"

"You are at risk of losing your friend, your sister, and someone who, despite his stupid actions, may not be what you think," Jade said. "At least, I hope not. I doubt they're dead. *Yet.* Sooner or later, Guru Deep will decide they're not worth the risk and trouble of keeping alive. I've restored you and tended you and advised you as best I can. I wish I could just let you lie down and sleep for a week. You've been through a lot, Branwen. Friend. Sister. Grúdaire. I hate to say it, but you are about to go through a hell of a lot more. It's all up to you now."

Branwen stood up. "Then let's get me ready for hell."

FECKNISS COULDN'T REMEMBER WHAT time he'd gotten home last night. He vaguely recalled looking out the window with Guru Deep. Then he'd swayed, and the the world had turned misty, foggy. Guru Deep had ordered him a taxi, but for all Feckniss knew, he had been carried up the stairs to his flat.

Now, early in the morning, returning to the Lotus, Feckniss felt the strangeness over the city too. Most people said nothing, only stared at the fog, as if afraid it was going to grab their wallets or their kids or their souls. The day's chill reached into you like a pickpocket and cut like a drunk surgeon. Around Feckniss, every person in London felt scared. If anyone was speaking, it was to talk about the explosion at First Call, the sadness the city felt at losing not only its favorite beer, but two of the key people behind the brewery.

I don't understand why they're scared, he thought. *Don't they know what has happened? Don't they realize all the amazing things to come?*

He knew what Guru Deep would say. That of course they didn't realize. Of course they didn't understand. They already lived in a fog, an eternal dream fog called life. They didn't know that if the fog went away, then the true light of the universe would shine and blaze. All the dream would burn away. Only the real would remain.

That's what Guru Deep would say. Feckniss smiled and opened the glass door of the Lotus.

Then he saw what scared him.

This morning his reflection had become even more wretched and twisted. Some of the yellowed teeth had fallen out. More of the thin hair was gone, showing a scalp covered in large greenish-brown spots. It chuckled at him. "Stupid Feckwit," said the reflection. "How's that zag when you should've zigged?"

Feckniss's joy at the morning, joy at last night's victory, all fell away. The reflection had been real. The rest was his own dream.

My own lie.

Across the lobby of the Lotus, he saw Nia Fox, standing near the central elevators. A woman was standing next to her, but when they saw Feckniss the woman went into the ground-floor women's toilets, leaving Nia alone.

He wanted to go to Nia, talk to her, be near her. His pulse quickened, and he couldn't stop looking at Nia Fox.

You have to stay away from her, Feckniss thought. Or was it the reflection talking now?

Nia looked at him as he came closer. In her eyes he saw again the serenity, but also something troubled.

Something scared.

She knows, Feckniss thought. *Or if she doesn't grasp the horror that I really am, she knows something is wrong with me.*

In the look that passed between them, Feckniss saw what could be. A conversation. An invitation to a drink. An evening of the best conversation he'd had in years, followed by a kiss that left them fulfilled and breathless, excited yet content that all, at last, was right with the world.

So much future passed between them. So many shared days and amazing times.

But that's not a future, Feckniss thought. *Not a real one. Not one that I could have. She is who she is. I am who I am. I wish I could be with her. Know her. Care for her. But all I can do is protect her—protect her from what I really am. And the only way to do that is to stay away from her. Forever.*

He gave a curt nod. "Good morning, Ms. Fox."

Her own reply was equally yet surprisingly distant. "Good morning, fellow assistant."

Feckniss stepped onto an open elevator. *Well,* he thought, *at least that's over with.*

But as the doors closed, the mask around Nia's face broke. He saw the pain etched there, the loneliness, and something else he could not describe or understand.

What was that? he thought. Then the elevator started upward. He stepped back—and his gaze fell to the polished brass elevator floor buttons in front of him.

His reflection stared back, the eyes calm like a bomb about to explode. "Well Feckwit," it said, "you really know how to let a girl down, huh?"

Feckniss stared back, revulsion rising in him like vomit. "Shut up, you arse," he said. "Just shut up."

When he arrived at forty-one, he stopped by his assistant's desk and pointed back where he'd come from. "Tell maintenance that elevator needs some work," he said. "All the buttons are smashed in, even the brass plating."

She nodded. He went to his office and closed the door. Feckniss ignored the piles on his desk. Instead he sat and stared at his hand.

"IT DOESN'T MATTER THAT I've got this snazzy black pantsuit," Branwen said when she rejoined Nia Fox in the lobby of the Lotus. "I look like hell frozen over and thawed. What do I do if someone notices?"

Nia chuckled. "All that time working here, and you didn't notice something?"

"What?"

"People here don't notice things. Stay behind me. Look confident and intent, like you know where you're going and needed to be there two minutes ago. The secret to working here is for people to believe that interrupting you is the surest way to ruin their day."

"Is that what you do?" Branwen asked. Then she turned her face away.

"What is it?" Nia said.

"My old boss," Branwen whispered.

The old man wheeled his cart to the elevator Feckniss had used. He hung a "CLOSED FOR REPAIRS" sign in front of the elevator doors.

Then he walked past the two women, barely nodding as he passed. "G'morning Ms. Fox," he said, in a voice little above a whisper.

Branwen stared at him as he walked away. "How did he not recognize me?"

"Because you aren't here," replied Nia, pressing the call button on another elevator.

"Umm."

"Let me explain." Nia smiled. "You were sacked. You left the Lotus. Since you no longer work here and have been banned from the premises, there is no way you could be here. Therefore, even if you are here, you aren't here. Simple. Besides, you were a janitor—and how many bigwigs ever notice the cleaning staff?"

"Are people working for Guru Deep really that spellbound?" Branwen asked as the two women got on to an elevator.

"I don't know about everyone else," Nia replied, bitterness in her voice, "but I certainly was."

"What happened?"

Nia shrugged. "Another story for another time," she said. "I need to keep my head clear. Thinking of that will put us at risk. I can't have that."

"Sorry."

"Not your fault," said Nia. "Unless you're actually Guru Deep in one hell of a disguise."

Branwen shook her head. "Orange makes me nauseous."

"There you go then."

The women grinned. "If this works," said Branwen, "I owe you big time."

"If this works," Nia replied, "we'll be too grateful to care."

"Grateful for what?"

"Being alive. Make no mistake, Branwen. The stakes aren't Guru Deep shutting down a company or ending a product line. At the basic business and accounting level, that's all First Call and GPS are to him."

"What's this about then?"

"Rucksack. Arthur and Zara are bonuses, collateral damage. Afterthoughts."

"That's my sister you're talking about."

"I'm not Guru Deep," Nia said. "But I can tell you how he thinks. Of course, if you don't want to know or don't want my help, well, I have a host of other ways I could be risking my neck right now."

"Guru Deep isn't going to keep them alive for long," said Branwen.

Nia shook her head. "I know I wouldn't."

"So why is he?"

"Guru Deep has them contained for now, as neutralized as he can make them without harming them, because he may need information. He knows they'll likely try to find a way to escape. He's far more confident that escape is impossible. He's accepting what risk there is because of the explosion at First

Call. He doesn't know what he doesn't know. If there's anything Guru Deep detests, it's being unaware of what's going on. They're alive as long as he wonders if they have another purpose."

The elevator doors opened, and the women stepped onto forty-one. Managers and assistants went about their silent tasks.

"Nia," said Branwen, "I really hate it here."

In a voice barely above a whisper, Nia replied, "So do I."

They went to Nia's desk. Branwen stared at the elevator behind Guru Deep's assistant. Nia unlocked a desk drawer and pulled out a file.

"Board of directors," said Branwen. "Well, I am here from the convention center's event services department, so we can discuss arrangements for your upcoming board meeting."

"Yes," Nia said with a smile. "Other than my, um, personal light reading, I thought we'd discuss particulars of the board members so you can factor in those details for your planning."

"What now? Are you taking me up Guru Deep's elevator?"

"Umm, no," said Nia. "No way we could do that unnoticed." She started walking away, and Branwen followed.

"Why are we heading toward Blanders's office?" Branwen asked.

"Because he's not here. Feckniss, Blanders, and Guru Deep left moments ago to visit First Call and evaluate the situation."

"This plan is making less and less sense all the time," said Branwen. "If I'm going to find a way into that secret prison room thingie, I need to go to Guru Deep's office to find out where it is, what access I need. Keys, passwords, magic spells, whatever. That's going to be there, not down here with some crony."

Nia said nothing, only knocked twice on Blanders's door. When there was no answer, Nia deftly produced a key, unlocked the door, and went inside. "Guru Deep has keys to all the offices here," Nia explained, shutting the door and walking behind Blanders's desk, stopping next to the large closet in the back corner. "Therefore I also have keys to all the offices. Which is how, one afternoon when everyone was gone with Guru Deep and I was here all alone, catching up paperwork, I indulged some colleague curiosity and discovered... this."

She leaned back and rolled her hands in front of her, pointing at the closet.

"I haven't been in a closet in years," said Branwen. "What use is one now?"

"It's not a closet," Nia said, smiling as she opened the door.

Branwen's mouth dropped open. "It's another elevator."

With a nod, Nia waved Branwen inside. "You have thirty minutes," she said. "Feckniss, Blanders, and Guru Deep will be back by then, and we'll still have to find a way to get you underground."

Branwen winked and tapped the wristwatch Jade London had also loaned her. "See you in twenty-five."

"Do you know what you're looking for?"

Branwen shrugged. "I'd better know it when I see it," she said, as the door shut her off from Nia Fox and took her to the forty-second floor of the Lotus.

* * * * *

ONCE INSIDE GURU DEEP'S empty office, Branwen made straight for his large wooden desk, where stacks of folders towered over the rich bright wood. *I think his desk is the size of our flat,* Branwen thought.

Behind the desk, on a small table in front of the window, a black lacquered wooden stand held a curved Japanese katana in its black scabbard, polished and resplendent. In front of the stand sat another katana. Its scabbard was dusty, chipped, and covered with something brown and dried. Except for a looped cord stretching from the scabbard where the blade entered, the dusty sword and the polished swords were identical twins.

What the hell?

Something about the swords pulled at her, but Branwen knew she didn't have time to wonder. Instead she shifted papers and lifted folders, searching and checking—but finding nothing.

"What am I looking for?" Branwen had asked Nia in the lobby, before they had seen Feckniss.

"Anything that has to do with last night," Nia had replied. "First Call, accidents, anything that mentions Rucksack and Arthur. There has to be something. You drop bread on the floor around here, there's going to be a form to fill out in triplicate. So there's got to be something. Just be careful. And be sure that you put everything back exactly the way you found it."

Precious time ticked away. After nineteen minutes, Branwen had found nothing.

Nineteen fewer minutes that Zara may have to live, Branwen reminded herself.

But there's nothing here.

Then she saw something.

The plain manila folder said simply, "Trub and Krausen Report."

Branwen picked it up. "Why would the CEO of a global corporate empire care about the fermentation debris and blow-off that you want to get rid of when brewing beer?"

No sooner had she finished speaking, when her eyes went wide.

"Of course," she said, opening the folder and reading the report.

Then closed it again in frustration.

Dammit. I thought for sure I'd find something.

She started to put the useless report back where she'd found it. Then she stopped, and opened the folder again.

"It talks about Krausen, always with a capital K, being an ongoing problem," she said. "And it talks about getting rid of Trub, with a capital T."

This is it.

Branwen nodded. "There's going to be paperwork," she said. "But that doesn't mean its meaning will be obvious. Since when does a company of this size ever speak plainly or say anything clearly?"

Trub is the gunk left at the bottom of a fermenter, she thought. It always stinks when we're rinsing it out of the carboys at home. Krausen is a sign that the yeast have fermentation in top gear. It makes a thick foam, and gases that blow off, leaving the fermenter and getting away from the beer. If it stayed, it'd cause headaches or make the beer taste bad. Trub is stuff brewers don't want... krausen is a sign of high activity—something Guru Deep doesn't want.

"Stuff we don't want," Branwen said out loud. "Nicknames. Trub and Krausen." *Like Malt and Hops.* "Arthur and Rucksack."

She read more—and smiled.

I know where they are.

She checked her watch. *It's been twenty-seven minutes,* she thought. *I have to get out of here.*

Branwen stuffed the folder down the back of her pants and pulled her jacket over it, then headed toward the elevator that would return her to Blanders's office. Then she stopped and turned around. Returning to the desk, she stood again in front of the small table with the two swords.

She picked up the dusty one.

"You don't belong here," she said.

Tucking the katana behind her as best she could, Branwen went to the elevator and stopped in front of the doors. *What a pretty plant,* she thought, looking at the tall potted plant next to the elevator box. She raised her hand—but before she could press the button, the light went on. A *ding* brought Branwen's world to a halt.

Behind the door, a voice.

She froze.

They're back!

The doors opened.

BLANDERS STEPPED OFF THE elevator first, and Feckniss followed. "Sir," Feckniss said, "what do we do about it?"

Instead of answering, Blanders stopped and massaged his right hand.

"Are you okay, sir?"

"I'm fine, Feckniss, fine. Must have a twinge from last night's excitement. Nothing a change won't fix. I need a break from this skin anyway."

He trusts me more than anyone, Feckniss thought, squinting at the white light.

When Guru Deep again stood before him, Feckniss smiled. "Always good to see you, sir. Umm..."

"What do you want to know, Feckniss?"

"Sir... I'm sorry if this is impertinent..."

"Go ahead."

"If you can look like anyone else, why not impersonate Arthur or Zara or anyone of strategic advantage, take their place, as it were? You could learn so much."

"An astute question," replied Guru Deep. "Unfortunately, my ability doesn't work that way. I am unable to assume a guise of any actual person. I can only take on the appearance of one who exists solely in my imagination." Guru Deep stared at Feckniss. "You seemed troubled, my protégé," said Guru Deep. "Is it what we found? We'll find a way into that office."

"That is troubling, yes, but..."

If he trusts you, trust him.

"The broken elevator, sir."

"What about it?"

Feckniss took a deep breath. "I did that."

Guru Deep silently stared at Feckniss for a moment. "That was an impressive punch," said Guru Deep at last. "But solid brass and steel? That should have broken your hand. Are you hurt?"

How can I explain this to him? Feckniss thought.

"That's what troubles me." Feckniss held up his hand. "There's not a scratch. No pain. Nothing wrong."

"I knew I chose well." Guru Deep smiled. "Tell me, Feckniss, what did you see when you looked at your hand in your reflection?"

"My reflection?" *He can't know! He couldn't possibly!* "Why would that matter?"

Guru Deep patted Feckniss on the shoulder. "You know as well as I do."

No! Feckniss dropped his head and closed his eyes. *He must be so disgusted. So disappointed.* "You've known?"

"All along. Before you knew. Does that scare you?"

Feckniss shuddered. "It's horrible. *I'm* horrible."

"It is a sign of your quality and good fortune."

"What do you mean?" Feckniss took a step back. "But it's twisted, and cruel... and... and... *me!*"

"We are both light and dark," said Guru Deep. "The essence of being human in the dream is learning to live with your light and with your shadow."

"Even you?"

How could you ask him that?

But Guru Deep only smiled. "Especially me." He guided Feckniss to the window. "Some would say that my shadow is currently locked in the basement. Part of freeing this world, Feckniss, means getting rid of that sort of shadow."

"What about mine?"

"One day, Feckniss, your shadow will be gone too. But not yet. For now, you do have it—but we must learn to use it. Harness its power. But it's part of you. I trust you, Feckniss. I accept you. All of you. It's time you did too. Now look at yourself."

Feckniss stared at his reflection. Guru Deep stared into the reflected yellow eyes and said, "Now hold up your hand."

Again Feckniss stared at the perfect skin, so pale he could see the veins beneath. No cuts, no bruising, not so much as a scratch.

But then he looked at his reflected hand.

"Swollen. Cut and bruised," said Guru Deep. "That first knuckle in particular looks broken and disjointed. But tell me, Feckniss, do you feel any pain?"

"Only at what I must look like to the world."

Guru Deep shook his head. "The world sees you as you are before me. Perfect. Flawless."

"The reflection shows my true self."

"The reflection shows your shadow. Nothing more. It is part of you, yes—but it is not all of you."

Feckniss stared at the two hands: the real and the reflected. "Does this mean that... I can't get hurt?"

"It does. You can push yourself past any limit, Feckniss, and you will suffer no injury. Perhaps you can't even die—though I'm in no hurry to test that theory. Any pain you would have suffered will exist only in your reflection. No consequences. No side effects." Guru Deep stepped to the window and touched the glass, right where Feckniss's face was reflected. "May I be completely honest with you, son?"

"You can always trust me, sir."

"I'm a little jealous. Not even I can withstand injury to the degree that you will learn. I knew you would go far, Feckniss. I knew you could go All The Way."

"All the way to what, sir?"

Guru Deep smiled. "To the end of the world," he said. "To the end of the dream and to the reality beyond. You are the perfect companion, the perfect partner I never could have hoped to ask for."

The smile fell off Guru Deep's face.

"Sir?"

Feckniss followed his leader's gaze to the desk. "What's wrong?"

Guru Deep strode to the desk and punched the intercom button.

"Sir?" said the voice of Nia Fox.

"Where is it?"

"Where is what, sir?"

"The sword."

Silence.

"Ms. Fox?" said Guru Deep again, irritation simmering in his voice. "What is the meaning of this?"

"I didn't realize you had returned, sir," she said, as if Guru Deep had wished her a most pleasant good morning. "You must have come up while I was away from my desk."

"Where is the sword?" said Guru Deep.

"I took it away for cleaning, sir."

"I've told you time and again that sword is never to be put away or removed. It is my finest trophy."

"I apologize for misunderstanding you, sir," said Nia Fox, "but I was never aware that you objected to the sword being cleaned."

"This is taking one liberty too far, my assistant. Why is it being cleaned?"

"Next week the Japanese ambassador is in London, and her delegation is meeting with you at the office." Nia's voice reminded Feckniss of his mum's, when she was explaining something to him as a child—a calm veneer concealing exasperation. "Seeing that sword so filthy would have been an insult and could cause irreparable harm to the new venture you seek in Japan. I gave the sword to a highly recommended expert. She will have it returned—in a presentable fashion, and with a proper stand—as soon as possible."

"The sooner the better," said Guru Deep. "In the future, anything regarding the swords is to be discussed with me first. As much as I appreciate your sense of self-direction, my assistant, you are perhaps the only person I've ever known who has initiative in overabundance."

"My apologies, sir," said Nia Fox.

Guru Deep ended the call. "No matter," he said, picking up the other, gleaming sword. "This was never going to be a fair fight anyway." Guru Deep drew the sword from its scabbard. The blade's singing hiss made Feckniss take a step back.

"But not yet." Guru Deep smiled and sheathed the sword, then put it back on the stand.

"Sir?" Feckniss asked. "What happened with the enemy in Kyoto? Blanders—you—said the swords had quite a story to tell."

Guru Deep smiled. "They do indeed. Their origins are legend, as are their deeds—and as are the only men who ever wielded them: Faddah Rucksack, my father, and me. Some say that one day in Japan, the earth shook, and a crack in the world led Rucksack to a sacred cherry tree. The tree split, and inside he found the swords. It's a lovely story. But the truth is that a master swordsmith designed and forged the swords for Faddah Rucksack, many centuries ago, as part of Rucksack saving Japan from a terrible threat. He wielded them until one day, in Kyoto, my father stole one sword. They dueled, and Rucksack was gravely injured. My father died soon after—but not before stealing the swords and leaving them to me.

I've had them ever since, as a reminder of what a threat Rucksack is to all I hold dear, and how I will not rest until he and his meddling are ended. Now, I'd love to tell you more, Feckniss. However, first you and Blanders have some business to tend to."

"Loose ends, sir?"

"We've learned all we can from the site of the explosion."

"We still need access to the brewmaster's office," said Feckniss.

"One way or another, we will get that," said Guru Deep. "I just may have a few ways to... motivate Arthur, before he stops being another pest to me."

With a flash of light, Guru Deep became Blanders again. "Let's finish our business, Feckniss," said Guru Deep, glancing at the sword as they went back to the elevator. "Then this evening, we have Trub and Krausen to dispose of." He shrugged. "Oh yes. And Sara too."

EVEN THOUGH THEY WERE gone, Branwen was still shaking. She exhaled and unwedged herself from behind the dark curtain she'd pulled in front of her, squeezed herself out of the space between the elevator box and the wall, then again shifted aside the tall plant placed there to cover the gap. She moved away from the elevator, into the middle of the office, away from the cramped corner where she'd struggled to breathe.

Out in the open space of the office, she tried to calm her racing heart and took in huge, deep breaths, hands on her knees as she breathed in and out, over and over.

They never knew I was here, she thought. *I can't believe I'm still in one piece. Not that I'm in a hurry to go back there. Worse than being crammed inside the brew kettle.*

The light went on, and the elevator dinged again.

No, Branwen thought.

The doors began to open. She stared at the space beyond the plant, and missed it with all her being.

I can't get there in time!

Nia Fox stepped out of the elevator. "You jackass," she said. "What were you thinking?"

"Thank goodness," said Branwen. "I thought—"

"I thought you and I were both about to wish for a fast death," Nia replied.

"I found out where they are though," said Branwen.

"Really?" said Nia. "Isn't a scabbard a tight fit for three people?"

"Huh?"

"The sword, dammit," said Nia. "It nearly ruined everything. At first I had no idea what he was talking about, but figured it had to be you. I barely covered my arse, let alone yours. Why did you take the sword?"

Branwen shrugged. "It's not his."

"This is a fine time for kindergarten morality."

"It's Rucksack's," said Branwen. "I remembered him mentioning it, the first time we met. His old swords. When I saw them here, I just... Something in me told me that I just couldn't leave this one. He needed it back."

Nia shook her head. "You'd better be right." She looked at the hilt and the looped cord dangling off the end of the scabbard where it met the sword. "What the hell's that?"

"If Rucksack tells me, you'll be the first to know."

The women got on the elevator and went over to Nia's desk. A notebook lay next to the open board of directors file.

"I thought that file thing was a ruse?" Branwen whispered.

"There's more than one ruse going on around here," Nia replied in a similar whisper. Then, in a louder voice that made heads turn, she said, "Guru Deep will want the sword returned in pristine condition."

"What the hell are you doing?" Branwen whispered. "Trying to make a spectacle out of me?"

"On the contrary, I'm making you invisible," Nia whispered. "I'm putting a spotlight on you right now so you'll be invisible later. By the time you reach the ground floor again, everyone will know about the expert transporting the sword for cleaning. Everyone will ignore you."

"How do you know?"

"No one will question someone carrying a prized possession of Guru Deep's. They will assume your worth because they believe they are unworthy." Nia smiled. "Plus there's a greater self-preservational pragmatism at work."

"What's that?"

"Who wants to get in the way of anyone with a katana?"

"Good point."

Nia chuckled. "I'm sharp, I am." Then she raised her voice again. "We know the sword will return to us better than the day the blade was forged. The Best Is Only The Beginning, as our Great Leader would say."

She stared hard at Branwen. "I look forward to your return. Now go about your task."

"What?" Branwen whispered. "Alone?"

Nia nodded. "I can't do any more than I have, I'm afraid. I'm due in meetings with Guru Deep the rest of the day, and any absence or delay would be noticed—and questioned. I'm sorry, Branwen, but you're on your own now."

THE ELEVATOR DOOR OPENED. Feckniss stepped into Guru Deep's office and picked up the sword.

He trusts me above all others, he thought. *He even sent me here unaccompanied, to retrieve the sword.*

"Do us a favor," said a voice, "and try to cut off yer own feckin head instead."

Feckniss stared at his reflection. "Would that make you feel better?"

"You idiot," it said back, "don't you realize that I'm you too?"

"You wish," said Feckniss, walking away without looking back. "Now, Guru Deep and I have work to do."

THE TRIO WORKED SILENTLY, and the pile in the corner of the room got bigger. After emptying the bookshelves, they had pulled the sheets off the bed and taken the linens from the bathroom. They'd ripped the upholstery from the couch and the overstuffed chairs.

Now they tried to figure out the last part of their conundrum.

"O' course there aren't any feckin matches," said Rucksack as he continued slowly walking along the wall, feeling the surface from eye level to the corner of the ceiling. "It's not like they *want* us to set things on fire. Rather the point."

Arthur pointed to the hill of paper and fabric. "Then how are we supposed to light one? And what in blazes are you doing now?"

"Figuring out the blazes part," Rucksack replied. "There's got to be somewhere we can get into the wall. Do that, and we can find some wiring. Find that, and we can get a spark. A spark is all we need."

"Why do you think this will work?" Zara asked. "What makes you so sure Guru Deep won't just let us barbecue ourselves to death in here?"

"If he wanted us dead, he already would have killed us," Rucksack replied. "We start a fire, keep any sprinklers off it, then no matter what, someone is going to have to come through that door and help us. That's our chance. Our only chance. Unless you can think o' a better way out o' here."

He's got me there, Arthur thought.

Rucksack thumped the wall. "Trouble is," he said, "I can't find anything. Not one damn crack or seam or weak point."

The radio clicked on.

"In two weeks," a voice said, "a vital, world-changing announcement from Guru Deep. And we'll be broadcasting it live, to the whole world."

"I hate that feckin radio," Rucksack said. "Never any good news."

But Arthur smiled. "No, Rucksack. It's great news. The best news."

"What do you mean?"

"It's a radio," Zara said, grinning too.

Arthur nodded. "It has a power cord."

Rucksack smiled. "Why Arthur," he said, "if we're not careful, we're going to start liking each other."

Zara grabbed the radio and turned it over. A thin black cable snaked from the table into the radio's housing.

Rucksack shrugged. "How are we going to...?"

Zara raised a crutch and began smashing the radio.

"Sometimes you need finesse," said Rucksack, nodding in approval. "And sometimes you just need a little brute force."

Arthur grabbed the insulated cord and yanked hard. It gave, and he smiled when he saw the bared wire at the end of the cable. "It's too short to reach the pile," he said. "Probably the only time I'm ever going to ask someone to bring me a Guru Deep guidebook, but if you would be so kind." When Rucksack did, the men looked at each other. "This is it," Arthur said. "Be ready."

He touched the wire to the paper.

Nothing happened.

Arthur tried again. No smoke. No fire. No current. Nothing.

"What's going on?" Rucksack said.

Arthur touched the wires.

"Be careful."

But Arthur shook his head. "There's no power," he said. "This is about as useful as a shoelace right now." He shook his head. "The power must have shut off from the source when the radio turned off."

"Keep the wire on the paper," Rucksack said. "That damn radio turns on all the time. Sooner or later there'll be something Guru Deep wants us to hear."

"Wait," said Zara. "There's something else."

"No," said Arthur. "We've looked at everything."

"Everything that was here," Zara said. "But not at what we brought with us."

"We packed light for this holiday," said Rucksack, "just got ourselves and what we're wearing."

Zara grinned. "And the flashlight," she said. "With its battery, as Guru Deep bragged, that held all that charge."

"O' course," said Rucksack, grabbing the light from his bed. "There must be a way to open this thing."

From outside the door, a booming sound reverberated through the room.

The trio stood up quickly. "Too late," Rucksack said. "How considerate o' them to knock. It's like they're our guests instead o' us being their hostages." His mouth was a hard line on his grim face. "Almost feckin sweet."

There was a scratching sound outside.

"Be ready," Arthur said. "If someone's coming in, then they're going to see the pile."

"Which isn't on fire," Zara reminded him.

"No," Arthur replied, nodding toward the flashlight, "but along with that, we'll have the element of surprise. We'll just have a moment to take advantage, but we've got to be quick and overwhelm them."

Rucksack nodded. He stood in front of the door, so he'd be seen immediately, while Zara and Arthur stepped to opposite sides of the entry.

When it opened, they jumped.

"What the hell are you doing?" said a voice they didn't expect. "And put down that damn light before you blind someone."

Branwen looked at the open mouths around her. "I'm glad to see you too," she said, lowering a broom.

"What are you doing here?" Arthur said. "And why is there a spray bottle tucked into your pants?"

"Maybe sometime you'll have something different to say to me," Branwen replied. "I'm rescuing you, of course."

Behind her, Arthur saw a man slumped on the floor. "You did that?"

Branwen glanced at the broom. "On my way here I stopped by the janitorial supply room for a few things. Brooms do more than sweep, you know." She stepped into the room. "We don't have much time."

Zara wrapped her arms around her sister. "Branwen!" she said. "I'm sorry! I'm so, so sorry! And I'm so glad you're not dead. You were right. I was wrong. I was—"

"I love you too, big sister," Branwen replied. "We have a lot to talk about. But right now, we have to get the hell out of here. Guru Deep... By the way, did you know that he and Blanders are the same person? He has some sort of ability to change his appearance."

"Yeah," said Rucksack. "We found that out the hard way."

"No matter," said Branwen. "I overheard Guru Deep and Feckniss saying they didn't need you anymore. I don't know how much time we have, but every second we're here is one less until he comes down here to kill you."

"What?" Rucksack said. "You'd think he'd just starve us. Or cut off the air or water."

Branwen shook her head. "I was hiding in his office, I heard everything. Including the sword he pulled out. His voice then... There's no way he'd let something or somebody else kill you, Rucksack. Whatever it is between you two, it's too personal. The only way he'll let you be dead is if it's at his own hand."

Arthur stared at Rucksack, wondering how he would react. Then Rucksack smiled. "That's good to know, Branwen," he said. "We just might be able to use that. But tell me, why were you in his office?"

"I had to find out where you were and how to get you out. Nia Fox snuck me in."

Rucksack nodded. "She's good at that."

"I found something else." Branwen pulled a strap off her shoulder and handed over the sword to Rucksack. "I believe this is yours."

Rucksack's eyes gleamed as he wrapped his hand around the scabbard. "My sword!" Then he stared at Branwen and added, "But where's the other one?"

"I only had time for one. And this one... it's like it called to me. The other sword is still in Guru Deep's office. Unless he's already gotten it and is on his way. Come on. We have to get out of here."

"Wait," said Rucksack.

"What?"

"How do we know you're really you?"

"Dammit," said Branwen. "I suppose I could explain I heard Guru Deep say that he can't impersonate actual people, and can only look like nonexistent people he imagines."

"If it's true," Rucksack replied, "that's good to know. But we don't know if it's true."

"Then ask me something that only Branwen would know."

"The day I met you and Zara and tried your homebrew for the first time," said Rucksack, "what did I say while you were pouring my beer?"

Branwen smiled. "The *night* we met you," she began, "while *Zara* poured your beer you said, 'You pour it like GPS.'"

Rucksack nodded. "Thank goodness you're you. Now let's get out o' here." Then he grinned. "Wait. Actually, there's one thing I need to do first."

Rucksack went to the wall across from the door and drew the ragged sword. The blade was shorter than Arthur expected—then he saw the tip of the blade. Instead of ending in an elegant, sharp point, the katana was jagged at a broken edge.

"Ah," said Rucksack, "my favorite one." He began scratching the jagged point into the wall.

Branwen stared at the pile of paper and cloth in the corner. "What's that?"

"Oh," Arthur said. "We were trying to start a fire to help us get out of here. I don't suppose you snagged a book of matches from that janitor closet?"

Branwen shrugged. "If only."

"I've got this," said Rucksack as he came back to the group. "Nothing like a diversion."

He walked to the pile, then threw the flashlight straight up into the air.

THE FLASHLIGHT ROSE IN the air, tumbling and spinning. Rucksack watched, standing completely still.

"What are you doing?" Zara asked.

He said nothing. The flashlight reached the apex of the throw and began to come back down. The little cylinder tumbled and tumbled, lower and lower.

In a blur, Rucksack pulled the sword from its scabbard and swung the blade.

The flashlight split into two pieces.

More importantly, sparks—created by the slash of the steel blade on the metal housing and the battery inside—rained onto the paper and fabric piled below.

Smoke rose. Soon, so did small orange flames.

Rucksack had returned the sword to its scabbard as quickly as he had drawn it, but it had been enough for Branwen to see. Before she could say anything though, Rucksack said, "Now run!"

They dashed through the empty corridors and into an elevator. The doors shut and they began to rise— and rise.

"My gods and goddesses," Rucksack said, "how deep down are we?"

"At least four hundred feet," Branwen replied. "That's my guess. As deep as the Lotus is tall."

Arthur nodded at Rucksack's sword. "You might want to have that ready."

"Good point," Rucksack replied. But instead of drawing the sword again, he looped the strange cord from the scabbard around the hilt, tightened it, then dropped the sword down casually. Holding the hilt, Rucksack tapped the point end of the scabbard on the floor, as if the sword were a mere walking stick.

"That's not exactly what I had in mind," said Arthur.

Rucksack's grin was thin and grim. "That's why I'm the one with the sword."

"Shouldn't you be ready to, you know, cut with it?" Zara asked.

"If that were the case, you should be really worried," replied Rucksack. "I only pull this blade when no option is left. That's how it was then. That's how it's going to be now." He nodded. "That said, get behind me. Leaving here could be a rough ride."

The elevator stopped. "Get ready, everyone."

With a *ding*, the doors opened.

Nobody moved.

"Branwen," said Rucksack, "where the hell are we?"

"Janitor closet, south side of the building."

"Right," said Rucksack. "I suppose you could have mentioned the elevator was hidden."

Before them were shelves of cleaning products. Zara chuckled. "That's a bit anti-climatic, don't you think?"

"We're not out yet," Arthur said quietly.

They left the elevator. When the doors shut behind them, all they saw was what looked like a regular door in the building.

In the corridor outside the closet, they could hear the sounds of people in the lobby. "We're on the back side of the main elevator bank," said Branwen.

"Don't tell me we have to go through the lobby to get out o' here," said Rucksack.

Branwen shook her head. "If we go the opposite way, a service door puts us near the street."

"Then let's move," Zara said.

As they started walking, they could hear running feet and someone saying, "Fire down below." Then Feckniss turned the corner and entered the corridor.

"Everyone!" said Rucksack. "Run!"

But before Branwen could move, Feckniss grabbed her arm. "You're not escaping, Rucksack!" he yelled. "Not any of you! Guru Deep! They got out! Guru Deep! The enemy—"

With her other hand, Branwen shoved the end of the broom into Feckniss's belly. He doubled over—then stood back up. "Can't hurt me," he said. His voice cracked and for a moment his eyes flashed yellow. "Can only hurt him."

Branwen kneed him in the balls. He laughed.

"Fine, you feckwitted Feckniss," she said.

Fury passed over his pale face. "What did you call me?"

She reached to her belt and grabbed the bottle hanging there. "Feckwit!" Branwen yelled, raising the bottle and spraying bleach into Feckniss's face.

"My eyes!" he screamed. "My eyes!" He let go of Branwen to grab his face.

Branwen opened the closet door and shoved him inside. "Well," she said, "I guess I can hurt something." She closed the door and wedged the stick of the broom against it, locking Feckniss in. "That won't hold him for long," she said.

"Not that it would help you now anyway," a voice boomed.

They all looked down the corridor. Guru Deep drew his sword and raised the blade.

"NO MATTER WHAT HAPPENS," said Rucksack, "run and keep running."

"No way," Arthur replied. "We're in this together."

"That's why you have to get Branwen out of here," said Rucksack. "She's everything now."

With a guttural cry that grew into a wall-shaking roar, Guru Deep ran forward. So did Rucksack, who said nothing, only raised his scabbarded sword and easily parried a blow meant to cut him in half.

"All you've accomplished is a swifter death," said Guru Deep. "Your escape has done nothing but save me an elevator ride."

"Shame you can't shut up long enough to save yourself some oxygen," Rucksack replied.

Soon the men were a blur. Guru Deep's attack was relentless, and Rucksack moved backward, defending and holding his own, but moving toward a dead end in the corridor.

"You can't run away forever," said Guru Deep.

"Is that what you thought I was doing all these years?" said Rucksack. "People think I aimlessly wander. No one ever supposes my destination requires a strange and winding path."

"You won't win," said Guru Deep. "I reduced you to nothing last night, Faddah Rucksack."

The *clang* and *thwack* of the sword and the scabbard rang up and down the corridor. "O' course you did. And you're putting on a good show today, I'll give you that. I'm still not back to my old strength. Sometimes I get so weak I can barely stand." Rucksack stumbled and lowered his sword. Guru Deep shouted and sprang forward, slashing horizontally.

Rucksack grinned and jumped backward, out of reach. "I'm getting stronger every day though," he said, faking a thrust. "This is where you're supposed to overpower me with your strength fueled by pure evil. While I, supposedly the hero o' old and hero o' always, display about as much ability and fortitude as an empty beer bottle."

"I'll take your head just for the sake of shutting you up," said Guru Deep as he slashed sideways at Rucksack's neck.

Ducking the blow with a smile, Rucksack said, "You'll have to pick out something else for your mantel." He whacked Guru Deep across the kneecaps, then turned the scabbard vertical and forced it upward. The blow took Guru Deep under the chin, and he staggered backward down the corridor.

Rucksack lunged forward. "You had the better o' me last night, just like Kyoto, there's no way around it." The sword and the scabbard swung. "I was exhausted. And you shot Zara. And, really, you just had me by the lads. Well played."

They locked swords, straining at each other and stepping closer and closer until they were nose to nose. Slowly Guru Deep pressed the sharp katana toward Rucksack's face.

"That was yesterday, when all seemed lost," said Rucksack, his teeth gritted and eyes ablaze, but his voice calm. "Today there's a bit o' hope. And that does wonders for your odds." Rucksack's breath fogged the steel of the katana. He grinned. "But you know what really gets me? How I know you're going to lose?"

"How?"

"My path is getting back what I lost so I can be what this world needs me to be." Rucksack pressed harder. Little by little, Guru Deep's sword began moving backward. Rucksack's eyes narrowed and his voice rumbled. "You know what I want?"

"What?"

"I want my feckin sword back, you jackass."

Rucksack spat in Guru Deep's eye.

Guru Deep gasped and stepped backward again, but Rucksack gave him no pause. Guru Deep swung his sword, faster and faster. The men's movements were a blur—but moment by moment, Guru Deep was losing his ground, moving backward step by step. Rucksack never attacked, only defended, but with every dodge and parry, every redirection and feint, soon the two men were standing in the lobby of the Lotus.

They paused. Guru Deep looked around, uncertain as people began to stare. He lowered the sword, keeping it ready yet out of sight.

"What's it going to be, Oh Great Shining Teeth That Need A Pint O' Toothpaste A Day?" said Rucksack. "Going to have at me in front o' all your associates? How will that be for business?"

"You won't leave here alive."

"You won't kill me," said Rucksack. "You'd get bored."

"You should've died in The Blast," said Guru Deep.

"I have a way o' disappointing expectations," said Rucksack. "I know, I know. I should've died in Kyoto too. It's a shame your dad only got to nick my swords. What a pity for you that I can't die in all the times and places and manners you see fit."

"One will suffice."

Guru Deep ran forward, back into the corridor, and raised his sword overhead. As Rucksack stepped forward he flung his scabbard upward, bashing Guru Deep across the knobs of his wrists as the Great Leader cried out in pain and fury.

The sword clattered onto the floor. Before Guru Deep could react, Rucksack stepped behind him, spun, and smacked Guru Deep on the back of the neck with the scabbard. The man in the orange suit crumpled to the floor.

Rucksack kneeled down. "You're going to pass out," he said. "But before you do, I want you to know something. You have a destiny too, Guru Deep, and it will never change: I will always stop you." Rucksack smiled. "One day it will indeed be just you and me. The way it was always meant to be. Maybe here in this grand wee lobby. Maybe in Kyoto again. Who knows. But no matter how you come at me, no matter what strategy or weapon you send my way, I will stop you. I will keep besting you until the day I stop you for good. For now, though, I'll settle for taking back my other sword—and then, and then, you arrogant bastard, my friends and I are going to do what you dread."

Guru Deep passed out. Rucksack sheathed the other katana, turned toward the service entrance, and ran like hell out of the Lotus.

"WILL WE BE SAFE here?" Zara asked as Branwen unlocked the flat. Everyone went inside.

"For now, as safe as we will be anywhere else," Branwen replied.

"Got room for one more?" said a voice in the hallway.

"I'm glad you're okay," said Branwen. "Oh, and you got your other sword back."

Rucksack smiled. "He practically gave it to me."

Inside, Branwen closed the door and said, "How long do you think we have?"

"Thirty minutes, tops," said Arthur. "They'll have your address. Guru Deep will surely have his people on the way to check your flat, and either contain or kill us if they find us here."

"Good point," said Branwen. "We'll need clothes, food, homebrewing gear. Just the essentials."

"Brewing gear?" said Zara. "We've got nowhere to go, and you're worried about homebrew?"

"Oh, we've got somewhere to go," said Branwen. She walked over to the table, where two boxes sat side by side. *Thank you Jade,* she thought. "Grab what you can, all of you," said Branwen, "starting with these."

"Where are we going?" Rucksack asked.

Branwen held up the first box, which was full of money. "We're going to rent a flat," Branwen said. She raised the second box. Inside was malted and roasted barley, a container of yeast slurry, and some bags of hops. "Then we're going to brew a batch of GPS like the world has never seen. Now let's get to work."

FECKNISS AND GURU DEEP stepped into the blackened, hot ruin of the underground prison. In the room beyond the open door, water dripped and thick swirling smoke obscured the room. In the walls, fans whirred and whined as they worked to clear the air.

"I should have stopped them," said Feckniss.

"I don't blame you," replied Guru Deep. "I blame myself. I let them live because I wanted to torment Rucksack. That was my flaw. My error. Our old enmity blurred my focus." He smiled. "But for the last time. When next Rucksack and I meet, I won't make that mistake again."

The room cleared more.

"When will that be?" asked Feckniss.

The fans took out the rest of the smoke, and at last the room was clear. The men stepped inside the room —then stopped.

The words were rough and angular, scratched in haste, but no less terrible:

BRING BACK THE BEER.

A bolt of fear coursed through Feckniss, but Guru Deep laughed. "I would expect it will be very, very soon."

IV

TWO WEEKS LATER, in a London that drank a beer it hated, the woman walked and rode and wandered all over the city. Everywhere she went, she stopped for a moment. Everywhere she stopped, she left something behind.

Wherever she left it, she gave no notice or got anyone's attention. If anything, she made sure no one was watching her.

Some secrets are best left in the plain open.

Her smile she took with her. Small and thin, but there. Her quiet joy, her growing hope, shone like candlelight. In the day it was easily unnoticed, but even if no one saw it shining, she knew it was there.

Whenever she left, someone saw the back of a woman in a long dark coat and a dark hat, camouflaged by the fog. She was a mirage. She was a ghost. She was really there, as real as real. Everyone saw her. No one saw her.

After the fog had closed in around where the woman had been, the people would then wonder who she was and why she had stopped there. At the stoop by their front door. At the outside table of the cafe or the pub. At the pocket of a man standing on the bus or a woman standing on the train. At park benches and the backs of taxis. All over London, she had paused.

Where she paused, the people found what she left.

A brown glass bottle, sealed with a black cap.

The cap was unadorned. The bottle was blank. Dark liquid lay inside, still yet also seeming to wink, to tap a finger to the side of the nose, to say, "*Shhh.* Not yet. But soon."

On the neck of each bottle had been tied a length of rough brown twine. On the twine was a note.

Each person read the note. Each person nodded and smiled. And either out loud to someone with them, or inside as a promise and a prayer, each person said, "I will."

"DO YOU REALLY THINK it will work?" Zara asked as she set a cup of tea in front of Branwen, then hung up her sister's coat and hat. Her walking was improving, and this morning was the first time she'd moved around without the crutches.

"I do," said Branwen as she sat down. "These past two weeks have proven what we suspected. People are resisting DSL more than Guru Deep expected. I'll bet my hops that announcement tomorrow is some sort of production ramp-up, or a temporary special, something like that. He needs to makes waves to tighten his grip on the world, but it's been more elusive than he expected." She raised the mug. "And thank you, by the way. My feet are killing me. Thank goodness that was the last of it. We've done what we can. Now we have to do the hardest part."

"What's that?" Zara asked.

"Trust."

Branwen picked up the box on the table. Most of the money was spent now, on their costs for the flat, food, and brewing ingredients. "We were able to do this because of the money in this box," she said. "What people gave us because they believe in us."

"In you, you mean," said Zara. She shook her head. "I'm sorry. I shouldn't have said that."

"It's okay. But Zara, people gave this to both of us."

"No, it's not okay." Zara sat down and looked at her sister. "All this time you've been leading us, little sister. I'm so proud of you. These past two weeks have been a blur. We've never brewed so hard in our lives. But you've not just been a brewer. You really are na Grúdairí. More than that. You've been like a captain. A general. You've led. All of us, all of this, wouldn't be happening without you. Rucksack was right. Gabsir was right. You are the key to GPS coming back. It's lost without you. You're a grúdaire through and through, and more. None of this has been easy for me, but I was wrong to be angry at you."

"I lied to you though," replied Branwen. "I'm so sorry for that. I hid this from you."

"But you aren't hiding it now. It makes me prouder than I could ever say, to see you are living who you are." Zara's smile was bittersweet. "I hope someday I can do that too."

Branwen squeezed Zara's hand. "You will, big sister. You will."

Arthur and Rucksack came into the flat and took off their coats. "Bloody fog," said Rucksack. "I've never seen London so dim and depressed."

Zara got them tea as well, and they all sat at the table together. "Everything is out, and we got what we needed," said Arthur. "I still can't believe we're doing that part."

Rucksack chuckled. "Guru Deep gets the credit for that part," he said. "It's all thanks to a little something he told me."

"Jade also confirmed," said Arthur. "It's done. Except for one thing."

"What happened?" Branwen asked.

"One o' the cases disappeared," said Rucksack. "We had finished unloading one, then turned around and the other was gone. No idea what happened to it."

"No point worrying about it," said Branwen.

"Now we wait for tomorrow," said Zara, "and Guru Deep's big announcement in the Lotus Plaza."

"Actually," said Arthur, "we have one more thing to do." He looked at Rucksack. "Starting with something that it's time to tell you."

"The message from my father."

"It only seems right that it's here. With everyone."

Rucksack closed his eyes and squeezed his left hand shut. "Okay."

"Jagathi's instruction was that when the time was right, the brewmaster of First Call was to tell you that your father forgives you."

Rucksack looked away.

Arthur continued. "But more than that. He said he knew it had to happen, and he wasn't sorry that it did. That it was part of your path. Part of what you had to learn, in order to truly achieve your destiny. He wanted you to know that the key to destiny was not in grand plans, but in living by the moment, accepting what came along for what it was, and doing what you could with what you had. If you could do that, then what happened would never happen again—and you would become who you wanted and needed to be."

A tear rolled down Rucksack's face.

"Maybe I'm learning something after all," he said simply. "Thank you."

Arthur leaned forward. "I once asked you to trust me, and you have. I cannot tell you how grateful I am for this. But in return I promised to tell you the truth, about me, about Samara, about the end of GPS. That time has come, and I am going to make good. But first I have to tell you something else: Tomorrow, we must go to First Call."

"Why?" said Zara. "That's beyond dangerous."

"It's also beyond necessary. There's something there, in the office, that I have to have in order for our plan to fully work."

"Then it is indeed time you came clean, Arthur," said Rucksack.

Arthur nodded. Then he told them everything.

ANOTHER DREARY LONDON MORNING misted and drizzled into a half-light that barely resembled day. After instructing his driver to wait in the alley where they had stopped, Feckniss had verified his device with the driver. Now he wandered around the wreckage and rubble of First Call Brewing, not looking for anything as much as he was looking away from one thing. His gaze always came back to it though. How it repelled them. How it eluded them. How it mocked them.

The scuffed metal box that had been Arthur's office so far had proven impenetrable. Drills, acids, picks, heavy equipment, tactically placed small explosives— all ineffective against whatever alloy comprised the thick shield. Feckniss had suggested it didn't matter how they broke into the box, since they were just going to destroy everything anyway. But Guru Deep had rejected the idea. Before destruction had to come understanding, he had said. Anything of use had to be known. Apprehension would determine destiny.

I still wish we could just blow the damn thing up, Feckniss thought. *At least then it wouldn't keep mocking me, taunting me to try again.*

A beam of light broke through the clouds. Feckniss turned away. His eyes were still sensitive after the damn ex-janitor had sprayed him in the face. He knew the damage could have been worse, but in a way it had been. *I couldn't even get used to the idea of being invincible,* he thought. *Then I find out I have a weakness.*

But that was all right. Sooner or later, he'd cross paths with her again.

Branwen, he thought. *What you do to me, I will return tenfold.*

Voices made him run, and he ducked down behind a pile of rubble. Peeking around, he saw all four of them, wearing hats and long coats, walking toward the former brewery. Rucksack. Zara. Arthur.

And Branwen.

Feckniss smiled. *There may be satisfaction sooner than I'd hoped.* His anger doubled when he thought not only of his own pain, but of the wrath that Nia Fox had faced in the aftermath of the sword fight and escape.

Guru Deep at first had blamed Nia Fox for the theft of Rucksack's sword. But Feckniss had spoken up for her, vouching for Nia, revealing that she had indeed been duped. Feckniss explained that Branwen had posed as a so-called expert on the sword by using her knowledge of Deep Inc. to foil everyone in the building, from the security staff in the lobby to the very assistant of Guru Deep himself.

The Great Leader's disappointment had been terrible to behold—but at least his rage had not found a home in consequences for Nia Fox. Guru Deep had accepted their stories, and for now Nia was still at her desk—at the least because Feckniss knew as well as Guru Deep that Nia was indispensable to him at such a precarious time in the company's strategies. The last thing Guru Deep wanted was to have to train up a new assistant, Feckniss had reminded him.

Feckniss feared for Nia though. Guru Deep's trust of his assistant always had been ironclad, but now when he looked at her or called her on the intercom, Feckniss could perceive the slightest doubt, the tiniest hesitation, the beginning of reluctance.

I may have bought Nia time, he thought, *but I don't know how much.*

If only I knew what had really happened—and how much I may have risked in helping her.

Now, Branwen and the others approached the metal box. Arthur stood in front of it, though from where he hid Feckniss couldn't see what the former brewmaster was doing.

Then a door opened, and Arthur went inside.

Go after him! Get inside! Overpower them all, destroy them all if you have to, but get inside and make that door stay open!

Feckniss's muscles tensed. He started to draw back so he could leap forward and sprint across the rubble.

He almost did.

And do what? he thought. *If I can get Arthur when he comes out, or get Branwen, then perhaps we can use them to get inside.* Feckniss smiled. *Or just get revenge. Guru Deep will find a way inside eventually. It doesn't have to be right now.*

Instead, he stayed still.

After a few minutes, Arthur came back out of the box. He held a thick file, and everyone seemed happy. The door closed. Arthur and the others began walking away from the office, their backs to Feckniss.

Go.

He rose quietly and moved like a shadow across the rubble without making a sound. He paused behind the box, looking for any indication of what Arthur had done, but found none.

It's time.

Feckniss pulled the device from his pocked. He pressed a button three times, the agreed signal.

As the foursome neared the curb, Feckniss ran like hell.

He was almost at them when Rucksack turned, pulling the sword off his shoulder. Arthur stepped away, putting the file behind his back. Zara picked up a chunk of brewery.

But Feckniss ignored them all, avoided them all, and barreled forward on the only path that mattered to him. She had no time to react. With one powerful sweep of his arm, Feckniss hit Branwen in the temple, picked her up as she fell, and kept running.

I'm stronger too! he thought. *Eyes be damned, I will be unstoppable!*

Perfectly timed with Feckniss's signal, the driver had adjusted his speed and course to arrive at the curb and spring the door switch just as Feckniss arrived. The car barely slowed as Feckniss threw Branwen and himself inside.

Then they were speeding away from the wreckage of First Call, and from the shouts of the three people left behind.

Branwen's head swung, then she looked up with vacant eyes. "You again," she said. "Fecking feckwit."

He slapped her. "You'll remain alive and in one piece," Feckniss said. "For now. And only out of my respect for Guru Deep. After today's announcement, though, he will decide your fate." Feckniss smiled. "And I will carry it out." He saw his reflection in the car window, and for a moment wondered if the sickly yellow glaze in the eyes was still just part of the reflection.

"Back to the Lotus," Feckniss said. "Take us to the platform at the Maya Plaza, where Guru Deep is preparing the future."

ARTHUR SUSPECTED THAT IN all the cities in the world, the moment a person needed a taxi one was nowhere to be found. He and the others ran from First Call, looking everywhere for a cab.

Now, at last, they found not just one—but two. Arthur flagged them both down.

"Why do we need two?" asked Rucksack.

"We're out of time," said Arthur. "You and Zara go back to the flat and get everything, then come to the Maya Plaza. Remember, this has to happen at ten o'clock, or it doesn't happen at all."

"Where are you going?" asked Zara.

"To play my part," replied Arthur. "This next bit is my responsibility. Get there as soon as you can."

"We have to help my sister," said Zara. "The hell with the plan."

Arthur shook his head. "Branwen has put everything she is into what we're doing today. She wouldn't want you to stop for her sake. It's true, and you know it as well as I do." Arthur stared Zara in the eye. "I've already lost my best friend in the world, the person who mattered to me more than anything," said Arthur. "And it was my fault. Zara, I will do everything in my power to save Branwen. I know the pain you feel and the pain you fear—and if I have to, I'll give my own life to save hers."

"But that bastard, he could be doing anything."

Arthur shook his head. "He's not. Branwen is by no means safe, but she's okay. For now. Guru Deep never knew Branwen needed to matter, and that's a mistake he wants to rectify. He'll have made it clear to his little minion that if she is found, she is to be unharmed. Guru Deep is going to be too busy finishing preparations for today's announcement—he'll trust that he has Branwen contained, and he'll deal with her later. That's our chance. It's the only chance we have, but it's what we've got."

"Then Rucksack should go with you."

"You need him more than I do right now," Arthur replied. "Your leg is stronger, but—"

"But my leg isn't strong enough for me to carry everything on my own." Zara looked away, bitterness in her eyes. "Fine."

"Do you need anything from the flat, Arthur?" said Rucksack.

Arthur patted the file and he patted his coat pockets. "I've got everything I need. Besides, Jade London will be in place soon too."

Arthur's taxi sped through London toward the Lotus and the sprawling green park surrounding the orange building. As the taxi wound through the streets, he thought about how they had worked together. How Branwen's brewing was paralleled only by her leadership. How they just might pull this off. And he thought of Gabsir, whom they had all mourned with every moment.

I'm going to make things right, my friend. If only I'd told you. Maybe we'd be doing this together.

Looking down at the thick file on his lap, Arthur kept thinking about the office. How something had looked different. He put those concerns out of his mind though—at least for now. *I have to focus on what's to come,* he thought. *For all our sakes.*

With a bittersweet smile, Arthur started taking things out of his pockets. When the taxi arrived at the Maya Plaza, a different person stepped out.

THE CAR ARRIVED AT the back of the Lotus, far away from the crowd gathering before the stage set up in the Maya Plaza. The driver came back with two people and a wheeled gurney. They covered her with a sheet. Feckniss led them around the back of the building and waited.

Guru Deep and Nia Fox walked out. In one hand, Nia held a clipboard. In the other hand, voices murmured and scratched over a two-way radio.

"All is on schedule," said Nia as the two walked west, toward the doors on the opposite end of the lobby. "The stage is assembled and final checks were just completed. Electricals and communication checks are being finalized at this moment. All relevant newspaper and radio media are setting up, and the public, due to our announcements and their innate curiosity, are in the plaza. We are ready, sir."

"Excellent as always," Guru Deep said. "And all personnel are out?"

"We are the last ones to leave the building," Nia replied. "When you and I walk out the doors, the Lotus will be locked down. No one in or out until you or I return."

"What about Feckniss?" Guru Deep asked.

"Feckniss was supposed to oversee the final preparations," Nia replied, a quaver in her voice. "But he left a while ago, saying he had an urgent matter to attend to.

"Where is he?"

"Here sir." Feckniss pointed to the gurney. "A last-minute difficulty came up, but I turned it into an opportunity."

Nia and Guru Deep turned and stared in surprise. "What the hell is that?" asked Guru Deep.

Feckniss pulled back the sheet. "The one you wanted." He explained what had happened.

Nia's eyes widened. "Is she—?"

"She is unconscious," Feckniss replied. He stared hard at Guru Deep. "But it wasn't easy."

"You'll have your chance. Your initiative and obedience impress me, Feckniss—as does your insight. I would expect nothing less." Guru Deep paused. "Take her to the back of the stage, and keep her bound, guarded, and quiet. We'll deal with her after the announcement." He turned to his assistant. "Ms. Fox, what do you think of Feckniss?"

Moments passed before Nia spoke. "I think, sir, that we can expect big surprises from him."

"Thank you," said Feckniss.

Guru Deep narrowed his eyes. "As long as they're ones I expect, that will be fine."

Nia's radio squawked. Then it squawked some more. She held the radio to her ear, trying to listen to the overlapping voices—then she began walking faster. "There's some sort of situation. We'd better get out there and get this done as soon as possible."

"What's the problem?" said Guru Deep.

"Unclear on the details, sir," said Nia Fox. "Security just reported a man and a woman slipping into the secure area near the stage."

NO GUARDS STOPPED THEM. No one looked at them twice. No one, in fact, noticed the woman and the man at all.

Anyone paying attention to the area cared far more about the hundreds of people teeming through the plaza, and about the dozens of media vans—with magazine, newspaper, and radio personnel from all over the world—set up at every available inch of space.

The crowd was far larger than expected, and more were arriving with every minute as ten o'clock came closer. Anyone paying attention also was far more curious about why so many of those people were carrying beer bottles, each sealed with a black cap, and each with a note tied on.

"I can't believe no one is stopping us," said the man. "Or confiscating the beer."

"I bet security is dying to." The woman chuckled. "But you forget. The Maya Plaza is a public park. No one can be stopped here. Besides, where better than a good park to enjoy a good beer? Guru Deep isn't as all-powerful as he likes to think."

The man nodded. "Let's remind him of that."

From the back of the growing crowd, the woman and the man took in the sight of all the people converging on the platform. Scaffolding elevated the simple stage, which was flanked on both sides by speakers. In the middle stood a metal microphone stand.

"Listen to the people," Rucksack said. "It's bloody working. I can hear it in the accents. I can smell it in the air. People are here from all over London. England. Scotland. Wales. Even Ireland. Feck, I think there's even some folks from feckin Europe. Maybe even the feckin USA."

"Spoken like a true lady," replied Zara. "By the way, you look good with long hair. And you know, you usually can't tell from the black clothes you wear, but that orange dress really brings out your figure."

"Orange was always my good color. Bloody wig itches worse than bedbugs though," said Rucksack, his long coat trailing behind him as they walked faster.

"What's with the black then?"

"A reminder," he said, his voice suddenly grave. "That I've still much to regain and much to put right. I've regained," he said, reaching back and tapping one of the scabbards. "Hopefully today I'll put some more right." He smiled. "Such a nice compliment from you though, Zara. If I didn't know better, you saucy chap, I'd think you were hitting on me."

Zara chuckled and looked down at her gray suit and orange tie. "Any sign of Branwen or Arthur?"

Rucksack shook his head. "Branwen is most likely backstage. Probably all they had time for. I see no direct sign o' Arthur." He pointed to the big, muscled men all over the stage and in front of it, between the platform and the people. "But judging by the way those familiar-looking security meatballs are trying not to look frantic, things are going to plan. For now."

"Then hitch up that dress," said Zara. "Arthur's doing his part. Let's do ours."

As they neared the middle of the crowd, Rucksack and Zara began to chant, roaring in unison with the people around them.

"Bring back GPS! Bring back the beer! Bring back GPS! Bring back the beer!"

FECKNISS LOOKED ALL AROUND. He had not expected this. No one had expected this. Staring out at the crowd was bad enough. But the crowd was ten times what they had anticipated, and even bigger than their worst-case scenario. *We don't have enough men to control them,* Feckniss thought. *Not even close.*

The sheer numbers alone were daunting, but the chanting...

The chanting didn't stop. Nor did it become aggressive or heated. They simply chanted, loudly but calmly. *They're like waves,* Feckniss thought. *Pounding on the beach and seeming to do nothing, but never stopping, never stopping...*

His radio crackled about how Guru Deep was almost in place. He looked at his watch. It was almost ten—and then Guru Deep would make his announcement. But would people listen? Would they interrupt? Interfere?

We can't have this chanting going out with the message. It'll ruin everything.

Sweat dampened Feckniss's clothes. *I hate being up here,* he thought. *I want to run. Have to get out of here—*

But he thought of how disappointed Guru Deep would be.

I have to get this under control.

Trying to stop his trembling, Feckniss walked onto the stage and went to the standing microphone. "People of London, th-thank you for coming," he said. His voice shook. So many people.

Staring at me. They're all staring at me. What do they see?

The chanting continued.

"G-Guru Deep w-will begin in a moment. I'm s-sure you all w-want to hear what he has to s-say."

The chanting continued.

Do they even know I'm up here?

Feckniss fought to steady his voice, to find the strength and command he had felt when he had taken Branwen. But there were so many people. So many. "If you can give me a moment of your time, I have a few announcements to make before the announcement."

The chanting continued. Then a voice rose above it.

"Shut up, boy."

Feckniss looked around. "Who said that?"

A tall woman in a dark coat, a hat atop her long hair, walked across the stage. At the sight of her, the chanting stopped.

No wonder, Feckniss thought. *Everyone must be too shocked—*

Feckniss heard the chatter on his radio. "She snuck in! Who the hell is that woman? Stop her! Get her out of here!"

The woman reached out a dark hand and took the microphone from Feckniss. "If you had something worth listening too, then maybe the people here would give a damn." The woman's voice was far deeper than Feckniss would have expected, and she continued to speak. "But I sure as hell have something to say that they want to hear."

The woman's eyes told Feckniss everything. The woman was afraid. Terrified. As if she'd been tucked away, out of sight, for the better part of a lifetime, and dreaded being in front of so many people, out in the wide world. But she was here, and with every word the courage in her voice beat back the fear.

But where is Guru Deep? He should be here by now, Feckniss thought. *Who the hell is this woman?* Then he began to recognize her.

Voices crackled on his radio. "What happened to Guru Deep?"

Another voice said, "Someone unauthorized was sighted near the Great Leader..."

Then another said, "We have visual. An unidentified person is pulling Guru Deep away from the stage. We are intercepting..."

The woman stared into Feckniss's soul. Her eyes narrowed, and her voice held a power like Guru Deep's.

"Now get out of here."

Feckniss stepped away from the mic. He walked backward, unable to take his eyes off the woman, unable to speak, unable to do anything but what he had been told.

Then the woman took off her hat—and her hair with it. The long coat dropped to the stage. The surprise at seeing the dead brewmaster hushed the audience. And standing before the crowd, before Feckniss, before the world, Arthur Celbridge, the last brewmaster of First Call, stood in a dark suit.

At the back of the stage, Feckniss forgot to look behind him. He slipped off the elevated platform, realizing too late that he had run out of room to backpedal. Arms flailing, grasping for anything, Feckniss plummeted through the air. His head smacked the ground below. The world turned as black as the only pint of GPS he'd ever had—but as it did, Feckniss saw his wristwatch.

Ten o'clock.

His radio crackled: "Get him off the stage! All of you! Now!"

Too late, Feckniss thought. *The world is already listening.*

Then Feckniss passed out, and Arthur began to speak.

"MY NAME IS ARTHUR Celbridge," he said, trying to sound brave but wincing as his voice cracked with nerves. "As you may have guessed, I am not dead after all." As he spoke, though, he wondered who would pull him down first. The burly men were converging now, two from the sides of the stage, two having climbed up from the grounds below. Their arms were bigger around than Arthur's head.

I'm so close, Arthur thought. *So close at last, after all these years. I'm ready. I had no idea how it might finally come about in the end, but it's here, and I'm here, and please oh please whatever might be up there watching over this world, please don't let it end like this.*

"Please," said Arthur, his voice booming around the plaza.

Of course, he remembered. *I have a microphone.*

"Help."

The stage seemed impossibly large and tall, yet also smaller than where Arthur stood. Too small to stand. Too big for anyone to help. Too unapproachable. Too terrifying. From out there in the sea of people, Arthur looked for ripples of change, of support. But saw none. People milled around. People stared. But none came.

The first burly man was reaching for Arthur. *You might have done a lot of desk work lately,* Arthur thought, *but heaving all those bags of grain and kegs of stout over the years has still left you with plenty of muscle. Time to use it.*

The punch knocked the first man backward. Not out, as Arthur had hoped, but back. It was a start—

But it had also been a distraction, all the second burly man had needed to grab Arthur's shoulders from behind. Arthur struggled, but the grip was already set. The third and fourth swung down and picked up Arthur's legs.

I'm going to be carried out of here like a sack of malt.

The first man stood and rubbed his face for a moment.

At least I've left him with a good bruise to remember me by.

"Not bad," said the man, his grin full of holes. "My turn."

His fist had to be bigger than the moon. It moved in a blur toward Arthur's face.

So much for my moment, Arthur thought.

From the crowd, a voice—a familiar voice, Arthur could've sworn he knew it—cried out again and again, "You heard the man! Help him! Help him!"

From the sea of people, ripples had come.

Then waves.

The fist stopped.

Arthur hadn't seen it happen, hadn't seen the people come onto the stage. The first man suddenly was moving backward, being pulled away by two men and by the woman who had stopped the fist, catching it as if it were a baseball. The grip on Arthur's shoulders disappeared. The other men disappeared in a swarm of people. He couldn't see their faces—but then he saw one, a blur of an older face, and long white hair—

It can't be, Arthur thought. *It can't be. But it must be, it must be—*

The old lady smacked one of the men with her umbrella.

It's not, Arthur thought. *Dammit. Why couldn't that have been you after all, Gabsir?*

Then like the sea, the wave of people receded. The people had returned to the crowd. The burly men were gone. Arthur stood on the stage alone.

They helped me, Arthur thought. *All these years I've been so afraid of people. But when I needed it most, they helped me. For all the times I've lived in fear, it's time I lived in something else.*

Mustering courage, Arthur once again stepped up to the microphone.

It's time, Arthur. All these years. All this isolation.

No more.

And with that, Arthur Ardclough Celbridge, the last and former brewmaster of First Call Brewing, a subsidiary of Deep Inc., began to speak for the last time.

"WHEN I WAS STILL too young to legally drink," Arthur began, this time his voice steady and calm, "I was already trying to work at First Call Brewing. It's the only thing I ever wanted. The only place I ever wanted to be. My dad taught me to make beer at home, and he told me I took to brewing like no one he'd ever seen. He told me I made beer as if it flowed through my veins.

"Every day, both before school and after school, I would go to the gates and wait for hours. Every day, a man named Gabsir Abrigs would eventually come to the gates and tell me to go away. After months of this, Gabsir asked me if I could carry a fifty-pound bag of malted barley. I told him I'd lift the bag with my teeth if I had to."

All around Lotus Plaza, the people were silent. Arthur tried to ignore not only them, but the millions of people around the world listening, and the millions more who would soon be reading these words in newspapers and magazines everywhere.

Now and again we get a chance to change the world, he thought. *Today is my moment—but the world isn't the only thing about to change.*

"I'd work in the brewery after school and homework, with an expectation from Gabsir that I would keep up with studies and family. Over time," Arthur continued, "I met everyone at the brewery. Men and women from all nations and cultures, young and old. It was a merry bunch. It was"—he paused, deep emotion surging through him—"the best time of my life.

"Eventually I met the brewmaster, an amazing woman named Samara. She took an interest in me, would often come around and help me with this or that, or just talk to me about my life and my day, how school was, what I liked and looked forward to. Little things. At the time I thought it was just someone being nice. Only as I got older did I realize that something else was happening. After all, the head of something that spans the entire world doesn't just drop everything to talk to some kid who barely knows malt from hops.

"Samara's true purpose became clear some years after I was grown, and working at First Call as a full-fledged grúdaire. This was right around the time when Deep Inc. was able to take control of First Call. I had been spending more and more time with Samara, learning the business and leadership side of brewing, and all the time having no idea why I was learning about the brewery beyond the moment-to-moment process of making beer.

"On that day, the day all the papers were signed and the ownership transferred, Samara told me her plans. Supported by Gabsir, she told me that I would follow her as brewmaster. And for that, she felt sorry for me."

Arthur paused. Murmurs went through the crowd. The feeling surged again, a double helix of conflicting, contrasting emotions—sadness and relief, longing and release, comfort and terror. *At long last,* Arthur thought, *the truth.*

"Samara confessed that leadership would now be far less about running a brewery and no longer about ensuring that Galway Pradesh Stout was what it must always be."

Shouts came up from the crowd, but Arthur pressed on. "First Call, and my leadership as brewmaster, now would be about something quite different: preventing Guru Deep from gaining influence in First Call. Blocking his every effort to warp us, or manipulate us, or make us and the beer less than it was supposed to be."

Arthur sighed. "But even that, she told me, would be futile—and it was not going to be my true purpose. Samara knew she could keep Guru Deep at bay during her tenure, but she knew in time that would become harder and harder. She knew we had two options. Ultimately, First Call would either have to regain its freedom, or it would die."

Arthur found Zara and Rucksack in the crowd, and they nodded at each other. "So Samara told me the terrible, terrible truth, a truth she carried in secret until her death. As she carried the secret, so have I, except that I have carried it alone. I could tell no one, not even Gabsir, my friend and longtime second-in-command. Sometimes I tried to deny it even to myself, but there is no denying the truth. First Call's choice was not to be destroyed or to regain its freedom."

Arthur took a deep breath, then continued. "The truth... is that it would have to do both. Just as illness took away Samara's life little by little, Guru Deep's budget cuts, combined with my and Samara's own efforts, gradually degraded First Call more and more and more. In order to be free again, First Call first would have to die. And I, the brewmaster, the leader, the one that every First Call brewery and all na Grúdairí looked to for guidance, example, leadership —I would be the one to strike the death blow."

Arthur reached down into the coat on the platform. He stood back up and raised high a thick beige file. "I struck the blow. But Samara handed me the weapon. She gave me something more though. She also gave me the tools to regain our freedom. The tools... to bring back the beer."

Some cheers went up from the crowd. "When Samara sold First Call to Deep Inc.," said Arthur, "people called it Samara's Folly. I hated it. Everyone hated it. People thought she had insulted the brewery, sold us out, mocked all that we had been. But she and I knew the truth. But knowing the truth and accepting the truth are rarely the same thing. For years I have railed against this fate that we chose—the decision to destroy what we hoped to save."

You've got them, Arthur thought. *Bring it home.*

"I wish I could say that my example has been strong, bold, and fearless." Arthur shook his head. "But I am not perfect. I have my own fears, my own weaknesses, and as a result I have made plenty of my own mistakes—some far worse than others. I have feigned weakness in order to hide purpose, but I have also lived in fear. Fear of being wrong. Fear of destroying what I loved, but being unable to save it."

"You have far more to fear now than you ever did," said a rumbling voice.

A flash of orange caught Arthur's eye. Guru Deep strode onto the stage.

GURU DEEP STOPPED NEXT to Arthur. They glared at each other. Then Guru Deep laughed.

"You finally left your office," he said, "and left wherever you've been hiding these last two weeks, but you are nothing more than a wet coaster, Arthur. Other than waving about your dirty laundry for a global audience, what do you think you're going to accomplish today?"

Arthur smiled. "I am going to bring back the beer. I am going to bring back First Call." He shook his head. "No, not me." He swept his arm out over the crowd. "We are. All of us."

Guru Deep laughed harder. "A noble quest, my dear former employee. But a failed one. You see, Arthur, former-brewmaster-of-nothing-anymore, I know something you don't."

"You usually think you do," Arthur replied. "What is it this time?"

Guru Deep's smile wavered a moment but came back bright as ever. "I have nothing to fear from you."

"Oh, but you do," Arthur replied. "A certain someone told me exactly what you fear: a man born of man, and a woman born of man." He smiled. "Well, I can't speak for the first part, but I'd say this man pulled off the part of a woman enough to be exactly what you need to fear."

Something in Guru Deep seemed to hesitate, to draw back a moment, but he leaned in close to Arthur instead. "No matter," said Guru Deep, then he looked only at the audience. "Now that my former colleague has harangued you with his tale of woe and weakness, let us come to why we are really here today. I appreciate the love you demonstrate for our beloved Deep's Special Lager and how it makes Every Night Special. No wonder you've all brought bottles of it with you today."

Guru Deep stopped. He looked at the audience. No one was looking at him.

Then he heard laughter.

Turning his head, Guru Deep saw what everyone was looking at.

Standing tall before the audience, Arthur had reached down into the coat again. Now he held up a brown bottle with a tag on it, identical to the ones everyone in the crowd held.

"But you..." Guru Deep stammered, but could not continue.

Arthur Celbridge smiled. "My fear, not you, was nearly my undoing and the undoing of all I hold dear," the brewmaster said. "I was terrified of failure. But no more." His smile outshone Guru Deep's brightest. For a moment, the clouds lost their absolute hold on the sky, and a few beams of sunlight escaped.

"Bring back GPS!" Arthur cried. "Bring back the beer!"

One person clapped.

Then two. Then four. Then more.

Soon, everyone in the crowd began to clap, then to hoot and shout.

Out of sight of the public, people scurried about backstage. Arthur heard someone say something about an unidentified person, and an empty gurney.

As the people quieted once more, Arthur said the only thing that was left to say.

"People of the world," he said, "you found the beers, all over London, all over the world. You suspected what was inside." He looked at Guru Deep. "And you knew it sure as hell wasn't DSL."

People laughed. Arthur lowered the bottle, held up the little tag, and continued. "'Enjoy this at Guru Deep's announcement in the Maya Plaza.' You came. Your time, is now." He flipped over the tag. "'Bring back the beer!'"

"GURU DEEP GAVE BRANWEN the idea," Zara said to Rucksack. "We thought, well, if he can use time and place to pull off something big, then so can we."

"Using the beer and the announcement to coordinate people," said Rucksack. "It's brilliant. Now to see if the tag's P.S. works."

Zara smiled. "Ready to get that frock off?"

"You minx," said Rucksack, "I thought you'd never ask."

Rucksack took off his coat and Zara unzipped his dress. He wore his usual black clothes underneath. He felt for the two swords, making sure each loop was secure around its hilt. He sighed, then took the loop off one hilt. "Just in case," he said.

Around them, everyone in the crowd raised their bottles high, and so did Rucksack and Zara. Light glinted off a sea of brown glass—but inside each bottle, something else glowed.

Arthur brought the mic close and said, "Open your bottles!"

A near-simultaneous hiss went up from the entire crowd, and along with it an aroma that was bitter and smooth, sharp and refreshing.

"I hope they like the beer," Zara said. "For Branwen's sake."

"I hope they brought the money," Rucksack replied, "for all our sakes."

And then they drank.

AS THE PERFECT DARK liquid washed over his palate and his soul, for the first time, Arthur realized he could see it all. The path he was to follow now. What was to come. Who would go with him. And where that would go.

If I'm seeing this, he thought, *what's everyone else seeing?*

From the silence as people drank their Galway Pradesh Stouts, something new came.

THE WORLD BEGAN COMING back. With it came many noises, all of them frantic and urgent. Branwen opened her eyes. The voices around her became people, men who were ignoring her while they scrambled around, paying desperate attention to something else.

Branwen tried to sit up, but tight straps held her down. She tried to call out, but nearly choked on the material stuffing and covering her mouth.

The sounds around her told her where she was.

Almost right where I need to be, she thought. *Dammit. Now if only I could do something.*

One by one, the voices went silent as man by man fell to the ground.

From behind, a hand pulled the fabric out of her mouth, then loosened the straps. Once Branwen was free, a jerk of her rescuer's head told her to follow.

"If you insist," said Branwen. "Though I certainly wouldn't have expected you."

THE SHOUTS AND THE clapping began. Branwen smiled her thanks to the person next to her, then looked up at the stage. Arthur stood, beaming, pride and calmness on his face. Guru Deep stood silent, quaking with an anger that wanted to burst the seams of his suit.

Branwen giggled and looked around the crowd. For minutes it went on, the people exalting, the people laughing and hugging, telling each other what they had seen, what they knew would be before them.

Then little silences came. More and more people stopped laughing and shouting. Instead, they began looking at the stage, their faces suddenly grim.

Branwen turned back toward the stage. When she saw, she fell silent too.

Guru Deep was standing at the microphone.

And he was smiling.

When all was quiet, Guru Deep began to speak. Behind him, a dazed Feckniss stood.

"People of London. People of the world." He raised his arms wide. "You have had a special moment today. A final grace note of something that is no more. What a wonderful way to say good-bye."

Someone in the crowd shouted, "We're bringing back the beer!"

Guru Deep shrugged. "Galway Pradesh Stout, its recipe, and its secrets are all the property of Deep Inc., as are all assets, facilities, properties, and equipment of the entity formerly known as First Call Brewing," he said. "As you know, that beer and its brewing company are no more."

"Reopen First Call!" someone else shouted. "Bring back GPS!"

"All First Call facilities will be dismantled and sold for materials." Guru Deep's smile got even bigger. "Or for scrap. All attempting to illegally produce this beer will be prosecuted to the fullest extent of the law. Starting with those responsible for the trespassing, assault, and copycat theft that has happened today. Arthur Celbridge, you made this abomination and sent it out to people. You are responsible. I have the right to do all that is in my power."

Next to Branwen, her rescuer held up a tagged GPS bottle and glared. "I'm going to shove this bottle up his—"

"You won't have to," Branwen replied, with a smile to rival Guru Deep's. "Arthur's not done yet."

But her smile faded when Guru Deep stepped back. With a nod from him, burly men came out from behind the stage. They circled around Arthur and stood still. Then they drew their guns. The men held them pointed down, almost casually, but with a stance and a glint in the eye that said they could just as easily put a hole in anyone's day, and then go back to standing still.

"What's our move?" said the rescuer.

Branwen shook her head. "Not your move," she said. "Mine."

"You are not going to do what I think you're going to do."

"If this becomes a mob rushing the stage, people are going to get killed." Branwen smiled. "But if one person goes—the one person Guru Deep could want right now—no one gets hurt."

"You don't know that."

"No one ever knows what happens next," said Branwen, "but I understand now."

"You understand what?" said the rescuer. "You'd better be..."

But Branwen didn't hear the rest. She'd already walked onto the stage.

NO ONE STOPPED HER. Standing on the stage, Branwen looked Guru Deep and Feckniss in the eye. "You have the wrong person," she said. "Arthur didn't make the GPS. I did." Murmurs went up from the crowd.

"You," said Guru Deep.

"I'm not tied up anymore, no," Branwen replied. Then she grinned. "As a former employee of Deep Inc., I must tell you: your severance package sucks."

People laughed. *A good sign,* Branwen thought.

"Your termination can be discussed later." Guru Deep nodded. "And you can share in Arthur's punishment."

More men with guns approached Branwen.

"Before you do anything with me and Arthur," said Branwen, nodding toward the back of the Maya Plaza, "you should check the mail first."

A small truck pulled up to the edge of the plaza. The bright red words "England Post" shone against yellow-gold paint.

A woman got out. Even from the stage, Branwen could recognize Jade London, and was certain the bartender-turned-postal-worker winked at her, just before she cried, "Special delivery for the brewmaster of First Call!"

Walking through the crowd, Jade climbed up the stage and walked toward Arthur. The men with guns stiffened, and one blocked her way. She didn't hesitate. Stopping inches from one man's face, she said, "Obstructing a postal carrier's delivery of the post is punishable to the fullest extent of the law."

The man sneered. "What law?"

Branwen hardly saw Jade move, only heard the flat smacking sound, a strangely soft *oomph*, and the man's gasp. He slid to his knees, cupping his crotch.

"The natural law," she replied. "No one ever gets between the English and their mail."

The other men stepped back. All of them looked uncertain about firing their weapons in public, and under such strange circumstances.

Jade handed Arthur a large envelope and said, "The instructions are for it to be opened immediately." Then she left the stage.

Arthur ripped open the envelope. He pulled out a letter—and also something smaller.

"What is this?" said Guru Deep.

Arthur said nothing. Just closed his eyes for a moment and breathed in deeply. Branwen thought she saw tears at the corners of the brewmaster's eyes.

Then Arthur stared at Guru Deep. For a moment

he expected the sting of the fear, but it was gone. He smiled. "Welcome to the end of the end," Arthur said. "And the beginning of the beginning."

He brushed aside the men, walked to the microphone, raised up the letter that was inside the envelope, and began to read.

AS JADE LONDON OPENED the back door of the truck, another truck arrived, then two more, then three more, then four more. Altogether, eleven mail delivery trucks were parked at the edge of the plaza. Arthur tried to ignore all the hustle and bustle going on at their back doors.

"This came express from Kenya," Arthur said into the microphone, "the land of my birth and ancestry."

```
Dear Brewmaster,

A dear mutual friend in London
received a bottle of your endeavor and
immediately informed me of the plan. I
suspect what you are trying to do, and
you have my fullest support. The
enclosed represents not only my own
support, but also that of others in my
community. Their names and other
details are below.

Should you ever return to Kenya, I
hope we may have a GPS together.

Yours in renewal.
```

Arthur paused a moment to let it sink in. "In addition to the signature of the person who sent this, the names of fifty other people are listed," he said at last. Then he held up the smaller piece of paper. "All of them contributed to the funds on this check."

"A check?" Guru Deep ran to Arthur. "For what?"

Arthur smiled. "To buy First Call, of course."

Guru Deep stepped back.

In the crowd, people were cheering, but not only for the letter and the check inside. The postal carriers, all ten, were now approaching the stage. Each pushed a cart. Each cart was loaded with fat bags of mail.

In front, Jade shouted again. "Special delivery for the brewmaster of First Call!"

One by one, the postal carriers heaved bag after bag onto the stage. "I hope I don't have to sign for each of these," said Arthur.

"Given the circumstances, we'll skip it," Jade said. "These have come from all over. London and England, of course. Wales and Scotland. Ireland. Egypt and Morocco. Germany and Sweden. Russia. India and Australia. Thailand and Japan. The USA and Canada. Guatemala and Brazil." She smiled. "And this is just the morning post and express items. I think it's safe to say there hasn't been this much global outpouring of support to London since The Blast."

Guru Deep kicked a bag. It didn't budge. "It doesn't matter," he said. "First Call is not for sale."

In the crowd below, people began coming forward. Arthur saw Zara and Rucksack come to the front and set empty bags on the ground in front of the platform. One by one, everyone in the crowd came up and placed an envelope in one of the bags. Each person would look at Arthur and Branwen, then say, "Bring back the beer."

Guru Deep went to the microphone. "First Call is not for sale," he repeated.

Setting aside a few opened letters and envelopes, Arthur went to the microphone as well. "Of course we'll have to do a proper count," he said, "but it's safe to say that each one of these envelopes contains funds from First Call supporters who want the brewery sold and made an independent company again, and who want the production of GPS to resume."

Guru Deep sneered. "Just because someone offers to buy something doesn't mean I am obligated to sell it."

Arthur smiled. "That, Guru Deep, depends on the offer."

"What do you mean?"

"Faddah Rucksack!" Arthur called. "The rules require a witness. Please come forward and serve in this capacity."

The burly men raised their guns.

Rucksack stepped onto the stage. "Put those down before you hurt yourselves," he said.

The men didn't budge.

"I might be known for talking a lot," said Rucksack, his voice rumbling like a tiger beginning to roar, "but I don't like to say the same thing twice."

The men laid down their guns. At a nod from Guru Deep, they left the stage.

Rucksack stood next to Arthur, who held up the thick file again. The paper had yellowed with time, but otherwise was in excellent condition.

"What is that?" Guru Deep said.

"This," Arthur replied, "is the original sales document that transferred ownership of First Call

Brewing to Deep Inc." He turned to the last page and showed it to Guru Deep. "As you see here, we have the relevant signatures. I recognize Brewmaster Samara's."

"And that's mine," Guru Deep replied. "Yes, yes, it's the document."

Arthur shuffled some pages. "You see, too, here, the section Conditions for Resale."

"Yes," said Guru Deep. "What of it?" Then his dark face turned pale.

Arthur continued. "Please state, for the record, the current valuation of First Call Brewing."

Guru Deep started to speak, but stopped when Arthur leaned forward. "And do remember, Guru Deep: the world is listening."

"Given the accuracy required of such a disclosure," Guru Deep replied slowly, "I'm afraid I must decline at this time. I simply don't know the number off the top of my head."

Arthur flipped some pages and tapped the document. "When a request is made by potential buyers, the terms of this agreement require such disclosure."

Guru Deep shrugged. "Then I have no way to help you. I'm sure my office can, in due course, with proper research..."

Then there were gasps.

Feckniss was standing at the microphone and speaking, a binder open in one hand—and a brown bottle in the other. The binder shook. Feckniss's face was so waxy and pale that Arthur thought the young man might throw up all over his orange tie.

"Thank you for your diligent honesty in helping us with the proceedings, Feckniss," Arthur said. "Given the recent damage to the London brewery and the fact that First Call currently has no product on the market and recently closed for business, such a low number only makes sense."

"I don't see what meaning any of this has." Guru Deep's voice scrabbled for authority. "A sale is not on the table."

"Incorrect," Arthur replied. "A sale has just been made."

"What are you talking about?"

Flipping another page, Arthur continued. "Everyone called the sale Samara's Folly. It was a farce and an insult, but by then she was already falling ill, so people curbed their cruelty. They still felt it though. And I don't blame them. Many's the time I cursed her decision too." Arthur tapped the page. "But then she told me why this section was there. What it really meant—and how it gave us the one thing we didn't have: a chance."

Arthur held the paper in front of Guru Deep. "Like I said earlier, in order to save the beer, first it had to be destroyed. The day you took over First Call, that day had come. Brewmaster Samara told me it would be terrible. That I would have to seem so weak, such a recluse, in order to ensure not First Call's success, but its failure."

He smiled. "But we owe so much to you, Guru Deep—that wonderful hubris of yours when Samara told you the section and exact wording that she insisted be included in the sale document. You, of course, were perfectly assured in your victory, so allowed it, if only as a further humiliation. But what she knew then, and what she told me as I trained to follow in her footsteps, was that she had insisted on this language to give us an escape hatch. A far-fetched fool's hope, a faint gleam in the dark. There would be little chance of there ever being an opportunity, much less success, but it was the only thing she could do at the time."

Guru Deep frowned. "You don't mean—"

"I mean exactly that." Arthur stepped forward. "Guru Deep, CEO, president, and chair of Deep Inc., I, Arthur Celbridge, brewmaster of First Call Brewing, on behalf of all na Grúdairí and supporters around the world, and before this witness, announce that I will purchase First Call Brewing from Deep Inc. as-is, for the price of three times the current valuation of the company."

Guru Deep's eyes widened. "Three times?"

"Three times." Arthur laughed. "Little did anyone know what Samara was really trying to do. But you know as well as I do, Guru Deep. Your company agreed to the terms: if an offer of at least three times the current valuation is received, then Deep Inc. is required to accept the offer and surrender all shares and ownership in the company." Arthur leaned closer to Guru Deep. "Do you accept?"

"You can't do this."

"You are required to answer," Arthur replied, "or else face breach of contract. Either will suffice. Oh, and do remember that once you accept, you, your employees, your associates, your shareholders, anyone with ties or backing from you, you are all forbidden, in any form or guise or structure or entity, ever to own so much as one share of First Call ever again. First Call will be held by its new shareholders from around the world, and by all na Grúdairí, as sole owners. So, you have been offered three times the current valuation. Do you accept this offer?"

Guru Deep stood still and silent, rage burning through his gaze. Then, his neck so stiff Arthur thought he could hear it creak, Guru Deep nodded. "Yes," he said, his weak voice barely a whisper, but loud enough for the entire world to hear.

This time, the yelling and cheering went on without stopping for a long, long time.

AS EVERYTHING HAPPENED IN front of him, Feckniss stood at the back of the stage, out of sight. Stunned and quiet, he swayed slightly. He'd dropped the binder, and it lay across his foot. He took another drink of stout. It was really, really good.

What was I thinking?

The brewmaster produced sale documents. Guru Deep protested, but Feckniss knew it would be to no avail. Feckniss knew the rules as well as anyone—and not even Guru Deep could flout those rules. Certainly not in front of the entire world.

Certainly not when I betrayed him, Feckniss thought.

He still didn't understand.

He'd woken up dazed, the cool dampness of the grass and earth oddly refreshing on his back. Nia Fox was kneeling next to him, near the back of the stage.

She helped me up, though she looked like she'd been in a fight herself. She handed me the bottle and the binder. Then she winked.

When the brewmaster had said for everyone to open their bottles and drink, Feckniss had done what he was good at: he did what he was told.

And now, standing at the back of the stage, forgotten for now, Feckniss followed orders again.

A voice said, "What happened?"

He turned, dazed, surprised, to see Nia Fox standing next to him.

"What do you mean?" he replied.

"Just now." She shifted her gaze toward the microphone, then back to him. "You could have stayed quiet. It all could have wound up in confusion and inaction. Guru Deep might have been able to delay things, or find a way to derail them. But instead, you forced his hand."

"I couldn't be quiet," he said. Tears hung in his eyes. He tried not to believe it, but he was certain Nia was holding his hand.

"Why?"

Her dark eyes locked onto his. *I can trust her,* he thought, forgetting all else. *It's crazy and I don't know why, but I know I can trust her.*

"Because I saw," he said. "When I drank that stout, for a moment I saw it all. My entire reality. And where it stood. Two paths, one like a shining silver rushing river, one dingy and gray, a muddy trickle. It was my life, Nia. I saw the choice I had to make. When I went to the microphone, I made a choice. But the worst part is, I don't know what I chose."

"What do you see now?"

Feckniss shook his head. He raised the bottle to his mouth, but it was empty. He sighed and set it down. "Nothing," he said. "I see and know... nothing. I betrayed Guru Deep, Nia. I don't have a future."

"You had courage," Nia said. "Bravery creates new paths."

"A coward is finally brave," Feckniss replied. "That never works out well. Shouldn't you be having me hauled down to those special rooms?"

Nia smiled and squeezed his hand. "From what I hear, they burned up. And if you've learned anything from working with Guru Deep," she replied, "you've learned that no one and nothing are what they seem."

"Does that include you?"

"You could resign," Nia said. "Get out of here. See the world. Be brave again—but really, just be yourself. Figure out who that is." She squeezed his hand. "I'd like to know. Maybe someday I could get out of here too."

"I won't get far." Feckniss shook his head. "Guru Deep won't let that happen."

"No matter what happens," Nia said, "I will promise you one thing."

"What's that?"

"You can always trust me, and you always have a friend in me."

"Why? Why do you care about what happens to me?"

"When the time is right, Feckniss, we just may get to find out." With one final press, Nia let go of his hand—and then she kissed his cheek. "Just promise me something, okay?"

"What?" Feckniss stared into Nia's eyes. And there he saw it. The fear. The hope that she was right. The pleading.

"Please don't tell Guru Deep how I've helped you."

Feckniss shook his head. "Never."

"Thank you." But in her eyes Feckniss could still see it. The pleading despair of someone trapped and without escape.

She has trusted me. Helped me. I must do the same. I will always do the same.

"You're safe with me," he said.

Nia smiled. Silently, they stood side by side and watched Guru Deep and Arthur Celbridge sign the papers that set First Call free. Then Feckniss turned to look at Nia again. He wanted to understand what he must do, wanted to know which path he would take.

But Nia had slipped away, and Feckniss was alone.

GURU DEEP'S FACE LOOKED like it would only ever scowl again, and that made Branwen smile. The man in the orange suit handed Arthur back his pen, then stepped away from the front of the stage.

"Now for two important decisions," said Arthur. "For starters, a personnel change. My own fears nearly destroyed the plan that could bring back GPS, and they cost me the life of my second and my friend, Gabsir Abrigs. As best I can, I must make that right, and I will spend the rest of my life trying to live up to his memory and redeem myself for my mistakes. Today, I announce that First Call is bringing on the first of potentially many new members of na Grúdairí." Arthur stretched out an arm. "Branwen 'Malt' Abby Porter, please come here."

Her legs feeling like they were no longer hers to control, Branwen came to Arthur's side.

"You did what I did not," Arthur said. "Your allegiance was to the beer, even when an old fool like me wouldn't see it. You have restored the secret of Galway Pradesh Stout, and made GPS once more the beer it is supposed to be. For that, and for who you are—and for who you will be—I name you part of na Grúdairí. I also name you my second, in honor of Gabsir, who brought you in when I would not, who trained you and taught you all he knew. He gave his life because of my actions and my mistakes. Together, you and I will work side by side to restore GPS to its proper place not only in the world, but in people's hearts."

The crowd shouted, "What is the secret?"

Arthur smiled. "If you want to answer, feel free."

Branwen stepped up to the microphone. "Have a GPS," she said, "and you will find out."

The people cheered.

Branwen felt a red rush in her cheeks. *They're clapping and yelling... for me,* she thought. *No, for the beer. It's always about the beer. And what people find there that they need. That's the secret.*

As the applause died down, Branwen took a step back.

"And now for my second decision," Arthur said. "As we all know, GPS is of the world, but its heart and home have been in exile during these dark, difficult years that Deep Inc. owned the company. Our damaged London brewery will be rebuilt better than ever. But it will no longer be our center of operations. First Call is going home. Effective immediately, I am relocating our global headquarters and primary brewery to New Galway, Ireland." Arthur smiled. "One more thing: We'll have GPS back on tap as soon as possible—and the first round is on me."

The applause went on for a long time.

"And now," said Arthur, "if you will excuse us, we have work to do."

With that, the crowd began to leave, and the myriad media personnel ended live broadcasts and began the hustle of working their stories for news agencies around the world. With a nod to Branwen and Rucksack, Arthur left the stage. Branwen followed, but Rucksack didn't move.

"Are you coming with us?" Branwen asked.

"I have one more thing to do first," said Rucksack as he walked toward the back of the stage.

GURU DEEP'S GAZE SKEWERED Feckniss. "You must choose," said Guru Deep. "Betrayal or renewal."

All Feckniss could see were the eyes, blazing and dark, furious and cold. *I have no will,* thought Feckniss. *How did I ever think I could stand up to Guru Deep?*

"He has another choice," said a voice. "The choice he's always had."

Rucksack stood between Feckniss and Guru Deep.

"You have no place here," said Guru Deep.

"I always have a place with those who need help finding their way," Rucksack replied. "Feckniss can choose the option he's always had." Rucksack looked to Feckniss. "Choose yourself. Choose to be free. The truth is still the truth: Your freedom is yours, as long as you accept it and live it."

Feckniss trembled. "I don't know what freedom is."

"All the more important," said Rucksack. "You can find out."

Feckniss looked from one man to the other. The man in orange. The man in black. Both with intense eyes, and each with a question.

"He has nothing to offer you that matters," said Rucksack. "But you can give something to yourself."

"What?"

"A chance."

"What do you mean?"

"You're scared," said Rucksack. "I understand. More than you'll ever know. There's a world out there, bigger than you can imagine and fuller than you can know in a hundred lifetimes. Yet the world is also small enough to get to know, and there are chances aplenty for you to find such experiences as you want, as you need, as you didn't know you wanted or needed." Rucksack took a step toward Feckniss. "All you have to do is go. Trust the world. Trust yourself. There are always choices. Reality or dream. Fear or love. We desire each, but the one that grows stronger, that one that can win out, is the one we follow." He held out his hand.

"I did you so much wrong," Feckniss said.

Rucksack shrugged. "You could do so much right."

Feckniss stood there. *Branwen is a grúdaire. She is her true self. Arthur made mistakes, and he lived in the shadow of weakness and fear, but ultimately he was true to his true self. But who am I? What am I? What is my true self? And if I don't know, where do I go?*

Guru Deep stepped forward. "What happened to your friend in India, Rucksack?"

Rucksack's eyes darkened, and his voice rumbled like a tiger. "That's o' no consequence here."

"Of course not." Guru Deep sneered. "Just like Kyoto wasn't. Because you're going to change the path of decision and destiny, right?"

"No," Rucksack replied. "I understand now. Decision and destiny aren't up to me. I try too hard. Always have been. Decision and destiny are up to each person facing their own fates and choices. My job isn't to do that for others. It's to help them do it themselves —then get out o' their way."

Guru Deep leaned closer, his face inches from Rucksack's. "What happens to most people around you? They tend to fall victim to the world. To your lies, and the lies of the dream they exist in." Guru Deep turned and stared at Feckniss. "He has nothing to offer you but delusion and death, Feckniss. I'm asking you. I'm begging you, son, stay with me."

"I betrayed you."

Guru Deep smiled, but Feckniss saw no warmth there. "You want to make amends, don't you?"

"But the world."

"Will one day be no more."

"But what about Operation—"

"No matter what, Feckniss, I will be here. Where do you want to be?"

Rucksack smiled. "All these years you've been trying, Guru Deep, and the world keeps on keeping on. Maybe that dream is more real than you think."

"You'll find out the truth soon enough, Rucksack."

"I live the truth, Guru Deep." Now the men stood so close their noses were almost touching. "As long as I live, I will make sure the world does too."

Feckniss reached down and picked up his beer bottle. In the afternoon light, his reflection stared back at him. The face was neutral, blank but not calm. A strange look in the eyes made Feckniss stare harder.

Pleading, he thought. *I'm pleading with myself. To make an impossible choice.*

Once more Feckniss saw the two paths: one shiny, one dark. But he didn't know which he was on.

Pleading. For an end to the solitude. For protection. For a way out.

And he saw it again, the pleading. Not his own.

Nia's. The shadow of weakness and fear...

Feckniss understood. For once, he knew what to do and where his path lay.

He dropped the bottle.

The glass shattered on the stage. The sound made both Rucksack and Guru Deep turn and look at him.

"I don't know what to do," Feckniss said. His shoulders slumped. "I am where I am. I don't know where else to go."

Guru Deep smiled. "That will do," he said, putting his right arm around the younger man's shoulders. "You know exactly where to go. Where you belong." Guru Deep paused and smiled at Rucksack, a dark gleam in his eyes. "Right by my side."

The two men took a few steps away from Rucksack.

"Oh, silly me," said Guru Deep. He stopped and turned. "Despite today's losses, I'll take what victory I can." His smile broadened. "After all, even the tiniest victory can lead to complete triumph. The crowd is gone, and there is still one bit of unfinished business to tend to. I might lose all else, Faddah Rucksack, but I can still at least see you dead." The barrel of the pistol flashed in the sunlight, which was getting stronger with each moment, as Guru Deep aimed.

In Rucksack's eyes Feckniss saw the moment of hesitation. Then Rucksack's left hand flew up over his back, to the splotched hilt of the ragged katana.

Guru Deep squeezed the trigger—

But before he could fire, the broken sword sliced a long cut across Guru Deep's right hand.

The pistol clattered on the stage. Guru Deep jumped backward, cradling his injured hand as he bellowed in pain. Then Guru Deep's eyes narrowed. He lunged to pick up the pistol—

Only to be met by a knee in the face.

Feckniss had no idea where the other sister had come from. As Guru Deep steadied himself and wiped the blood from his nose, Zara stepped back on her healed leg and braced herself, feet wide.

"Ah, Sara," said Guru Deep. Rage distorted his smile. "You're fired." He rushed toward her.

Zara said nothing, only bent low, her entire body unfolding as her left fist flew. The uppercut lifted Guru Deep, knocking him backward as his chin reached for the sky. When his head dropped back down, she stepped forward, drew back her right fist, and punched him in the third eye. He staggered into Feckniss's arms.

"My name," she said, "is Zara."

She smiled and stood at Rucksack's side. Hatred blazed in Guru Deep's eyes. Feckniss felt the Great Leader tense, ready to lunge again for the gun.

Rucksack reached back with his right hand, removing the loop from the other sword and drawing the blade in a single, fluid motion. The air whistled and roared as he swung down. The unbroken katana sliced the pistol in two.

"Go clean yourself up," said Rucksack quietly, holding one sword up and pointing the other at Guru Deep. "And go now. Before I change my mind about you keeping that hand."

Feckniss put his arm around Guru Deep and began leading the Great Leader back toward the Lotus, which was still swathed in shadow. Guru Deep turned and stared at Rucksack. "You're still alive and I have not yet brought down the dream," said Guru Deep. "But soon, Rucksack. Soon."

"There are so many lies he's told you," Rucksack said to Feckniss. "And so many truths he can't bear to admit to himself. But you can turn away from all that. Feckniss, you can still choose. As long as you draw breath, you can make a better choice. And I promise, Feckniss, I promise that the day you change your mind, I will be there."

Feckniss said nothing, only walked back to the Lotus with Guru Deep. He gave one last look at Faddah Rucksack, who was walking around the platform, slicing every fallen gun into pieces before he left the stage.

V

THE FOUR OF THEM had squished in around the small table in the kitchen of Zara and Branwen's former flat. *It's a little uncomfortable,* Branwen thought, *but better too much closeness now, given what's to come.*

The past week had been a blur, filled with nonstop phone calls and visits, conversations and paperwork. So. Much. Paperwork. At one point Branwen remembered saying to Arthur that she thought she had blisters on her fingers from where she'd been holding the pen. The brewmaster's wink and reply still puzzled her: "Better get used to it."

I guess it'll make sense someday, Branwen thought, staring at the person who once had refused even to look at her, and now was her boss, her mentor. And was smiling at her.

Zara uncapped the bottles and passed them around to Arthur, Branwen, and Rucksack.

"To bringing back the beer," said Rucksack.

"To the love of friendship and family," said Zara.

"To new beginnings," said Branwen.

Arthur paused a moment, as if unable to speak. Finally he said, "To absent friends."

They clinked bottles and took long swallows of Galway Pradesh Stout.

"He would have thought it was perfect," said Rucksack, lowering his bottle.

"I'll never forgive myself," Arthur replied. "Gabsir died because of me. Because of the plan and my fear."

"Gabsir never had any regrets," Rucksack replied. "He lived a long, full life, doing what he loved. And he, more than anyone, would have hoped that when he died, it would mean something to someone. He would have gladly given his life to bring back GPS, and to help his friends."

"I'll never stop living for him," Arthur said. "He was my best friend. I'll never live in that fear again. Hard though I'm sure it will be, I'm going to try to live in love, to live in hope. For Gabsir. For me. And for all that I still have to do."

"I know what you're trying to say," said Branwen. "But I won't be Gabsir."

"That's not what I meant," Arthur replied. "Training you, helping you find your way, that is how I can help First Call and honor Gabsir. I understand now. He thought the world of you."

"How do you know?"

Arthur took a long drink of stout. "As we've gone through the offices to pull out everything getting moved to New Galway, I found something he'd left in my office... before. A letter about you."

"What does it say?"

"It's *about* you, but it's *for* me," said Arthur, voice firm but eyes smiling. "Let's just say that Gabsir has very firm ideas about your present—and your future." He grinned. "When the time is right, I'll show you."

Zara squeezed Branwen's hand. "I'm proud of you, little sis. I'll miss you, but it's time."

"I'm going to miss you too," Branwen said. "But I'll be back when the London brewery is getting going again. And there are always holidays."

"Don't think you've got to do all the traveling," said Zara with a grin. "I'll be heading your way too."

"What do you mean?"

"You aren't the only one figuring out dreams and futures," Zara replied. "Everyone kept saying what I didn't want to hear: my path wasn't to be na Grúdairí."

"But we also knew you had something else before you," said Rucksack.

Zara nodded. "Yes, I just had to see it too. Amazing how obvious it was."

"I wouldn't be where I am if it wasn't for you," Branwen said. "I'll do anything I can to help. What are you going to do now?"

Zara grinned. "Make more yous."

Branwen sat back. "I don't understand."

"I am a decent brewer," Zara said, "but a far better guide. A better teacher. My path isn't to make beer, little sis. My path is to make brewers."

"My offer still stands," Arthur said. "We have our own training programs, and you could run all of it. Train all the prospective na Grúdairí in all the world."

"My polite refusal still stands," Zara replied. "First Call and Galway Pradesh Stout are a crucial part of the world. But I understand: I can't revolve around one beer. The future that's coming, there are many things to bring about in the world. There are other beers than GPS. I need to bring about the brewers who can bring about those beers. So I'm opening my own school, here in London." Zara smiled. "New Galway may be the heart and home of GPS, but I'm going to make London the heart and home of every new beer and brewery to come for the next fifty years."

"A lofty goal," said Rucksack, raising his bottle. "Something tells me you won't want for students."

"If you're not careful, Rucksack," Zara said, "you may just find another beer you'd actually drink."

Rucksack grinned. "If ever I do, you'll be the first to know."

They savored their last beer together, the final minutes of mutual company. At long last but all too soon, Arthur looked at the clock and said it was time for him and Branwen to catch their train to the coast, so they could take the ferry to Ireland and from there board a train to New Galway.

"Why aren't you flying?" Rucksack asked as they stood and shared hugs and handshakes.

"Something about the First Brewer," Arthur said. "When all of you fled from Asia all those eons ago. The boat ride over. I've always wanted to know what that felt like, to travel some of where Jagathi traveled. To feel for a moment his mind and soul."

"Something in one o' Dad's old journals?" Rucksack said.

Arthur shook his hand. "No. Something Gabsir told

me once, something he had seen somewhere."

Rucksack started to say something but stopped. "Tell me how it goes," he said, his voice strangely thick. "Maybe we can swap stories sometime."

Arthur smiled. "You're always welcome in New Galway, Faddah Rucksack. Son of the First Brewer."

"Thank you," Rucksack said with a nod. "Now if you'll excuse me, I also have somewhere to be." He stopped at the door. "Zara," he said, "I hope you'll keep the poster. I do enjoy the likeness."

After he left, Zara looked at Arthur and Branwen and said, "Before you go, I have to know one thing."

"What?" said Branwen.

"That day when Feckniss took you. Who freed you?"

Branwen smiled. "I promised I wouldn't say," she replied. "A lot depends on it."

"Fine," said Zara, shaking her head. "A consolation prize, then. What's the secret to GPS?"

Branwen smiled. "Funny thing is, you already know."

"Come on," Zara replied. "You're being all evasive and trying to sound lofty and profound. Tell me."

"That's just it," Branwen said. "The secret really is obvious. It really is simple. Everyone already knows. It's just that there's a big difference between knowing a secret and living it." She hugged her sister tightly. "I love you, big sis." Then she whispered something in Zara's ear.

Zara's eyes widened. "I knew it," she said. "And I love you too."

As Branwen left the flat for the last time, her sister sketched plans for her brewing school.

"Are you ready?" Arthur asked.

Branwen smiled, and gently closed the door.

FOR THE ENTIRE PAST week, Feckniss felt like he had done nothing but paperwork. He'd hardly left his office, which was streaked with black from his latest high-priority project. He hadn't been out and about in London. Hadn't even gone home.

And he hadn't seen Guru Deep at all.

Nia Fox had circulated a memo explaining that the manager Blanders was transferring to another division in another country, and that Guru Deep would be unavailable for an undetermined amount of time, owing to a special project that was requiring his full attention in his office.

"What about me?" Feckniss had said, shaking the memo. "Did he say anything about needing me?"

In her eyes, Feckniss saw a mix of relief and pity, fear and concern. And perhaps, just perhaps, the tiniest gleam of hope, though for what he didn't know.

Nia shrugged, and all the emotion Feckniss thought he'd seen was gone. "He'll send for you when he's ready," she said. "Guru Deep knows."

She turned away.

Whatever had happened, or hadn't happened, or he only thought had happened, it was over. He didn't know why, but still he looked at her and said, softly, "It's still true. Always. You can trust me."

Feckniss waited, but Nia didn't say or do anything. She kept her back turned, but he saw her trembling.

Back in his office, Feckniss stared at his desk and all the paperwork. Behind him, he knew, London was darkening. But he wouldn't look at the window.

A gleam caught his eye. Ignoring the work before him, Feckniss opened his desk drawer. He took out the dark brush and can of black paint. *No reflections,* he thought. *If I can't see you, you can't hurt me.*

Feckniss painted over the gleam, then looked around the office, where random black smudges covered everywhere some cruel light had threatened to make him see himself.

In the curtains that he would not open, he still was watched himself. One face was blank, expressionless, like a terrible egg waiting to hatch. The other laughed maniacally, and its yellow eyes flashed, and its face was covered in cracks that seeped blood.

Feckniss finished painting, sat back down to his mound of paperwork, and secretly prayed that soon Guru Deep would call for him again.

THE MAN SET A pint before Rucksack, then sat across from him and took a long pull off his own pint.

"Funny," Rucksack said, "that wasn't on tap. Jade's always full o' surprises—though it's a shame she's moving on now. I'll have to find her all over again. She swears up and down she had nothing to do with freeing Branwen. At first I thought it was Nia Fox, but now it all makes sense."

The man pulled the brim of a hat down over his forehead. "Always kept back my own stash. Just in case."

"I knew it had to be you. The brewing supplies. Jade London didn't know about that. The missing beer. Arthur saying things in his office were different. And someone had to help Branwen get away from Feckniss and Guru Deep's goons."

"I will neither confirm nor deny any involvement."

"Then tell me one thing." Rucksack leaned forward. "How did you survive, Gabsir?"

"It's what I do," Gabsir replied. "That and make beer."

"I once knew someone else who was incredibly good at those two things," said Rucksack, deliberate and careful. "Until one terrible day when he stopped being good at the first one." Rucksack took a long swallow of the pint. "As good as he ever made."

"Thank you," said Gabsir, taking a long pull of his own beer. "I like to think I've had a lot of practice."

"Brewing? Or surviving?"

"A bit of both."

Rucksack set down the pint. "Are you going back?"

"To First Call?" Gabsir shook his head. "Arthur has what he needs, and so does Branwen. They need to find their own way now, free of some daft old man who couldn't outrun an explosion."

"It would mean the world to Arthur to know you're still alive." Rucksack looked away for a moment. "It certainly means a lot to me."

Gabsir shrugged. "When the time is right, he'll know. For now, he needs to believe what he believes, to help him focus. To help him find whatever redemption he needs. Sometimes the best way to help people is to stay out of their way. No matter how much it hurts."

Rucksack absorbed the bittersweet words, then nodded. "Where are you going to go?"

"I've got some wandering to do," Gabsir replied. "Places to see. Things to tend to. Unfinished business to see about finishing. After all, when you're my age you don't know how much time you have left. Yet no matter how little or how much, it always seems like it's both never enough and yet all the time in the world, all at the same time."

"I never told you before, Gabsir, but sometimes you remind me o' Dad," said Rucksack. His voice became softer, and he looked away. "There are so many things I want to ask you."

Gabsir saw the question burning in Rucksack's eyes. A tense silence hung between them. "That's a higher compliment than I deserve, but I thank you all the same," said Gabsir. "We have much in common, Faddah Rucksack. I am just doing what I must as best I can." Gabsir sighed. "I have many questions for you too. In time I am sure we will understand each other better." Gabsir drained the rest of his pint. "But not yet. Though I look forward to our next meeting."

"What are you talking about?"

Gabsir nodded and Rucksack turned. Two men walked over. Their faces were generic to the point of being indistinct, as if any attempt to remember who they were would slide right off your memory. One of the men held a silver tray. They stopped beside Rucksack. The second man said, "Letter for you, sir."

"And no," said the first man. "Before you ask, it's not a trick."

Rucksack nodded. "I figured you buggers would know better." He picked up the letter, opened it, and read. Soon he noticed nothing but the paper.

"Oh bugger. I have to leave for Kathmandu. Now," he said, still staring at the flowing script on the page. "I have some unfinished business too. Or rather, I thought with great sadness that it was finished, but now I can be hopeful that it is unfinished." Rucksack looked up.

The chair across from him was empty.

AS NIGHT TOOK OVER London, Guru Deep sat at his desk, straightened his orange suit, and checked that his teeth and nose were back in place. He'd always healed quickly, but that damn janitor had been far more trouble than he'd ever expected. There would come a time, he knew, when he would rebalance the scales. Not yet, but at least it no longer hurt to smile when he thought about that future vengeance.

Guru Deep pulled the bandage off his right hand, and the smile vanished. The cut had healed, but it had left a white, jagged scar, like a fractured river. He frowned at his hands. He had tried and tried to keep up the change, but the illusion was too difficult, the reality too extensive and inherent. It had taken too much energy—energy perhaps that had distracted him from finishing the strategy the way he'd intended. But no matter. Guru Deep knew tomorrow was always another day—until the wonderful moment when finally it wouldn't be.

He reached into a drawer, unlocked the secret compartment inside, and set three items on his desk. Closing the drawer, Guru Deep sighed, then for a moment he closed his eyes. "Damn you," he said. "You told me what would happen. 'Never cease your course, then only a man born of man and a woman born of man shall harm Guru Deep.' And now I have indeed been harmed by a woman born of man. But this man born of man? I will find him, and I will stop him before he ever can harm me."

Guru Deep opened his eyes. The sight of his right hand made him gasp.

The white scar was the least of it now. The right hand was smaller than the left, covered in twisted, bumpy scars and irregular lumps that distorted his stiff fingers. Instead of the rich nut-brown of the rest of his skin, the hand was pale, broken only by the marring of a horrific raw red-pink scar that covered his palm.

Opening the box he had taken from the drawer, Guru Deep pulled out a pair of white gloves.

"What you began," he said, his voice hard and full of old, simmering rage, "I will finish."

He set aside the box. For a few silent moments, he stared at what was underneath. Clenching and unclenching his stiff gloved hands, he picked up the thin file on top, marked OPERATION LAST DREAM, and set it aside.

For now.

Then he opened the thick file, marked on the front with the words "FADDAH RUCKSACK," and began from the beginning.

THANK YOU FOR READING!

Please tell your friends about this story and review it at your favorite bookstore. Reviews are the best way readers discover great new books, and I would truly appreciate it. Even a couple of sentences is a big help. Here's a list:

anthonystclair.com/lotus

MORE FROM THE RUCKSACK UNIVERSE

The Martini of Destiny
anthonystclair.com/martini

Home Sweet Road
anthonystclair.com/homesweetroad

Forever the Road
anthonystclair.com/forevertheroad

Eugene, Oregon, is home to a remarkable brewing community, and I'm fortunate to write about it in other parts of my work. Many local brewers patiently answered my questions about the brewing process and brewing industry. My thanks to Hanns Anderson from McMenamins High Street, Jamie Floyd from Ninkasi Brewing, Matt Van Wyk from Alesong Brewing, and Jason Carriere from Falling Sky Brewing for reducing the number of times I might make an arse of myself. Sometimes I may have taken artistic license, but any outright errors are mine and mine alone. Next time you're in the Northwest, look for some of their beers.

My Chief Reader and team of Beta Readers (Taylor Rutledge, Robin FitzClemen, and Bonnie Donaghy) came through with numerous things that needed addressing in earlier versions of the manuscript, and as always I'm grateful for their diligence, attention to detail, and their desire that my stories be the best they can be. Thank you.

Scott Alexander Jones did his usual crack job on copy editing, and Bonnie Donaghy designed an amazing cover. My gratitude to them both for helping these books stand out. Thanks to Crissy Hennesay Bartell and Ger Killeen for advising me on the Irish language, and for making it clear how important the different accent marks are. Katherine Donaghy of Urban Design London also gave me context on how London is, how London was, and what to consider when building my post-Blast world.

Above all, thanks to my friends and family, who have been there and encouraged me all these years. Especially to my wife Jodie, for helping me find the courage to choose to take the path I was meant to take, and to my kids Connor and Aster, for all the paths ahead.

Anthony St. Clair
Eugene, Oregon
2016

ABOUT THE AUTHOR

Anthony St. Clair has walked with hairy coos in the Scottish Highlands, choked on seafood in Australia, and watched the full moon rise over Mt. Everest in Tibet. Anthony's travels have also taken him around the sights and beers of Thailand, Japan, India, Canada, Ireland, the USA, Cambodia, China and Nepal. He and his wife live in Oregon and gave their kids passports when they were babies. Learn more and connect:

www.anthonystclair.com